Lovers

The world's sexiest bachelors!

Latin Lovers

THE HEAT OF PASSION
by
Lynne Graham

THE RIGHT CHOICE
by
Catherine George

VENGEFUL SEDUCTION
by
Cathy Williams

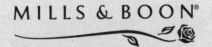

MILLS & BOON®

MILLS & BOON and MILLS & BOON with the Rose Device are registered trademarks of the publisher.
Harlequin Mills & Boon Limited,
Eton House, 18-24 Paradise Road, Richmond, Surrey, TW9 1SR

LATIN LOVERS
© by Harlequin Enterprises II B.V., 2000

The Heat of Passion, The Right Choice and *Vengeful Seduction* were first published in Great Britain by Mills & Boon Limited in separate, single volumes.

The Heat of Passion © Lynne Graham 1995
The Right Choice © Catherine George 1996
Vengeful Seduction © Cathy Williams 1995

ISBN 0 263 82413 6

05-0003

Printed and bound in Spain
by Litografía Rosés S.A., Barcelona

Lynne Graham was born in Northern Ireland and has been a keen Mills & Boon® reader since her teens. She is very happily married with an understanding husband, who has learned to cook since she started to write! Her five children keep her on her toes. She has a very large old English sheepdog, which knocks everything over, and two cats. When time allows, Lynn is a keen gardener.

THE HEAT OF PASSION
by
LYNNE GRAHAM

CHAPTER ONE

EBONY-BLACK hair against a crisp linen pillow, brown skin against a blindingly white sheet, and tiger's eyes burning with blatant cruelty and triumph into hers. In horrified rejection of the imagery that had sprung into her mind, Jessica shuddered violently, dimly aware that she was still in the grip of severe shock.

Abruptly, she was dredged from her turmoil by the insistent shrill of the telephone in the hall. Reluctantly she answered the summons, carefully shutting the lounge door behind her so that her father was not disturbed.

'Jessica…?'

She froze, her stunningly beautiful face white as snow between the silken wings of her silver-blonde hair. Her breath caught in her throat in a strangled gasp. The receiver dropped from her nerveless fingers and swung towards the floor.

That voice, that truly unforgettable voice…deep, dark and rich as golden honey. He said her name as no one else had ever said it. She hadn't heard him speak in six long years and yet recognition was instantaneous and terrifying. Her throat closing over, she bent down to retrieve the phone.

'I am so sorry to have startled you,' Carlo Saracini purred, lying between his even white teeth.

Her own teeth clenched. She wanted to reach down the telephone line and slap him stupid. And feeling that way again…feeling that alien surge of raw violent hatred which he alone invoked…scared her rigid. Her mouth went dry. 'What do you want?'

'I'm in a very generous mood,' he imparted with a

5

husky edge to his slow slightly accented drawl. 'I'm prepared to offer you a meeting—'

Her fingers clenched like talons round the receiver. 'A
meeting…why?'

'Can it be that you haven't seen your father yet?' he
murmured.

She went white. 'I've seen him,' she whispered, not
troubling to add that Gerald Amory was still in the room
next door.

'Embezzlement is a very serious offence.'

'He had gambling debts,' Jessica protested in a feverish undertone. 'He panicked…he didn't mean to take the
money from the firm! He was borrowing it—'

'Euphemistically speaking,' Carlo inserted with more
than an edge of mockery.

'Amory's used to belong to him,' Jessica reminded
him with helpless bitterness.

'But it doesn't now,' Carlo traded softly. 'Now it be-
longs to me.'

Jessica's teeth gritted. Six years ago, burdened by the
demands of a wife with expensive tastes, ageing ma-
chinery and falling profits, Gerald Amory had allowed
Carlo to buy the family firm. Duly reinstalled as chief
executive, her father had seemed content and, with new
equipment and unparalleled export opportunities through
the parent conglomerate, Amory Engineering had
thrived.

Guilt stabbed like a knife into Jessica. If it had not
been for her, Carlo Saracini would never have come into
their lives. If it had not been for her the firm would still
have belonged to her father. If it had not been for her,
Gerald Amory would not now be facing criminal charges
for embezzlement. Nausea stirred in her stomach,
churned up by a current of raw loathing so powerful, she
could taste it.

'Dad intended to repay the money…if it hadn't have

been for the audit, you wouldn't even have found out!' she said in desperation.

'Why do you think I spring occasional surprise audits on my companies?' Carlo enquired gently. 'Employees like your father get greedy and sometimes they get caught as he has with their hands trapped in the till.'

Jessica trembled, her heartbeat thundering deafeningly in her eardrums. His deliberate cruelty appalled her. 'He wasn't greedy…he was desperate!'

'I'm willing to meet you tonight. I'm staying at the Deangate Hall. I'm sure I don't need to tell you which suite I'll be occupying. Eight,' he specified. 'I will wait one minute past the hour, no more. If you're not there, there'll be no second chance, *cara*.'

Aghast at the site he had specified and absolutely enraged by his instinctive sadism, Jessica gasped, 'Don't waste your time! I'll see you in hell before I set foot inside that hotel again!'

'You must have been quite a sight limping out on one shoe that afternoon,' Carlo mused provocatively. 'The chambermaid found the other one under the bed. I still have it. Cinderella's slipper—'

'How dare you?' she seethed down the phone in outrage.

'And as I recall it, you damned near left something far more intimate behind,' Carlo breathed reflectively.

Scarlet to her hairline, Jessica slammed down the receiver before she could be further reminded of her own appalling, inexcusable weakness that day. No, the very last thing she wanted to think about right now was that day at the Deangate, six years ago.

No more, she wanted to scream, no more. But of course, she wouldn't. Jessica didn't scream. Jessica hated to lose control. She had grown up sobbing silently behind closed doors, covering her ears from the sound of her mother screaming at her poor father. And she had sworn then that she would be different and that her own fiery temper would be subdued by every means within her power. She would be strong without passion. And if she stayed away from the passion, she would not be hurt.

The worst thing of all now had to be looking back, seeing how she had broken her own rules and how she had suffered accordingly. Struggling to escape those frightening echoes from the past, Jessica returned to her father.

Grey with strain, he glanced up and began talking again, not even acknowledging that she had been out of the room, so cocooned in his own problems that he might as well have been on another planet.

'I had to hand over all my keys...even my car keys. I wasn't allowed to enter my own office again,' Gerald Amory relived painfully. 'Then I was escorted out of the building by two security guards...it was a nightmare!'

Those must have been Carlo's instructions. Hadn't her father deserved just a little bit more consideration? Couldn't he have been allowed to retain even a tiny sliver of dignity?

'Dad...' Her voice suspended by choking tears, Jessica darted across the room to offer comfort but her father pulled away from her.

'I would have treated a thief the same way—' The admission was stark.

'You're not a thief!'

But Gerald Amory made no response.

Every which way Jessica looked, she felt responsible. She should have been there for her father, should have seen that he was in trouble. A week after Carlo had bought Amory Engineering, Jessica's mother had walked out and started a divorce. The amount of cash from the sale had proved too severe a temptation for Carole Amory. Bad as the marriage had been, Gerald Amory had been utterly devastated. Her father had adored her mother. He had been terrifyingly loyal and forgiving through her every extra-marital affair. He would have done anything to keep her...he had crawled, begged, pleaded. The only person relieved by Carole's departure had been her daughter.

But she should have seen the immense vacuum that had opened up in her father's life. She had watched him turn into a workaholic, living and breathing business and profit because that was all he had left. Why hadn't it occurred to her that, as the firm thrived and made all the money her greedy mother could ever have wanted, her father must have bitterly resented the fact that the firm was no longer his and that those healthy profits had come too late to sustain his shaky marriage?

But gambling...?

'It was somewhere to go, something to do,' he proffered while she stared back at him aghast. 'And then I started losing and I thought I couldn't go on losing forever...'

The silence went on and on and then abruptly and without any warning, Gerald Amory rose heavily from his seat and moved with the shambling gait of a much older man towards the front door.

'Where are you going?' Jessica demanded, her violet eyes almost purple with the strength of her distress.

'Home...I need to be on my own, Jess...please understand that.'

In despair, she hurried down the path after him, 'Dad, we can cope better with this together! Please stay,' she pleaded.

'I'm sorry. Not now, Jess,' he breathed tightly, unable to look at her.

Cope with the shame, the publicity, the court case? With the loss of his home, his job, his self-respect? Would he be able to cope? It was a tall order, she registered dully, especially for a man of his age. But what alternative was there? You coped, you survived. If Jessica had learnt anything in recent years, it was that truth. Yet struggle as she did she could no longer keep her mind fully focused on her father's problems. The past was surging back to her, the past she had buried six years ago...

The day she had met Carlo Saracini she had been in London, shopping for her trousseau in the company of a friend. It had been less than two months before her wedding to Simon. She hadn't been wearing her engagement ring. One of the stones had worked loose and it had been in the jeweller's for repair.

She had been standing chatting to Leah at a busy intersection, waiting on the lights changing so they could cross. Somebody behind her in the crowd had pushed her and she had fallen into the road, practically beneath the wheels of Carlo's chauffeur-driven limousine.

She didn't remember falling. She had knocked herself out. What she did remember was coming dizzily back to consciousness before the ambulance arrived and focusing on the most extraordinary golden eyes above hers. She had been suffering from concussion. As a child she had had a story-book about a tiger with eyes that were pools of brilliant gold. So, naturally she had stared. She had never before seen eyes that shade.

'Stay still...don't speak.' Carlo had been rapping out autocratic instructions in every direction, including hers.

'I'm fine—'

'Keep quiet,' she had been told.

'It's only my head and I want to get up...' She had begun trying to move.

A brown hand like a giant weight had forestalled such daring.

'Look...I want to get up,' she had said again, embarrassed eyes flickering over the gathering crowd of onlookers.

'You are not getting up...you could have injured your spine.'

Her temper had begun to spark. 'My spine is OK...I'm OK—'

'We will have a doctor tell us that.' He had continued to stare down at her with the most phenomenal intensity and then he had run a forefinger almost caressingly along her delicate jawbone. 'I shall never forgive myself for hurting something so incredibly beautiful…'

Leah had been totally useless, having hysterics somewhere in the background. Jessica had found herself in a private ambulance, accompanied not by her friend but by Carlo.

'She will follow in my car,' he had asserted, getting in the way of the paramedics while simultaneously telling them what to do.

She just hadn't had the strength to fight Carlo Saracini off that day. Her head had been aching fit to burst and her stomach churning with nausea. She had shut her eyes to escape, telling herself that this volatile and domineering foreigner was simply attempting to make amends for an accident which hadn't been his fault in the first place.

She had been taken to a clinic, subjected to an alarmingly thorough examination against her will and tucked into a bed in a very expensively decorated room.

'I want to go home,' she had protested to the nurse. 'This is so unnecessary.'

Carlo had strode through the door, splintering waves of vibrant physical energy that seemed to charge the very atmosphere and drive out all tranquility.

'Where's Leah?' she had whispered, shaken that he was still around.

'I had her taken home. She was too distressed to be of any assistance. I understand that your parents are abroad and will not be home until tomorrow. Do you wish me to contact them?'

'I don't even know your name,' she had begun through clenched teeth.

'Carlo Saracini,' he had murmured with a slashing and brilliant smile. 'How do you feel?'

'I just want to go home…don't you ever listen to anything people say?'

'Not if I don't want to hear it,' Carlo had admitted.

'Look, all this…' She had indicated the fancy room
with embarrassment. 'It's not necessary. I fell into the
road. Your car didn't touch me. It's not as if I'm going
to sue you or anything, and all this fuss—'

'Is my wish,' he had inserted silkily, scanning her
slender shape beneath the bedclothes with blatant appreciation, making her cheeks ignite into sudden colour and
sweeping up to her face with yet another smile. 'I can't
take my eyes off you. You may have noticed that. Then,
you must be accustomed to a great deal of male attention.'

'Not since I got engaged,' she had muttered stiffly,
infuriated by the fashion in which he was openly looking
her over as if she were an object on a supermarket shelf
there for the taking.

He had stilled, golden eyes narrowing and flaring.
'You belong to another man?'

'I belong to no man, Mr Saracini!' Jessica had
snapped.

'You will belong to me,' he had murmured with utter
conviction.

She had honestly thought he was nuts. Nobody had
ever talked to her like that before. Mind you, she had
been to Greece once on holiday and had noted that rad-
ical feminism had yet to find a foothold there. But that
a male dressed with such apparent sophistication in a
superbly tailored mohair and silk blend suit, a male who
spoke with an air of culture and education, should make
such primitive statements had astonished her.

'I'm getting married in six weeks,' she had informed
him flatly, involuntarily studying his strikingly male features before she realised what she was doing and hurriedly looked away again.

'We'll see…' And Carlo had laughed indulgently, the

way you laughed when a child said something innocently amusing.

Jessica sank back to the present and discovered that she was shivering. Her first thought was for her father. No matter what he said, he shouldn't be alone. Grabbing up a coat, she let herself out of the tiny cottage she rented and climbed into her car to drive over to his house.

'But your father's at work, Mrs Turner. What would he be doing home at this time of the day?' Her father's housekeeper studied her with a questioning frown.

Jessica swallowed hard, fighting to keep her face unconcerned. 'I thought he was finishing early.'

'Well, he didn't mention it to me.'

'I'll catch him later.' Jessica climbed back into her car.

Dear God, where had her father gone? She must have been out of her mind to let him wander off like that in the state he was in! Another little voice asked her what she was doing. Her father had said he needed time on his own. She was not his keeper. Shouldn't she respect his wishes? But the nagging sense of urgency nibbling at her nerve-endings wouldn't leave her alone.

Reluctantly she went home again. Carlo...she couldn't get Carlo out of her mind. Would she go to the Deangate Hall Hotel to crawl and beg and plead as once her father had done with her mother? Her stomach gave a sensitive heave. What would be the point? She *knew* Carlo Saracini. There was no way he would let her father off the hook. Carlo wanted revenge. He couldn't touch Jessica but he knew just how deep the bond was between father and daughter. It would be a sweeter revenge than any that dark Machiavellian intellect might have calculated.

'Some day you will come to me on your knees and beg me to take you...and I will break you.'

As she remembered, perspiration dampened her short upper lip.

Carlo Saracini had destroyed her life. He had hacked to pieces everything she held dear. Her love for Simon, her happiness, her tranquillity…and in the end her self-respect. She had fought him to the very last shred of her endurance and then had learnt the secret of her own frailty in a shattering hour of self-discovery. Shuddering with disgust, she shut out the memories but the humiliation and the shame lived on as strongly as ever.

Carlo was one hundred per cent predator. Ruthless, unforgiving, utterly intolerant of those weaker than himself. She would never ever forget the way he had looked at her on her wedding-day. With smouldering incredulous fury and naked hatred. The Alpha male, fabulously rich, indecently successful and stunningly handsome…rejected. Right up until the very last moment Carlo had expected her to change her mind and fling herself at his feet.

'I will never forgive you.'

Carlo Saracini's parting assurance outside the church door. She had been shaking so badly by that stage, Simon had practically been holding her upright. She looked like a ghost in the wedding photographs. Simon had assured her that he had forgiven her but as she lived day in, day out with the farce of her marriage, she had never been able to forgive herself.

Jessica raised an unsteady hand to her pounding temples, struggling with the greatest of difficulty to regain her concentration. Why on earth hadn't she realised before now that her father was in trouble? She had been too involved in her own problems, she acknowledged wretchedly.

Simon had been ill for a long time before his death. His business had crashed in the recession, leaving nothing but debts. Her father had urged her to come home but she had refused. She hadn't wanted to turn into the Daddy's little girl she had been before her marriage. She hadn't even had a job in those days. All she had ever thought about as a teenager was marrying Simon and having children. She shoved that particular recollection away with helpless bitterness.

Carlo had invited her to the Deangate to gloat over her father's downfall. A sadist to the backbone, he wanted to experience her pain personally. Why should she give him the satisfaction when she knew that he would not allow her father to go unpunished? No way was she going to keep that appointment at the Deangate Hotel!

Jessica climbed out of her car. It was dark and cold and wet, just like that other day long ago, that day she couldn't bear to remember. She straightened slight shoulders, tightened the sash on her serviceable beige raincoat and lifted her head high as she crossed the car park. *This* was for her father. *This* was her duty. So what if she felt physically sick at the prospect of seeing Carlo Saracini again? She owed this meeting to her father.

If the opportunity to watch her squirm gave Carlo a kick, maybe…just maybe it might be possible to persuade him to mitigate the severity of the punishment he was doubtless planning. Naturally the money would have to be repaid. And the only way that could be done would be by the sale of her father's home. And since houses didn't sell overnight, Carlo would have to be prepared to allow time for that sale to take place. All that she would ask would be that he did not drag her father through court and utterly destroy him.

Was that so much to ask? she wondered tautly as she approached the reception desk of the Deangate Hotel. Yes, it was a great deal to ask of a male of Carlo's ilk.

'Can I help you?' a smiling receptionist asked, jolting her out of her reverie.

'My name is Turner. I have an appointment with Mr Saracini at eight,' Jessica advanced with all the appearance of a job-hunter, mentioning an interview.

'I'll call up...Mrs Turner.' The young woman's eyes flicked over the wedding-ring on Jessica's hand.

Jessica moved away a step or two, a nervous hand brushing up to check the sleek severity of the French pleat she had employed to confine her eye-catching hair.

'I'm sorry, Mrs Turner...'

Jessica turned back. 'Is there a problem?'

'Mr Saracini...' The brunette cleared her throat awkwardly.

'Yes?' Jessica pressed tightly.

'He says that he does not recognise your name—'

'I beg your pardon?' Jessica breathed in deeply, hot pink abruptly washing her ivory pale complexion as she belatedly understood. Carlo had taken exception to her marital name. One slim hand braced on the edge of the desk. She swallowed hard on her fury. 'Try Amory,' she suggested thinly.

'Amory?' the receptionist repeated with a perplexed look.

'Just tell Mr Saracini that a Miss Amory is here,' Jessica enunciated between gritted teeth.

'You can go up,' she was told ten seconds later.

The lift disgorged two couples in full evening dress. She walked in, her heart in her throat. The Deangate Hotel was one of the most expensive country house establishments in Britain. It lay five miles out of Barton and few locals had the income required to avail themselves of such unashamed luxury. Jessica had always hated the place. This was where her mother had come to meet men. This was where she had trysted with her lovers. And there was a peculiar agony to Jessica's awareness that it was in this very same establishment that she had forever lost her claim to the moral high ground.

Had she been smug and pious in those days? Her mother had once accused her of that…

'You're just like your father,' Carole had condemned with bitter resentment. 'You're so bloody virtuous, you ought to be wearing a halo! So smug, you make me sick! But you won't get through life like that. Some day you're going to fall off your pedestal and fall flat on your pious little face and it'll serve you damned well right!'

And she had fallen, boy, had she fallen. With an inner shudder of distaste, Jessica stepped out of the lift, outraged by the direction of her thoughts. She had come here without allowing herself to think of what she had to face at journey's end but the eerie familiarity of her surroundings was like a razor twisting inside her.

Six years ago, she had stalked along this corridor in a rage to tackle Carlo Saracini. And even this length of time after the event it was quite impossible for her to explain how she had very nearly ended up in his bed. The two of them…like animals, her clothing half off, his hands on her body, her hands on his. Obscene, she reflected with a stab of revulsion. And had it not been for the noisy entrance of the chambermaid into the lounge next door to the bedroom, that disgusting incident might have gone considerably further than it had.

Youth had given her an edge, she appreciated now. Youth often knew no fear. That had been her strength at the beginning. She really hadn't realised what she was up against. Carlo Saracini, a shark in a sleepy backwater. Superbly clever, insidiously calculating and terrifyingly dangerous. Fear might have protected her, but she hadn't learnt to fear him until it was far too late.

But she was scared now, scared enough to please even the most merciless sadist. Not scared for herself…but for her father. An old-fashioned gentleman, who had grown up in a far different world from Carlo Saracini's.

She came to a halt in front of the door and briefly

closed her eyes. Crawl, she told herself. That's what he wants. And if he gets what he wants, maybe destroying her father would seem less appealing. She knocked the door and braced herself. It was opened almost immediately by a young man.

'Come in, Miss Amory,' he said gravely.

The lounge of the suite was unchanged. Her fluttering gaze fell on an overstuffed lemon brocade sofa and helplessly she thought, It started there. Her skin burned.

She heard Carlo say something in Greek. The product of a marriage between an Italian and a Greek, Carlo was equally at home in either language. Her spine stiffened. He strolled into view and the door slid softly shut behind her.

Jessica couldn't take her eyes off him. He repelled her. Every earthy, oversexed inch of him absolutely repelled her and there was a certain deadly attraction to that amount of revulsion, she told herself. He moved with the grace of a prowling tiger. He had the face of a dark fallen angel and the stunning magnetism of a very physical male.

She studied the dark planes of his impassive features, the clear golden eyes set beneath winged black brows and the savagely high cheekbones which lent such fierce strength to his face. Her gaze glossed over the stubborn jut of a decidedly Greek nose and the wide perfection of his narrow mouth before hurriedly falling away.

'I bet he's a voracious lover,' her mother had murmured throatily the first time she met him. 'He has an incredible sexual charge. I could feel it fifty feet away…any woman with red blood in her veins would. What's wrong with *you*?'

Jessica shivered. The red blood in her veins was chilling fast. Carlo was so cold. Although he betrayed nothing visually, she could feel that. And for some reason she couldn't understand that made her feel physically cold and threatened.

Suddenly the silence was something she might drown in and she leapt into speech. 'Why did you invite me here?'

'Take off your coat.'

Her tongue crept out and moistened her dry lower lip. 'I'm not staying—'

'Go, then,' he murmured with a dismissive flick of one lean hand. 'You waste my time—'

Her teeth clenched. She undid her sash, dropped the coat off her shoulders and cast it aside. 'I asked you why you invited me here.'

'I wanted to look at you.' Burnished golden eyes skimmed over her slender figure, resting on the surprisingly full thrust of her breasts above her tiny waist and sliding with insulting cool down over the feminine swell of her hips.

Jessica had never been at ease with her own body. Her voluptuous curves and her silver-blonde hair drew male eyes like beacons. Both attracted the wrong kind of male attention. She looked like her mother and she despised that awareness. If she hadn't possessed a distressingly opulent shape and unnaturally bright hair which ironically was entirely natural, she would never have caught Carlo Saracini's attention six years ago.

Her eyes glittered like brilliant amethysts as she withstood his inspection with her chin as high as she could hold it.

'Would you like a drink?' he drawled.

'No, thank you.'

He poured himself a glass of champagne. 'I hate to celebrate alone but I understand that you're afraid of touching alcohol around me. I'm surprised you're still that naïve,' he remarked softly.

'What are you celebrating?' She ignored the dig about alcohol, drawing on every scrap of icy dignity she possessed.

'You're a widow,' he delivered with smooth emphasis.

Jessica was shattered by his candour, brutally reminded that Carlo had no inhibitions and, similarly, little respect for ordinary standards of decent behaviour.

'My father—'

Carlo straightened to his full six feet three inches and shifted a silencing hand, dark golden eyes gleaming over her pallor. 'He stole from me and from his employees. We know that. Do we really need to discuss it?'

'Do you have to be so callous?' Jessica demanded, abruptly unfreezing from the spot to move forward in unconscious appeal. 'He made a huge error of judgement—'

'The prisons are full of people who make huge errors,' Carlo incised, his nostrils flaring. 'Theft? Such a sordid crime and yet so personal—'

'P-personal?' Involuntarily, she stammered.

'It was for your sake alone that I bought Amory Engineering at an inflated price. What you might call a gesture of good faith towards your family—'

'Good faith?' A choked laugh fell from her lips as she studied him with unhidden loathing and disbelief. 'You don't know what good faith is. It was blackmail. You tried to put pressure on me by playing on my family's financial position—'

'I was demonstrating that I look after *my own*,' Carlo cut in with ruthless precision.

'*Your own*?' she repeated with revulsion. 'I was never yours!'

A winged ebony brow was elevated. 'You were mine the first moment our eyes met but you were too stupid and craven to face that reality—'

'How dare you!'

'How dare you enter this room where you lay with me and try to deny what happened here between us?' Carlo demanded with blistering contempt.

She wanted to hit him. She wanted to scream back from the depths of her humiliation. But she wouldn't allow herself to be drawn. 'My father—' she said very deliberately.

'Was the most cosseted employee I have ever had,' Carlo interrupted. 'I allowed him complete autonomy over a company which was no longer his and in return I expected loyalty, not common theft.'

'He can sell his house and pay back every penny!' Jessica swore furiously. 'Isn't that enough for you?'

'Your family home carries two mortgages. Why do you think he stole?' Carlo returned drily. 'I wish to hear no more on the subject.'

'He's desperately ashamed of himself.' Jessica hadn't known that the house was mortgaged. She concealed her dismay with difficulty.

'This subject bores me.' Carlo sent her a grim glance. 'I have no interest in your father except as a means to an end. You can't influence my judgement with sentimental pleas. There is no sentiment in business—'

'So you simply brought me here to gloat?' she gathered with flashing eyes and a look of glowing scorn. 'You make me sick, Carlo. I will stand by my father through whatever you throw at him—'

'You like weak men, don't you?' he said silkily. 'Men who need mothering and support, men who make you feel that you're the one in the driver's seat. Maybe if I'd wept and plucked violin strings instead of demanded, you would have come to me instead...'

'Don't be crass.' Jessica was trembling with a rage that was becoming increasingly hard to control. 'I would never have *come* to you. I hated you for your primitive macho outlook and—'

'I am not primitive.' The insertion was immensely quiet but the temperature had shot up. 'I have Greek blood.'

For a split-second she was tempted to laugh. So vast

an amount of blatant pride and arrogance dwelt in that
assurance. But then she clashed with golden eyes that
burned with the ferocity of a tiger about to pounce and
all desire to laugh was stolen from her. Instantly the
alarm bells rang in a frantic peal inside her head. That
ferocious, utterly terrifying temper... She found herself
instinctively glancing round to measure the distance to
the door.

'And you are not my equal. You proved that six years
ago!' he shot at her. 'Most conclusively did you prove
your stupidity—'

Her small hands clenched into fists. 'If you call me
stupid just one more time, Carlo, I won't be responsible
for what I do!'

'*Per Dio*,' he murmured with a brilliant, slashing
smile. 'If I push a little more, will you rip off my shirt
and beg me to take you the way you did the last time?'

'Dear God, how can you talk to me like that?'

'Easily. Then,' Carlo spread two very expressive
hands, 'I have no respect for you. What did you expect?'

The rage was beginning to gain on her self-control.
She was having a very tough time holding it in.

'You behaved like a whore—'

'You swine!' she positively spat at him, powered by
a tremendous wave of aggression.

'You were true neither to me nor to Turner,' Carlo
drawled with caustic bite. 'He offered marriage. I offered
something less secure. You went for the wedding-ring.
And you lost.'

'I married the man I loved...I didn't lose *anything*!'
Jessica slung back hotly, her adrenalin pumping madly
through her veins.

Carlo threw his darkly handsome head back and
laughed uproariously. 'Are you telling me that you
didn't think of me in the dark of night? That you didn't
crave the passion I alone could give you? If you'd re-

sponded to him the way you responded to me, he'd have run away from you in terror!'

Jessica launched herself at him like a lioness. Two incredibly powerful hands snapped round her wrists and held her back. An insolent smile curved his hard mouth. 'You dress like a fifty-year-old spinster but you're a little animal at heart, aren't you, *cara*? I scratch the surface of that ladylike exterior and I find teeth and claws. I like that. It excites me—'

'You filthy swine...*shut up*!' she screamed.

'And it excites the hell out of you too!' Long fingers hauled her closer as she attempted to kick him. He caught both flailing hands in one large male hand and pinned them behind her back, forcing her closer, staring with sardonic amusement down into her blazing violet eyes and pressing a long muscular thigh against her stomach as she twisted and tried to apply a well-aimed knee. 'All that howling sexual frustration just begging to be released. I could take you now here...up against the wall, on the floor, anywhere and you'd love it!' he asserted with rawly offensive confidence. 'Is that what you want?'

CHAPTER TWO

'NEVER!' Jessica gasped breathlessly, searing his dark, savage visage with all the tortured fury of her ignominious and powerless position. 'The very idea of you touching me again makes me feel physically sick!'

'One lesson wasn't enough for you, was it?' Carlo murmured huskily, narrowed eyes raking over her outraged features. 'Don't you remember what it was like when I made love to you?'

'That wasn't love,' Jessica vented fiercely. 'That was *lust!*'

'And you have a problem with that…I don't,' Carlo confided in a black velvet purr. And then, with a sardonic laugh, he released her when she was least expecting the gesture and thrust her carelessly back from him.

Jessica was trembling and in considerable distress. She had lost control. Physical and mental control. And that terrified her. Six years ago, she had been twenty, barely out of the teen years and considerably more naïve and foolish than she considered herself to be now. The last few minutes were like a blackout inside her mind. She didn't want to examine them. He had made her so angry she had become violent and that knowledge literally filled her with shame and horror.

Her body felt peculiar. Her heartbeat was still madly accelerated. Her breasts were suddenly extraordinarily sensitive. She was maddeningly aware that the lace cup of her bra was chafing her nipples and that her skin felt stretched and tight. Horrified by what had happened to her body, she studied the floor, fighting to relocate her composure.

'Let's get down to business,' Carlo suggested drily. 'We've wasted enough time.'

'Business?' Her brow furrowed.

'I invited you here for one reason only. You *could* be of use to me. I need a woman to play a role. A woman I can trust to play that role to the best of her ability and do exactly as she's told. And I think that that woman could be you—'

Her lashes fluttered in bemusement. 'I don't think I follow.'

'If you are prepared to place yourself without question in my hands for a period, not exceeding three months, I will consider treating your father's offence with sympathy, understanding and forgiveness...' Carlo stated quietly.

Sympathy, understanding and forgiveness. Alien emotions where Carlo was concerned. Her temples were throbbing. Her concentration was blown. She studied him with perceptible incomprehension, temporarily drained of all emotion. She just didn't know what he was talking about.

'This role,' Carlo selected smoothly, letting champagne froth down into another glass. 'It would entail considerable intimacy—'

'Intimacy?' she whispered shakily.

Carlo slotted the glass into her nerveless fingers. He surveyed her with immense satisfaction. 'Intimacy,' he repeated lazily, making a sexual banquet of the word and the long-drawn-out syllables were like a set of taunting fingers on her spine.

'What...what exactly are you offering me?' Jessica framed jerkily.

'You would have to agree before I told you the details.' Carlo dealt her a cool, steady glance, silky black lashes low over hooded, very dark eyes.

'That's ridiculous.'

'Unusual.' Carlo shifted a broad shoulder in a slight

shrug. 'But I don't trust you. Why should I? And it is not as though you have moral scruples, is it? And even if you had,' he pointed out, 'you do have your father to consider.'

She tensed, forcing herself to concentrate. 'Are you talking about some kind of job?'

Carlo's mouth curved wryly. 'You could call it that.'

'And would it entail breaking the law?' she prompted flatly.

'What do you take me for, *cara*?'

'Would it?' she persisted.

'No.'

Jessica cleared her throat. 'You mentioned intimacy…were you talking about sexual intimacy?' she pursued, tight-lipped and rigid. 'Or was that just your idea of a joke?'

His strong jawline hardened. 'There would be nothing remotely humorous about the exercise, that I can assure you. And yes, I was referring to sexual intimacy. The part you would play would not be credible without it.'

Dear heaven, why was she actually standing here listening to this nonsense? Her oval face set with distaste and rejection as her imagination ran absolutely rampant. Was he suggesting that she become some sort of business spy, sleeping with some competitor to gain information? An insane idea, but why else the secrecy? A kind of job that would last no longer than three months which would entail sex. How utterly revolting! A hysterical laugh clogged up her throat though. Her level of sexual experience lifted such a proposition to the heights of a tragi-comic black joke…but then Carlo was not to know that.

Jessica threw back her shoulders. 'Clearly you need a hooker—'

'*Madre di Dio*…what are you saying to me?' Carlo shot her a black glance of naked hauteur. 'Are you crazy? I need a woman who can at the very least behave like a lady—'

'And you don't know any?' Jessica cut in. 'Now why doesn't that surprise me? And how many beds are you expecting this *lady* to climb into at your request?'

Dark golden eyes narrowed. 'What the hell are you talking about?'

Jessica reddened, suddenly uncertain.

'The only bed you would be expected to warm would be mine,' Carlo spelt out very drily.

Jessica went white and looked back at him in disbelief. Setting down the untouched champagne, she reached for her coat with an unsteady hand. 'Quite out of the question,' she told him with bitter clarity. 'I have no intention of selling my body to keep my father out of prison! Why the cloak and dagger approach, Carlo? Couldn't you just have asked me to be your mistress? Well, the answer is no...no, no, *no*! I'd sooner take to the streets!'

Brilliant dark eyes raked over her impassively. 'Go, then...I have nothing more to say to you.'

'But I'm not finished yet,' Jessica asserted with venom. 'Six years ago, you came into my life like a dark shadow and you tried to destroy it. There is no human being alive whom I hate more than you! And why did you set out to wreck my life? Out of nothing more than overweening conceit, selfishness and lust. It didn't matter to you that I was engaged to another man or that I loved that man. It didn't matter that you might hurt him as much as you hurt me.'

'You hurt him, not I,' Carlo returned without emotion.

Jessica shuddered with the force of her own teeming emotions. 'You set out to ruin our relationship—'

'If you had truly loved him, I would have been without power. The power I had *you gave me...*'

Hot pink flushed her slanted cheekbones. 'I did not!'

'With every look, every breath you took in my radius.

Your hunger drew me,' Carlo condemned without conscience.

'*No!*' She stared back at him in stark distress and reproach, her father's plight forgotten as he plunged her back into the past, heaping her with more guilt and an even greater sense of responsibility for all that had gone wrong.

'Did it give your ego a kick?' Carlo sent her a look of blazing contempt. 'You play with fire, you get burnt, *cara.*'

Jessica's knees felt like cotton wool. She was shattered by Carlo's view of what had happened between them. He was accusing her of having encouraged him when she had fought his ruthless pursuit every step of the way. Only at the last when she was at the very end of her strength had she failed.

'I came here and I shouldn't have come.' White and drawn, she turned away. 'We hate each other, Carlo. I don't think you realise the extent of the damage you did six years ago and I expect that even if you did you wouldn't care—'

'*You walked away from me...*'

And it was still there, an intensity of disbelief and banked-down fury. She couldn't understand the strength of his emotion after all this time. It wasn't as though Carlo Saracini had fallen in love with her. Right from the beginning, it had been a rawly sexual wanting on his side. The way he looked at her, the way he touched her, the way he talked to her. Predator and victim. Passion and pain. That was what he had offered her. And she hadn't walked away...she had run as if the hounds of hell were on her tail.

'I still don't think I deserve the offer you just made,' Jessica breathed not quite steadily. 'You sit there in your ivory tower, wrapped in all your money, and you have the sensitivity of a butcher where feelings are concerned.' Tears stung her amethyst eyes but she held her head proudly high.

'That is a gross untruth,' Carlo slashed back at her rawly.

'You walk over people. You manipulate them. You push them around. My father really liked you six years ago. You see, he couldn't see through you as I could. Oh, yes, he thought you were a hell of a guy!' she proffered in a choked voice of distaste. 'But you don't give a snap of your fingers for what he's going through now, do you? All you can see is an opportunity to humiliate me further. And I will not give you that weapon, Carlo. You see, I have my pride too.'

He was pale beneath his naturally olive skintone but he wouldn't give an inch. And she hadn't expected him to. Censure rarely came his way. In receipt of it, he silently seethed, presumably thinking it beneath his dignity to defend himself against such charges.

Eyes as flaming gold as the heart of a fire burned her face. 'Were you happy with him?'

On her passage to the door, she froze and slowly turned. He hadn't absorbed a thing she had said. Pain dug lines of stress into her face. He was asking about Simon. She looked away. 'He was my best friend,' she said finally.

'And this…this being a best friend is your ideal of marriage?' Carlo demanded, his usually fluent English curiously letting him down.

No, but it was what she had ended up with, she reflected sadly. Her troubled eyes slid back to him and collided with questioning gold and something twisted tight deep down inside her stomach. The atmosphere fairly throbbed with undertones. She stopped breathing, was sentenced to sudden stillness, every bone in her body pulling taut. For a split-second, she experienced the most extraordinary physical pull in his direction and resisted it with every last remaining drop of self-discipline. But that split-second shook her inside out.

'I would have been your lover, your soul, your survival,' Carlo gritted, and the anger was there, the anger she had feared, suddenly flaring up at her without warning in a blazing wall of antagonism that made her step back. Burnished golden eyes alive with derision and fury bit into her with a look as physical as a blow.

'Get out of here,' Carlo told her roughly. 'Get out of here before I lose my temper and show you just how sensitive I can be!'

Jessica required only that one invitation. On unsteady legs, she backed out in haste. Out in the corridor, she closed her eyes and breathed in slowly and deeply. She felt bereft, alone, wretched, and the sensations were intense. Carlo confused her, cast her into turmoil. He always had. They were opposites in every way but just for a moment...for a strange and highly disturbing moment she had recognised an utterly inexplicable pang of empathy. She had wanted to put her arms round him.

Crazy, unbelievable, just one of those mad tricks of the mind when one's emotions were on a high, she translated inwardly. After all, would she pet a sabre-toothed tiger plotting to put her on his dinner menu? But she could not escape the feeling that she had hurt him. And yet wasn't that what she had always wanted to do?

When she was with Carlo Saracini she didn't know herself. It had always been that way. With other people she was introverted and quiet, never bitchy or hot-tempered and certainly not violent. Dear heaven, she thought as she recalled the manner in which she had launched herself at him like a screaming shrew. He drew out everything that was bad in her character. He made her feel as though she could turn into a woman like her mother...wasn't that what frightened her the most?

She got into her car without remembering leaving the hotel. She didn't start the engine. She stared out the windscreen unseeingly. The way she had felt when he touched her six years ago still haunted her. And every so often she *made* herself draw those memories out to reinforce her own disgust and shame. Not only did she look like her mother, she had found that she could *behave* like her too. That had been the most devastating discovery of all. That there was this weakness inside her, this ability to forget everything...loyalty, self-restraint, even love...and lose all control in a man's arms.

Sometimes, Jessica had even told herself that she ought to be grateful for that sordid incident with Carlo. She had been afraid then that if she didn't remain constantly on her guard, virtually policing even her thoughts, she too might easily turn into a slut. If it hadn't been for that noise next door, Carlo wouldn't have stopped, she knew that. Sex was a terrifyingly powerful force if you knew yourself to be as vulnerable as Jessica felt herself to be. One weak moment in the vicinity of a male like Carlo and that would be that. She had been incredibly lucky to escape unscathed.

Only somehow, she thought now on a tide of bitter pain, it had never occurred to her that she might be just as unscathed six years on, after five years of marriage. Untouched by human hand. A virgin, no less. And wouldn't Carlo just love to know that, she reflected painfully, shuddering at the very idea. He would find it hilarious.

Jessica drifted out of her thoughts to find herself sitting shivering inside a very cold car with all the windows fogged up. She drove off but somewhere down deep in her mind was an image of Carlo as she had last seen him in the hotel suite. Angry, contemptuous...*bitter*? What the heck did he have to be bitter about? Had he really imagined she would accept that grossly insulting offer? Three months in Carlo's bed, working out her penance for daring to marry another man. What a monumental ego he must have! And the utterly peculiar way he had gone about making that offer… Her head was thumping again, tension twisting through her like a steel wire.

It was too late to go barging in on her father. Tomorrow morning first thing, she would be on his doorstep, and if he hadn't seen a lawyer yet she would see that he did. It was a crisis and she was good in a crisis. For years it seemed her life had lurched from one crisis to another.

She was about to phone her father when the doorbell went. She peered through the peephole and recognised the broad, weathered features of the heavily built man on the other side of the door.

'Dr Guthrie…?' Her brow furrowed. Henry Guthrie was one of her father's oldest friends. He and his wife ran a private nursing home.

'I tried to ring you earlier but you were out,' he proffered.

'What's wrong?' she demanded, anxiously scanning his troubled face.

'Your father's going to stay with us for a day or two until I can get him sorted out—'

'But why…I mean, I gather you know what's happened…but what's the matter with him?' Jessica prompted sickly.

Henry Guthrie sighed. 'Gerald's been receiving treatment for depression for some months now—'

She paled. 'He didn't tell me…'

'He's been quietly going off the rails ever since your mother died.'

She shut her eyes and groaned. Four months ago, they had received news of her mother's death in a car crash. From the day she walked out until the day she died, neither Jessica nor her father had had any contact with Carole. Her mother hadn't wanted any contact. She had wiped them both out of her life and had embarked on a new life abroad.

'But he seemed to take it so *well*,' she protested shakily.

'Didn't it ever occur to you that he took it too well?' the older man murmured. 'I think that he still hoped that she would come back. But when she died, he had to finally face that she was gone. That's when the depression came and the gambling started. Now I understand he's got himself in one hell of a mess—'

'Yes,' she whispered, tears stinging her eyes.

'He just can't cope with it, Jess,' Dr Guthrie sighed. 'He took some sleeping tablets this afternoon—'

Jessica gasped at him in horror. 'He did what?'

'Not enough to kill him but then, he didn't have enough. His housekeeper found him lying in the hall and thought he'd had a heart attack...'

Jessica collapsed down on the sofa behind her, sick to her stomach, and bowed her head.

'She rang me. I saw the tablets and contacted his own doctor, worked out how many he must have taken and between us...well, we decided the nursing home would be a better choice than the local hospital.'

Tracks of moisture ran unchecked down her cheeks. She wanted to thank the older man for exercising that discretion but she couldn't find her voice.

'Now when he came to, he swore he hadn't been trying to harm himself. He said he was just desperate to stop his mind going round and round and get some sleep and when the first pills didn't do the trick, he took a few more...'

'Do you b-believe him?'

'I'll know better what to think in a few days when we've talked some more,' he confessed wryly. 'Well...now I'm here to ask you how to get in touch with this character, Saracini—'

'Carlo?' she gasped.

'Do you think he'd see me? I want to tell him that

Gerald needs criminal charges right now like he needs a hole in the head!' he delivered grimly.

Jessica was barely thinking straight. But one awareness dominated the morass of emotions tearing her apart. Tonight she might have lost her father. And even if it hadn't been a suicide attempt, in his current condition, who was to say he mightn't make such an attempt this week or next week or the week after? If he wasn't coping now, how could she expect him to cope when the police were involved and the news of his disgrace leaked out? How could he handle all the horrors still to come?

She cleared her throat. 'There aren't going to be any criminal charges. I...I saw Carlo tonight and he was very understanding—'

'He wasn't very understanding when he had Gerald tossed out of the building!'

'I explained how much strain Dad had been under. There won't be any court case,' she repeated unsteadily, her slender hands twisting together as she made her decision.

'But what about the money? I gather that Gerald has no hope of paying all of it back...'

'Carlo is prepared to write it off—'

'He must be a very decent sort of man.' Dr Guthrie shook his head. 'I honestly thought he would want to nail your father's hide to the wall as an example to the rest of his employees...'

An inward quaking at that particular image assailed Jessica. She tasted cold fear but this time it was not only for her father, it was for herself as well.

The older man smothered a yawn and stood up. 'I'll pass on the good news to Gerald.'

'I'll come and see him tomorrow.'

Dr Guthrie grimaced. 'Would you be terribly hurt if I advised you to give him a couple of days to get himself together again?'

'No,' she lied.

'He feels he's let you down and I don't think he wants you to see him until he has himself under control again.'

'No problem,' she said stiffly.

'He still has a lot to handle, Jess. He's lost his job and his self-respect.'

As soon as the older man had gone, Jessica dialled the Deangate Hotel with clumsy fingers. She asked for Carlo's suite. He answered the call with a growl of impatience in his voice.

'It's me…' she said tightly. 'I've changed my mind.'

Silence buzzed on the line for long seconds. It went on and on and on while she trembled at her end of the phone with a heady mix of fear and despair. Maybe Carlo had never expected her to accept…maybe Carlo had been playing some sort of game with her.

'I'll send a car over to collect you.' There was no emotion whatsoever in his response. She couldn't believe her ears.

'When?'

'Now.'

'*Now*?' she echoed incredulously.

'Now,' he repeated, his accent more pronounced than she had ever heard it. 'I waited six years. I won't wait one hour or one day longer.'

'I can't come over to your hotel at this time of night,' Jessica gasped.

'Why not?' His deep, dark voice thickened audibly. 'You won't be going home again…'

Jessica was shattered. *Now…tonight*?

'And if you don't come tonight, the deal's off.'

'That's totally unreasonable!'

'But what I want,' Carlo asserted.

'You can't always have what you want—'

'Can't I?' He laughed softly and the phone went dead.

CHAPTER THREE

JESSICA kept the car waiting an hour. She packed as though she was going away for the weekend. In the back of her mind, a voice kept on saying, You can't be doing this…you can't have agreed. The unknown beckoned with all the welcome of a black, endless tunnel. She lifted a photo of Simon off the nightstand and stared at it tautly. It had been taken the day he opened the photographic studio. Unusually, he was wearing a suit. A slim, fair man of medium height with gentle brown eyes.

'It doesn't matter to me…that sort of thing is really not important,' Simon had soothed when she sobbed out her shame and despair after that dreadful afternoon when she had almost ended up sharing Carlo Saracini's bed. 'Of course I forgive you.'

Simon and his family had moved next door when she was ten and he was fourteen. He had been the odd one out in his large, extrovert family. Quiet and unambitious, his greatest interest wildlife photography. Simon had been an oddity to his rugby-mad father and brothers. And Jessica had been a lonely child, painfully conscious from an early age that her mother had no time for her or her father.

Simon had heard Jessica sobbing her heart out in the summer house the day she came home early from school and saw Carole half-undressed with a strange man. Simon had climbed over the wall and she had been so shocked by what she had seen that she had told him. He had been very kind and comforting. He had put his arm round her and listened, showing her the easy affection she craved.

The adult world had come to her door that day. Simon had explained that she mustn't tell her father or anyone else about that accidental glimpse. He had been naïve too in his assumption that her mother didn't make a habit of that sort of thing. Jessica hadn't been very much older before she had learnt that there was always another man in Carole's life and that her father simply tried to pretend not to know about those men.

Indeed she had soon realised that her mother's frequent affairs were food for the juiciest gossip in town. That knowledge had been an agonising humiliation to live with during the sensitive teen years.

And throughout it all, Simon had been there for her. Her best friend, her adolescent hero. By the time she had reached seventeen, both their families had begun to view them as inseparable. But, looking back, she now recalled that Simon had never talked of love or marriage or children with her, not until his family and other people began teasing them repeatedly about when they planned to tie the knot.

He had actually gone down to work in London for over a year, coming back on only odd weekends, and she had thought she was losing him, had actually wondered if Simon had ever been hers to lose, if indeed he was striving to break away from the popular belief that they were childhood sweethearts destined to marry.

Then out of the blue, the Christmas she was eighteen, Simon had asked her to get engaged. Even when he'd carefully stressed his wish for a long engagement, Jessica had been ecstatic, convinced that together they were a match made in heaven. There was nothing she could not tell Simon, nothing, it seemed, that they could not discuss. In every way they had seemed to complement each other, unlike her parents who didn't have a single thought in common.

Dear God, but she had been so innocent, she reflected now, tucking the photo into her overnight bag. Blind right to the bitter end. When had it finally occurred to her that the average male would have lifted the roof when his bride-to-be very nearly fell into another man's bed a week before the wedding? Her betrayal *should* have mattered to Simon. It *should* have been important to him. And forgiveness *should* not have come so quickly and easily to his lips. Ironically, Jessica had been far more upset than Simon had been. She had wanted to cancel the wedding but Simon had pleaded with her, telling her how much he needed her, and in the end, she had allowed herself to be persuaded…

The limousine ate up the miles back to the hotel and with every mile her tension mounted another unbearable notch. Not only was she being forced to face a savage humiliation, but also to accept the necessity of bargaining with Carlo for her father's sake. She did not yet know if Carlo would even agree to what she had already promised in his name.

Jessica didn't approach the night receptionist. With the chauffeur bringing up the rear with her bag and waving away the proffered attentions of the porter, she was terrified of being asked where she was going and why she wasn't signing the hotel register. The man flicked her a glance, said nothing, and then her pale cheeks fired on a worse thought. Did he think she was a call-girl? Didn't hotels discreetly ignore those sort of comings and goings?

A waiter opened the door of Carlo's suite.

Carlo was standing by the fireplace, talking on the phone in rapid Italian. He looked past Jessica and made a signal to his chauffeur, briefly connected with Jessica's taut stance several steps inside the room and said carelessly in an aside, 'I was about to dine without you, *cara.*'

Her gaze fell on the table exquisitely set for two. She hadn't eaten since breakfast but she did not feel hungry.

The waiter lit the candelabra, dimmed the lights and then uncorked the wine and hovered.

Carlo cast the phone aside and crossed the room in a couple of long strides. Confident hands undid the sash at her waist, parted her coat and slid it off her tense shoulders as if she were a doll to be undressed.

'Pour the wine and leave us,' he murmured to the waiter, a hand touching her narrow back as he walked her to the table, tugged out a chair and sat her down.

With a not quite steady hand she reached for her glass as soon as it was filled.

'One glass only,' Carlo decreed with dark satire. 'I would hate to be accused of getting you drunk a second time.'

Heat crawled up her slender throat. She couldn't meet his eyes. She couldn't think of anything beyond the fact that she was here in Carlo's suite and expected to share his bed tonight. 'I think the receptionist thought I was a call-girl.'

'Surely not?' Carlo parried silkily. 'A high-class hooker would never be so badly dressed.'

Her teeth clenched. 'I didn't come here to be insulted.'

'I think you came here to take whatever I choose to hand out,' Carlo flicked back, skimming her taupe skirt and blouse with a curled lip. 'When you kept me waiting, I mistakenly assumed you were dressing up for the occasion—'

A choked laugh that was no laugh at all escaped her. 'What occasion?'

'I ordered all your favourite foods.'

So he had. She hadn't noticed. He had to have a phenomenal memory.

'I remember everything about you.'

He sounded as if he expected a round of applause.

'We have to talk about my father,' she opened in a rush.

'You haven't met my eyes once since you entered this room.'

Involuntarily, she clashed with glittering gold alive with impatience above a set jawline. Evidently she was not delivering the required responses.

'This won't work if you can't do better than this,' he said drily, unfeelingly.

'Don't threaten me…' she warned tautly, great violet eyes nailed to his hard dark features. 'I function even less efficiently under threat. Now…can we talk about my father?'

'I prefer to eat to the accompaniment of *light* conversation.'

Her gaze damned him to hell and back. She dug into the pâté with sudden appetite. She worked through the next two courses without speaking unless forced. If anyone lost their appetite it was Carlo, finally thrusting his plate away with an imprecation and tossing aside his napkin as he rose from the table.

'You sulk like a little girl.'

'I am not sulking, Carlo.' Jessica embarked slowly on her dessert, it having long since occurred to her that the longer she spent eating, the longer she stayed out of the bedroom. 'You wanted me here. I came. You wanted me to eat. I am eating.'

'I won't prosecute your father.' The statement was coolly unemotional.

'He can't pay back the money—'

'He must,' Carlo's tough jawline set hard. 'The money must be returned.'

'*How*?' she demanded bitterly. 'He has no job and he's not likely to get another one. And even if he sells everything he has, he will still owe you money.'

'I will give him another position, then.'

Startled by that most unexpectedly generous offer, she stared at him. 'Where?'

'Not here. He needs a fresh start for this second

chance. Leave it with me,' he drawled. 'I will find him something.'

'And the money?' she prompted.

'He repays,' Carlo repeated grimly. 'If he is as sorry and as ashamed as you protest, he will want to repay it. He will not wish to be further in my debt.'

'But—?'

'In addition,' Carlo cut across her interruption drily, 'the offer of continuing employment will be conditional on his agreement to seek help for his addiction—'

'He's not addicted!' Jessica jumped to her father's defence.

'Any man capable of gambling so far above his own income is an addict. He requires therapy to ensure he can withstand future temptation. Now, are you satisfied?' he demanded shortly, dismissively, making her suspect that he had conceded more than he had planned to concede.

Yet Jessica had hoped for more. She had wanted the debt wiped out as she had promised Dr Guthrie. Whether it was unreasonable or not, she wanted every practical cause of stress removed from her father's path. 'You're getting me pretty cheap, aren't you?' she said shakily and then, the instant she saw the dark fury leap into his set features, she wished she had bitten her tongue and stayed silent.

'You want to go on the payroll for three months for sharing my bed?' Carlo threw back at her with a flash of even white teeth. 'A contract maybe, complete with severance pay and an assurance that you retain any jewellery or clothes that I buy you? OK, that is fine by me.' He moved an expressive brown hand in a gesture that made it very clear that it was anything but fine with him. 'I have heard of such contracts in America. But do tell me now up-front, what price do *you* put on that perfect body of yours?'

She wondered sickly whether, if someone handcuffed

his talkative hands behind his back, he would still be able to articulate. 'You know that's not what I meant.'

'Do I?' Nostrils flaring, he surveyed her with derisive dark eyes.

She rested her brow down on the heel of one unsteady hand. It was almost one in the morning. That wouldn't bother Carlo. He had reserves of energy unknown to less advantaged mortals. She wanted to go to bed but the prospect of bed was fraught with far more alarming possibilities than she could face. 'At this moment,' she whispered, 'all I need to know is what you expect from me over the next three months.'

Silence fell. Since silence was rare from Carlo's corner, she looked up.

Carlo cleared his throat, tension thrumming from his poised stance by the window. 'I want you to pretend to be my fiancée—'

She couldn't hide her astonishment. 'Why?'

'I have my reasons,' he parried, the anger gone and replaced by a set gravity which disturbed her.

'I don't see why you can't tell me—'

'I will tell you only this,' he breathed shortly, his golden eyes grim and distant as he studied her. 'I have been estranged from my father for some years and now he is dying. I wish to spend some time with him and, to facilitate this wish, I require a fiancée to accompany me to his home.'

Shaken by the unemotional explanation, Jessica studied him in turn, helplessly, maddeningly curious about why a pretend fiancée should be a necessary requirement of such a visit. She presumed he was intending a reconciliation with his father. Why muddy the water with the presence of a fake fiancée, for goodness' sake? Especially when his father was dying...a stranger would surely be even less welcome in those circumstances?

Her smooth brow furrowed. 'Once you told me that you had no family.'

'In the sense of the true meaning of the word "family",' he stressed, 'that was the truth. My mother died when I was fourteen. I was sent off to school. My father remarried and after a while he chose to forget my existence. He had his life and I my own until, some years ago, we met again at his instigation...' His strong features shadowed, his eyes night-dark and impassive. 'And what happened between us then severed all familial ties,' he completed harshly.

There were so many questions she wanted answered that she was on the edge of her seat. 'What happened?' she finally prompted in frustration when it was clear that he had no intention of continuing.

Carlo cast her a sardonic smile. 'Like all women, you are incurably inquisitive. Knowledge is a weapon in a calculating woman's hands. Do you think I don't know that?' he gibed, scanning her sudden pallor with derision. 'I don't spill my guts to anyone, *cara*...I never have and I never will.'

He made her feel like a peeping tom with a door slammed shut on her prying fingers. It hurt, humiliated.

'I only require one thing from you. A good act. My father is not a stupid man. He will not be easily deceived.'

'I don't want to deceive anyone.'

'That's why we really will be lovers by the time we arrive. Intimacy, like sexual chemistry, is something that can be *felt*,' Carlo asserted with husky conviction. 'The sole deception will be the pretence of love and of course...my intention to marry you.'

Lovers... She stiffened helplessly at the threat of what was yet to come. Arrive where? she might have asked, had not her nervous tension been too heightened for her to care at that moment. But still she longed to know why he was prepared to put on such an elaborate deception for his father's benefit. And then cynicism suggested his motive. His father was dying, presumably a wealthy man. Was Saracini Senior attaching conditions to his heir's inheritance? Was he demanding that Carlo settle down and marry? Could anyone be that old-fashioned these days? And was cold, hard cash at the foot of Carlo's deception?

'I think it's time we went to bed.'

Jessica froze. Carlo reached down for her hands and drew her up slowly, almost tauntingly. 'You're trembling…why? You've been married for years; you are not without experience.' Predictably, the reference to her marital status darkened his glittering eyes, hardened his mouth and roughened his syllables.

'That doesn't make any difference!'

'*Dio…*' he swore, running a familiar forefinger down the buttons lining her silk blouse and then pausing to flick up to the top one and slide it loose, allowing himself access to the shadowed valley between her breasts. 'Of course it makes a difference. Were you a faithful wife?'

He towered over her. His broad shoulders blocked out the light. She felt trapped and cornered and told herself that that was why she could barely get air into her lungs. A blunt fingertip, very dark against her pale skin, hovered and she stopped breathing altogether. 'Of c-course I was—'

'Really? I find that hard to believe,' Carlo murmured softly as his fingers hit on the next button.

'Why?' she gasped half an octave higher.

'You weren't faithful before the wedding…why afterwards?' he prompted. 'If you had been my bride, I would have killed you. I certainly wouldn't have gone ahead and still married you.'

I would have killed you. Said softly, conversationally but with incredible certainty. A buzzing sound filled her eardrums as a hand brushed across the swell of her breasts. All of a sudden she felt light-headed and dizzy but her breasts felt full and heavy.

'Did you tell him about what happened between us?' Carlo asked.

'Yes!'

'So you told him the whole truth and nothing but the truth. I bet you didn't,' Carlo guessed with cruel and merciless amusement. 'I doubt if you gave him a blow-by-blow account…he'd never have recovered from it.'

'I don't want to talk about this!' Jessica slung at him tremulously and then, belatedly registering that her blouse was now hanging open, she backed away from him so fast, the side table behind her dug painfully into her hipbone. 'Carlo…I met you again less than five hours ago—'

'Who's counting? I'm not. I would have been at this stage four and a half hours ago if you hadn't been so stubborn—'

'That's disgusting!' she threw back in raw outrage.

'But truthful…don't you know yet how the male mind works?'

She was starting to find out. Carlo was surveying her with smouldering golden eyes, hot with unhidden desire. And the sexual charge her mother had once mentioned was like fireworks in the heavy atmosphere. She edged round the table beneath that tracking, utterly ruthless gaze. 'Carlo…please…not tonight… I mean—' the tip of her pink tongue snaked out to moisten her lower lip '—I mean, you can't really want to do this—'

'I do.' He bent down and shattered what remained of her fast-fleeing composure by letting his own tongue follow the path her own had taken along the full curve of her sultry lower lip, and heat surged between her thighs in a sensation long buried but never forgotten. She leapt back as though he had struck her and sent a lamp flying, her heart thumping like a jack-hammer against her breastbone.

He ignored the crash and caught her arm before she could busy herself reaching down for the broken pieces.

'I want a bath!' she exclaimed in desperation.

'And maybe you'd like me to go downstairs and smoke even though I don't smoke while you prepare yourself for bed like some blushing bride!' Carlo whipped back with lancing satire.

'Yes…what a good idea,' Jessica slung back at him bitterly. 'And maybe if you're very lucky you can find a whore in the bar, because clearly that's the only kind of woman you're accustomed to!' she completed with the shrill edge of hysteria in her shaking voice.

An electrifying silence fell. Carlo dropped her arm as though she had burnt him. Beneath her distraught gaze, he had tautened. Dark colour had highlighted his blunt cheekbones. 'Is that how you think I am treating you?' he gritted back at her.

'What do you think?' After that one explosion, Jessica was drained.

'That was not my intention.' He released his breath in a hiss.

Dully, she looked back at him, her lack of conviction in that assurance clearly visible.

'I'll go downstairs,' Carlo intoned flatly. 'I suppose I may hope that when I return, you will not have broken out into a rash or got blind drunk in my absence.'

'I beg your pardon?'

'Cary Grant and Doris Day…*That Touch of Mink*,' Carlo supplied sardonically. 'Haven't you ever seen that movie?'

'I'm afraid not,' she admitted tightly.

'I don't think I'll buy a video. You're doing just great on your own.'

And he was gone. And she couldn't quite work out how she had managed the feat. Smothering a yawn, she wandered into the bedroom, wondered if he realised that his biggest challenge would be keeping her awake. She rooted through her bag, dug out what she required and went into the bathroom without once looking at the bed.

Maybe he would meet some loose woman down in the bar.

Carlo was very, very good-looking. Funny, how she had sort of blocked that out over the years. Along with so much else. The cliff edge excitement he generated. The swift, volatile changes of mood. She didn't want to think about that afternoon six years ago. The turmoil, the passion, the sobbing utterly soul-shattering pleasure of his mouth and his hands on her body. Briefly she closed her eyes, her skin flaming. She really hadn't realised that the episode could have been anything that special on Carlo's scale of experience.

But evidently it had been. Otherwise why would he be so blatantly impatient to get her into bed? Then, on his terms, nothing very much had happened that long-ago day. A few heated caresses, a little disarranged clothing. But their lovemaking had not gone to its natural conclusion. Carlo had been deprived of that ultimate triumph. And had she come across as some sort of raving sex bomb? She crept into the enormous bed as warmly clad as a great-granny ready for the Blitz in the middle of the night, sheathed from throat to toe in brushed cotton. Why should she make it easy for him?

Tears burned her eyes and crept slowly down her cheeks into the pillow. It was sheer farce...all of it. You are not without experience, Carlo had blithely assumed. A sob tore painfully at her throat. Six years ago she had honestly believed that she had a terribly low sex-drive. Simon had confined himself to occasional rather chaste kisses. Simon had never asked for more. And she had decided that in that field they were as well suited as in every other. Sex did not play a part in their relationship before their marriage. She had been proud of that fact, certain that their bonds were built on far more sturdy foundations than those formed by couples in the heat of passion.

It was frighteningly ironic that Carlo had found her

an unbearable temptation then. She just hadn't had a clue
how to handle that. It had been an entirely new experience to meet a male who couldn't take his eyes off her,
who would use the smallest excuse to touch her and who
could turn her scarlet over a dinner table in company
just by looking at her.

Yes…Carlo had *wanted* her. It had been Simon who
hadn't wanted her. Simon who got exceedingly drunk on
their wedding-night and who continued to drink throughout their fancy honeymoon in the Caribbean without
consummating their marriage.

Jessica had gone through hell, reading his lack of interest and his drunkenness as her punishment for her
shameless behaviour with Carlo. Guilt had tortured her
into a ceaseless circle of blame and unending mortification. It had torn her apart night after night…the belief
that she was reaping exactly what she deserved and that
she had hurt Simon so badly that he couldn't even bring
himself to touch her.

Who did you talk to about something so deeply personal and private? Simon had refused to talk about it,
had withdrawn into a shell if she'd dared, and once or
twice had taken off for days on end to avoid the subject.
Her best friend had stopped being her best friend and
become a moody, rarely sober stranger. It took her an
incredibly long time to realise that Simon did not want
her as a man wanted a woman and that, if she accepted
that status quo, he was quite happy to live in a sham
marriage and go back to being her best friend again.

She fell asleep wondering how long Carlo would devote to not smoking downstairs and whether he was already regretting their agreement. Regardless, she slept
like a log, flattened by complete exhaustion.

And Carlo laughed with a rich appreciation that would
have stunned her when he came back upstairs.

CHAPTER FOUR

JESSICA woke up from a long, dreamless sleep, gloriously relaxed. And then she opened her eyes. Carlo was less than six inches away. Dark golden eyes raked mockingly over her startled face. Relaxation vanished. Tension took its place.

'I don't think a woman has ever fallen asleep waiting for me before. You could be seriously bad for my ego—'

Jessica sat up with a falsely bright smile. 'Gosh, is that the time?' she gasped. 'Why didn't you wake me?'

Carlo dealt her a genuinely amused smile that quite transformed his powerful dark features. He anchored one hand in the tumbled fall of her silver hair before she could take evasive action. 'Don't worry about it. You're not in an all-girls dorm and sleeping late doesn't mean you miss breakfast,' he murmured, deliberately mimicking her schoolgirlish speech. 'Why did I ever call you stupid?'

Breathlessly, Jessica attempted to keep some space between them. 'I don't know.'

'You outgunned Doris Day last night,' he said softly, appreciatively. 'You stitched me up like a professional. I went out of here feeling like a cross between an oversexed and clumsy teenager and a complete bastard.'

'If the c-cap fits—'

His free hand curved to one slanted cheekbone, his gaze probing her wide violet eyes intently. 'And then you got into bed and slept like the dead. When you're asleep with your hair lying over the pillows, you look about sixteen. And incredibly untouched...' His husky voice deepened. 'Like a story-book princess. The day

49

we met, you looked just like that lying on the road in a white summer dress with a lace collar. Then you opened your eyes and they were the colour of pansies after the rain... *Madre di Dio*, I never wanted any woman in my life as I wanted you then!'

His deep, rich voice had a hypnotic quality that made her quiver. His palm felt warm against her cheekbone and her feathery lashes dropped low over her gaze, screening her sudden confusion from him. Every breath she inhaled seemed inadequate.

'I never had to fight for a woman before either...but I love to be challenged and you made yourself a challenge with your frigid little smiles and your icy stares,' he told her. 'I knew that that wasn't the real Jessica. It was an act, a deception—'

'No!' she objected shakily. 'You saw something that wasn't there, a woman you created in your own mind, who never existed except in your imagination!'

'She existed here in this bed. She came alive in my arms. Passionate, fearless and irresistible. And I want her back again.'

Jerkily, she ducked her head away, but he wouldn't let her escape his hold. Her angry eyes clashed with suddenly thunderous gold and the long fingers in her silky hair tightened their grip. 'You are very stubborn,' he grated.

'And you're an egotistical jerk! I won't give you what you want. I'll play the part of your fiancée but the acting stops at the bedroom door,' Jessica slammed back at him, imperious in her fury.

'Like hell it will.' Carlo's enunciation was succinct.

'You want your pound of flesh?' Jessica demanded hotly. 'OK, take it!' She wrenched her hair free of his hold, flung herself flat on the bed again and said, 'Well, what are you waiting for?'

She tensed as his dark head lowered, eyes wide glimmering with defiance and scorn, breathing stilled. He wouldn't get any enjoyment out of it, she promised herself. If his idea of entertainment was making love to an inanimate body, let him go ahead.

Carlo took her mouth in an explosion of silencing heat, his dark head blocking out the light, his hands on her shoulders hard and rough. The heat was like a red-hot wire shooting through her and she gripped his arms frantically in a last-ditch attempt to break the connection. But he wouldn't let her go.

Her hands curled into fists and struck blindly out at his chest. In response, he darted a powerful hand under her limbs and flattened her to the bed. There was a rich, enveloping darkness beckoning behind her closed eyelids and she knew what it was and she fought it, struggling for breath, for control, for anything that would wipe out the sensations he was forcing her to feel.

But her body was treacherous in pursuit of those same sensations. Her nipples tautened into tight little buds, her thighs trembled and every inch of her quivered with anticipation. Excitement was taking over in hot, drugging little spirals that peaked as he stabbed his tongue deep into the moist interior of her mouth. Her hands tangled in his hair and she kissed him back, passionately and wildly, twisting up to him to get closer.

Hard hands wrenched the nightdress from her shoulders, down her arms, effectively imprisoning her, and she couldn't bear it, her hands tugging for freedom from the sleeves. But no sooner had she freed herself than he pinned her wrists to the sheet with an earthy sound of amusement.

The tip of his tongue flicked over the thrust of one swollen nipple and a sob of tortured sound escaped her. His lips enclosed the aching bud slowly, teasingly, and her back arched, her teeth gritting. 'No!' she almost sobbed.

'Yes...' Carlo said thickly, exploring the proud swell of her flesh with his mouth and his tongue and his teeth until she was torn from that last shred of control and frantic only for continuance.

He released her hands and eased her out of her night-dress in one smooth movement. Long, sure fingers caressed her now tender breasts, playing on the sensitivity he had awakened, and a low moan of growing frustration escaped her. Dragging him down to her, she found his mouth again for herself, a long sigh of pleasure torn from her as the black curls of hair on his chest rubbed an abrasive course against her erect nipples.

A blunt forefinger traced the length of one slender thigh and she trembled, jerked as he slid his hand over the flat, silky skin of her belly. It was as if a hot wire were tightening inside her. She couldn't stay still. He made love to her mouth slowly, erotically, every thrust of his tongue making her quiver with unbearable need. She gripped his shoulders, felt the heavy thud of his heartbeat against her, and craved more, shuddering with wave after wave of raw excitement as he lazily trailed one hand through the silvery curls at the apex of her thighs.

He lifted his head and looked down at her hectically flushed face and nibbled teasingly at the reddened curve of her lower lip. She was pitched on an agonising high of arousal as his fingertips flirted with the smooth skin of one inner thigh, maddeningly refusing to touch her where she ached to be touched.

'Please...' she panted, lost to everything but the screaming demands of her own body.

'Are you begging me?' Carlo whispered in a black velvet undertone, his breath fanning her cheek, burnished golden eyes scanning glazed amethyst.

'Carlo...' She trembled against him.

'Tell me.' His dark head lowered and his carnal mouth found an incredibly sensitive spot below one small ear, sending shivers of hot, burning need running through her.

'Don't stop!' She didn't recognise the desperate edge in her own voice.

And suddenly she was free. Carlo lounged back against the pillows and watched her with hooded, calculating, dark-as-night eyes. Wildly disorientated, she stared back, not understanding, not comprehending anything but the painful ache of her own hotly aroused body.

'Never dare to tell me again that you don't want me,' Carlo murmured softly, sibilantly, studying her with chilling detachment. 'I can make you want me. You're a very sensual woman. You were made for passion—'

Too late she understood, and she dragged the crumpled sheet over her exposed limbs in an agony of mortification. 'No...' she said sickly, stricken by such cruelty.

'Yes. Six years ago I could make you burn just by looking at you—'

'That's a lie!'

'Your skin would flush, your eyes would fire and you'd shift in your seat like a cat being forced over hot coals. You wanted me then...you just wouldn't admit it,' he condemned fiercely.

Stunned, she buried her hot face in the pillow.

'At first, I didn't think of you as a tease. You were so patently unawakened. I knew you were a virgin—'

'*Stop it*!' she gasped.

'But then came that afternoon here when we only made it on to this self-same bed by a mighty feat of self-control on my part. If we hadn't been disturbed, I'd have had you,' he reminded her callously. 'After that, you were *mine*.'

'No, I wasn't!' she cried in turmoil.

'No woman, inexperienced or otherwise, responds like that to one man and then marries another a week later, still busily maintaining that she madly loves the unfortunate groom. At least, no honest, decent woman…' he gibed.

'Shut up, Carlo!' There was a sob in her voice. Initially she *had* gone to Simon, determined that their marriage should not take place. Confessing all, she had expected Simon to be outraged. Instead he had asked her if she loved Carlo. And she had uttered a vehement no. Nothing in the emotions Carlo aroused had fitted her concept of love. She had seen only lust and a terrifying self-seeking greed for pleasure in what had happened between them. She had grown up watching her mother demonstrate those same traits.

Carole had always done what she wanted, taken what she wanted, careless of the pain she caused others. And Jessica had seen the same frightening stamp on her own behaviour with Carlo. She had seen what she believed she might become without Simon to hold her steady. What Carlo had made her feel had petrified her. And Simon's love offered unconditionally had seemed a safe sanctuary. At the time she had been desperately, humbly grateful for his seeming loyalty, his pleas and assurances about needing her…and not being able to face the future without her.

Hard fingers abruptly closed round her wrist. Dully she lifted her head. Carlo wrenched off her wedding-ring and sent it skimming across the room. 'You don't need that in my bed. He wasn't very much on your mind anyway, was he, *cara*?' he breathed with an insolent smile.

'Why do you have to be so *cruel*?'

'I have a photographic memory of you walking down the aisle in your virginal white dress to marry another man!' he raked back at her.

'Well, why should that have bothered you? You didn't want to marry me!'

'That rankled, did it?' Carlo incised.

'I hated you...how could it? And I certainly had no desire to be your travelling tart!'

'*Scusi*?' He looked blank.

'Forget it,' she mumbled, but *she* never had. That day it had been the last straw when Carlo smoothly suggested she travel round the world with him.

He had said he would 'look after her'. That she could have 'anything her heart desired'. That, unfortunately, he wasn't 'into marriage or serious commitment', as he had put it.

That sadly, 'such arrangements didn't last forever', but he could promise that she would 'have a wonderful time while it did'.

And if that hadn't qualified as an offer to be a travelling tart, she didn't know what did. It had set the final seal of humiliation on their brief intimacy. Carlo hadn't loved her, hadn't cared about her...hadn't even respected her. She had just been a stupid girl from a small town very nearly conned into his bed for an hour of entertainment. And then there had been the unholy delight he had demonstrated at the idea of taking her from Simon.

She listened to him running the shower in the bathroom, endured the only slowly subsiding ache in her unsatisfied body. Well, now she knew, didn't she? She knew now that she was still every bit as vulnerable as she had feared. And Carlo had proved his point, she reflected bitterly, stiff with self-loathing. She did *want* him, probably much as a drug addict craved a fix, knowing that it was dangerous and self-destructive but unable to kill the craving. And if it was humanly possible she hated him more than ever for forcing her to concede that reality. The next three months were going to be a one-way ticket to hell. An exercise in constant humiliation.

Half an hour later, after phoning Dr Guthrie to learn that her father had spent an undisturbed night, she joined Carlo for breakfast. As she crossed the room towards him, clad in tailored ski pants and a loose green sweater, she was furiously conscious of his critical appraisal.

'Today we go down to London and buy you a new wardrobe and a ring,' he drawled flatly. 'Thursday, we fly to the Caribbean—'

'The Caribbean?' she repeated, losing some of her carefully applied cool front. 'Is that where your father lives?'

He ignored the question. 'That gives you three days to tie up your own affairs here.'

'What about my job?' she suddenly demanded.

'You work?' Carlo elevated a brow.

'I'm a legal secretary. I'm on holiday right now because my boss is,' she conceded slowly, biting at her lower lip. 'He's not likely to give me three months' leave—'

'Tell him you've found more interesting employment.'

'You don't give a damn about me losing my job, do you?' Jessica splintered back.

Impassive dark eyes rested on her angry face. 'When this is over, you can pick yourself a new position in any one of my companies.'

His complete lack of emotion chilled her. There is no sentiment in business, he had told her. A cold, scared sensation deep down inside drove away her appetite.

'No, thanks,' Jessica said jerkily. 'I'll never be *that* desperate.'

A phone buzzed and Carlo rose fluidly upright.

She found her attention roamed after him, disobedient to her brain. He was wearing an Italian-cut grey suit that fitted him like a glove and screamed expense, sheathing long, lean thighs and squaring broad muscular shoulders. Briefly she squeezed her eyes shut, despising herself.

What was she doing? Dear heaven, what was she doing? It was as if he had conjured up the dark side of her character and it was insidiously taking her over. Her skin heated, disturbing recollections of an hour past filling her conscious mind, and so real were those images that she could *feel* the touch of his hands on her flesh, *feel* the hot, hungry onslaught of his mouth on hers. With a trembling hand she poured herself another coffee, mortified by her own lack of mental discipline. It was time she got herself back under control…but just how easy was that going to be with Carlo calling all the shots? Perspiration dampened her brow.

A manservant showed Jessica into a beautiful bedroom. He reappeared several times, laden with the day's shopping, and offered to unpack for her. Her skin warming, Jessica said thank you but no and as soon as he was gone she locked the door behind him.

Before today she had not appreciated that the purchase of clothes could be embarrassing…until Carlo took her shopping, that was. She had been trailed round, thrust in and out of every outfit which attracted him and forced to parade like a concubine for his appraisal in the kind of revealing clothes she would never have chosen for herself.

The ring on her engagement finger was a stunningly noticeable diamond cluster that literally weighed down her hand. She also had diamond earrings and a slender gold watch that had undoubtedly cost thousands, although nothing as indiscreet as price had been mentioned in Cartier within her hearing.

'What about an ankle chain?' she had said, meaning to be sarcastic.

But Carlo had found that idea a distinct turn-on. For a split-second his businesslike detachment had evaporated. Heated golden eyes had scanned her assessingly, a sensual curve tinging his expressive mouth. 'I believe I'll shop for that item on my own,' he had murmured in a black velvet purr of anticipation.

You really couldn't afford to be sarcastic with Carlo.

'We'll dine out tonight,' he had decreed after the limousine had dropped them off at his London apartment.

An hour and a half later, she regarded her reflection in the mirror with scorn. The sapphire-blue cocktail dress lovingly defined every breath she drew, never mind her body. It was the kind of dress which screamed 'I want to be noticed,' and Jessica had never suffered from such a need.

But you're playing a part, she reminded herself doggedly, surveying the ring with a curled lip. And maybe if she could prove to Carlo that she could play that part well, he would be less keen to force her into bed. A subconscious voice told her she was tilting at windmills but Jessica did not easily accept defeat.

Nor did Carlo. Involuntarily she recalled the sheer bloody-minded ferocity of his pursuit six years ago.

He had insisted on driving her home personally from the clinic the next day. He had already alerted her parents without her knowledge. Her father had greeted Carlo as though he had snatched his beloved daughter from the jaws of death and her mother's usual expression of boredom had evaporated the same second she saw Carlo.

He had stayed for dinner. He had talked business with her father and, when her mother had made some fleeting reference to the wedding, Carlo had smiled. 'Jessica's too young for marriage—'

'Far too young,' Carole had chipped in, making no secret of the fact that she had little time for Simon Turner.

Later, her mother had come to her room. 'Well, well, well,' she had said mockingly. 'So you've found yourself a millionaire.'

'I haven't found myself anything!' Jessica had dismissed with distaste.

'Sometimes I think I must have been handed the

wrong baby at the hospital.' Carole Amory had grimaced. 'What's the matter with you?'

'Nothing. I just don't like him.'

'What a shame. I've invited him to join the rest of our guests next weekend.'

'*Mother*!'

'He's loaded, darling. He might just decide to invest in Amory's if we play our cards right. So be nice to him for your Daddy's sake. It was pretty obvious to me that the only thing Carlo Saracini is really interested in is you.'

Flowers had arrived for her every day the following week, each card adorned only with a slashed initial 'C'. Then he had phoned and asked her out to dinner. She had refused and he had laughed. The following evening she had found herself smiling glacially across a table at him, with her parents seated on either side as Carlo returned their hospitality at the Deangate.

With spectacular speed and efficiency, not to mention breathtaking effrontery, Carlo had broken into their lives, offering her father business contacts and advice, flattering the older man with his interest. Her mother had raged at her when she'd attempted to persuade her father that Carlo Saracini was not a man he wanted to know.

'If the firm goes into receivership, it'll be your fault!' Carole had told Jessica furiously. 'Carlo could help us…but he's not going to help if you offend him!'

Jessica had been shaken to appreciate that the family firm was on such rocky foundations. And the idea that Carlo Saracini had the power to make or break Amory's had horrified her. She hadn't trusted him an inch but her continuing attempts to warn off her father had fallen on deaf ears.

'He knows four times as much as I knew at the same age,' Gerald Amory had said admiringly. 'And he's already put me in touch with a couple of very useful people.'

Carlo had become a regular visitor to her home. Had she ever actually been naïve enough to believe that Carlo might simply invest in Amory's? Yes, she had been.

'I can help your father…' Carlo had drawled softly the night he had called when she was at home alone. 'Take off that ring and you'll find out how generous I can be.'

'I'm not for sale, Mr Saracini, and my engagement to Simon is not some bargaining counter in a sordid deal,' she flashed back, stiff with outrage.

Carlo had anchored one powerful hand round her wrist and yanked her up against him. 'Isn't it?' he had murmured fiercely, dark golden eyes searching her furious face. 'You know how much I want you—'

'Because you can't have me!' she had rebutted, struggling to pull free from the disturbing proximity of his lean, all male body. 'That's the only reason you say you want me, isn't it? I'm not interested and your ego can't take that lying down!'

'But you are interested,' Carlo had breathed almost amusedly. 'Do you really think I don't know when a woman wants me, *cara*?'

'I love Simon!' she had slung back.

'Who treats you like a little sister—'

'That's not true—'

'Then tell me when he last kissed you like *this*…' And before she could forestall him, Carlo had crushed her mouth under his and it had been like being struck by forked lightning. Terrifying.

Jessica sank back to the present and found her fingers shakily touching her lips. She saw more clearly now than she had seen then. Just as Carlo had, ironically, seen more as an outsider looking on. Carlo alone had registered the lack of sexual tension between Jessica and Simon. But Carlo had cynically misread her behaviour. He had believed she was using Simon as a weapon against him, using Simon and her fast approaching wedding to pressure him into offering her more. And in return, Carlo had used Amory's to balance the equation.

Lifting the phone, she rang Dr Guthrie to ask after her father and was delighted to hear that her father was still angrily insisting that he had had no thought of harming himself but that he was, none the less, greatly relieved to be told that he was no longer facing prosecution.

She joined Carlo in the lounge with a ramrod-straight back and a rigidly uncommunicative face, unaware that her amethyst eyes sparkled with all the angry turmoil she was struggling to hide.

Lean and lithe in his dinner-jacket, Carlo strolled forward, a faint flush highlighting his hard cheekbones as he scanned her with hooded eyes. 'Let your hair down. I don't like it up.'

'Tough.' Jessica tilted her chin.

It was a mistake. Carlo caught her to him with one hard hand and ruthlessly released her hair from the sleek plait she had confined it in. A mass of silver cascaded untidily to her shoulders, framing her outraged face and glittering eyes.

'You look messy now…as if you just got out of my bed,' Carlo delineated in a scorching purr of satisfaction. 'I think that's more the look we're aiming for…and *this*—' He lifted her hand and tugged off the diamond ring. 'While I appreciate your enthusiasm, I don't want to see you wearing it until we take off for the Caribbean.'

Colour surged painfully up her slender throat. 'I hate you, Carlo,' she enunciated with husky clarity.

'If you want your father off the hook, *cara*…' Carlo let the smooth words hang threateningly in the air between them. 'You really are going to have to work on your attitude.'

Jessica turned paper-white.

Carlo surveyed her with pitiless dark eyes, his pow-

erful features hard and unyielding. 'You're useless to me
if you can't act the part with conviction.'

Shattered by the sheer cruelty of that uncompromising
reminder, Jessica couldn't even find her voice, but inside
herself she seethed with a combustible mix of mortified
pride, thwarted fury and helpless fear.

Carlo let the silence drag. He spread both hands in a
fluid motion. 'Do you want to go home again?'

Jessica trembled. She wanted to slap him hard. Her
feathery lashes lowered over her expressive eyes. He
didn't have to humiliate her like this. He didn't have to
hold her father over her as if he were flexing a whip
over a wild animal. Hatred powered through her slight
frame but with the greatest difficulty she held it in.

'No, I don't want to go home,' she muttered grittily.

'Good,' Carlo retorted drily.

He handed her a comb in the limousine.

'You didn't need to threaten me,' she said tightly.

'This isn't a game. I don't want any temperamental
displays in my father's home. Your act has to be credible.'

But why, she wanted to demand. Why…why was
such a deception necessary? It could only be for money,
she decided. Carlo's father must want him to marry and,
unwilling to sacrifice his freedom in the long term, Carlo
was prepared to deceive in the short term. Her eyes filled
with scorn and disgust.

He took her to a fashionable restaurant where their
entrance attracted a discreet wave of turned heads and
murmured comment. Studying the menu, Jessica was
vaguely surprised to register that she was really hungry.

'Don't you think it's time you told me something
about your father?' she prompted.

'Where do you want me to begin?' His clipped tone
was not encouraging.

'I'm not likely to put on much of an act without *some*
background information. You said that he was dying—'

'Heart disease,' Carlo filled in flatly. 'He's in a wheel-chair—'

Jessica felt suddenly very insensitive. 'Can nothing be—?'

'The last operation failed. He is not strong enough for another.'

Jessica swallowed. 'Is his wife still alive?'

Unexpectedly, Carlo laughed, but the sound was curiously sardonic. 'Very much so. Sunny is considerably younger than my father.' His handsome mouth hardened, a tiny muscle pulling tight at the corner of his lips, adding a chilling gravity to his dark features. 'She is his fourth wife.'

'His *fourth*?' she couldn't help echoing weakly. 'Do you have brothers and sisters?'

'One sister, much older than I, born of his first marriage. I did have a half-brother but he was drowned in a boating accident several years back,' Carlo proffered without emotion.

'I'm sorry.'

'Don't be. He was so much older, I barely knew him.'

Jessica was silenced. Carlo was describing an impossibly fragmented family tree quite alien to her.

'My sister, Marika, lived with my father. She has never married. They live on a tiny cay in the Turks and Caicos Islands.'

'Were you born there?'

'I was born in Greece. After my mother's death, I was sent to school in Italy.'

'Why so far away?'

'I didn't like my new stepmother any more than she liked me,' Carlo said drily.

A tall, rake-thin brunette with huge dark eyes and a ripe, sultry mouth stopped by their table. Ignoring Jessica, she spoke to Carlo in Italian. His response, whatever it was, was not to the other woman's taste. Her cheeks flamed, her eyes widening. She sent Jessica a

scorching look of loathing but her dark eyes were full
of pain and jealousy before she shrugged and walked
back to a table nearby.

'And who was that?' Jessica couldn't help asking.

'Nobody you need concern yourself with,' Carlo said
dismissively.

Jessica could feel the brunette's eyes burning into her
profile. Uncomfortable with the sensation, she concentrated on her meal.

She felt claustrophobic in the limousine.

'Who was that woman?' she heard herself ask again
as they entered the apartment. Disturbingly, she found
that she could think of nothing else.

'Jealous, *cara*?' Carlo cast her a mocking, slanting
smile.

Her slender frame taut with disbelief, Jessica very
nearly choked. '*Jealous*? Are you crazy?'

Before she could move away, Carlo linked his arms
round her narrow shoulders and gazed down at her with
eyes the colour of molten gold. 'You're the crazy one,'
he murmured huskily. 'No woman has ever made me
want her as I want you.'

Her breath snarled up in her throat. She was caught
unprepared.

'Would you fight for me the way I would fight for
you?' Carlo enquired in the same deep-pitched tone of
intimacy. 'I should have kidnapped you six years ago...'

'S-stop it, Carlo!' Jessica relocated her voice clumsily,
every bone in her body tensing under the perceived
threat.

Instead, he dropped his arms to her waist, bent and
swept her up off her feet. At the same instant he covered
her startled lips with a dark, fierce hunger that devoured.
She felt the leap of response inside her and fought it to
the last ditch.

He laid her down on a bed in the moonlight. 'I don't

want this, Carlo,' she protested tautly. 'It isn't enough for me.'

He slung his tie aside, shrugged fluidly out of his jacket and came down beside her. 'What would be enough?' he demanded darkly, harshly, and before she could roll away out of reach to the other side of the wide bed he brought both hands down hard on hers, imprisoning her. 'What did *he* have that I didn't? What could *he* give you that I couldn't?'

Stunned by the seething anger she had ignited, Jessica stared up at him. He was talking about Simon again. 'It wasn't like that. You couldn't understand—'

'Then bloody make me understand!' Carlo invited in raw challenge. 'Was he a better lover than I was?'

Torn by a pain she had never shared with another living soul, Jessica wrenched her head to one side, seeking to evade his glittering scrutiny. 'Carlo…'

'I want to know,' he intoned, twisting one powerful hand into her hair to force her eyes back to his. 'So you tell me, what was it about him that made him so special?'

'I'm not going to talk about this!' Tears stung her eyes in a blinding surge.

'I want to talk about it. I offered you everything I had to give and you walked away…' Carlo returned with smouldering bite. 'And yet it was *me* you wanted—'

'*No!*' she gasped.

'*Si*…' Carlo snarled down at her.

'Wanting isn't enough!' she suddenly screamed back at him.

'But without it, there's nothing,' Carlo pointed out with devastating simplicity.

And the reality of that fact was like a knife twisting inside her. A tortured sob escaped her convulsed throat. She had had a marriage that was five years of nothing.

'Don't cry…' Carlo smoothed a not quite steady hand over her damp cheek and she found herself turning into the seductive warmth of that caress like a homing pigeon.

The awareness that she could not restrain her physical impulses this close to him merely added to her torment. She was her mother's daughter, a little voice said, and a sick sense of shame stirred inside her. Carlo had eased a supportive hand beneath her shoulder blades to raise her up and her fingers accidentally brushed against his broad chest and heat sprang up beneath her fingertips, the raw heat of his flesh below the thin silk shirt.

He trembled, and for some reason that made her want to do it again. He muttered something rough into the veil of her hair and she let her hand stay where it was, listening to the ruptured rasp of his breathing and feeling the thunderous crash of his heartbeat against her palm.

The atmosphere was explosive, abruptly, inexplicably exhilarating as adrenalin surged through her veins. She let her fingers spread and flex and without warning Carlo groaned, sweeping her with a sudden current of live-wire excitement.

'*Maledizione*!' Carlo muttered thickly, dragged her lithely back down on the bed. 'With you I have less control than a teenager!'

He was shaking in the circle of her arms. When had she closed her arms round him? It didn't seem important. Briefly, crazily, she experienced an extraordinary sense of power. A heartbeat later it was torn from her by the burning assault of his hungry mouth. Her body leapt into throbbing life and rational thought ended for long, timeless minutes.

The scent of him was so achingly familiar it was an aphrodisiac. His shirt was open and she found the sleek, smooth brown skin of his shoulder with her tongue and he shuddered against her, chest to breast, thigh to thigh in a pagan feast of agonising, uncontrollable excitement. Carlo rolled over and wrenched violently at her dress. She heard something tear. It meant nothing to her.

With a ragged gasp of pleasure he bent over her bared breasts, shaping her, touching her. She closed her eyes, arched her slender throat and was lost in a world of sensory overdrive, more powerful and more primitive than anything she had ever dreamt of experiencing. Scorching heat surged through her shivering body in an unstoppable surge.

Her hands fluttered over every part of him she could reach, torn between the black silk luxuriance of his hair and the oiled smoothness of the muscles flexing on his back. She wanted to touch him everywhere at once, burned to explore him as intimately as he was exploring her.

Her nails skidded down the long sweep of his back and he moaned against her mouth, biting erotically at her lower lip in punishment. Rawly impatient hands dealt with the scrap of silk that was all that shielded her from him. When he found the damp, eager heat of her, a wild cry escaped her. She was poised like a diver on the edge of a deep, beckoning abyss and she knew she would throw herself off even though she couldn't swim. The sheer primitive need she was controlled by was closer to agony than ecstasy.

'You're *mine*…from this moment on,' Carlo spelt out roughly, 'you are mine.'

She collided with glittering dark eyes, unreadable in the moonlight, and her mouth ran suddenly dry, a shaft of returning sanity tightening her every muscle in rejection.

But his hand slid over her quivering body, shattering her with her own response. There was a buzzing sound somewhere in the background. She closed it out but after a while Carlo began to tense. Abruptly, he lifted his dark head and swore viciously under his breath. A second later, he rolled away from her and the light went on as he answered the phone.

It took several seconds for Jessica to appreciate that

Carlo was talking in fast, urgent Italian. He cast aside the phone, his starkly handsome features pale and rigidly cast, his brilliant dark eyes hooded. Without a word or a glance, he strode out of the room.

Jessica was in a passion-induced daze, only slowly fumbling her way back to the real world. But at Carlo's exit she sat up. Dear God, had he had bad news about his father? In confusion she absorbed her own nudity and, hurriedly vacating the bed, found a robe to pull on. She wanted to go to Carlo, offer sympathy and comfort, and the instant she recognised that need within her, she collapsed down on the edge of the mattress and covered her face with unsteady hands.

Dear heaven, what was happening to her? What was going on inside her head? For six years she had told herself that she hated this man and yet a mere second ago her most driving urge had been to rush to his side and ease his pain by whatever means were within her power. Suddenly, she was plunged into complete turmoil by the conflicting signals between her thoughts and her emotions. Fearfully she sought to rationalise her feelings.

So much had happened so fast, she told herself weakly. This whole situation put her under severe strain. In addition, she was deeply ashamed of the fact that she could not withstand Carlo's blatant sexuality. Really it was hardly surprising, she decided, that her emotions should become wildly confused as well. She was only now learning the kind of things that most women already knew by their late teens. Desire was not love but maybe her puritanical inner self wanted her to behave as though it were. Was that what was the matter with her?

She didn't know how long she had been sitting there when she glanced up and saw Carlo framed in the doorway. He was still and silent as a statue.

Jessica swallowed hard, intimidated by his aggressive stance. 'What's wrong?'

Carlo released his breath with an audible hiss. 'Why didn't you tell me that your father was in a nursing home?' he demanded.

'How did you find out?' Sharply disconcerted, Jessica stared at him wide-eyed.

'My PA, Spiros, attempted to contact him this evening. He called to let me know and I have just finished speaking to Dr Guthrie on the phone.'

Jessica lost every scrap of colour.

'Why didn't you tell me?' Carlo thundered with sudden raw condemnation. 'Why didn't you tell me that he was in an unstable frame of mind?'

Jessica rose unsteadily upright, shattered by his fury. 'I didn't think—'

'What didn't you think? That it would make any difference to me?' Carlo's outrage was so great, he could barely vocalise the question. Strain had etched lines into his sun-bronzed skin, flattened his sensual mouth. 'Is this your opinion of me? That I would happily drive a man to suicide?'

Jessica trembled. Voiced like that, it sounded appalling. 'I only thought you wouldn't consider it… relevant—'

'Relevant.' Carlo only got the repetition out with the greatest of visible difficulty, his accent scissoring along the syllables like a cut-throat razor.

'My father insists that he was not trying to harm himself,' she heard herself protesting weakly. Carlo was looking at her as if he had never seen her before. And it was equally obvious that he did not like what he did see.

'Last night you made no attempt to tell me that your father was in such extreme distress…not once did you even hint of such a danger!' he spelt out with sizzling disbelief.

'I didn't think you'd care.'

Carlo went white and spun away from her, both hands

clenched into fists. 'I don't think I have ever been closer to physical violence than I am now,' he bit out in seething incredulity. 'How dare you say to me that I would not have cared? *Dio*…to think I almost made love to you! What did I ever do that you should view me in such a light?'

Jessica bent her head, attacked by sudden shame and confusion. Carlo was so absolutely appalled by what he had learnt. 'I…I—'

'Had I known of your father's state of mind, I would have done everything within my power to reduce his distress. *Everything*,' he stressed, surveying her with scorching intensity. 'Did you really believe that my desire for you would outweigh the worth of a man's life? Or even the smallest risk of him taking that life?'

'No, I didn't…' Jessica was shaking.

Carlo's golden eyes raked her with derision. 'Or were you just looking for a damned good excuse to come back to me without sacrificing your precious pride?'

She flinched as though she had been struck but she was in no condition to respond. When *had* she turned Carlo into the very image of vicious corruption inside her own head? When and on what grounds had she shorn him of every decent human emotion? Dear God, why had she deceived herself that way? For she had deceived herself. She saw that now. Had it been easier to blacken Carlo and blame him for everything sooner than face the extent of her own culpability? And worst of all, had she done that purely to avoid coming to terms with what Carlo made her feel?

'You said that there was no sentiment in business,' she attempted desperately to defend herself. 'You said that you had no interest in my father except as a means to an end and that the subject bored you.'

Reminded of those harsh words, Carlo swung away from her. 'I had no idea of your father's depression, no knowledge of your parents' divorce or of your mother's death,' he muttered less aggressively.

Jessica couldn't think straight. She felt sick inside. She saw quite clearly that last night at the Deangate she should instantly have told Carlo what had happened to her father. Yet she had not even considered telling him. She had been so punch-drunk on her image of Carlo as a sadist that she had remained silent.

'I should have told you,' she heard herself whisper.

Carlo wasn't even listening. 'I will meet with your father tomorrow and set his mind at rest. I will not have him on my conscience,' he asserted, shooting her a glance of smouldering condemnation. 'And to further that end I will tell him that I have offered you a job as my secretary.'

'That's what I intended to—'

'Believe me,' Carlo cut in fiercely, 'had I known yesterday what I know now, I would never have touched you! Just to think of you lying in my bed smugly thinking that you were sacrificing yourself for your father's life…' His teeth gritted and he spread his hands in violent rejection of the idea, his dark features pale and taut. 'That disgusts me, but it also makes me want to shake you until your teeth rattle!'

'Don't you dare!' Jessica gasped.

Carlo reached out a punitive hand and hauled her up against him without warning, his sheer strength intimidating her. Flaming golden eyes clashed with hers and she stopped breathing. 'You're not a martyr, *cara*… you're a coward!' he seethed down at her with lancing derision. 'You want me every bit as much as I want you but you haven't got the guts to admit it!'

'Let go of me!' Jessica suddenly sobbed in turmoil.

Carlo released her so abruptly, she fell back against the bed. Spinning on his heel, he strode out of the room. Picking herself up, Jessica slammed the door after him and then she leant back against it, tears streaming down her convulsed face, trapped in a morass of pain and emotional turmoil. She understood the turmoil but she didn't understand the pain. She could not explain to herself why it should hurt so much when Carlo looked at her with distaste and derision.

CHAPTER FIVE

'…A TREMENDOUS opportunity for me,' Gerald Amory continued with satisfaction. 'A challenge is exactly what I need right now, and I've always liked Scotland.'

Jessica gave her excited father a strained smile. Carlo had offered him the management of an ailing engineering company in Glasgow. And her father, seemingly a broken man mere days ago, had been so boosted by Carlo's apparent faith in his abilities that he was a changed personality. There was a new spring in his step and a look of energy in his tautened features that she hadn't seen in a very long time.

'He couldn't have been more understanding,' Gerald murmured, not for the first time. 'But obviously I couldn't let him write off the money I took from Amory's.'

Jessica gave him a look of shock. 'Carlo suggested that?'

'Yes, but I couldn't let him do it. I have some very valuable antiques in this house and I intend to clear the lot. I want to start with a clean sheet. I should have done it years ago. I should never have stayed in this house with all its memories of your mother,' he said with a wry grimace. 'Nor should I have agreed to stay on at Amory's, not when I felt like a dog in the manger. That was taking the easy way out. I should have restructured my life then and moved on just as your mother did. I expect to be free of my debt to Carlo within two years and who knows, with a little belt tightening, maybe sooner!'

This was said with such good cheer that Jessica simply stared, but she was inwardly digesting the astonishing news that Carlo had tried to persuade him that there was no necessity for him to return the money he had stolen.

'As for Amory's and my abrupt departure...' Gerald sighed. 'Everybody thought I had been suddenly taken ill and that's why I was rushed out of the building. Of course my secretary and the chief accountant know the truth but neither of them will talk. I've been very fortunate, although I'm not quite as slow on the uptake as you and Carlo seem to imagine, Jess...'

In receipt of his suggestive smile, Jessica said, 'Meaning?'

'Even when I finally managed to convince Carlo that yes, I had reached a very low ebb but no, I did not intend to put an end to my existence,' Gerald Amory asserted squarely, 'Carlo was still set on being extraordinarily generous. And I can think of only one reason for that.'

Jessica sat very taut.

'He has to be in love with you.'

Jessica forced a laugh. 'He offered me a job, Dad. That's all!'

Her father shook his head with a rueful smile. 'You're a very junior employee at Fulton and Greenbury and he's a tycoon. You don't even know how to use a computer, Jess. I don't think he's shipping you out to the Caribbean to stay with his family for your secretarial skills alone. At least, if he is, he's in for a very frustrating time of it!'

Jessica didn't know what to say but her father didn't seem to expect any response. He was an astute man and she should have known he would pick holes in so thin a cover story. Carlo in love with her? She couldn't even summon up any amusement at the idea. She hadn't seen or heard from Carlo since that night, three days earlier.

He had been gone when she breakfasted the next morning and she had been driven home to the cottage.

Spiros, Carlo's PA, had phoned her yesterday to tell her when she would be picked up to be taken to the airport tomorrow. He had also dropped the news that Carlo would only be meeting up with them in Miami for the final leg of the journey.

Now, as her father took his leave, eager to embark on the challenges ahead of him, Jessica was left to cope with her own confusion. Astonishingly, Carlo had gone to great lengths to help her father without hurting his pride. He had been far more generous than she could ever have expected. She had grossly underestimated Carlo. But then, she reflected ruefully, Carlo had not displayed an honourable or more appealing side to his character six years ago. Carlo had been ruthless, arrogant and aggressive. Feeling threatened, she had clung all the harder to her belief that she loved Simon.

She had loved Simon for a good half of her life and had been too inhibited by her mother's promiscuous example to question Simon's lack of sexual interest in her before their marriage. She had been grateful for his restraint, for what she had seen as his *respect* for her. For the first time she openly acknowledged that Simon had cruelly betrayed her trust.

He should have told her the truth. He shouldn't have pretended. He had had no right to use her simply to silence his family's suspicions, plunging them both into deep unhappiness and endless pretences. Why had she blamed Carlo for the misery of her marriage? she now asked herself. The reality was that her marriage would have been a disaster even if she had never met Carlo…only, having met Carlo and confessed all to Simon, she had given Simon an excuse to hide behind. Simon had allowed her to believe that her moral lapse with Carlo was what kept him from her bed. It had been a very long time before he'd admitted the truth.

And in the interim of tortured guilt she had hated Carlo and kept on hating him with quite irrational fervour. Carlo had become the focus for her bitter dissatisfaction with her life. But common sense told her that she could never have been that attracted to a man she truly hated. No, what she had really hated was the uncontrollable chemistry she experienced in Carlo's radius, a powerful sexual attraction that she couldn't handle and was deeply ashamed of feeling.

So where did that leave her now? She had scarcely slept the last few nights. She couldn't get Carlo out of her mind and that, frankly, terrified her.

Jessica boarded the luxurious jet at Miami and surveyed her superbly comfortable surroundings with a faint frown line between her brows. 'Nothing like travelling in style.'

Spiros laughed. 'Mr Philippides likes his guests to be comfortable.'

'Who is Mr Philippides?' Jessica enquired of the likeable young Greek, who had unbent from his strict formality with every hour of the travel they had shared.

Spiros sent her an incredulous glance. 'You are joking, yes?'

'Why should I be joking?' Jessica dropped into her seat and wondered when Carlo intended to show. Her nervous tension was heightening by the second.

Spiros frowned and leant forward. 'Lukas Philippides is Carlo's father, Miss Amory,' he proffered awkwardly. 'Of course, you knew...you are pulling my foot—'

'Leg,' Jessica corrected, frozen to stillness by shock.

Spiros chuckled. 'Who has not heard of Lukas Philippides?'

'Who indeed?' she mumbled through a dry mouth. Lukas Philippides was one of the richest men in the world and in recent years he had lived like a recluse, encouraging the media to concoct wildly unlikely stories about him and compare him to the late Howard Hughes.

Spiros was studying her closely. 'You really didn't

know,' he realised with unhidden astonishment. 'But the relationship is widely known. Carlo dropped the Philippides name and took his mother's many years ago.'

Damn Carlo for his refusal to fill her in on the most basic facts! That was her first thought. Her standing as his supposed fiancée might very easily have fallen at the first ditch had she betrayed her ignorance in the wrong company. Lukas Philippides was dying and the media had yet to stumble on that scoop. All that money, an amount of money beyond her comprehension, was shortly to be up for grabs. Carlo had been playing for far higher stakes than she could ever have imagined, she thought sickly. Wealth beyond avarice, the kind of inheritance many would kill for...never mind lie and deceive.

Jessica was badly shaken. Carlo's fury that she had failed to tell him of her father's depression, his astonishing kindness towards her father from that point...both those things had demonstrated a new side to Carlo's volatile nature. But now she found her most recent assumptions being flung into chaos all over again.

Had Lukas Philippides demanded that his son marry before he could inherit? She could think of no other reason for Carlo's deception. And how likely was it that a man like Lukas Philippides would find a twenty-six-year-old widow without any assets an acceptable match for his only surviving son and heir? The plot thickens, she thought hysterically. What the hell had she got herself into?

The stewardess was speaking. Jessica lifted her head as Carlo appeared. He dropped down with fluid energy into the seat opposite her. His impact was incredibly physical. In a lightweight, exquisitely cut cream suit that threw his exotic darkness into prominence, he was shatteringly sleek and beautiful in an entirely masculine way. Undoubtedly not a single female head had failed to turn on his passage here. This proximity to Carlo was like being struck by lightning.

Her body reacted involuntarily to the powerful sexuality he emanated. Beneath her silk camisole she could feel her nipples tighten into hard little points and a quiver ran through her as she attempted to remove her eyes from the magnetic gold allure of his. Her heartbeat thudded in her eardrums and it was suddenly impossible to breathe in the rushing silence.

'You missed me,' Carlo positively purred, stretching out his long, lean thighs in an attitude of indolent relaxation as the jet engines whined up to take-off. He rested his dark head back and surveyed her from below a screen of lush black lashes, hooding his gaze to a sliver of gleaming awareness. 'I can feel the heat from here.'

A hectic flush coloured her cheekbones. Her soft mouth tightened. She felt entrapped by her own weakness, as easily read as a pre-teen suffering from a giant crush. Carlo let his eyes wander with sensual intensity over her, his attention lingering shamelessly on the taut buds of her tilted breasts plainly visible beneath her camisole. She threw up her chin. 'It's the air-conditioning!' she snapped in outrage.

Carlo was still laughing when they were airborne. He twisted his head and said something to Spiros, who was seated behind him. The younger man left his seat as the stewardess appeared with a tray of drinks and her attention was so entirely pinned to Carlo that she very nearly spilt Jessica's.

But she might as well not have existed. Carlo's attention was centred with smouldering potency on Jessica. Releasing his belt, he slid upright and settled down beside her. Removing her drink from her nerveless fingers, he pulled her out of her seat with easy strength and yanked her down on top of him. He took her by surprise, and she collapsed across his hard thighs in a tangle of limbs.

'What the hell—?'

Both lean hands pinned to her cheekbones, he drove his tongue deep into her mouth in a hot, erotic invasion that sent her every sense into instant, shuddering melt-down. With a husky groan, he repeated the assault in a blatant imitation of a far more intimate possession and a tight, coiled spring of need fired her every skin cell. She couldn't get enough of him. He was a feast after a famine, the heat of the tropics after a long, endless winter and she was helplessly greedy for every sensation so long denied.

'There's a very comfortable bed in the cabin.' His palms still framing her face, brilliant golden eyes, blazing with desire, scanned hers.

Simultaneously, her nostrils flared. Obsession. A definable aroma of the exclusive perfume clung to him. Her stomach twisted painfully. Carlo had been in close bodily contact with another woman. Nausea doused her excitement. She jerked her head free and slid upright on wobbly legs.

'No doubt you're very familiar with those kinds of facilities.'

An ebony brow elevated. 'Do you want the truth or a polite fiction? Of course there have been women in my life, but never more than one at a time.'

Furiously she turned her head away. All she could smell was that perfume and it was turning her stomach now, reminding her what a fool she was in this male's presence. He made her wanton, reckless. It was one thing to acknowledge his attraction, another thing entirely to accept that that same attraction could humiliate her. Her lips still stung from the carnal imprint of his, her unsatisfied body still ached. But she was torturingly certain that Carlo was not suffering from similar rigours of celibacy. Carlo had been with another woman…and why not?

This was the son of one of the twentieth century's

most renowned womanisers. Four wives and innumerable mistresses. And six years ago Carlo had acted like a real chip off the old block, offering her nothing but sex and the good life and the cool assurance that marriage wouldn't feature anywhere in the equation. Perhaps it was time she reminded herself that all Carlo was doing now was putting a sensual gloss on their supposed relationship for his father's benefit.

'What do you want from me?'

The answer came inwardly. Much more than you will give… It shook her.

'Together we're sexual dynamite. Why deny yourself the pleasure I can give you?' Grimly amused dark eyes rested assessingly on her taut profile and unexpectedly she turned and caught the gleam of mockery.

'You didn't expect me to go into that cabin with you…did you?'

'I like watching you torment yourself,' Carlo confided, the full intensity of his probing gaze resting on her. 'You're a fascinatingly complex little creature. Passionate and repressed. Wild and inhibited. And secretive, intensely secretive…'

Her lips compressed bloodlessly. 'I don't know what you mean.'

Carlo laced lean brown fingers calmly round his glass and surveyed her as if she were a specimen under a microscope. 'What made you what you are? What goes on inside that beautiful head? Most of my women have told me the story of their lives by the end of the second date. But you tell me nothing and you never did. Not about your family, not about your marriage. You keep it all locked up tight inside…'

'I am not one of your women, Carlo.' But it was a shaken retort. She was appalled by the direction of the conversation. It was an attack on the privacy she cherished.

'If it were not for your father, I wouldn't even know

how your late husband died.' Carlo seemed to be selecting his words with immense care. 'I find it surpassingly strange that this great love that encompassed so many years of your life should never, ever be mentioned even accidentally. But I've yet to hear his name pass your lips.'

She stared at him with huge amethyst eyes dark with pain. 'I don't want to talk about it—'

'But isn't that unnatural? He's only been dead a year and I understand that you nursed him for many months beforehand,' Carlo continued with merciless persistence. 'Leukaemia…that must have been a harrowing experience…'

Jerkily, Jessica swung away from him. She wanted him to shut up. She wanted to cover her ears. She wanted to run away but there was no place to go. Carlo had chosen to stage his interrogation well. She folded her arms. 'It's none of your business.'

'But I've made it my business,' Carlo pointed out gently. 'By the time we part, all of my questions will have been satisfied. I will know everything about you.'

It was a threat. In defiance of her own inner insecurity, she thrust up her chin. 'And do you plan to be similarly expansive?'

'I doubt it. I tend to keep my own counsel.'

She flung her head back, silver hair flying back from her exquisite face. 'Even to the ridiculous extent of not telling me *who* your father is?'

'So the penny finally dropped.' Carlo's expressive mouth curved into a sardonic smile.

'Spiros told me and I'd like to know why you didn't!'

'It's not an announcement I've had to make in recent years. It is of no importance,' he asserted.

And suddenly she understood and she was speared by a sharp pang of pain. 'You didn't trust me, did you?' she condemned shakily. 'You knew I didn't know and you didn't trust me enough to tell me!'

A broad shoulder lifted in a fluid shrug. He met her distressed gaze unflinchingly. 'It did cross my mind that you could sell the information for hundreds of thousands of pounds in the right quarter. His death will create havoc on the international money market. Fore-knowledge would give certain speculators the opportunity to make a fortune. And even if you had simply chosen to approach a tabloid, you could still have made more than sufficient money to clear your father's obligations to me.'

Jessica looked at him, incredulous and deeply wounded. 'And you think that I would have done that?'

'Let us say that I saw no reason to take an unnecessary risk.'

Numbly she shook her head. 'Dear God, what sort of woman do you think I am?'

'Tough. Been there, done that,' he traded with dry mockery. 'Delicate wrapping round a steel backbone.'

'I would never have done something so disgusting!' Jessica told him vehemently. 'I do have some standards.'

Golden eyes glittered over her tautened figure. 'Then where were they six years ago, *cara*?'

Her stomach turned over, every muscle tightening as though to ward off a punch. 'I made a mistake…a dread-ful, inexcusable mistake—'

Carlo vented a sardonic laugh and drained his glass, the hard planes of his dark features chillingly set. 'Are you calling me a mistake…or *him*?' he drawled softly.

Although she was trembling, she stood her ground. 'What do you think?'

'That I will never forgive you either way.'

Sharply disconcerted, she collided with gleaming gold and it was like ice sliding slowly down her tautened spinal cord, the most frightening chill spreading with sick certainty through her limbs. The colour drained from her face.

'You're telling yourself right now that you don't want

or need my forgiveness,' Carlo murmured with shattering accuracy. 'But you will find that you do. You already look for me when I'm not there, don't you, *cara*? How did you sleep the last few nights? Did you expect me to call and wonder why I didn't? And just how did you feel when you first saw me today…elated? Sexually excited? You're halfway to falling in love with me already. I recognise all the symptoms and this is where I normally beat a strategic retreat in an affair…but not with you.'

Throughout she had stood there, entrapped by the wicked allure of his beautiful eyes and the hypnotic mastery of his rich, dark voice. She was transfixed by fascination, had to struggle just to unglue her tongue from the roof of her dry mouth. 'You're out of your mind,' she whispered. 'I could never love you.'

'I will settle for nothing less,' Carlo told her softly in the steadily thickening atmosphere.

'You belong in a cave, Carlo!' Jessica managed a laugh that sounded oddly forced even to her own ears. 'Do you honestly imagine that I have so little control over my own emotions?'

Carlo dealt her an insolent smile that made her palms itch to slap him hard. 'I hate to be crude but you have very little control over your body—'

Fury seized hold of her and she snatched up her glass and flicked the contents over him.

'And even less over your temper.' He withdrew a silk handkerchief and calmly wiped the drops from his cheekbones. 'In fact you are quite appallingly juvenile in your reactions when you do lose your head. Like a child hitting out blindly in a tantrum,' he mused reflectively. 'Almost as though you haven't allowed yourself the luxury of freely letting go of your anger very often…so you really can't handle it, can you?'

The insight inherent in that careless stab dismayed her and she stepped hurriedly back from him. 'Has the game-playing moved into the field of therapy now?' she asked with sarcasm dripping from every syllable.

'One,' Carlo itemised, 'this is not a game for me. And two, I'm more into shock treatment than therapy. I lack the necessary patience. When I want something, I want it yesterday.'

Frustration currented through her. She needed to fight back but was now too afraid that in anger she might be guilty of revealing too much. Disturbingly, Carlo smiled, his cool composure untouched. 'You should go and lie down for a while. I'll wake you up before we land on Grand Turk.'

'I don't want to lie down.' Every fibre rebelled from the concept of retreat. 'Is Grand Turk where your father lives?'

'He lives on Paradiso Cay which he owns.'

With determination, Jessica took a seat again. If she talked, she would not be required to think about Carlo's unashamed lust for revenge. 'And how long has he lived there?'

'Five years. He bought Paradiso when ill-health became a feature of his life,' Carlo said unemotionally.

'You are so filled with compassion.'

'He is not a man who inspires compassion,' Carlo fielded drily. 'And he would be furious if he was given it. He has lived his life exactly as he wanted to live it. He has never followed medical advice. He smokes, he drinks, he loves the richest of foods and his sexual appetite was once legendary. He would tell you that childhood deprivation made him greedy for the luxuries but the reality is that Lukas has never seen the need for temperance in any field and never, to my knowledge, considered any human being's needs above his own—'

Jessica swallowed hard. 'You're describing a monster, Carlo.'

Quite spontaneously, Carlo laughed. 'To you, perhaps,

for restraint in all things is your holy icon, isn't it?
Everything neat and tidy, nothing unpredictable…'

She dredged her startled gaze from him. 'You were
talking about your father—'

'He's volatile, fiercely proud, and no doubt bitterly
resents his failing strength. He will fight for life to the
very last moment and will probably die cursing all who
survive him.'

'Does that include you?'

'I would hope not.' Carlo's strong features shadowed
and then he shrugged with Latin acceptance. 'But I
would not like to make a career out of second-guessing
Lukas. He loves surprising people. A pussycat one moment, a predator the next—'

'A lot like you, then,' she muttered in a 'forewarned
is forearmed' tone.

'At least what you see is what you get with me.'

But what did she see? she questioned, flipping her
vulnerable eyes away out of his probing reach. So kind
to her father, so unrelentingly cruel to her. He had waited
until they were airborne before he told her what he had
in store for her. But he couldn't make her love him.
Liking and respect and sharing were the prelude to loving. 'Everything neat and tidy, nothing unpredictable…'
Her teeth gritted. She wanted to tear his honey-smooth
drawl out of her head, no matter how much it hurt!

How could he have thought that she might sell the
revelation that his father was dying to the highest bidder? She shuddered with revulsion. Of course, she had
been hurt. Nobody could easily accept such a charge.
So, he didn't trust her as far as he could throw her…but
what had made *him* like that? She remembered him saying that knowledge was a weapon in a woman's hands
and that had come straight from the gut! Clearly at some
stage Carlo had got badly burned by a member of her
sex and the memory rankled, kept him on his guard,

made him cynical and suspicious…so, who's playing the therapy game now, Jess?

Why was she allowing him to wind her up like this? What did any of this matter to her? All that lay between her and Carlo was sex. A demeaning passion on her side, lust on his. Though maybe lust was too strong a word. Evidently, Carlo was more powered by a desire for revenge than by his sex drive. Sex was simply the channel through which he planned to trap her. Did he really think he could make her fall in love with him?

Dear heaven, all that intellectual wheeling and dealing seemed to fail him when it came to human emotions, and to actually have the supreme self-assurance to forewarn her of his expectations…! Jessica smothered a laugh and then her nostrils flared with renewed distaste.

'You stink of perfume, Carlo. I think you should have a shower.' The suggestion simply leapt right off her tongue and it was hard to say which of them was most taken aback by it.

'*Scusi*?' Carlo lapsed into Italian, surveying her with cool enquiry.

Jessica wrinkled her nose. 'It's tacky, like lipstick on your collar.'

'What the hell are you talking about?'

'The lady left her signature, *caro*,' she dropped with dulcet sweetness. 'Her perfume. It's all over you.'

Carlo's eyes splintered into hers, alight with disturbing mockery. A slumbrous smile of staggering charisma glued her gaze to him. 'What a wonderful private eye you would make…I can see you sheltering from the rain in a doorway, watching out for the evidence of some poor bastard cheating on his wife! Unhappily for you, Jessica I am not a married man—'

'I haven't the slightest desire to know what you were doing last night!' she vented in disgust.

'It can't have been last night,' Carlo drawled. 'I had a shower this morning.'

Jessica flew upright, infuriated by his mockery. 'Do you really think I gave a damn when or with whom?'

Carlo stretched out with positive indolence, his eyes a mere glimmer of light below the luxuriant veil of his ridiculously long lashes. 'One of my PAs from the New York office. Five foot ten inches tall, Titian hair…my besetting sin,' he confided softly, reflectively, his eloquent mouth taking on a sensual slant. 'She was as wild and hot as I was. I got laid in my coffee break—'

Frozen by appalled disbelief that he could actually be confessing to such behaviour, Jessica was welded to the spot. Her vocal cords were strangled.

'And at lunchtime. She was *insatiable*,' Carlo savoured. 'Sadly the lift on the way up to my suite was occupied…that's always been one of my fantasies, but unless I close off and empty some building it looks like going unfulfilled. I'm not into audience participation. Still, we made the best of the floor, the bed, the bath, the walls, the kitchen table…and then she called up a friend and that is *really* when the fun got started…you're lucky I made the flight…'

Functioning on automatic pilot, Jessica backed away. She felt butchered. He might as well have been wielding a knife without giving her an anaesthetic. She was in agony and scared of throwing up in front of him.

'You don't want to hear about the truly perverted things we did?' Carlo raised an ebony brow in apparent surprise and then sighed. 'Good, I'm afraid my imagination is fast running out of fuel. Here…catch!'

A gift-wrapped box landed at her feet but she barely saw it before she was forced to whirl into the washroom and lose her lunch in the most humiliating fashion possible. She heard Carlo mutter a startled imprecation in her wake and wished she had had time to close the door. Just about the last thing she expected from him was help. But Carlo took over, pressing a cold cloth to her perspiring brow and offering her a glass of water to rinse out her mouth. Then he swept up her still shivering and weak body, kicked open a door and laid her down on a bed.

Her eyes skidded over him, haunted, bruised.

'*Madre di Dio*!' he launched down at her with a groan. 'It was a joke!'

She shut her eyes, too shattered to comprehend and then abruptly she rolled over, curling into a defensive foetal position as far away from him as she could get.

'It never happened! You think I'm some sort of pervert?' Carlo grated in frustration. 'I made it up...all of it! I was joking! I gave you what you seemed to expect. I do have a red-headed Amazon on my staff but she happens to be built like a tank and the happily married mother of four kids. I will never, ever buy you perfume again...'

Her nose wrinkled to force back the flood of tears threatening. The aftermath of shock, but she would sooner have been boiled alive than cry in front of him. 'If you were hanging off the edge of a cliff, I'd stand on your fingers,' she told him jerkily.

She heard paper tearing. A bottle of Obsession landed beside her.

'The name caught my eye,' he raked down at her, 'and the stupid bitch behind the counter sprayed some of it round me. That was yesterday and I still can't get rid of it!'

A long silence stretched. Her teeth bit into the hand she had wedged against her mouth but she couldn't stop the faint tremors still racking through her.

'I am sorry.' He sounded frustrated, furious and out of his depth. 'I didn't intend to upset you.'

Pull the other one, she thought bitterly, forcing herself to face head-on the extent of her self-betrayal. He tells you he's been with another woman and you go to pieces and start throwing up. Anguish trammelled through her afresh.

'There has been no woman in my bed for many weeks. Is that what you want to hear?'

No, what she really wanted to hear, she registered in agony, was that there had been no other woman in *six years*. Carlo had concentrated her mind wonderfully. She didn't have any secrets from herself now. No secret and no proud pretence could survive after what he had just put her through. She could not bear to think of him with another woman...all these years had not once permitted herself to envisage that reality, had not even dreamt that that reality could be so tormentingly painful to her.

Deep down inside her subconscious, Carlo had been *hers* alone. And until now she had never even known that that crazy belief existed inside her. But now the horrendous possessiveness she had discovered twisted like a knife in an open wound. She had no right to feel possessive about Carlo, no excuse to be torn apart by the most bitter and violent jealousy.

Beside her the mattress gave. 'What are you thinking?' Carlo demanded.

'Bastard!' she gasped helplessly.

'Was Turner unfaithful?'

One and one make two. Two and two make four. Carlo was already acting on signals received and computing possibilities like a champion downhill skier racing triumphantly for the finishing line. She couldn't even be bothered going through the motions of attempting to throw him off the scent. 'No,' she said wearily.

But she had grown up in the shadow of constant infidelity. Her mother had been quite unashamed of her promiscuity. Sexual freedom had been a destructive drug she was hooked on, and the older Jessica got, the more blatantly Carole had flaunted her beliefs and her men.

Jessica had found that even more deeply offensive than the screaming fits of abuse her father had regularly withstood. Forced to live in the turmoil of her parents' deeply destructive marriage, she had also been forced to stand silent and blind on the sidelines, neither commenting nor taking sides. Perhaps that was when she had begun to repress her own emotions.

'You wanted to know why I never talk about my family,' she said flatly. 'Well, here goes. My mother was once asked to leave the Deangate Hotel because the management suspected her of soliciting.'

'Soliciting?' Carlo repeated the term as though it was foreign to him.

'She used to pick up men in the bar and go up to their rooms. Not for money, for kicks. Sometimes she brought them home…the first time, I was ten,' Jessica confided shakily, 'I didn't know she was home. I was doing my homework in the kitchen and then I heard her laughing. I went upstairs and she was doing a strip for this guy…'

Carlo expelled his breath in a hiss. 'What did you do?'

'I ran away and told Simon. He told me not to tell.' An embittered laugh yanked painfully at her aching throat. 'I never told. I never told once. Daddy's little princess wasn't supposed to know about things like that. But God knows, everybody else knew my mother was the local tart. The boys at school used to laugh about her and ask me to do all sorts of…interesting things with them…after all, I was the daughter of a gifted amateur. Have you got a tape recorder running, Carlo? I would hate you to miss any of this—'

'Stop it,' he grated roughly, his arms tightening round her even though she was fiercely resisting his embrace.

'I never went out on a single date because I knew what would be expected of me. And I never had a female best friend. My mother was so notorious, nobody wanted their daughter to risk coming to my house, and how could I possibly be a *nice*, decent girl with a family background like that? Dad adored her…can you believe that?' Jessica muttered sickly. 'He pretended it wasn't happening and that meant that I had to pretend too…except with Simon. Am I mentioning his name enough for you, Carlo?'

'I don't want to hear it again,' he gritted out tautly, running a hand down her rigid back. 'Stop treating me like a leper! Why didn't your father divorce her?'

'He loved her.'

'That isn't love, it's masochism—'

'She didn't want a divorce until you bought the firm,' Jessica whispered grimly. 'There was finally enough cash to finance her escape in style. She walked out a week later and took Dad for just about all of it. I think he thought she'd go off on a spree and then come back…but she never came back…never so much as looked back—'

'And that hurt?'

'Yes.' For the very first time, she admitted to herself that it had. Even though her mother had never shown her affection, Carole's departure and years of silence had rammed the message of her disinterest home harder than anything else had. And it had hurt, but Jessica had buried that hurt.

'Go to sleep,' Carlo urged huskily.

Utterly drained, her mind floating free behind her heavy eyelids, she let her body relax into the sheltering heat of him and she slept.

CHAPTER SIX

JESSICA woke up with a start, a groan of remembered embarrassment escaping her as she sat up. She had felt half-dead when Carlo had all but carried her on to the helicopter. She had been wishing she were dead by the time she was hauled off it again, sick and in a state of collapse. Her impressions had been fleeting.

She recalled the cluster of security men converging on the helipad, blurred glimpses of an incredibly large white villa and heat that only increased the non-stop pounding behind her temples. Jet lag had finally caught up with her. A rueful grimace slanted her face as she gingerly slid out of bed to gratefully appreciate that the ground beneath her feet was no longer rocking. It was dark outside. Locating the bedside light, she glanced at her watch. Eight in the evening.

The housekeeper—at least she assumed the warm, matronly woman who had come to her assistance was the housekeeper—had been a merciful saviour. She had taken charge, banishing Carlo and helping Jessica into bed. Nor had her care ended there. Oblivious to Jessica's mortified assurances that she would be all right, the older woman had still been sitting by the bed when she finally fell asleep.

But what had possessed her yesterday? Why had she told Carlo about the misery of her adolescent years? She had told Carlo things that she had not even told Simon, things that she had never shared with anyone. And at the time she had felt curiously lightened of the burden of those unpleasant recollections, almost as though she was exorcising them and finally putting them into the

92

past where they belonged. In a weak moment she had surrendered her most private memories...so why didn't she feel bad about that?

She explored the huge, opulently furnished room, complete with brocaded sofas, magnificent flower arrangements and an exquisite antique escritoire with tiny drawers filled with luxury notepaper. The adjoining bathroom and dressing-room were equally impressive. Her very cases had been unpacked and her clothing hung.

Some of her tension evaporated. There were no male accoutrements anywhere to be seen. The décor was defiantly feminine. Contrary to her expectations, she was clearly not sharing a room with Carlo. That made her breathe a little easier.

She was emerging from the shower, towelling her hair, when she thought she heard someone in the bedroom. Employing the fleecy robe supplied for her use, she hurriedly donned it.

A tall woman in a figure-hugging backless gown the shade of ripe Hamburg grapes was standing by the windows. As she turned, her waist-length torrent of curling copper hair flew round her narrow white shoulders and great green eyes with the luminosity of jewels fixed on Jessica. Without doubt, she was one of the most beautiful women Jessica had ever seen.

'I'm Sunny,' she murmured, her gaze pinned to Jessica with disturbing intensity. 'Welcome to Paradiso.'

'Jessica Amory.' Jessica struggled not to feel self-conscious about her wet hair, bare feet and scrubbed face. Sunny Philippides, her hostess, no more than a handful of years her senior and as British as she was herself. Was an unannounced invasion the usual way she greeted her guests?

Sunny strolled about the room, her pale hands touching this, adjusting that before passing by Jessica to wander into the dressing-room and skim a hand through the garments visible and then walk back out again without a shade of discomfiture. 'Did Carlo buy the clothes as a prop for the masquerade?'

'I'm sorry. I don't follow.' Jessica maintained her composure but underneath her tension was heightening.

Sunny laughed and sent her a gleaming look of amusement from below her artfully darkened copper lashes. 'I *know*…I know it's a masquerade. How much is he paying you? If you're good, I'll double it!'

'I don't know what you're talking about,' Jessica returned drily.

'Even the walls have ears…is that what he told you?' Sunny drifted fluidly over to the door. 'But you don't need to keep up the act with me. After all, I am aware that you only met Carlo for the first time last week…'

'I've known Carlo for six years.'

Sunny stilled and turned. 'That's impossible.'

Jessica's irritation was rising steadily. 'Why is it impossible?'

'You were married and Carlo…' Thrown by Jessica's announcement, Sunny frowned and then elevated an imperious brow. 'Oh that's the story is it? Clever. Lukas will appreciate it. Dinner's at nine. Don't be late,' she instructed as if she was addressing an employee.

Jessica's knees sagged as the door shut. And what was all that about? Where had Sunny got her information from? How had she known that Jessica had been married? Had Carlo told them? But surely Carlo would not have told his father's wife that the engagement was a fake? Had Sunny simply been trying to trip her up?

With a furious frown of frustration, Jessica set about drying her hair and dressing, choosing a sleek gold satin and chiffon gown which she had thought was quite over the top until she saw the villa…and Sunny. 'How much is he paying you? If you're good, I'll double it.' The hint that Sunny and Carlo were in partnership had been clear. Jessica swallowed hard, her stomach clenching. Carlo had some explaining to do.

Carlo…who didn't want to explain anything. Was his reluctance to explain based on the reality that the truth was distinctly unsavoury? With a hiss of impatience Jessica asked herself where her wild imagination was taking her now. She was not the melodramatic type. A recollection of that stupid scene on the jet replayed and her skin heated. She didn't want to think about that. Right now there were more important things.

A dark-skinned maid escorted her along a mile of corridors, down a palatial gilded staircase and into a drawing-room. Jessica registered her first mistake as a plump woman in a black dress adorned by an opulent diamond brooch moved forward to greet her. Not the housekeeper, she guessed, her cheekbones colouring. Marika, Carlo's sister.

'How are you feeling? I was going to send a tray up to you later. I thought you would sleep for hours.' With a firm hand she drew Jessica deeper into the room. 'She looks much better, doesn't she, Carlo? Sunny, this is Jessica…'

Sunny extended a languid hand as though they had not yet met. 'Do let me see your ring,' she enthused, holding onto Jessica's fingers with a surprisingly steely grip. 'It's gorgeous. Your choice or Carlo's?'

'A shared choice,' Jessica breathed, removing her hand again, but before she could move away Sunny tucked her arm chumily into hers so that they stood side by side.

'What do we look like together?' Sunny giggled. 'She's so *small*, Carlo!'

Carlo strolled forward, dark and devastating in an off white dinner jacket. His golden eyes burned as scorchingly bright as flames, a tiny muscle pulling at the sensual line of his mouth. Jessica sensed his faint tension but his slanting smile was a masterpiece of cool.

'How do you feel, *cara*?'

Sunny's hand dropped away. With relief, Jessica moved out of reach. 'As if I never want to board a helicopter again.'

Carlo lifted her hand and pressed his mouth hotly to the sensitive skin on the inside of her wrist. As she collided breathlessly with his hooded eyes, her every nerve-ending ran riot. 'You look ravishing,' he murmured huskily.

Act one, scene one...the Latin lover, Jessica thought tautly. He drew her down onto a sofa and signalled for a drink to be brought to her and as she took her seat, she glimpsed Sunny's furious face. Jessica looked away again. Marika started talking doggedly about clothes, seating herself beside Jessica and effectively blocking her sister-in-law from view. Carlo wandered over and stood at the windows with his back to them. Seconds later, Sunny drifted over to his side.

A humming sound turned Jessica's head. A big, broadly built man seated in a wheelchair had appeared in the doorway. Lukas Philippides had thick silver hair and a deeply lined, fleshy face. He was struggling for breath but furiously waving away the uniformed male nurse beside him. Sunken dark eyes scanned the room and centred on Jessica with perceptible force.

He lifted a hand. 'Come here,' he commanded brusquely like an old-fashioned potentate.

Helplessly, Jessica sought out Carlo. He was smiling with genuine amusement. She stood up under the glare of the huge chandelier above, her head high, her shoulders back and moved forward.

'She walks like a queen, Carlo!' Lukas Philippides subjected her to a thorough top to toe assessment. 'Small. Good breasts. Quick temper,' he concluded, reading Jessica's flashing eyes with accuracy.

'Would you like to check my teeth?' Jessica enquired.

Lukas stared at her for a startled moment and then

gave a great shout of appreciative laughter. 'Spirit and a sense of humour...I like that. But can you give Carlo sons?' he demanded bluntly. 'That is the most important thing.'

Carlo banded an arm to her taut spine. 'Not to me.'

'Five years of marriage and no children,' Lukas argued fiercely. 'You think about that, Carlo...send her for some tests or something and then I'll keep quiet!'

Jessica could not quite believe that this utterly revolting conversation was carrying on above her head. Carlo said something in rapid Greek and his father snapped back at him and then cast both hands in the air with an attitude of blistering contempt.

Dinner was announced.

As they left the room in the wake of Lukas, Jessica hissed at Carlo, 'I want to talk to you!'

'You want to fight, we do it in private,' he gritted down at her roughly, a dark anger seething in his flashing sidewise glance.

And what the blue blazes did he have to smoulder about?

She asked him.

'The thought of you lying under Turner for five bloody years!' he slashed back down at her with visible distaste. 'Unproductive or otherwise.'

Jessica went white.

The dining table was circular. It was a relief to find Marika seated to one side of her. She couldn't bring herself to look at Carlo again.

'Children are very important to Greek men of my father's generation,' Carlo's sister murmured with a sigh. 'It was not his intention to hurt your feelings.'

A lie if ever there was one, even if it was meant kindly. After half an hour watching Lukas Philippides in action, it was crystal-clear that he didn't give a damn what he said or how it was received. The mere fact that Jessica was female put her in an inferior position.

Sunny was different in her husband's presence. She smiled and chattered gaily, putting on a show of great friendliness towards Jessica. She ate very little but her wine glass required constant replenishment. Father and son talked in Greek. Marika made polite, rather anxious conversation, her attention frequently straying to her sister-in-law.

Jessica was sipping her coffee when it happened. With a guttural sound of fury, Lukas reached out, snatched up his wife's glass and flung it violently against the wall. Quite unconcerned, Sunny smothered a yawn with a polite hand.

'I think I'll turn in,' Sunny said as a poker-faced manservant began to quietly pick up the broken shards of glass.

Lukas grunted something rough in Greek and lit a fat cigar, unconcerned by the shattering silence. He gave his daughter an impatient nod.

'Would you like some fresh air, Jessica?' Marika murmured brightly on cue. 'We could walk on the terrace.'

Jessica's last view of Lukas was of him choking on the cigar and wheezing, and with the best will in the world she couldn't experience much in the way of compassion.

'My father is not a sensitive man,' Marika said with careful emphasis as soon as the doors closed behind them. 'Don't let him upset you. I wish you could have witnessed his delight and satisfaction when he learnt of your engagement. My brother is thirty-three and the news was most welcome. We were beginning to fear that he would never marry.'

'How long is it since Carlo last saw your father? Carlo doesn't talk much about his family,' Jessica added hurriedly, fearful that she had made a slip.

But his sister's plump face merely looked sad and resigned. 'Over nine years. Of course, I have always kept in touch with Carlo. I would say I was going shopping and we would meet up in Miami. I am deeply attached to Carlo,' she shared with great warmth. 'Ever since he was a little boy. I was seventeen when he was born and he was the most beautiful baby…'

They strolled along the paved terrace beneath the starry night sky while Marika gave her chapter and verse on Carlo's baby years. Her pride was touching, as was her pleasure in sharing such titbits with the woman she believed to be her brother's bride-to-be. Jessica felt horribly guilty. Marika was so kind and trusting, clearly not even dreaming that there was anything strange about her brother's sudden engagement.

'What was his mother like?' she asked encouragingly.

'She was very beautiful. Then, Lukas would not have married her otherwise,' Marika chuckled, and then her smile dimmed. 'I think, for a while, he really loved Sofia, but he wanted more children and she couldn't have them. That's why he divorced her. It was a very bitter divorce. Carlo wanted to live with his mother but my father would not allow Sofia to take Carlo away—'

'Why not?'

'Carlo was his son,' sighed Marika. 'Unfortunately, Carlo was very protective of Sofia and he blamed his father for hurting her. That's when the trouble between them began. Lukas was furious…his young son, daring to condemn him. Then Lukas remarried and Sofia died. Carlo hadn't seen his mother in many months and that made him even more bitter. Eventually he was sent off to school. When he was eighteen, he took his mother's name and I have never known my father as angry as he was then. For Lukas, it was the most base insult. He is immensely proud of the Philippides name.'

But father and son had got together again nine years ago and Jessica was insatiably curious about what had occurred to upset the apple cart then. Sufficient to sever all familial ties, to employ Carlo's phraseology.

'He forgave him, though…didn't he?' Jessica fished,

and then suddenly despised herself for trying to draw his sister into telling her more.

There was no mistaking Marika's tightening features. Her gentle dark eyes hardened. 'Did he? I don't think so,' she said reflectively. 'But this time, yes. My father very much wants to win his son back to his side. He is aware of how little time may be left to him. He will not admit it but he is very proud of the success Carlo has achieved without his help.'

Hail the conquering hero, the return of the prodigal to the celebration feast.

Suddenly Marika laughed and leant closer to Jessica to whisper, 'I tell you a secret. Lukas has a library of Press cuttings on Carlo but Carlo would never believe it unless he saw with his own eyes.'

Her homely face tightened and she patted the younger woman's arm. 'I am very happy that Carlo has found it possible to love again. I feared that he would never marry. A weaker man might have had his faith in women destroyed forever by such treachery but—'

What treachery? Jessica was on the brink of asking when a manservant emerged from the villa and spoke to Marika.

'Please excuse me. My father wants me.'

'I think I'll go to bed,' Jessica said, but as Marika sped off at an obedient trot she decided instead to stay outdoors a little longer. The slight breeze was deliciously welcome and her brain was engaged on such frantic activity that she knew she had no hope of sleeping.

Some woman Carlo had loved had betrayed him. Jessica ached at the image of Carlo loving a woman that deeply. It hurt, yes, she acknowledged grudgingly, it really hurt.

Why did that knowledge hurt her? Ego? He had not loved Jessica, had laid no heart at her feet, had made no concessions to her self-respect or pride and had employed no heated persuasions. He had offered her the vacant space in his bed and the time limit of his boredom. A cool, arrogant, take-it-or-leave-it choice. Was that why it had been so easy to run away?

Leaning on the terrace railing, she let her cool hands press against her hot cheeks. She had gone to the Deangate that day in a colossal rage. Calling into her father's office, she had found him sitting with his head in his hands.

'I've sold Amory's,' he had muttered as if he couldn't quite believe it himself. 'I've sold to Carlo. Without finance, the firm was going to sink. I had no choice. Better money in the bank than bankruptcy...and I suppose your mother will be pleased.'

Like a madwoman, Jessica had hammered on the door of Carlo's suite. He had opened it himself.

'Take a long, slow deep breath,' Carlo had suggested, reading her furiously flushed face with ease. 'I gather your father's told you—'

'How dare you steal Amory's from him?' she had blitzed.

Carlo had poured her a brandy and handed it to her in silence.

She had downed it in one, outraged by his cool.

'I didn't steal it, I bought it. For far more than it's worth in its current state of efficiency,' he had drawled. 'And I am not a man known for my generosity. If it weren't for you, I wouldn't have bought. Your father doesn't realise how fortunate he is to possess such an asset.'

'What the hell have I got to do with it?'

'If you had surrendered *last* week,' Carlo had spelt out gently, 'I would have given him the finance he requires to survive and he would still have owned his business.'

Sick with horror, Jessica had stared back at him. He had cruelly laid the responsibility for the loss of

Amory's on her shoulders. And there had been worse to come.

'This week, as you may have guessed, that offer was concluded and I bought instead,' he had continued lazily. 'And by next week, I will no longer be prepared to consider offering your father the opportunity of staying on as managing director—'

'That's blackmail,' she had whispered incredulously.

'That's business,' Carlo had asserted.

And Jessica had gone crazy, appalled and outraged that he could use her father to pressure her. A violent row had ensued. She had been so furious, she had no memory of her abuse, but Carlo had lost his temper too. Her attempt to slap his face had landed her on her back on the sofa with Carlo on top of her...and then it had begun, in raw mutual anger that, terrifyingly swiftly, had turned into the scorching heat of an uncontrollable passion.

A passion that was insanity to her in the aftermath of shame and disbelief. But he had not held her down and forced her to submit to his mouth and the heated caress of his hands. She had been a full participant. Hating him, wanting him, needing him, hating herself. He had unleashed a woman she did not know and did not want to remember afterwards. When they were interrupted, she had been fathoms deep in shock.

But Carlo had blazed with triumph. He had skated an insolently intimate hand across her breast in an arrogant display of sexual possession. 'You tell Turner tonight. It's over now. Why did you fight me? From the first, I *knew* it would come to this.'

And she had lain there listening while she died inside at both what she had almost done and what he wanted to make of her. She had hated Carlo with boiling ferocity at that moment of biting humiliation. She had been repulsed by the future he had offered her so casually. But that had not been why she had run out of the Deangate like a madwoman.

No, far from it. She had run in terror from her own physical response to Carlo, absolutely convinced that she was as oversexed and immoral as her mother. Carlo had been the very first temptation she had ever had to withstand and she had not withstood him. From the moment he touched her she had been a lost cause, burning with a passion that equalled his and utterly, hopelessly submerged in her own sexuality. And then, she acknowledged, she had not been able to cope with that discovery.

Only maturity had brought her closer to understanding. She was a normal healthy woman but for six years she had been forced to repress and deny all her physical urges. Simon's complete indifference to her as a woman had been deeply wounding on every level, a secret shame that had destroyed her faith in her own femininity. Carlo had taught her that she had sexual needs but she had been bitterly ashamed and afraid of those same needs at the age of twenty.

But she owed no other man loyalty now, and why should she be ashamed, she suddenly asked herself angrily—why should she be ashamed of experiencing the natural physical promptings of that side of her nature? Sexual attraction made the world go round. Without it, the human race would die out.

She was not like her mother, ready to jump into bed with any man who took her fancy, she told herself fiercely. If she had been like Carole she would have found it out by now, would have experienced this attraction with a whole host of other men and would surely have ended up having affairs. That she had not told her that she was not as vulnerable as she had once feared, no…not vulnerable at all in that sense.

Take Carlo out of the picture and she could live like a nun. Only Carlo could turn her inside out with one burning glance, only Carlo had the ability to infiltrate her mind with erotic thoughts and melt her to molten honey in his arms. For the very first time in her life she was attempting to understand the sheer driving force of sexual desire and accept it, rather than run in terror and shame from it. But accepting that those promptings existed did not mean that she wanted to act on them.

Slowly, she straightened and made her way back to her bedroom. As she opened the door, she saw that a light was burning. Carlo, minus his jacket and tie, was reclining on her bed.

On the brink of verbal attack she belatedly recalled that she had told him that she wanted to speak to him. 'I gather this is as private as we can get,' she said coolly. 'I had a visit from your stepmother before dinner and very interesting it was too.'

The dark planes of his features were impassive.

'*She* suggested that our engagement was a masquerade and asked me how much you were paying me,' Jessica volunteered. 'She then offered to double it.'

'She was fishing,' Carlo dismissed carelessly.

'Was she? She seemed to be basing her convictions on the belief that we only met for the first time last week—'

'I wonder where she got that from.' But Carlo did not seem particularly interested in the subject, his veiled dark eyes intent on Jessica as she stood there at the foot of the bed. Her heartbeat skidded at the thickening of the atmosphere.

'I told her I'd known you for six years and I think she then assumed that I was suggesting we had been having an affair while I was married but she still thought it was a fairy-story,' Jessica relayed in an increasing rush as Carlo sprang gracefully off the bed and moved towards her. 'What I would like to know is why she was so convinced that we—'

'Ignore her.'

'Carlo, I really would like to go to bed,' she began.

'Your luggage has already been moved.'

Her eyes widened. 'Moved where?'

'My room…where else?' Carlo responded drily, casting open the door in expectation. 'Do you really think it would be credible that we sleep apart?'

But when she had trekked quite to the far side of the villa it occurred to her that *someone* had been very keen to keep them apart, by night at least. Marika?

Carlo had an entire suite of rooms, complete with twin bathrooms. Like an automaton, Jessica took her night attire into one, changed and ten minutes later slid into the wide, empty bed and over to the furthest edge of it. She doubted that some eleventh-hour miracle would save her tonight. Carlo reappeared and shed his towelling robe in an untidy heap on the floor. He looked at her, blazing all-male satisfaction, and she shrank under the sheet.

He stood half in shadow, half in light, the long, muscular planes of his golden body a glorious vision of rampant masculinity, and she felt her own hunger stirring, insidious as a secret invader. Her skin flushed hotly and she closed her eyes, stricken by that hunger and her own sudden blinding shyness.

As he came down on the bed beside her, her mouth ran dry. She felt boneless, scared. Dear God, how was she going to get out of this? If he made love to her, would he be able to tell she was a virgin? Surely not, she told herself, preferring to think of the aftermath rather than what might come before. She had read that a woman's first experience of sex was often a very big disappointment.

Carlo stared down at her in total silence, smouldering golden eyes hungrily scanning her face. Slowly, he raised a blunt forefinger and skimmed it along the voluptuous line of her lower lip. 'Why are you so shy?' he whispered in wonderment.

'S-shy?' She forced a jerky laugh. She could have told

him. Every other time he had touched her, he had taken her by surprise. There hadn't been time for considered thought. *This* was different. 'Don't be ridiculous!'

'You look as if you're running a fever, too.' Leaning over her, Carlo flicked one pink cheek mockingly.

'I don't want to do this,' Jessica said fiercely.

'You're no virgin…' Carlo breathed with sudden shocking insolence, his starkly handsome features darkening, brilliant eyes hard. 'You gave that to *him*. You gave to him what should have been mine—'

He was so damn primitive and arrogant. What should have been *his*…how dared he say that after the way he had treated her that day? Did her supposed lack of virginity take the edge off his triumph, dull the pleasure of his conquest? Well, he would never hear from her lips that he had been her first lover. She would take that secret to the grave with her.

'Tough!' The retaliation just erupted from between her clenched teeth.

Dark blood slashed his cheekbones and she paled, knowing instinctively that she had never pushed Carlo closer to violence and realising rather too late that that was the very last mood she wanted him in.

A pair of hard hands sank to her slim hips. He jerked her into the hard heat of his very masculine length, bringing her into direct contact with the full force of his arousal.

'If you hurt me I'll…I'll scream the place down!' Jessica gasped, energised by both that contact and his mood.

'Hurt you? What sort of an animal do you think I am?' Frowning in disbelief, Carlo studied her with probing golden eyes and his sensual mouth firmed.

A very male animal, she thought fearfully.

'I have no intention of hurting you,' Carlo asserted drily, and lowered his dark head.

He took her parted lips in a hot, hungry surge of passion. He knotted a hand into her hair, holding her there as though he feared she might seek to evade him, but the instant their mouths met Jessica went limp, bowing to the inevitable. Within seconds the fear was burned away by the heat of his mouth. She quivered in response, and thought became far too much of a challenge.

He bent his dark head over the full swell of her breasts and her fingers speared helplessly into his thick black hair. His lips pulled on a taut pink nipple and a whimper of sound escaped from her convulsed throat. He lingered there, toying with her sensitive flesh until every skin cell went on red alert and every nerve-ending tautened in sizzling anticipation. Her hands gripped his smooth brown shoulders and skimmed in near-desperation over the tautness of the muscles flexing in his back.

She felt as if she was being consumed. There was no breathing space between one spasm of response and the next. Sensation took over and she was mindless in the grip of it. His mouth on her breast was an unbelievable pleasure, but when he began to employ his tongue and the teasing edge of his teeth she went crazy, possessed by a hunger so intense she was lost to all else. She twisted restively beneath him, too hot to stay still, sobbed out his name, drove her fingers into his hair, wantonly, wildly out of control.

'We have all night,' Carlo muttered thickly, lifting his head.

She focused on him with the blankness of passion's grip and simply, instinctively reached for him again because he had dared to stop and she couldn't bear that.

With a husky laugh, Carlo caught her to him. 'Slow down,' he urged softly.

She ran exploring fingers through the curling black hair on his chest, tracing the superb musculature rippling below his golden skin. She heard the startled hiss of his breath escaping and then he took her hand and thrust it down to the hard swell of his erection, shocking her, startling her.

'Touch me,' he invited with an earthy groan.

He was velvet-smooth and hot and hard and she was helplessly alarmed by the sheer size of him. She looked up at him, dredged from the hold of passion by the bite of her own ignorance and sudden shyness.

Carlo dealt her a sudden vibrantly amused smile and moved against her, pure sexual licence barely contained. 'I'll teach you some time...but what an extraordinary gap in your education.' He punctuated the comment by driving her flat again with the force of his mouth.

Sanity trickled away again like sand through a mesh grid. He kissed her breathless, long, deep, drugging kisses that stole the soul from her body and melted her into a quivering length of subservience.

Only then did he lift his head again and slide with aching slowness down the length of her extended body, making love to every part of her he could reach. The tip of his tongue dipped into her navel and she whimpered with an intolerable desire, jack-knifing wildly under the taunting, teasing fingers skimming her unbearably tender nipples. She couldn't stay still but he forced her still with powerful hands, forcing her to endure every maddening second of his tormenting assault.

Her entire body was possessed by an electrifying excitement and yet simultaneously one gigantic ache expressing the raw agony of her need. By the time he parted her thighs and let knowing fingers brush against the honeyed centre of that ache, she was at screaming pitch and she cried out his name, her hips moving with a rhythm that required no enforced learning. It came as naturally as the air in her lungs.

He was touching her now as she had never been touched and she was on fire, convinced she was being tortured to death by pleasure. She sobbed just to breathe, her heartbeat thundering madly against her breastbone, the blood in her veins racing insanely in accompaniment. She couldn't bear it…

'You're very tight,' Carlo muttered thickly, hesitating.

Her body was at screaming pitch. Instinctively she pulled him down to her, desperate for contact, any form of continuing contact. Untensing, he followed her lead, his hands tipping her up, spreading her thighs. He entered her with one fierce thrust and then stilled, every muscle ferociously taut as he groaned with the nakedness of his pleasure. It hurt so much, Jessica almost passed out with the sheer shock of being forced back to reality.

She twisted her head away to hide her reaction, thankfully feeling the edge of the pain fade away. Carlo uttered a feverish imprecation and stopped.

'I'm hurting you—'

'*No!*'

'Relax then,' he instructed unevenly.

Pushing his hands beneath her hips, he plunged deeper still into her damp sheath in a rawly powerful invasion. This time there was no pain. In fact he dragged a sob of incredulous delight from her. The pleasure came back in powerful waves, shooting through her in a rejuvenating burst of energy.

He moved with restraint and then slowly, he began to drive into her harder and faster with a shuddering savagery that sent her finally rocketing into an explosive climax of such intensity that a wild cry escaped her and her quivering body writhed uncontrollably under the hard onslaught of his. Groaning her name, Carlo slammed into her one last time and then jerked violently with the force of his own release.

Rolling on to his back, Carlo carried her with him, binding her into his arms so tightly she could barely breathe. Jessica was in a daze, a complete daze, and she lay like a boneless rag doll on top of him, her face buried in the hollow of one broad shoulder, her nostrils flaring sensuously at the hot, moist scent of him.

She was in seventh heaven. In the back of her mind she was already wondering when he would do it again. Her face burned. She was a shameless hussy but she couldn't help it. Nothing could have prepared her for that amount of pleasure. Still in shock at her own response, she felt drugged and incapable, incredibly tender towards him.

Her mouth curved in a silent caress against his bronzed skin. And then it hit her like a bolt of lightning. I love him. A quiver of disbelief ran through her. Carlo instantly tautened his grip on her. I love every rotten thing about him, she registered in growing horror. His temper, his arrogance, his sheer bloody persistence. Mentally, she felt like the ground had suddenly vanished from beneath her feet. The silence began to get to her in her new and tender state of vulnerability.

Carlo was thinking. Strange, how she could literally *feel* Carlo thinking manipulative thoughts, practically see all those little cogs and wheels spinning ever faster in that far too clever brain of his.

'Extraordinary,' Carlo murmured softly. 'You felt like a virgin. If it were not for that ring you used to wear, I would be one hundred per cent convinced I had just become your first lover.'

Tense as a bow string, Jessica uttered a strangled laugh. 'Don't be ridiculous—'

'Was I hallucinating? I hurt you—'

She tensed in horror. 'You were rough,' she muttered hurriedly.

Carlo shifted lithely on to his side, taking her with him. She collided with the full force of blazing golden eyes and paled but she was still determined to silence the smallest suspicion he might have. 'It's been a very long time since—'

'Rough…' Carlo sent her a slashing, primal look of thwarted fury and abruptly freed her. He sprang out of bed. 'I need a shower.'

She turned over and found a cool spot on the pillow. Not the most generous of comments, she registered belatedly, scarlet washing her cheekbones. Oh, what a tangled web, she thought guiltily. Deception didn't come naturally to her but a current of fierce pride and loyalty to Simon's memory kept her silent.

'What the hell is this?'

The wrathful incredulity in Carlo's growled demand lifted her pale head. At arms length, Carlo extended a framed photo. He was possessed by such ferocious incredulity, he couldn't hold it steady.

It was of Simon. Her jaw dropped. It had been at the foot of her overnight bag, one of the pieces of luggage she had packed to come here. She had not intended to bring it, indeed had completely forgotten its existence until this moment.

'Where did you get it?' she demanded.

'It was on the dressing-table!' Carlo unleashed, spitting out every syllable with a flash of white teeth.

'I didn't put it there!'

'But you brought it out here with you!' Carlo seethed, flinging it violently aside. 'Into my bedroom—'

'I did not bring it into your bedroom!' Jessica gasped unsteadily.

Carlo strode forward and swooped on her in a tempest of rage. He scared her half to death and she fought with flailing arms and flying fists to fight him off. He dropped her from a height on to a sofa that had all the bounce of a rock. 'You sleep here...I do not want you in my bed!' he delivered.

She was stark naked and absolutely humiliated. He yanked a blanket out of a closet and threw it at her. Clumsily hauling it round her, she headed for the door. 'I am not staying here to be insulted...you primitive bloody man!' she scorched back at him.

'You put one toe in that corridor and the electronic

surveillance picks you up on camera. My father's security men will have one hell of a laugh. Go ahead!'

She hesitated and then snatched her fingers back from the door-handle as though she had been burnt. Without a single glance in his direction, she made it back to the sofa, rigid-backed but literally shaking with the force of her own fury.

'I thought you might see it that way,' Carlo drawled with blatant amusement, temper cooled by the ridiculous picture she made. 'Learn to look on sleeping in my bed in my arms as a privilege—'

'You hateful bastard!' Jessica screamed back at him.

'And by the way…you love it rough!' Carlo shot at her for good measure.

'*Shut up, Carlo!*'

I do not love him, she told herself ferociously, huddling into a ball, the blanket tangled uncomfortably round her. I do not love him. I hate him! I hate him so much I could burst wide open with it! *He's jealous.* Carlo was wildly jealous of Simon. How come it had taken her this long to appreciate something that obvious? In the darkness, she smiled, fists unclenching. She didn't care if she didn't sleep a wink. She was fairly certain that he wouldn't either.

CHAPTER SEVEN

LUNCH was being served outdoors beneath the leafy splendour of a ring of flame trees. Beyond them, flight after flight of shallow steps adorned with classical statues descended to the white beach below. Lukas Philippides dealt Jessica a fiercely amused scrutiny. Flustered, she dropped down into her seat. One of the maids had awakened her and she hadn't had much time to get ready.

When she glanced up again, Carlo's brilliant golden eyes were wandering with indolent satisfaction over her in a look as blatantly physical as a caress. A deep flush of awareness carmined her skin, making her desperately conscious of the unfamiliar ache between her thighs. Erotic recollections surfaced and she fought them to the last ditch, feverishly embarrassed by her own lack of mental discipline.

While she slept, Carlo had shifted her off the sofa and back into his bed. Out of consideration for her comfort and his own unjustifiable behaviour the night before…or out of a need to set the scene to keep their deception intact? At what stage had she chosen to overlook the fact that it had always been Carlo's stated intent to make love to her for the benefit of that self-same deception? A deep unease assailed Jessica. Now they *were* lovers, she was far more powerfully aware of the masquerade they were engaged in and she was forced to question Carlo's motives.

Was Carlo simply trying to please his dying father? Or was there a far more mercenary reasoning behind it all? Yesterday she had tried very hard not to think about that. Today, she found that she could think of little else.

Sunny sauntered up, clad in a flowing dress and sun-hat, looking vaguely reminiscent of a Twenties film star-let on a picnic. Picturesque and quite stunningly beau-tiful, she took her seat. Both Lukas and Carlo had watched her progress across the lawn. You had to hand it to her, Jessica thought sourly. Sunny knew how to make an entrance.

Last night, Jessica had wondered if Sunny had a prob-lem with drink and if that might explain her strange visit to her room and her even stranger remarks. But she hadn't behaved then as though she had been over-indulging. Neither her speech nor her movement had been impaired. Yet Carlo had been surprisingly uncon-cerned by his stepmother's conviction that their engage-ment was a fake.

'A toast…' Lukas announced, raising his glass of wine. 'To Carlo and Jessica. The wedding will take place on Tuesday.'

Jessica's hand jerked and sent her glass over. A pool of red wine spread across the white tablecloth. She col-lided with Carlo's hooded dark eyes and read the warn-ing there. To say nothing, do nothing.

Sunny sighed and laid a soft hand on her husband's sleeve. 'I think you've shocked your son, Lukas. Don't you think this should be *his* decision?' she prompted with a small, deprecating smile. 'I hope you don't mind me speaking up—'

Lukas shook off her hand irritably. 'Since when have I wanted your opinion on anything?' he demanded rudely.

'My thanks,' Carlo murmured softly into the throb-bing silence. 'But Jessica and I are not intending to marry until next year.'

'This year, next year!' Lukas responded with abrasive

bite. 'You think to deprive me of a father's right to see his son marry?' It was a thunderous demand of disbelief.

Carlo tautened, his dark features clenching hard. He said something in Greek but Lukas slashed a despotic hand through the air and retorted in English, hot temper flushing his drawn face at the threat of his authority being further challenged.

'Enough!' he ground out angrily. 'It is arranged. Already the invitations go out. You people! A little surprise and where is your gratitude?'

As his bloodshot gaze raked the table, seeking dissension, Jessica studied the stained tablecloth. Dear heaven, why hadn't either she or Carlo seen the threat of this in advance? Lukas Philippides was dying. It was surely not that unreasonable of him to want the wedding of his son to take place here and now while he could still enjoy it? So simple, so understandable a wish, that she marvelled that such a danger had not previously occurred to either of them. But somehow, heaven knew how, she conceded dazedly, Carlo was going to have to get them back out of this tight corner! And he only had three days in which to accomplish that feat...

'We will fly to Miami to find a dress,' Marika announced cheerfully.

'You pick a designer,' Lukas interrupted with a curled lip. 'But he will fly here.'

'I really cannot arrange a wedding in that timespan,' Sunny said thinly, coldly.

'What's it got to do with you?' Lukas snorted. 'Marika will take care of it all.'

It was without doubt the most strained meal Jessica had ever endured. When Lukas went off to rest, as was apparently his habit in the afternoon, she left the table with relief and started for the steps.

'Jessica...'

Halfway down, she spun, stilled by Carlo's voice. He drew level with her, very tall and very lean and very dark and quite extravagantly gorgeous in the first casual clothing she had ever seen him in. Faded jeans sleekly encased his narrow hips and long, powerful legs, a short-sleeved cotton shirt open at his brown throat. Hurriedly, Jessica dragged her gaze from him. And then, above at the top of the steps, she saw Sunny standing there, watching them. She looked furious.

'And how do you plan to get us out of the wedding?' Jessica enquired tightly.

Carlo threw back his black head and suddenly laughed. 'I don't!'

She couldn't believe what she was hearing and looked back at him in shock.

'The only escape would be to tell the truth,' Carlo pointed out gently. 'And that is quite out of the question.'

'You could tell him that you're not sure of your feelings for me!' Jessica protested tautly.

Carlo moved on down the steps in front of her. 'That would be the very last excuse I would offer—'

'*But why*?' Jessica demanded in furious frustration. 'He's been married four times himself! Surely he would understand?'

Carlo didn't respond. Infuriatingly, he moved fluidly on down to the beach. She caught up with him breathlessly.

'Let's go sailing,' he suggested lazily as if the previous conversation had been most definitely concluded.

'*Carlo*!' Jessica gritted, struggling to match her pace to the long stride heading in the direction of the wooden jetty where a large and immaculate white yacht was moored.

'We get married, then we divorce,' Carlo breathed impatiently. 'No big deal!'

Jessica couldn't credit his attitude. 'It's a heck of a big deal to me!'

Carlo stilled and scanned her with hooded dark eyes.

'Really, *cara*? You married Turner without love…why not me?'

Attacked by such open derision, she paled. 'That…that isn't true.'

'If you had really loved him, you would never have allowed me to lay a finger upon you,' Carlo murmured drily.

'You're trying to change the subject—'

'Why should I need to? We made a deal. Three months of your freedom,' Carlo reminded her, his sun-bronzed profile hardening. 'And having seen my father, I think it highly unlikely that he will survive half that period.'

Involuntarily, she felt his pain at that estimation. It was there in his roughened voice and tautening features, but Jessica felt that pain on a deeper level, her own feelings for Carlo heightening her sensitivity. He really did care about his father. For the first time, she acknowledged that truth and the unlikelihood of Carlo's cherishing purely mercenary motives for their fake engagement. Maybe it was all just as it seemed on the surface. Lukas was delighted at the idea of Carlo marrying and Carlo was prepared to pretend to give that pleasure.

'I'm sorry,' she muttered, her throat thickening. 'You must wish you had come here years ago—'

'No. It is only working now on these terms,' Carlo retorted flatly. 'Lukas and I have never got on. I believe it is often so with father and son. Only the lack of time brings us together. It makes me more tolerant and him more generous…'

With a mighty effort of will, she fought an overwhelming urge to close her arms round him. 'You must have known that he might demand that you marry me—'

'Yes.' Carlo shrugged a shoulder with Latin casualness. 'It is a small thing if it contents him.'

'But it is not a small thing to me, Carlo.' They were strolling towards the yacht.

She stared down at the sea, deep blue and then blindingly silver where the sun's glare hit the water. One false marriage was enough in any woman's life. She refused to make a second. What Carlo wished to do to placate his father was his business, she told herself, staving off an unwilling stab of sympathy. He had no right to ask such a thing from her, especially when he coolly admitted that he had foreseen this situation arising and had not bothered to warn her.

'I will not hold you a day after his death.'

The assurance hit her like a cruel blow and she despised herself for reeling from that reality as though it were a surprise. She loved him, hopelessly, helplessly, but that did not mean making a sacrificial lamb of herself. Some day not too far in the future, Lukas would die and it would all be over. The deception would end, and with it the affair. She did not want a fake wedding-ring to add to her bitterness.

But didn't she owe Carlo something for the immense kindness and tact he had employed with her *own* father? OK, they had made a deal but Carlo could have fulfilled the terms far less generously. A deal...dear God, she reflected painfully, had the giving of her body last night merely been part of the deal as well? Her stomach heaved at the suspicion.

Carlo planted his hands to her waist, taking her by surprise, and swung her with ease on to the gleaming wooden deck of the yacht. Two crewmen emerged. The men talked and Jessica planted her unsteady hands on the shining brass guard rail. Drawn by a need she could not suppress, her troubled gaze clung to Carlo's strong, masculine profile. He was such a mixture of opposites. Kind and cruel. Understanding and judgemental. Tender and rough. Quick-tempered, calculating, secretive but capable of far more true emotions than she had ever believed. And he hated her.

He hated her for marrying another man. She had cast

a slur on his manhood, injured his precious pride and he was still seething with a sense of injustice. But how many women would have thrown themselves gratefully into his arms six years ago after the treatment she had received? And by what God given right did Carlo imagine that she should have swallowed such arrogance when on every other level they had been mortal enemies? Yet she could not imagine Carlo behaving now as he had behaved then.

'Do you like sailing?' Linking his arms round her, Carlo drew her back into disturbing connection with every vibrant line of his long, muscular length.

'I haven't done much.' Feeling manipulated, Jessica stiffened, fighting the flood of heat threatening to consume her. 'Don't change the subject.'

'There is nothing more to say,' he breathed, pressing her closer still, the palm of one lean hand splaying across her taut stomach as he bent over her. 'There is also little that I would not do to assuage my father's fear—'

'Fear?' She frowned.

Perceptibly, he tensed. 'His fear that I might not marry—'

'But why should he fear that?' She wanted him to tell her what his sister had already told her.

'As a man who married for the first time as a teenager, he cannot comprehend my single state.'

Disappointment assailed her. He was lying to her…or at the very least mounting a cover-up. He did not confide in her. It shook her that they could have shared something so intimate last night and yet he could still hold her at a distance. Her own emotions were not similarly disciplined. She had lost all ability to stand back and be rational. She was too involved now.

'He doesn't seem particularly happy in his own marriage,' she said drily.

'Sunny is forty years his junior. Would you expect a match made in heaven? He's content enough. He only ever looked for two things from your sex. An ability to decorate the bedroom, and to reproduce.'

Jessica was chilled. Presumably Sunny had married for money and position but she reckoned that the red-head paid for her pleasures. Now she asked herself if Carlo wanted any more from a woman than his father ever had. Right now, Carlo was using her, and last night he had used her body as well. Why didn't she face that harsh reality head-on?

He had brought her here to pretend to be his fiancée but she was being forced into deeper deception with every hour that passed. And he had yet to explain *why* to her satisfaction. How did she know whether or not his principal motivation was connected with the terms of his inheritance? He wasn't going to admit it, was he?

And suddenly, she wondered if that might be why Sunny had attempted to the best of her limited influence over Lukas to hold off the wedding…why Sunny might have been so keen to prove that their engagement was a fake. Were Carlo and Sunny competing in the same competition? How was Lukas's immense wealth tied up?

The blood chilled in Jessica's veins. She didn't know what to think, swerved from one moment to the next, but now she recognised how much making love with Carlo had increased her sense of insecurity. She could live with the deception if it was just a matter of pleasing a dying man…she could not live with it or herself on any other terms. It would be too unbearably, cruelly humiliating.

'You're astoundingly quiet.' Without warning, his lean brown hands moved up to her breasts, cupping them, and she quivered violently, her rigidity evaporating in a surge of heat.

'You're wearing a bra,' he complained.

'Don't!' she gasped, sudden tears lashing the back of her eyes. Dear lord, she felt so vulnerable now. She craved his touch helplessly but then she wondered how much *this* meant to him. A little light relief on an island where there was no other sexual outlet for his desires, or did he get even more of a kick out of her wanton response? Revenge…how much did that play a part in his apparent hunger for her?

Dropping his hands, Carlo spun her easily round to face him. Surprising lines of strain were engraved between his expressive mouth and arrogant nose. She met dark golden eyes that riveted her bonelessly in place. 'I want to forget Paradiso and its occupants for an afternoon.' Carlo pushed back the silver hair curving her cheekbones and framed her uncertain face with both hands. 'When I make love with you, I forget everything else. It is the sweetest oblivion I know,' he stated huskily.

Her heart jumped behind her breastbone. She turned to watch the two crewmen unfurling the sails, wretchedly aware of just how badly she wanted to believe him. The yacht sailed round Paradiso. Since the cay encompassed little more than a square mile of territory that didn't take long. Jessica let Carlo show her down into a comfortable cabin and display the range of swimwear available for her use. She took her time selecting a bikini in the least daring design. When she climbed the companionway, she saw the crewmen speeding away in the motorboat.

'Why have they gone?'

'To leave us in privacy,' Carlo advanced, amused by her question, intent golden eyes lazily skimming over the full thrust of her breasts and the rounded swell of her hips.

A deep flush warmed her skin.

He stripped off his shirt and cast it carelessly aside.

He had a truly magnificent torso. Her tongue stole out to moisten her dry lips as he embarked on his jeans. She expected him to reveal swimming briefs beneath but

Carlo skimmed off down to bare golden flesh. 'I never wear anything when I'm swimming.'

'So I see.' Magnetised by the view, she stared like a schoolgirl as he executed a perfect dive off the yacht and broke into a fast crawl that cut through the water.

A less able swimmer, she got into the water by way of the steps provided. The sea was deliciously warm. After a little exercise, she let herself float, heat beating down on her wet body like a rejuvenating drug.

Carlo surfaced beside her. 'You're not very active.'

'Don't pull me under or anything smart like that!' she warned nervously.

He kissed her instead, and in the sudden blinding grip of sensation she forgot to paddle and was hauled upright again by Carlo before she slid beneath the surface. 'Float,' he suggested gently, amusedly.

Half an hour later, she was reclining on a sun-lounger, a Daiquiri clasped in one hand, as she let relaxation seep luxuriously through her every limb. She opened her eyes behind her sunglasses when the glorious heat was abruptly reduced by Carlo's arrangement of a parasol above her. 'Spoilsport,' she muttered.

'You'll burn...and if you burn,' Carlo said with single-minded cool, 'I won't be able to touch you.'

'I would prefer to burn—'

'Liar.' He reached for her with hands that brooked no argument and she trembled as the sunwarmed heat of his body met electrifyingly with hers. He had dispensed with the towel he had knotted round his lean hips.

'Don't you think you should put some clothes on?' she gasped.

'I think you need a few anatomy lessons,' he laughed softly, indolently, scanning her hot cheeks. 'Did he undress in the dark?'

'That is a disgusting question!' Jessica was suddenly infuriated by the sheer blaze of his sexual confidence. Did he think desire would make a mindless slave out of her? Did he think he could use sex to blind her to everything else?

'And to return to the subject you keep dropping,' she snapped. 'I don't want to go through with a fake wedding.'

Carlo gazed down at her and slowly, erotically moved on her, forcing her into raw acquaintance with his arousal. 'Sometimes we all have to do things we don't want to do.'

'Meaning that you don't either?' In quite irrational annoyance, her mouth tightened as she fought to suppress the shivering hunger he was invoking in her with such insulting ease.

'A wedding-ring has to be about the last reward I would want to give you—'

Her amethyst eyes widened to their fullest extent. '*Reward*? You consider going through a disgusting parody of a wedding ceremony a reward?'

Untouched by her fury, Carlo cast her a grim smile. 'Parody or not, it will still be a true marriage and you will still be my wife...for a while.'

'You smirking, self-satisfied toad!' Jessica launched up at him. 'You think that's a reward? It's a punishment! Unlike you, I have some respect for the sacrament of marriage. It's not just a useful ploy to me...you'd use anything and anybody to get what you want!'

Hooded dark eyes surveyed her. Abruptly, he lifted himself fluidly from her and vaulted upright, contempt in every angle of his bearing. 'Would I?' he parried drily. 'Six years ago, I could have told your father how *close* we had become and I am quite sure he would have strained every sinew sooner than watch you marry Turner!'

Her furious gaze dropped from him. She had never thought of that possibility. His derisive withdrawal exercised a similarly disturbing effect on her. She felt bereft.

'I could have personally dealt with Turner. I could have made marrying you such a humiliation that *he* would have been forced to save face by calling off the wedding!' Carlo continued with biting conviction. 'I did neither of those things. I kept quiet. I stood back…I allowed you to make your own decision—'

'Damn you!' Jessica gasped. 'There was no decision. You treated me like a whore!'

'That is not true.'

'Yes, it is. And don't you dare forget the background of blackmail and pressure that came before it!' Jessica urged bitterly. 'I never have. You made no attempt to understand how I felt. I had betrayed Simon. I had done something unforgivable to a man I believed I loved. I was confused and ashamed and I couldn't handle it. And what did you do? You gloated. You didn't care about how anybody felt, except yourself. You said that was true of your father but it was equally true of you then!'

Carlo was standing stock-still, his piercing gaze wholly pinned to her distressed face. 'You said…the man you *believed* you loved. So you finally admit it,' he grated, throwing his ebony head back. 'You finally admit that you didn't love him.'

Jessica whirled away, cursing her impulsive tongue and the descent into temper which removed all restraint. Her knuckles showed white as she curved her unsteady hands fiercely round the rail. 'I thought I loved him…later I realised that I didn't…at least,' she stumbled in her turmoil, 'not the way I should have loved him.'

'Later!' Carlo ejaculated with lancing contempt. He followed it up with something that sounded exceedingly rude in Greek.

In anguish, Jessica closed her eyes, breathing deeply. She had loved Simon as a friend. Had their marriage been normal, she might have continued to believe that she loved him, but when they had lived month after month with separate bedrooms and the relationship of a brother and sister, she had had too much time in which to analyse the fact that sexually Simon did not attract her and that, if she offered herself, tried to talk to him about the lack of a physical relationship, she did it out of guilt and the belief that that willingness was the very least she owed him. Ironically, that attitude had kept Simon at even more of a distance until he fell ill and sex became the least of their worries, she conceded sadly.

'I did not treat you like a whore—'

'Ten days ago, you called me one for what we did that day! And that is how you treated me,' she condemned starkly, sticking to her point. 'I was only twenty and I had no experience of a man like you. You are the one who took advantage, Carlo—'

'I wanted you.' The assurance was harsh, immoveable, no admission of fault.

Her mouth twisted painfully. 'Regardless of cost or decency? I paid in spades for what I did. Loyalty is very important to me. I could hardly live with myself and all for what…a little entertainment for you, so that you could prove that I *was* susceptible? Was it worth it?' she demanded shakily.

'No,' he murmured, suddenly very quiet. 'Looking back, I see that it was not worth the cost.'

Involuntarily she looked at him. His chiselled profile might have been carved from marble. All of a sudden she wanted him to argue the point, which was crazy. He should never have touched her that day but then neither one of them had been in control. She saw that now. Carlo had been as possessed as she was by the passion that had flared up between them. But that didn't mean she forgave him for his behaviour afterwards.

He sailed the yacht back in alone. She couldn't wait to get off it. She couldn't cope with Carlo's moody introspection. Silence from Carlo was not golden. She felt shut out, banished. She had the lowering suspicion that he could barely bring himself to look at her and without the false strength of anger and bitterness over the past she found that she was weak and horribly vulnerable to the chill in the air.

She spent ages getting ready for dinner, lazing in a bath for a full hour and fussing unnecessarily with her hair. The dress she chose was black. It suited her mood, a long dark sheath hugging every curve. She would rival Sunny, she thought wryly.

Lukas was absent from the dinner-table. 'He's resting in bed,' Marika explained. 'There has been too much excitement.'

Sunny, brilliant as a butterfly in emerald lace, laughed thinly. 'Excitement? Here on this godforsaken rock? You've got to be joking!'

'This is a difficult time for all of us,' Marika murmured.

'He's dying but I might as well be dead too,' Sunny complained bitterly. 'I hate this place.'

'Nobody's keeping you here.' Marika's plump face was flushed with rare anger.

'Well, thank you very much!' Shooting Marika a look of outrage, Sunny rose from the table and stalked from the room.

'I should not have said that,' Marika whispered in distress, tears blurring her brown eyes.

Carlo said something in Greek and patted his sister's hand. She squeezed his fingers gratefully, her lips wobbling into a rueful smile.

'I shall go and sit with Lukas,' Carlo announced before dessert was served. He strode out of the room without a backward glance in Jessica's direction.

Jessica went off to explore after dinner, wandering through beautifully furnished and decorated reception rooms that were lifeless. She was delighted to come upon a library and, locating the English section, selected a Jane Austen she hadn't read for several years. But Miss Austen failed her for the very first time. Jessica found it impossible to concentrate.

Standing up again, she cast the novel aside and stepped through the curtains to open the french windows that featured in virtually every room. She walked along the terrace. As she passed by open doors, she caught Sunny's voice clear as a bell.

'You can't love her, Carlo…you *can't* possibly love her!' she was arguing shrilly. 'And he can't force you to marry her!'

'Control yourself,' Carlo breathed fiercely. 'Have you any idea what he would do to you if he knew you were here with me?'

'You want me…not her!' Sunny told him. 'I love you…you know I do! Look at the risks I've taken!'

Carlo said something that might have been a swear word.

Jessica had stopped dead in her tracks. There was a curious ringing in her eardrums. She couldn't breathe. The curtains weren't drawn. She could see them. Carlo had his back to her. Sunny had flung herself into a chair to sob hysterically.

'Why don't you tell him that you don't want to marry her?' she demanded wildly. 'You're the only one of us who can afford to stand up to him. He'll give you whatever you want.'

'I doubt very much that that includes his wife, cast-off or otherwise,' Carlo said very drily.

'God forgive me, I can't wait for him to die!' Sunny sobbed.

CHAPTER EIGHT

AN INVOLUNTARY moan escaped Jessica and Carlo spun fluidly round. But by then Jessica had already fled, her sole desire to escape. She raced down the steps that led into the gardens, her breath sobbing in her throat.

'Jessica!'

Lights came on, illuminating the outdoors. Jessica kept on running blindly, heedless of the shrubs that tore at her. The heel of one of her shoes snapped when she stumbled. She kicked it off and then bent to rip off the other one. She headed for the steps that would take her to the beach, down and down and down again, far too fast for safety but truly not caring whether or not she fell and hurt herself. Carlo was behind her. She could hear his pursuit and she moved as if the devil were on her heels.

She tore on to the beach and instantly into the cloaking cover of the trees, struggling desperately not to gasp for oxygen, her hand crammed against her convulsing mouth.

'Jessica!' Carlo roared, and she froze in her hiding place.

She watched him stride down the beach, lean hands on hips, a desperate urgency in his very aggressive movement. Maybe he would tie a big rock to her ankle and drown her if he found her. The secret she had learnt was undoubtedly the biggest danger he had ever faced. He moved off towards the jetty and immediately she set off again in the opposite direction.

Her dress tore on a branch, scraping her abdomen painfully. Pulling free, she kept going until she couldn't keep going any longer. Her breasts heaving with the effort of breathing, she collapsed where she stood. The agony folded in and she shuddered and shook, hugging herself with trembling arms, rocking back and forth without realising it.

Carlo and Sunny. His father's wife. It was obscene, unbearable. How could she have been so blind? Sunny hadn't been confused when she came to Jessica's room. Sunny had known that Jessica was simply a pawn on the board. Did Lukas suspect that his wife and his son were having an affair? Was that why Jessica had been required as a smoke-screen for this visit?

Jessica covered her face and wanted to die. No wonder Sunny had attempted to hold off the wedding. She was in love with Carlo. Dear God...no wonder Carlo had refused to tell her the truth. No decent human being would have agreed to such a deception.

Carlo was even prepared to go to the lengths of marrying her to be convincing! Carlo had made love to her last night while the woman he really loved slept under the same roof. Jessica was a mass of pain and wounded emotion. Sunny had been responsible for that room miles away from Carlo. Sunny had been jealous. Sunny hadn't wanted the deception to go that far. But then Carlo was cleverer. Carlo had been determined to play the masquerade for real for his shrewd father's benefit. And he hadn't drawn the line at driving poor, stupid Jessica mad with desire and ensuring that she fulfilled the agreement to the very last letter.

A twig snapped. That was her only warning. Her swollen eyes opened. Carlo was hunkered down in front of her. 'Go away!' she gasped.

He ignored her. An unexpectedly gentle hand lifted one of her bare feet and he groaned. 'You've cut your feet to ribbons...you're bleeding!'

Dimly she was aware of the stinging of her maltreated flesh but it was her heart and her pride and her ability to trust that was causing her the most unimaginable pain. She bowed her head down on her raised knees, tight as a spring with tension.

Carlo swore succinctly. 'Come here!' A powerful hand closed round one scratched forearm.

'No!' Her voice broke right down the middle as she reeled back, desperate to avoid the contact.

'I have the feeling that I have been condemned to Death Row without the right to appeal.'

'That's w-where you ought to be!' she condemned strickenly. 'It's vile! The two of you waiting like ghouls for him to die…I feel dirty, dear God, I feel soiled and you w-wouldn't believe how dumb and stupid I feel!'

She loved him. That was the full extent of her stupidity. She deserved everything that had happened to her. She deserved to be used and abused. Her own pride and self-discipline should have protected her.

Carlo expelled his breath in a hiss and leapt upright again. His lean powerful length was rigid.

'Just g-get me off this island!' Jessica sobbed.

'Isn't life a bitch?' Carlo breathed. 'The woman I don't want is obsessed by me and the woman I do want spends her whole time running in the wrong direction.'

It was too late. Didn't he see that? Was his estimation of her intelligence so low that he could think he could fool her again?

'*Dio*…what sort of bastard do you think I am?' he demanded with sudden ferocious hostility.

'I suppose if it weren't for the money the two of you would have got together openly a long time ago,' Jessica mumbled sickly.

'Would you just listen to me?' he demanded rawly.

He was about to tell the truth and she didn't want to hear it. She did not want to hear how his love for Sunny had overcome family loyalty and every decent feeling. 'I don't want to know!' she burst out. 'Not any of it!'

'I could beat you for that,' Carlo bit out with blatant

frustration. 'There is nothing between Sunny and me. There never has been. There never will be.'

That did grab her attention. She lifted her tear-swollen face and stared. Carlo was standing several feet away, the moonlight picking out the grim lines of his darkly handsome features.

'It didn't sound like that.'

'Six months ago, I met Sunny for the first time at a party in Rome. She knew Lukas was dying. She's been chasing me ever since—'

'Chasing you?' Jessica echoed.

'The first couple of times I ran into her, I took her out to dinner, purely and simply because she's my father's wife,' Carlo spelt out with sardonic bite. 'But Sunny read that differently. She took it as encouragement. She showed up at my apartment one night in London and asked for a bed for the night, told me this stupid story about being afraid to stay in a hotel alone since some friend of hers was raped. I fell for it…but the only bed Sunny wanted into was mine…'

Jessica swallowed hard. 'And?'

'She told me she was in love with me and I had her driven to a hotel in the middle of the night. But Sunny's very persistent because no man has ever rejected her,' Carlo murmured with an expressive grimace. 'Sunny is one of the reasons I brought you here. I wanted her kept at a distance—'

'So you needed me as a…a buffer—'

'It would be a little difficult for her to get into my bed when it was already occupied,' Carlo said very drily.

Bemusedly, she struggled to recall what Carlo had said in that emotional scene she had stumbled on, and she realised that Carlo had said nothing that did not fit the story he had told her. Her head ached at the effort of concentration. She was almost afraid to give way to the intensity of her relief.

'She's so beautiful,' she muttered.

Carlo said nothing. In the silence, all she could hear was the thunder of her own heart and the soft rushing of the surf.

'A storm in a teacup, then,' she said uncomfortably. 'I'm sorry, I assumed—'

'The worst? Don't you always?' Carlo drawled.

As he extended a lean hand down to her, Jessica allowed him to pull her up. The force of her distress had left her badly shaken. Relieved as she had been by Carlo's confidences, she still felt frighteningly raw and vulnerable. Badly needing to believe that he did not find Sunny desirable, she looked up into his hard features but she could read nothing there, knew that what Carlo did not volunteer, she would never guess. Carlo did not easily reveal his emotions.

He tugged her back along the beach. She could feel the pain in her abused feet now and the sting of the scratches on her arms and stomach. At the foot of the steps, he surveyed her limping gait and groaned. Bending, he hoisted her over one shoulder.

'You *can't* carry me up there!' she objected.

But he did, although by the time they reached the top every muscle in his superbly built body was feverishly taut and she could feel the dampness of perspiration sticking his silk shirt to his skin. 'No more steps,' he muttered raggedly.

He set her down in the lift that gave his father access to the gardens and sent the doors winging shut. He lounged back fluidly against the stainless steel wall and surveyed her with sudden uninhibited intensity.

The dark vibrancy of his magnetism was potent. Jessica collided with smouldering golden eyes and her heart skipped a beat and began to race instead. A slow, sensual smile curved his handsome mouth. He reached out and deftly flicked open the control panel. He touched a button and the lift swooshed to a halt and he hit another before the doors could open.

Arranged on the wall opposite, Jessica felt a quivering heaviness enter her lower limbs as Carlo closed the distance between them. He braced his hands on either side of her and drove her head back with the force of his mouth, his kiss like a fiery brand of ownership. He unleashed a hunger that was primitive in its intensity, sending a burst of scorching heat shooting through her veins.

'Somebody might—' she gasped as he released her reddened lips.

'If I don't have you now,' Carlo said thickly, 'I'll die.'

His hands wrenched down the straps of her sleeveless dress and she glanced down, shocked to see her own bared breasts, helplessly shy of him and yet unbearably aroused by his impatience. With a groan, Carlo lifted her and suckled at an erect pink nipple and her hands clenched fiercely into his shoulders, an involuntary moan of excitement torn from her. Her head fell back as his tormenting mouth bit at her sensitive flesh with a knowing eroticism that drove her out of her mind with excitement.

She was boneless in his grasp, a wanton creature drunk on sensation. A lean hand skimmed beneath the flimsy silken fabric of her gown, following the upward curve of a slender thigh and lingering there with devastating effect.

'You drive me crazy,' Carlo groaned, sinking to his knees to slowly tug down the scrap of lace that was all that divided him from her. 'You always drove me crazy.'

He buried his mouth hotly in the triangle of silver curls he had revealed and she started sliding down the wall until he gripped her thighs. 'No…' she mumbled in shock.

He didn't listen and a split-second later she stopped thinking altogether, thrown into a vortex of extraordinary excitement by what he was doing. She gasped his name, speared her fingers wildly into his tousled black hair and surrendered absolutely to the pleasure, losing all track of time.

When Carlo drew level with her again, she was inflamed to fever pitch, not a bone or a muscle in her body obedient to even the most confused command. He wound her arms round him and took her swollen mouth in a savage admission of need and then he lifted her, wrapping her thighs round his narrow waist and entered her in one compelling thrust.

Stilling, he shuddered against her, fighting for control. 'It's never been like this for me...*never!*' he rasped.

I love you... She found it on her lips and kept it there, instinct reining the confession back. Bracing her spine against the steel wall, he began to move again, fast and slow, smooth and rough until she was possessed by the primal rhythm and the explosive, uncontrollable hunger. As she reached an intolerable peak of excitement, she sank her teeth into his shoulder and was flung over the edge into quivering, whimpering fulfilment at the same time as he was.

His breathing pattern roughly audible, Carlo dealt her a shattered glance and slowly lowered her limp body to the floor again, glittering golden eyes still pinned to her. He dropped a kiss on to her brow and began rearranging her dress with hands that were uncharacteristically clumsy.

'We'd better get out of here.' He indicated the red light flashing behind the open control panel, readjusting whatever he had previously put out of place at speed. 'Security will be on their way.'

'What?' she moaned in horror.

The doors opened. Carlo grabbed her while she was still reeling incredulously from what she had allowed him to do. A few feet out of the lift, they were on to a staircase. Dear heaven, she acknowledged dazedly, that shameless woman in the lift had been her! She was pole-axed, barely functioning on automatic pilot.

Carlo dragged her into their bedroom, closed the door and slumped back against it. His narrowed gaze swept her hectically flushed features and then he burst out laughing. After a startled moment, she saw the humour of that indecently adolescent flight of theirs from authority and was overcome by helpless giggles.

'Like guilty teenagers!' Unselfconsciously, Carlo wiped at his damp eyes, fighting to rein back his laughter. 'I've never done anything like that in my life before.'

All threat of constraint banished, Jessica met his ruefully amused dark eyes and knew she had never loved him more than she loved him at that moment.

Abruptly, Carlo muttered an imprecation. 'I forgot about your poor feet.'

'I wasn't thinking about them,' she murmured shyly.

He took her into his bathroom and produced a medical kit. He made her sit on the edge of the bath and soak her feet. Then he crouched down and patted them dry with a fleecy towel. He was incredibly gentle and she watched him minister to her needs with growing astonishment. What a mixture of opposites he was, she thought painfully. The antiseptic he dabbed on stung like mad and tears sprang involuntarily to her eyes.

'You shouldn't swim for a couple of days.'

'Fine.'

Carlo swept her up and carried her back to the bedroom to deposit her on the bed. He sank down on the edge of the mattress and lifted the phone. 'Are you hungry?'

She discovered that she was. He ordered sandwiches.

As she stretched out, Carlo noticed the tear on her dress for the first time. Before she could object, he had peeled her out of it and discovered the angry scratch across her stomach. 'Please…not the antiseptic,' she begged in total cowardice.

Carlo grinned and pressed his lips tenderly to the abrasion, making her muscles clench suddenly tight with awareness. Lifting his dark head, he scrutinised her with sudden gravity. A tiny muscle pulsing at the corner of his compressed mouth. 'Last night,' he breathed. 'Last night when I saw that photograph of your late husband, I was insanely jealous.'

Entrapped by his dark eyes, she was shaken by his honesty.

'You knew,' he saw. 'I'm surprised you didn't throw it in my teeth.'

'In the mood you were in, I might just have ended up out in the corridor.'

'You chose him over me.' Carlo had shed his sense of humour and would not allow her to lightly flip the subject. 'That is why I felt jealous. If I had not known you then, he would merely be a part of your past.'

'I didn't choose—'

'You did...you chose,' he asserted, allowing her no escape from that fact.

A knock on the door announced the arrival of supper. Jessica had rarely been so grateful for an interruption. Carlo collected the tray and settled it on the foot of the bed.

'I refuse to accept that I am second best,' Carlo continued tautly in the throbbing silence. 'For that is what you want me to accept...I cannot do it.'

All relaxation banished, Jessica slid upright and reached for her robe.

'You say nothing,' he commented with flaring impatience.

'Maybe I don't want to fight with you—'

'No, you evade my every invitation for you to talk about your marriage. You close me out of five years of your life! You slam the door shut in my face—'

'I am not about to run Simon down just to please you,' Jessica muttered shakily.

'I do not expect that from you. I am not a child unable to face harsh realities. But I find your refusal to discuss

Turner…peculiar,' Carlo selected, reaching for a sandwich, entirely at his ease. 'My life is now an open book to you—'

Her teeth gritted. 'Only because I stumbled accidentally between the covers.'

'I did not want my past to come between us,' Carlo stated levelly. 'You force me to be blunt. OK. Your father intimated that your marriage had not been a happy one.'

Taken by surprise, Jessica froze.

'And he was not talking about your husband's illness. He made that clear—'

'He had no right to imply that—'

'You were not blissfully happy with your *best friend*,' Carlo incised with scorn.

Jessica rolled off the bed, cornered by his persistence. 'I will not discuss Simon with you.'

'Why not? He is dead. He cannot be hurt.' Carlo dealt her an expectant stare.

'You say I made a choice. Why don't you look to your own behaviour during those six weeks?' she demanded. 'You might be surprised at what you see!'

'I behaved like a bastard,' Carlo growled the admission to her back a second before she vanished into the bathroom. 'But you didn't encourage me to be anything else. You made me angry and frustrated and you challenged me. You made it an all-out fight between us and I know only one way to fight…and that is to win!'

She ran a bath for herself. She needed the space. In full flood, Carlo was a talented interrogator. The water stung her feet like mad but a masochistic part of her rejoiced in the pain. She deserved it. She kept on letting her guard down around Carlo and manipulative swine that he was, he sensed that every time it happened and demanded answers he had no right to expect.

Once, she had been grossly disloyal to Simon with Carlo. Ultimately that hadn't mattered, except in so far as she had contravened her own high principles. But she could not be disloyal to Simon's memory. How could she tell a male as rawly virile and passionate as Carlo that Simon had failed to consummate their marriage? He would laugh, wouldn't he? He would kill himself laughing. He would be triumphant, possessed of the knowledge that her marriage had been pure farce from start to finish and that he, after all, had become her first lover. She felt that she owed Simon's memory something more than that.

She emerged to an empty bedroom and instead of being relieved felt deserted. Furious at her own increasing emotional dependency on Carlo, she compressed her lips. She could not afford to look for Carlo when he was not there. Some day not too far in the future, he would not be there at all.

Unintentionally, she recalled the passion they had shared and reddened fiercely, still barely able to credit that that wanton woman had been her. Carlo touched her and that was that. Nothing else mattered. Sooner or later, she would pay a heavy price for such memories, she acknowledged painfully. The fact that Carlo had finally contrived to fulfil his fantasy of having sex in a lift was unlikely to be a recollection she cherished with pride...when he was gone.

'Some day you will come to me on your knees and beg me to take you...and I will break you.' Jessica shivered, suddenly cold and scared. Just a few short days ago, Carlo had still been talking in the same vein. And though he had yet to discover it, he had already won. She loved him. Whatever happened, she was going to be very badly hurt.

Another knock sounded on the door. It was fresh sandwiches and sweetly fragrant coffee, ordered by Carlo on her behalf. The pretty dark-skinned maid passed on the message that Carlo was with his father.

'I'm sorry you had to be bothered so late.' It was two in the morning and Jessica felt guilty.

'But I work the night shift here, ma'am.' The woman smiled. 'This is my job.'

The night shift, Jessica reflected, slowly shaking her head. A night shift of staff for round-the-clock service. It was like living in a top-flight hotel. Then she wondered if Lukas had taken a turn for the worse and frowned.

Carlo returned about ten minutes later. 'How is Lukas?' she asked.

'A consummate insomniac,' Carlo sighed. 'Problems have arisen over a shipping deal in Athens. He's asked me to fly out there and take care of them. I'll be leaving at seven and I expect to be back the night before the wedding.'

Disappointment enveloped her and she fought to conceal it.

'You'll miss me,' Carlo asserted with teeth-clenching conviction.

He slid into bed beside her and tugged her into his arms with determination. His lean, muscular frame felt surprisingly tense. 'Something occurred to me earlier.' He lifted his head. 'Are you on the Pill?'

It was Jessica's turn to tense. 'No.'

Carlo expelled his breath in a hiss. 'I didn't protect you this time…I'm sorry.'

She flushed, made some feverish calculations and decided that the risk of pregnancy was so small as to be most unlikely. 'There isn't very much chance—'

'Russian roulette,' Carlo groaned. 'I have never been that careless.'

Jessica was stiffening. 'I really don't think you have anything to worry about.'

It would be very foolish to forget the true parameters of their relationship, she appreciated. Passion had intervened to blur those limits but there was something hor-

ribly realistic about Carlo's alarm at the prospect of re-
percussions.

'We'll see.' Carlo looked fatalistic and shrugged a
smooth brown shoulder. 'Perhaps it is just as well that
we will be getting married.'

'It won't be a real marriage.'

'What is real and what unreal?' Carlo murmured
wryly above her downbent head. 'I am not sure I know
any more.'

'I thought you knew everything—'

'I have moments of occasional insanity—'

'In lifts?' The quip flew off her tongue, embarrassing
her.

'Only with you,' Carlo muttered with earthy amusement, splaying a determined hand across her bottom and
bringing her into closer connection with his highly
aroused body. Her eyes widened in shock at his readiness to make love again. It occurred to her that she was
at the very foot of the learning curve in this particular
field.

Carlo surveyed her with unhidden satisfaction. 'You
really are the most gloriously passionate woman...I find
you irresistible.'

Sexually, not intellectually, she affixed, rather bitterly
aware that a fortnight ago she would have wanted to hit
him for looking at her with that air of arrogant ownership
but now she was busy drowning in dark golden eyes and
longing for the heat of that expert mouth on hers. Her
mother had spoken with the wisdom of a seer six years
ago. This time she really had fallen flat on her face.

'You look ravishing.' Surveying Jessica, Marika sighed
with heartfelt satisfaction. 'My brother will worship at
your feet.'

Jessica tautened. She could not imagine Carlo wor-
shipping her. Carlo's instincts were far more basic, but
then his sister was a hopeless romantic. Jessica at-

tempted to scan her reflection without being gripped by
any similar fantasies. She wouldn't have objected to
wearing a smart suit. But she had not envisaged wearing
anything that remotely resembled a wedding-dress.

And here she was, sheathed in the most devastatingly
bridal concoction she had ever seen. Sizzling white with
a superb beaded Elizabethan collar, the whole covered
with magnificent embroidery and even sweeping down
into a small train. Her mistake had been protesting the
unsuitability of such a gown within Lukas's hearing. She
had never dreamt he would even interest himself in what
she wore.

'All my wives wore white,' Lukas had interrupted
loudly. 'It's part of the show—'

'But I'm a widow—'

'A merry one?' Lukas had chuckled with great amusement at his own timeworn joke. 'We don't advertise
these things. You wear white.'

Recalling her intense mortification, she began to peel
off the dress. Marika handled it with reverence, turning
to a hovering maid for assistance lest the smallest damage be done to the delicate fabric. As Carlo's sister left
to dress for dinner, Jessica realised that in less than
twenty-four hours she would be married. Married to the
man she loved but who did not love her, married as part
of a deal to please a dying old man. It was crazy…why
had she allowed Carlo to persuade her to play along?

Jessica was putting the finishing touches to her make-
up when the door opened without warning. Sunny
strolled in, clad in a glistening grey sheath dress. Jessica
hadn't laid eyes on Sunny for over forty-eight hours, not
since seeing her with Carlo. Over breakfast the next
morning, Marika had informed her that Sunny had flown
to Miami on one of her regular shopping trips.

'Do you want something?' she asked drily, infuriated
by the fashion in which Sunny simply walked in without
knocking.

Green eyes glittered coldly over her. Sunny uttered a brittle laugh. 'All of a sudden you're very sure of your-self, aren't you?'

Jessica looked back at her, refusing to be discomfited. Calmly, she stood up and crossed the room to slide her feet into shoes but behind the cool front, her nervous tension was running at an all-time high. Physically Sunny had an impact that took even Jessica's breath away. Carlo was undeniably aware of this woman's beauty. Could he really be quite untouched by her desire for him?

'You saw us together the other night,' Sunny mur-mured with faintly patronising amusement. 'Didn't that bother you at all?'

With a not quite steady hand, Jessica lifted a silver-backed brush that belonged to Carlo from the dressing-table and ran it through her hair slowly. 'I saw nothing that bothered me,' she lied.

'You're in love with him too, aren't you? Poor Jessica. I can imagine what he's told you. I can also imagine just how much you wanted to believe him—'

Jessica took a deep breath. 'If you don't mind, I'd like to finish getting ready.'

'If you don't mind…you're so polite!' Sunny scanned her with wide, wondering eyes. 'He won't have told you the truth. The truth is that *neither* of us matters a damn to him right now. Carlo's one priority is keeping his darling daddy happy.'

'Why shouldn't it be?' Jessica said defensively. 'He hasn't got much time left with him.'

'And his inheritance is conditional on his mar-riage…did you know that?' Sunny prompted gently. 'Right now, Carlo has to play you along and keep you happy. He needs a bride and it seems he's found one, dumb enough to shut her eyes to reality.'

The floor rocked under Jessica's feet. She turned pale. 'I don't believe you,' she said shakily.

'You are naïve…and you haven't a clue how the men in this family operate.' Sunny's exquisite face twisted with derisive amusement. 'I understand Carlo. You don't understand him at all. Carlo wants me and he fully intends to have me…but he won't put a foot wrong while his father is still alive. All that keeps Carlo from me now is Lukas…and of course, the money…'

As the door shut on Sunny's exit Jessica closed her eyes tightly in anguish. She felt physically sick. Carlo had lied to her. He was not marrying her purely to please his father. He was marrying her for entirely mercenary motives. And yet he had fooled her brilliantly into believing everything he had told her!

In a wild passion of despair and turmoil, Jessica hauled her cases out of a closet in the dressing-room and began dragging her clothes out and packing them. She refused to be used like that…she absolutely refused!

'What the hell are you doing?'

On her knees beside the cases, Jessica glanced up. Carlo was a big dark silhouette filling the doorway. Hooded ebony eyes dug into her like aggressive question marks as he stared down at her in disbelief.

'I'm not going through with the wedding!' she gasped.

CHAPTER NINE

CARLO scanned the wildness in her amethyst eyes for a fulminating ten seconds, a muscle jerking tight at his hard jawline. 'I don't know what the hell you think you're playing at but the wedding goes ahead tomorrow…even if I have to drag you through it by the hair!'

'No. Sunny told me why you *had* to get married!' Jessica slung rawly. 'And I refuse to be part of it!'

'Why do I have to get married?' Carlo invited very softly. 'I really would like to know.'

'You lied to me,' Jessica condemned fiercely. 'Everything you told me was a lie…you played on my sympathy when all the time you were just using me—'

'Do you ever get to the punchline?'

'You *have* to be married to inherit your father's money!'

After a staggered pause, Carlo threw back his dark imperious head and laughed uproariously, utterly incredulous at the charge.

It was not the reaction Jessica had expected. Her mouth fell open.

'*Dio*…is that the best she could do?' His amusement spent, Carlo studied Jessica with narrowed eyes, his hard mouth compressing. 'And you believed her, didn't you?'

Suddenly less sure, Jessica said, 'I—'

Carlo cut across her. 'I have been my father's heir since the day I was born because his blood runs in my veins. And no matter what bitterness or resentment lay between us that has never changed. Why would he demand that I marry?'

'Because he wants you to settle down,' Jessica suggested tremulously.

'Lukas Philippides wants me to do what he never did himself?' Carlo elevated a sardonic winged brow. 'Settle down? He didn't settle down through four marriages and countless mistresses…why should he seek to interfere in my private life?'

Jessica was not prepared to cede the point without a fight. 'Well, then, you tell me why both your father and your sister are so damned glad that you're getting married?' she demanded, shooting what she knew to be the last bolt in her argument.

His hard features perceptibly darkened, his mouth tightening as though she had drawn blood. Glittering golden eyes rested on her coldly. 'OK, I'll tell you. Ten years ago, my father went to bed with the woman I had asked to marry me—'

'He *what*?' Jessica mumbled in shock, certain she could not have heard him correctly.

'Thus a decade of mutual silence,' Carlo pointed out grimly.

'But how…I mean, *why*?' she whispered.

'Lukas invited me to visit him. I brought my fiancée with me,' Carlo murmured in a flat, unemotional tone. 'You see Lukas now, a shadow of the man he was then. In those days he was still virile and attractive to women. He wanted me to work for him. That was why the red carpet came out. My half-brother was a drunk, useless in business. Lukas wanted me back to take his place. I refused. I knew it wouldn't work. He was furious and Bella was furious too. She loved the lifestyle he was offering…the constant parties, the bottomless well of money. I wasn't one quarter as wealthy then as I am now—'

'But still—' Jessica found herself still arguing her

own disbelief, she was so shattered by the very idea of what he was telling her.

'Lukas made a play for Bella. She was flattered and he took her to bed—'

Jessica was appalled. Dear God, he had been twenty-three years old! How could any father have done that to his own son and how could any woman sink that low?

'I found them together,' Carlo volunteered in the dragging silence. 'And I was devastated. I knew *he* couldn't be trusted with any beautiful woman but I had assumed that I could trust *her*—'

'How could they do that to you?' Jessica felt physically sick.

'Lukas can't help competing and he doesn't always think ahead. He was settling old scores, showing the young dog that the old dog still had a trick or two up his sleeve. Bella?' Carlo's mouth compressed. 'One of the wealthiest men in the world told her he wanted her and she was knocked sideways by the idea. She was dumb enough to think he would marry her but he dumped her a couple of weeks later. He knew he'd gone too far—'

'But how could you ever forgive him?'

'Because he doesn't know any better. Like a bull in a china shop, he creates havoc and lets other people pay the price, but ultimately, he's still my father.' Carlo surveyed her pale, troubled face. 'Now you know why my father and my sister are so damned glad I'm getting married,' he derided harshly. 'It buries that tacky little episode with Bella.'

Jessica was still in shock, stricken by an awareness of the pain that must have been inflicted by a cheap little gold-digger who had her eye on a richer quarry. Carlo was so proud and at that age he must have been far more vulnerable.

'You were so quick to accept the word of a most

unreliable character witness…incredibly quick,' Carlo condemned her now with contempt. 'Sunny is jealous and will do just about anything to cause trouble between us. Didn't that occur to you?'

She hadn't taken time to think. She had acted on impulse. Now her loss of faith in him seemed heinous. Her cheeks flamed. 'I'm sorry…'

'I really believed I was getting somewhere with you,' Carlo breathed harshly. 'And I was wrong. I open my heart to you and you still kick me in the teeth. You have no faith, no trust to give. As far as you're concerned, I'm still the bastard you decided I was six years ago and as far as I'm concerned I might as well be from now on!'

Her throat was convulsing. There was a pain in his dark, clenched features that she had never seen before. It cut her up inside. 'I said I was sorry! It's this situation—'

Carlo swung on his heel, unmoved by her unhidden distress. 'Your father's waiting downstairs for you—'

'My father?' she echoed weakly.

'I picked him up on the way through London. I thought you would want him here.'

She swallowed hard. 'I—'

'You'd better tidy yourself up before dinner,' Carlo cut her off with bite.

Why *had* she listened to Sunny? In retrospect, it seemed very foolish of her to have placed credence in anything the other woman said. Sunny was not reliable. Sunny had set her sights on Carlo and she was jealous. Jessica covered her face with shaking hands. And she herself was inclined to be jealous of Sunny, she acknowledged. Had it been easier to latch on to the accusation about his inheritance than confront him with Sunny's confident belief that only filial loyalty prevented

Carlo from admitting that he *did* want his father's wife?
Sunny had been horribly convincing.

But Carlo was right. She didn't trust him. No faith,
no trust. Had Simon done that to her as well? She had
trusted Simon from childhood and he had let her down
badly by using her, uncaring of how much he might hurt
her. He had been too weak to care and he had depended
on her loyalty and her pride to keep her quiet and carry
on the pretence of their marriage. Suddenly she knew
that she owed Carlo that truth, no matter how distressing
she found sharing it.

In the bedroom, Carlo was halfway into a shirt, muscles flexed across his smooth brown back as he shrugged
into it, and her mouth ran dry. 'Carlo…' she whispered.
'I think I should tell you about my marriage—'

'You can keep him like some holy icon inside your
heart.' He spun round and sent her a chilling glance of
impassivity. 'I'm not competing with a ghost—'

'You wouldn't be competing—'

'You don't understand,' Carlo breathed with cold dark
eyes that froze her out. 'Simon's the past and as irrelevant as yesterday's newspaper to me. What is important
is trust and you haven't got any to give. You hadn't any
six years ago either!'

'Don't throw that up to me now. You said you'd never
forgive me on the way over here,' she reminded him
shakily. 'That does not create an atmosphere of trust.'

'I'll see you downstairs.' Carlo snatched up his dinner-jacket and strode to the door. 'You'd better wash
your face. Your mascara's running.'

Jessica smacked her coiled fist against the wall in frustration as the door slammed and then curved the injured
member into her stomach, wincing with pain.
Sometimes, Carlo was so hatefully superior that she
wanted to hit him! Loving him didn't wipe out that
temptation. And now he had brought her father over as

if this were a normal wedding. Dazedly she shook her head.

Gerald Amory was chatting animatedly to Marika when she entered the drawing-room and Jessica barely had time to kiss his cheek before Lukas arrived and her father was taken over. Throughout dinner, Carlo's father shot questions at her father, demanding his opinions on business practices and frequently censuring them. Gerald Amory stood up to the interrogation well, wry amusement in his gaze when he caught Jessica's anxious look.

'Well, I wouldn't employ you,' Lukas grumbled over his coffee. 'I don't believe in feather-bedding my workers—'

'The EC rulings won't give you much choice,' Gerald Amory dared.

After dinner, she was left alone with her father.

'Am I to believe you've finally taken leave of your wits?' he teased. 'I never thought I'd see the day that you did anything at reckless speed and here you are rushing into marriage within weeks of meeting Carlo again!'

Jessica tensed. 'What did he tell you?'

'Oh he was very persuasive,' Gerald laughed. 'Never shut up about you the whole flight!'

'Really?' Jessica encouraged.

'Told me he fell in love with you at first sight six years ago and never recovered. Very impressive stuff, it was,' her father recalled with a fond smile. 'He did explain that his father's condition was pressing you both into a quick marriage but he stressed that he could have married you a couple of weeks ago just as happily!' he chuckled.

Her strained smile glazed over. Dear heaven, Carlo had laid on the I-love-your-daughter routine with a trowel. Very impressive indeed.

'Carlo's a rather more complex character than I ever

appreciated,' Gerald admitted. 'I always thought of him as very cool and controlled. He is in business. But in love…he's all emotion and reaction. So, now you tell me how you feel.'

Jessica took a deep breath. 'I'm crazy about him.'

'And you're much more reserved than he is…did your mother and I do that to you?' he sighed regretfully.

She went to bed about eleven. There was no sign of Carlo. She lay sleepless in the darkness waiting for him. But he didn't come and she was hurt. Why was it that when she finally decided to open *her* heart, Carlo closed her out? It was impossible to believe that tomorrow was her wedding-day. But then it wasn't a real wedding-day, she reminded herself wretchedly.

The next morning she was served breakfast in bed. There was an air of strong excitement in the household and from dawn overhead the ceaseless racket of rotor blades as guests were flown in for the festivities.

It was to be a very small wedding, Marika had explained. Just relatives, her father's closest business associates and executive staff and of course Carlo's friends. It was rather sad that she listed not one single person as a friend of her father's. Like someone in a dream, Jessica let herself be fussed over and dressed. She was merely playing a part, she told herself repeatedly, just going through the expected motions to please everybody.

'It's time,' Marika said from the door with a misty smile.

'Their idea of a small do wouldn't be ours,' her father shared out of the corner of his mouth on their passage down the huge main staircase. All the staff were in the main hall to see her.

And a minute later, as the music sounded up and she had a startled glimpse of the hundreds of people packed into the vast ballroom with standing room only at the back, she understood what he meant. Every head seemed to turn, a rippling sigh of comment accompanying their passing. Her pallor was banished by colour as Carlo swung round impatiently to unsmilingly watch her approach. Like the condemned man, she thought furiously, on the brink of being forced to walk the plank!

The ceremony seemed endless and it was conducted in both Greek and English. Carlo slotted the ring on her finger with a cool, steady hand. And it was done. He was not invited to kiss the bride and, although the opportunity came as she turned to face him, he took no advantage of it. His darkly handsome features were starkly set.

Her throat tightening, she glanced away and caught a no more cheering view of Lukas beaming with satisfaction and Sunny beside him, her stunning face wearing a set smile.

'Well, I'm glad that farce is over,' Jessica hissed before they made their exit.

Carlo swung her round like a doll and brought his mouth crashing down on hers in punishment, his powerful hands biting painfully into her wrists. She knew he was furious. She knew she wasn't supposed to enjoy it. But her body had other ideas. It went into instant meltdown like he had thrown a self-destruct button.

'No farce,' Carlo murmured softly, nastily as he lifted his dark head again and smiled for the assembled audience. 'You are my wife now, legally, morally and in every other way.'

There were no speeches over the banquet which followed. Lukas, she was informed by her father, didn't like speeches. Many toasts were offered and made. Jessica began to notice that Carlo's attention was frequently directed at Sunny. He did it cleverly, covertly, but he did it all the same, she noted painfully.

Sunny, ravishing in silver and gold, her bright hair an

eyecatching beacon every time she moved her head. 'Titian hair…my besetting sin,' Carlo had once confided. Jessica's stomach clenched. Why did she have to remember that now? An hour ago, Sunny had looked frozen, but now she was effervescent and glowing like a blazing torch.

After the meal, Carlo whirled her on to the empty floor while everybody sat back and watched. Jessica was desperately self-conscious. She had never danced with him before and was suddenly tortured by the lack of such small experiences in their relationship. They had never had a courtship, never dated and yet she loved him with a passion that burned and flamed more with every increasingly insecure moment.

'When are you going to start talking to me again?' she whispered.

'Have I stopped? You mean I might actually have something to say that you might want to hear?'

'I said I was sorry…what do you want me to do? Crawl?'

'I think I might enjoy that,' Carlo admitted.

'Well, I'm not about to do it…dream on!'

As he bound her closer, she felt his breath on her cheek and clashed with smouldering golden eyes and an explicitly sexual scrutiny. 'If you want me in your bed tonight, you'll have to do better than that—'

Her skin flamed scarlet and she trembled, cursing her innate and inescapable physical awareness of him. He could feel it. She knew that. 'I can do without you in my bed.'

He laughed huskily. 'You're as much a slave to the passion as I am!'

But I want more; I want it all, a little voice screamed inside her head.

'I counted the hours I was away from you,' Carlo

suddenly groaned above her head. 'And then I found you packing—'

She missed a step but he carried her on effortlessly. Through the light fabric of her gown, she could feel the thrust of his arousal and her knees went weak, her breath feathering dangerously short in her dry throat. Her nipples were tight little points that ached under the tight bodice. 'I'm sorry…'

'I'm getting more forgiving by the second,' Carlo gritted, binding her even closer so that she was in contact with every inch of his powerful body.

She was trembling by the time they came off the floor but radiant. Lukas beckoned to her as Carlo dropped her hand. Her father-in-law indicated that he wanted her to bend her head. 'What would you say if I told you I wasn't leaving him a *drachma*?'

Still radiant, she laughed. 'I'd say he doesn't need your money.'

'You love him. Make him happy. That's all I want,' Lukas growled.

Across the room, Sunny was the centre of a crowd of bedazzled men. Jessica saw Carlo several yards away and his hooded dark eyes were trained on Sunny. Suddenly sick, Jessica looked away. Lukas had already moved on but Marika appeared at her elbow.

'Men find Sunny quite irresistible, don't they?' Jessica remarked helplessly.

'Men like my father,' Marika conceded wryly. 'She's an expensive adornment, other men envy. That's why Lukas married her when his health was failing. He gets to show her off; she gets to spend the money. And I have to admit that in recent months she's surprised me—'

'How?'

'She's been leading a very restricted life here on Paradiso and she's handled it better than I expected,'

Marika conceded. 'Then she knows her freedom is on the horizon, and Sunny isn't the kind of woman likely to be on her own for long. Right now, she's probably looking out for her next meal ticket and I can't really blame her. Lukas forced her to sign a pre-nuptial contract. When he dies, she gets next to nothing.'

Marika clearly had no idea that Sunny had already targeted Lukas's replacement and that she was keeping it in the family, so as to speak. Only Jessica had got in her way.

Carlo's sister sighed, still watching Sunny flirting like mad with her admirers. 'I wonder why she's upset today.'

'Upset?' Sunny looked anything but upset to Jessica's untutored gaze. The redhead appeared to be revelling in all the attention she was receiving.

'Something's bothering her. She's drinking too much,' Marika proffered. 'She knows how my father feels about that. She's usually more careful.'

Carlo crossed the room with a brilliant smile that tore at Jessica's heartstrings. 'What are you doing over here? Come on...I want you to meet my friends.'

The afternoon wore on and the party became more riotous. Jessica didn't know what time it was when she overheard Marika say something to Carlo in Greek. She caught Sunny's name and Carlo's sudden tension. His hard jawline squared.

Where was Sunny? It had been some time since Jessica had last seen her. A split-second later, Carlo strode off.

'Where's he going?' she asked his sister.

Marika compressed her lips. 'I asked him to find Sunny. She's drunk and when she's drunk, she can be...indiscreet,' she selected the word curtly.

Jessica hesitated only a moment before setting off in pursuit. She saw Carlo at the top of the stairs and hurried after him. He clearly knew exactly where he was going and she almost lost him down one corridor, catching up round a corner just in time to see him throw wide a door.

Before she saw for herself the scene that had met his eyes, she heard him explode into guttural Greek. Sunny was half out of her dress on a bed and a highly embarrassed young man was spluttering fervent apologies and struggling to get back into his jacket beside the bed. Carlo stood there with clenched fists, a dark flush highlighting his blazing eyes.

'You don't want me,' Sunny slurred, fumbling clumsily to right her dress. 'Why should you care?'

As the young man took advantage of Carlo's stasis to flee, Jessica was almost knocked flying. Her gasp as she grabbed at the door-handle to steady herself turned both Carlo and Sunny's heads.

Sunny gave an inebriated giggle. 'If it isn't the blushing bride...come on, why don't you? It's open house!'

Carlo was rigid, his dark, strong face utterly impassive. 'Go back downstairs, Jessica.'

'She's not that sensitive.' Sunny laughed again. 'I know all about her, Carlo. I found the file in Lukas's desk. Her mother was a nymphomaniac and her daddy's a thief. You weren't too choosy, were you?'

'Shut up!' Carlo gritted furiously as every scrap of colour drained from Jessica's shattered face.

'And her first husband was gay,' Sunny giggled, unconcerned. 'You must be a real shock to the old system after an experience like that!'

Carlo stilled. His fiercely narrowed gaze slewed at speed back to Jessica and simply stayed there. 'Gay?' he practically whispered in disbelief.

Jessica unfroze and whirled out of the room. She was outraged and devastated at one and the same time. Lukas Philippides must have had her investigated. Where else could Sunny have obtained such information? All along

Lukas had known about her background. She felt invaded and violated, horrified that such information should have fallen into Sunny's grasping hands, cheap fodder for her spite.

Carlo caught her back on the landing before she could head for the sanctuary of their bedroom. A far from gentle hand closed round her forearm. 'Pull yourself together!' he warned her with barely subdued ferocity.

He wasn't laughing. He looked furious, rage threatening to seethe up through the cracks. Jessica felt torn in two. Last night, she had wanted to tell Carlo the story of her marriage and he had denied her the opportunity. She was humiliated by the manner in which Sunny had deprived her of that right.

Carlo's hands curved powerfully into her shoulders. His dark face pale and set. 'Is it true?' he demanded.

'None of your blasted business!' she gasped. 'Why don't you go ask Sunny for the same sleazy invasion of my life and read it for yourself?'

'I might just do that.' Carlo released her with pronounced reluctance and bit out, '*Dio*…if it is true, I don't think I'll be responsible for my actions!'

He made her rejoin the party, his arm an iron vice clamped to her rigid spine. He held her so close she could feel the tremors of repressed rage still shuddering through him. 'Smile,' he instructed harshly.

Later she remembered nothing of the last couple of hours of the wedding. Did she smile? She could not understand why Carlo should be so angry. Surely the right to anger was hers alone? It was her privacy which had been crudely and shockingly invaded. A nymphomaniac, Sunny had called her mother. That more than anything else made Jessica feel physically sick with humiliation.

'To think I thought the impossibility of a honeymoon unfortunate,' Carlo drawled in a murderously quiet tone as he flung off his jacket and tie. 'In these circumstances, it would have been grotesque!'

Jessica was stationed by the window, her slender back defensively turned to him.

'You're like Pandora's box...what else don't I know?' Carlo enquired with flat emphasis.

'I wasn't the only one who kept secrets,' she reminded him tautly. 'Just when were you going to tell me that Sunny was after you?'

'That was different.'

'How dare your father have me investigated?' Jessica suddenly gasped with renewed outrage.

Carlo released his breath in a hiss. 'I should have expected that—'

'Is that all you've got to say about it?' Jessica demanded hotly.

'It's done now,' Carlo pointed out drily. 'And I wish I had done it myself—'

Jessica turned in disbelief. 'I beg your pardon?'

'I will request that he has it destroyed. His security must be getting very lax if Sunny was able to get her hands on his private papers.' Carlo shot her pale face a look of grim challenge. 'So now you start at the beginning and tell me everything.'

She stiffened, antagonism leaping through her. 'Last night you weren't interested—'

'Last night I had no idea what you were hiding.'

'I hid nothing. My marriage was my business.'

Carlo dealt her a seething stare, an antagonism equal to her own firing the atmosphere. 'Six years ago, you made it mine.'

She went rigid but she held her head high. 'When I told Simon what had happened between us, he said that it didn't matter to him—'

'He said what?' Carlo broke in incredulously.

Her throat closed over, her voice emerging unevenly.

'I wanted to cancel the wedding. He begged me not to. He told me that he needed me...couldn't imagine life without me. He said he forgave me absolutely,' she recited with a quivering lower lip, 'and that there was no reason for me to ruin our future just because of one silly mistake.'

'And you swallowed that...*Dio*!' Carlo framed with gathering temper, spreading his hands wide as if to appeal for some shred of sanity from her.

Hot moisture smarted behind her eyes. 'I thought that he loved me enough to forgive me and I didn't want to let him down—'

'You married him because you felt sorry for him!' Carlo stabbed back at her.

'I felt safe with him. I thought he cared. I really thought we could be happy!' she returned with feverish emphasis. 'Our relationship had never been based on sex. What happened with you...it frightened me, and the way you reacted afterwards—'

'Go ahead, blame it all on me!' Carlo slashed back ferociously.

Jessica spun back to the window before the tears could fall. 'What I did with you,' she repeated shakily, 'well, it was the sort of thing my mother would have done, and in the Deangate Hotel of all places, which *she* used to haunt. It was my worst nightmare come true. I behaved like her and it terrified me—'

'I hardly touched you!' Carlo cut in ruthlessly.

'That didn't change how I felt. It was the fact that I lost control that was scary, the fact that I wanted you to make love to me,' she admitted brokenly.

'I want to hear about your marriage,' Carlo told her rawly.

Jessica drew in a deep shuddering breath of air. 'Simon got very drunk on our wedding-night. And every night after it. I thought it was my fault...that he just couldn't bring himself to touch me because of you. And he let me think that…he let me think that for so long!' she gasped painfully. 'It was hell. We didn't even share a bedroom when we came home and when I tried to talk to him about it he walked out and stayed away…'

Carlo uttered a ground-out imprecation and she shivered.

'He wouldn't go to marriage guidance or anything. He refused to admit that there was a problem…'

'Why the hell didn't you leave him?' Carlo roared at her.

A sob caught in her throat. 'Guilt. I did think it was my fault. It wasn't until he became ill that he admitted that he was impotent…and that he had never wanted any woman physically,' she recounted jerkily. 'Some people just don't have a sex drive and I believe that Simon was one of them. I don't think he was gay but apparently, before he asked me to get engaged, there had been rumours about him. He was terrified of his family and friends thinking that he was gay…that's why he married me. He used me to hide behind. It stopped people wondering—'

'And this is the bastard you called your best friend?' Carlo murmured tautly.

A choked laugh escaped her. She was shaking. Remembering brought all the pain and suffering back. 'He was until I married him,' she muttered with unconcealed bitterness.

'Did you ever consider walking out?'

'Not once he was ill,' she whispered. 'I felt cheated but I felt I'd asked for what I got—'

'You owed him nothing. He knew about me before he married you. You gave him a free choice. What choice did he give you?'

She wiped shakily at her overflowing eyes. 'None,' she conceded.

'He lied by omission. He deceived you. Why do you still seek to defend him at your own expense?' She was stunned when she felt his arms close round her. Momentarily she went rigid. Carlo drew her firmly back into the hard heat of his powerful body. 'Don't cry...I can't bear it when you cry,' he said roughly.

'I thought I loved him,' she mumbled fiercely. 'I grew up thinking I loved him and I would have trusted him with my life. Not much of a judge of character, was I?'

'You were very young and I was arrogant,' Carlo breathed. 'I never once thought of how you must have felt that day. I couldn't believe that you would still marry him. You said that I never thought of the damage I was causing...you were right. I only thought of winning.'

'Why are you being so understanding?'

Turning her round, he studied her with intent golden eyes that glittered with all-male satisfaction. 'It takes an accomplished liar to recall her lies,' he murmured with fierce amusement. 'Four days ago you lied to me after I made love to you...why did you lie?'

Too late, she remembered her denial of her own in-experience. Her pallor was put to flight by hot colour.

'You were a virgin. Why pretend otherwise?'

'I felt I owed that to Simon's memory,' she whispered, stiff with mortification.

'And maybe you didn't want to give me the pleasure of knowing that I was the first,' Carlo completed shrewdly, but he smiled none the less.

The one lie she could tell Carlo and be magnificently, generously forgiven for, she realised dazedly. Why had she ever thought he would laugh when she told him about her unconsummated marriage?

The joy of conquest had just been made all the sweeter for Carlo. On that level, Carlo was primitive. She understood him perfectly. She had never belonged to any other man in the physical sense. On Carlo's terms that meant she belonged that much more to him. All jealousy was magically banished. Simon had not, after all, managed to *take* what Carlo had regarded as his by right six years ago.

'Let's go down to the beach,' Carlo suggested softly.

In bemusement she blinked. 'The beach?'

'This house suffocates me.'

A rueful grin slowly tilted her mouth. 'You want me to go down to the beach got up like this?'

Carlo flipped her round and suggestively ran down the zip.

Breathlessly she tugged a shocking pink sundress from the closet and slid her feet into flatties. She felt extraordinarily carefree as she walked out on to the terrace to join him. Carlo had changed into jeans and removed the bottle of champagne from the ice bucket beside the bed.

He dropped an arm round her bare shoulders. 'Come on.'

'What did you do with that shoe I left behind six years ago?' she heard herself ask. She had always wondered.

'It's about somewhere.'

'Oh.'

'Did you think I might have had it dipped in pure gold and placed in a glass case?' he teased.

'It was one of my favourite shoes.'

'What did you do with the one you had left?'

'Dumped it.'

'There you are, then,' Carlo mocked. 'I was more sentimental than you were.'

'I thought you'd laugh about Simon.'

'Why? It wasn't funny. He put you through a lot of pain and you didn't deserve that. I'm not a sadist. Although two weeks ago I was outraged by the idea that you had been blissfully happy with him. A lot can change in two weeks…'

'Yes,' she conceded, her voice a whisper of sound.

'Although I'm still desperate to know how you define a "travelling tart"!' he confided.

'You offered me a life of luxury on the move in return for sex!' she snapped.

'I couldn't stay in England forever. I wanted you to myself. What was wrong with that? We hardly knew each other. I didn't know whether or not the attraction between us would last. I was honest with you—'

'You were an ignorant, egocentric swine!' Jessica returned with spirit.

Carlo shifted a broad shoulder. 'Possibly I could have wrapped it up a little more tactfully but I was angry with you and uncertain of my own feelings. Once bitten, twice shy…after Bella,' he admitted drily. 'I didn't want to make another mistake. I wasn't going to make promises I might not keep. It never at any stage crossed my mind that you might still marry Simon. I thought *that* was over from the moment you melted in my arms…and if he had been any other man it would have been.'

'Did you love her very much?' she couldn't prevent herself from asking.

'Who?'

'Bella!'

'At the time, I believed I did. Now I think she might just have been a trophy on my arm. Like Sunny, she was stunningly eye-catching,' Carlo mused softly. 'Lukas always went for women like that, the kind of women other men would kill to have. What was underneath didn't count. Maybe that's why I chose Bella…maybe in my own way I was competing too. I was a lot more like Lukas then than I like to admit.'

'Like Sunny, she was stunningly eye-catching…' He said it so carelessly. He did not deny the strength of

Sunny's physical appeal. Jessica endured a fresh stab of insecurity. She recalled Carlo's blazing fury when he found the redhead with that young man…and Sunny's almost taunting amusement. Then she told herself off. Carlo had given her no cause to distrust him and she was being foolish.

'Were you shocked by what—?' she began.

Carlo stilled and pulled her close. 'Shut up,' he said softly. 'I want to kiss you.'

Helplessly, she smiled. 'You don't usually ask in advance.'

He splayed a masterful hand over the rounded swell of her hips and pressed her into the hard heat of his lean thighs. 'Fate had it in for me when it served you up six years ago.'

The scent and the feel of him made her tremble. And when it came, it was the most devastating kiss. It stole the soul from her body and rocked her from her head to her toes. He released her reddened lips slowly and stared down at her, glittering dark eyes sweeping her rapt face with satisfaction.

They walked along the beach in a curiously peaceful silence. It was a gorgeous night. She kicked off her shoes and walked into the surf whispering on to the shore. The water was warm but cool on her hot feet, gloriously soothing to toes cooped up in stilettos all day.

'Come here,' Carlo said thickly.

She turned with quicksilver grace and looked across at him and the simple pleasure of the water was forgotten. She looked…and she ached with a need that ran far deeper than desire. Her feet carried her back as though he had yanked a string. It was an irresistible pull. He reached for her and she was boneless with anticipation, adrenalin racing through her veins, heat surging between her thighs. For the very first time, she rejoiced in her own response, neither unnerved by nor ashamed of it.

In fact, she drowned in the meeting of their mouths as desperate as he was for that fierce contact. In the midst of it he shed his shirt; she wriggled feverishly out of her dress. Her breasts felt heavy, swollen, and a soft gasp was torn from her throat as he discovered for himself that she had not bothered to wear a bra. He groaned his approval, shaping her aching flesh with hungry hands, his thumbs glancing over her painfully aroused nipples before he crushed her against his hair-roughened chest.

He shuddered and lifted his head. 'Every time I touch you, I want you more than I did the last time…but this time I want to go slow—'

'Next time.' Reaching up, she framed his hard cheekbones with loving fingertips and drew him back down to her again, incredibly hungry for the scorching heat of his mouth. Daringly, she employed a tactic he had taught her. She ran the tip of her tongue along the curve of his lower lip.

'Slow,' he intoned raggedly, and snatched her up to kiss her breathless.

For an endless passage of time it was a battle of wills. Her hands fluttered over every part of him she could reach. She was driven by a deep atavistic need to possess and be possessed, to wipe out days of fevered uncertainty and terrible tension with the passion that made him uniquely hers. She would not be controlled but the jerk of his responsive muscles beneath his smooth bronzed skin, the rawness of his breathing and the thunder of his heart against her exploring fingertips defeated her. His blatant excitement was the most shattering seduction of all.

They came down on the sand in a tangle of limbs, neither one of them able to part for a second. He skimmed off her lace panties with a powerfully impatient hand and she opened her arms to him in an electrifying state of quivering readiness, every inch of her burning and screaming for the fulfillment that only he could give her.

'*Madre di Dio…*' Carlo rasped, coming up for air. 'Did I teach you to do this to me?'

Empowered by a dizzying sense of her own sensuality, Jessica took the opportunity to run her fingers down that intriguing little silky furrow of hair arrowing down over his taut stomach and she found him with shy and shivering pleasure, velvety smooth and hard and… suddenly she was flat on her back, deprived of further journeys of discovery.

She giggled, full of joy and the most wonderful sense of freedom. In retribution, he let his tongue and his teeth rove over her unbearably sensitised breasts and she gritted her teeth and her back arched in agonised response.

'I can't bear it…' she gasped.

'You will,' he assured her.

Her hips began to lift in an expression of need as old as time. He stroked his fingertips over the very heart of her and laughed softly when she moaned, teasing her with the honeyed sweetness of an expert lover, determined to drive her to the outer edge of pleasure before they enjoyed that final union. Time had no meaning. She surrendered to the shuddering instinctive responses that controlled her, lost in the ever-increasing fever of her own excitement.

And when he came to her it was like dying and being reborn in a flash flood of wild sensation. Everything was sharper, hotter and more intense, her body trained to an extraordinary pitch of sensitivity. It was agony and ecstasy, each glorious moment building into an explosive, slow-burning climax that made her sob and gasp in wonder at the peak and then subside, still shivering in the aftermath of an intolerable pleasure.

Carlo smiled down at her, a very male smile of indolent satisfaction. He pressed his lips to her damp cheek and she felt moisture smart behind her eyes. In all her life, she could never recall feeling so outrageously happy.

They washed the sand off in the sea, drank champagne in great thirsty gulps and a little while later made love again. Jessica was more than a little tipsy by the time they strolled down to the jetty and boarded the yacht.

'We'll go sailing all day tomorrow,' Carlo promised.

'And the day after,' she whispered, gripped by this terrible fear that such contentment could not possibly be sustained with other people around.

'If you like.' He led her gently into a cabin, exquisitely furnished with a very large double bed.

She tripped on the edge of a rug and he caught her before she fell. 'I'm drunk on you,' she said, losing herself in the smouldering golden eyes.

'How do you feel about renegotiating our divorce?'

'P-pardon?' She froze.

'As in not having one until we feel the need…*if* we feel the need.' A brilliant smile slashed his gorgeous mouth.

She melted into him with bone-sagging relief. 'I'll think about it,' she said all the same.

The sun was high in the sky when she surfaced from a deep sleep to hear Carlo on the phone.

'What are you doing?'

'Ordering breakfast.'

She was sprawled on top of him, her tousled silver head resting on his chest. It had been the most incredible night. She was adrift on a sea of love so all encompassing it closed out everything else in the world.

'How does being married feel this time?' He ran a caressing finger along one exposed cheekbone and she stretched and tightened her grip on him.

'Good.'

'How to damn with faint praise.'

She smiled voluptuously. 'Fantastic.'

Fast-moving steps sounded somewhere above them. Carlo tensed. Then Marika's voice cried his name.

Carlo sprang out of bed, reached for his jeans and yanked open the door.

Jessica scrambled up but there was no clothing within her grasp. Carlo left the cabin. She heard the swift exchange of Greek, the sob in his sister's shaking voice.

'Lukas has had another attack...' Pale, every facial muscle savagely clenched, Carlo sent Jessica a fleeting, almost blank glance that told her he was already a thousand miles away from her in mind and body.

The honeymoon, she registered, was over.

CHAPTER TEN

JESSICA shivered in spite of the heat. Lukas had left careful instructions for his burial and he had chosen to come back to Greece to the sunbaked hillside where his own parents had been laid to rest. The funeral was small, strictly family but the Press were just beyond the graveyard, a sea of hungry wolves, restrained only by the strong police presence.

'It is time to go.' Marika briefly leant on Jessica's extended arm for support and then straightened again. 'I didn't know I would miss him like this,' she whispered, shaking her greying head. 'But all my life he has been there. For fifty years telling me what to do…I feel lost.'

She wasn't the only one who felt lost. Jessica felt deserted and superfluous to requirements. For days she had told herself not to be childish, not to be selfish, not to expect Carlo to find time for her when his every waking moment was filled with ceaseless demands for his attention. She had innocently expected to make herself useful but had learnt that anything she could do could inevitably be done far more efficiently by a member of his staff. Carlo hadn't just lost a father…Carlo had inherited a vast empire, quaking in the turmoil of Lukas's sudden death.

Carlo had also inherited the devastated and publicly inconsolable widow, Jessica thought grimly. Dear heaven, she *tried* to feel some sense of compassion for Sunny but she had noticed that Sunny invariably wept only in Carlo's vicinity. It was hard to believe that she could be genuinely distressed by her husband's death but if she wasn't, she was certainly putting on a very good show. And there was no doubt that Carlo was impressed by that display. His attitude to Sunny had warmed and softened.

Sunny drooped in unrelieved black beside the grave, a wispy little silk hanky dabbing behind her veil. Carlo hesitated on his way past in a phalanx of male relatives and then paused. Jessica stiffened and looked away, walking ahead with Marika. The cameras went off in a blaze. Jessica flinched.

'Ignore them, Mrs Philippides,' the security man flanking her said. 'You'll soon get used to it.'

But Jessica could not believe that she ever would. From the instant they had left Paradiso Cay she had understood why Lukas had bought an island. At every airport, in every public place, the Press surrounded them in a stifling surge.

'You're hot news,' he sighed as she was slotted into a limousine.

All she wanted to be was hot news to Carlo, who no longer even travelled in the same car with her, it seemed. Nor did he sleep in the same bed very often. He worked through the night, ate at extraordinary hours and never went anywhere with less than three executives tagging on his heels. When she tried to see him, she learnt that she was in the way, and if she hovered and he forgot she was there, she felt humiliated.

'I think I'll go to bed,' Marika mumbled when they reached the opulent house and surrounding estate outside Athens which had once been Lukas's permanent home.

Sunny had made it into Carlo's car. Jessica watched from the window as Sunny was helped out, the very picture of feminine fragility. Jessica's teeth gritted. Maybe I should practise sobbing and throwing hysterics! Childish, you're being childish, the little voice said. She is his father's widow and he takes that tie too seriously to ignore her apparent distress.

Sunny was just an irritation, she told herself in exasperation. A symptom, not the source of the illness. Carlo had married Jessica to please Lukas and now Lukas was dead. She was bitterly aware that the only hold she seemed to have on Carlo was sexual and even that seemed to be on the wane. She had this sinking feeling that their relationship was running fast to its natural conclusion. 'I won't hold you a day after his death,' Carlo had said just days ago. How much strength could she take now from the casual assurance that he wasn't planning on an immediate divorce? Those words had been prompted by the heat of passion on their wedding night.

'Carlo...' She intercepted him in the echoing grandeur of the hall.

'What time do you want to eat?' Sunny talked over her as if she wasn't there.

'Seven.' Hooded dark eyes flicked to Jessica and lingered. 'Hello, stranger,' he said softly.

She moved forward.

'Mr Philippides, the London office is on the line—'

'When would you like this Press release made?'

The twin enquiries from staff stole his attention. He moved on and something simply exploded inside Jessica. 'The next time you want to see me, *you* make an appointment!' she snapped and spun on her heel, stalking back into the drawing-room.

'Bed...by midnight, I promise,' Carlo murmured with soft amusement.

She spun. He had followed her. But they were not truly alone. Just beyond the doorway, his staff awaited them.

'Is it always going to be like this?' she whispered in sudden desperation.

'No, but it will take time to restore calm. Lukas kept a very tight rein on his holdings. He believed in the personal touch. Right to the end he was working an eighteen-hour day,' Carlo drawled wryly. 'He thought he had more time. This is not the smooth transition he envisaged. Everybody's hitting the panic button.'

He should have been exhausted but he wasn't. If anything his aura of vibrant energy was more noticeable. It was beginning to dawn on Jessica that Carlo Saracini no longer existed. This was Lukas Philippides' son, driven, committed and absolutely in his element, she sensed, and the pace was speed up or fall out. Was there a place for her in this new life of his?

Right now, her position felt exceedingly precarious, and that hurt her pride. Jessica bitterly resented the idea that she was slavishly hanging around just waiting for Carlo to take the time and the trouble to reassure her that he *did* want her to stay. And even then, how long did he want her for? Carlo was not in love with her. He had taken his revenge. He had used her to make his father happy. When his hunger for her body faded as it surely would, how could they possibly have any sort of a future together?

She had to dine alone with Sunny. Marika had not emerged from her suite. Faced with Sunny, Jessica wished she had stayed in hers.

'You look terrible,' Sunny sighed, scanning Jessica's shadowed eyes and pallor. 'You should have gone to bed too.'

With a helplessly curled lip, Jessica wondered how the redhead could weep without reddening her eyes. 'I'm not tired,' she said.

'You want me out, don't you?' Sunny guessed. 'But I'm not going anywhere.'

Jessica ignored her.

'You're stuck with me,' Sunny told her with an amused smile. 'I've got nowhere to go. Lukas didn't leave me a bean. I signed a watertight pre-nuptial contract. I'm Carlo's responsibility now.'

Jessica's amethyst eyes flamed. 'And you intend to play it for all you're worth, don't you?'

'Ask Carlo if he wants me to leave,' Sunny suggested softly. 'You see, he doesn't. Carlo likes having me around. He always makes time for me. Haven't you noticed that? It won't be very long before he admits to himself how he really feels about me—'

'I don't want to hear any more of this, Sunny,' Jessica broke in tautly but with dignity.

'But it's the truth. You don't want to see it but Carlo *is* using you. You're the one who's going to be hurt and humiliated,' Sunny asserted confidently. 'Not me. I know the score. I know Carlo—'

'So you keep telling me.'

'He married you to keep Lukas happy, and now Lukas is gone he doesn't need you any more. It's that simple.'

'Carlo is not in love with you,' Jessica told her shortly.

'But he wants me.' Sunny gave her a brilliant smile. 'That's enough, don't you think?'

Jessica rose from the table and walked out of the room. She would not argue with Sunny, thereby lending credibility to her wild claims. For they were wild claims, weren't they? Carlo had yet to betray any sign of *wanting* Sunny. Restively she paced the bedroom floor. She was upset, no point denying that! Sunny was so confident of Carlo…although she hadn't been that night she was drunk, Jessica reminded herself. Then Sunny had said, 'You don't want me…why should you care?' But possibly that had just been a deliberate taunt, a scene engineered to pierce Carlo's tough hide.

Dear heaven, what was she thinking? That it was all true…that Carlo was cold-bloodedly using her? She remembered their wedding-night and could not believe that that had all been pretence. But Jessica reminded herself that Carlo had openly admitted that he had brought her here to keep Sunny at bay. That did not suggest that Carlo was one hundred per cent sure of his ability to withstand the lure of what he already knew was blatantly on offer to him…should he choose to extend a welcoming hand.

She could hardly believe it when Carlo actually made it to bed as he had promised. She sat up, watching him undress with helplessly hungry eyes, but she felt cold inside, resentful that it took the dark of night and his highly sexed nature to bring Carlo to her.

'Is it true that Sunny's staying?' she asked finally because she had to ask, she *had* to know.

The silence stretched; her heartbeat accelerated.

'For the moment, yes,' Carlo murmured.

Jessica took a deep breath. 'Naturally I'm not suggesting you throw her out…but your father owned other houses.'

Carlo sent her a narrowed shrewd glance, his beautifully cut mouth compressing. 'For the moment, she stays here.'

Jessica swallowed hard and then said, 'So you expect me to live with a woman who says she's in love with you and who doesn't seem to give a damn who knows it? Don't you think that's asking a little too much…or is there some special reason why I have to put up with her?'

'*Dio!*' Carlo ground out with sudden savage impatience. 'My father is barely in his grave—'

'Where Sunny wanted him to be.' The interruption leapt recklessly from Jessica's tongue.

Golden eyes blazed over her. 'Like all of us, she says things in distress which she does not mean.'

'She's a damned good actress, I'll give her that!' Jessica snapped back. 'And she's playing you like a fish on a line!'

Pure outrage darkened and hardened Carlo's strong

features. 'At this moment, Sunny is my responsibility. She is my father's widow. If I threw her out, where would she go and to whom? I wouldn't do it. She has as much right to be here as you have. She's scared of the future. That is why she is clinging to me.'

'And maybe you enjoy that,' Jessica condemned shakily. 'Macho man and the poor fragile little woman who hangs on his every word. With Sunny beside you, you could turn into a megalomaniac overnight!'

'I'll tell you what I don't enjoy now. Your jealousy,' Carlo returned with blistering derision. 'At least Sunny knows when to shut up and be feminine and warm…'

Jessica went white, lowering her lashes over shocked and wounded eyes. Carlo had turned on her with a biting cruelty unfamiliar to her.

'All I wanted tonight was the sweet oblivion of your body—'

'Sex,' Jessica countered with a shudder of mingled rage and pain.

'Why not? You're my wife,' Carlo slung back at her harshly.

Dear God, was that all their marriage meant to him? Was she just an available body? Or was she merely a temporary substitute for Sunny until such time as he deemed it acceptable for him to bed his father's widow? Jessica was devastated by the suspicion but when Carlo compared her unfavourably to Sunny suspicion found foundation in fact. It was not as though Carlo loved his wife, not as though they had married for any of the more usual reasons… She was in agony.

'I don't want you,' she mumbled.

'Then you won't object if I find someone who does, will you?' Carlo delivered with cut-glass precision but he slammed the door so hard that she wouldn't have been surprised if it fell off its hinges.

He doesn't mean it…he's being dramatic…he can't

stand it when you say you don't want him, she told herself. Then she burst into tears but that made her feel worse. She propped her chin on her hand and reflected for a long time. Where were her wits? Why had she thrown a scene like that?

Carlo might not be showing it but he was under immense strain. He hadn't even had twelve hours' breathing space to grieve for Lukas and he had been flung in at the deep end of his father's vast business empire and forced to take charge. She shouldn't have attacked him about Sunny. He had wanted warmth and why not? Right now, the bedroom was the only place they were alone, the only place he could relax, and she had driven him away!

Sunny didn't give up the chase easily. She knew Carlo was not in love with his wife and that encouraged her. She was just trying to cause trouble by playing on Jessica's insecurity and Carlo's infuriating sense of what was due to his father's widow. What a fool she would be to allow a bimbo like Sunny to come between her and Carlo!

Jessica slid out of bed and pulled on a lacy peignoir. He had said that she didn't trust him, that she didn't have faith, and she was about to prove him wrong for a change. When life was calmer, she would tell him what she was having to take from Sunny and then he might understand just how offensive she found the situation. She was a big girl, wasn't she? She could deal with Sunny herself.

The house was silent but the corridors fully lit. Wryly, it occurred to her that she couldn't go barging into all the bedrooms in search of Carlo. But maybe he hadn't gone to bed yet. As she descended the main staircase, she saw a dim light showing below the library door and thought, Bingo!

Only she didn't hit the jackpot she expected when she

quietly turned the handle and opened the door, intending to surprise him. Every muscle in her slender body jerked painfully tight. There was a roaring in her eardrums and for a split-second she thought she was going to pass out.

Carlo was sprawled along a comfortable sofa with Sunny in his arms. Both of them were fast asleep in the indolent, relaxed positions of lovers, Sunny's wonderful hair trailing like a banner across his chest, one of her hands resting loosely on his shoulder.

Later, she didn't recall actually stepping back and closing the door again, but she did recall her absolute terror of them waking up and seeing her standing there, gaping at them. She mounted the stairs again, returned to their bedroom and lifted the phone.

'I want a car to the airport now. Mr Philippides is asleep. There's no need to disturb him.' An hysterical laugh nearly choked her at that point. She reckoned that it would have taken an avalanche to disturb either of them. Lying there totally at peace on the same day as the very funeral. Dear God, how could he?

He had to *want* her, just as she had said. Maybe they hadn't even made love yet…Carlo had still been clothed, Sunny in one of her drapy white silk nightgowns. Did it matter? They had looked like bloody Romeo and Juliet, she thought sickly, so torn apart by what she had seen, she was still shaking all over with shock.

'So what *can* I tell him?' Gerald Amory enquired thinly.

'Nothing.' Jessica kept on sipping at her cup of coffee, holding it like a barrier in front of her drawn face.

'All right,' her father spelt out flatly. 'I can accept that you made a mistake rushing into marriage with him, but at least you could have the gumption to tell him that to his face instead of running away and hiding!'

She chewed nervously at her lower lip. It hurt that her father should be on Carlo's side. But how did she tell her father the truth? If she did, he would probably feel he couldn't work for Carlo any more, and he might throw up his new job and then where would he be?

'Are you pregnant?'

Jessica stared in astonishment.

Gerald sighed. 'Carlo thought you might be…hormones putting you round the twist or some such thing.'

'I am not pregnant or crazy, thank you very much!'

'Well, you look awful. You've lost a lot of weight.'

Silence fell, uneasy, tense.

'Every time he phones me, I feel worse,' her father persisted. 'He knows that we're in contact with each other. He knows that I know where you are.'

If she had had the energy left, she would have hated Carlo for putting her in such a position. What on earth was he playing at? In the six weeks since she had left Greece, it had become painfully obvious that Carlo had no intention of going public with his relationship with his former stepmother. Maybe he thought it was too soon, or maybe Carlo was quite happy just to have Sunny in his bed in secret.

Having run the gamut of every possible conjecture, Jessica had learnt that ultimately it really didn't matter. Carlo wanted Sunny. Sheer uncontrollable lust, or love—what difference did it make? Jessica just wanted to be left alone with the most intolerable burden of misery she had ever endured.

'He's worried sick about you.'

'Breaking his heart, no doubt,' Jessica muttered tightly.

'Why can't you see him?'

Because pride was all she had left, and if she saw him she might let herself down badly. Carlo didn't know that she had fallen in love with him and she didn't want him to know.

Her father took his leave, close-mouthed and disapproving. Having come down to London on business, he was flying back to Glasgow where he had recently embarked on his new job. Jessica looked round her tiny flatlet, over-furnished with her possessions from the cottage. She hadn't been able to find a permanent secretarial position yet. She had signed up with a temping agency and with the aid of some savings was just about managing to survive. But one day blurred with terrifying blankness into the next.

It was around ten when someone knocked on the door. She was on her way to bed and grimaced. Her nextdoor neighbour, a rather pushy male in his late twenties, had been putting his all into trying to chat her up this week, calling round at odd times, refusing to take no for an answer…

Exasperated, she opened the door and then fell back a step, the colour draining from her cheeks, shock currenting through her in debilitating waves. Carlo dealt her a razor-edged smile from the vantage point of his greatly superior height and thrust the door shut behind him with a powerful hand.

'Your father was followed. I knew he would meet up with you sooner or later,' Carlo imparted grimly.

'You had no right to do that!'

But she couldn't take her eyes off him. In a superbly cut pearl-grey suit that sleekly outlined his lean, muscular physique, a white silk shirt highlighting the gold of his skin and the darkness of his hair, Carlo looked breathtakingly handsome. His impact slivered through her nerve-endings, leaving her disturbingly aware of his every movement and badly shaken. She felt horribly like a plant left to wither forgotten on a windowsill suddenly being tantalised with a jug of life-giving water.

'You are going to crawl by the time I'm finished with

you,' Carlo sizzled down at her, emanating temper and arrogance and self-satisfaction in perceptible waves.

'I don't think so.' Squaring her slight shoulders, Jessica slung him a look of pure scorn, denying the craving that he could evoke inside her even when he was demonstrating all in one go all the less pleasant characteristics of his powerful personality.

'You have a VCR?' Seeing it for himself, Carlo headed for it in one long stride and deposited two videotapes beside it. 'We'll probably still be sitting here at lunchtime tomorrow. You are going to watch and inwardly digest every unutterably boring hour of this just as I had to—'

'Carlo…w-what are you talking about?' she prompted, watching him feed in a tape with incredulous eyes.

'It was several weeks before it occurred to me that you might have taken off for a reason…as opposed to being just sheer bloody contrary!' he raked at her, suddenly sizzling with rage. 'And I was furious with you. I couldn't wait to get my hands on you. Then I dug out these tapes and I wanted to strangle you!'

The tip of her tongue snaked out to dry her lips. What the blazes was he rattling on about? What were those tapes? The TV screen came alive with a most disorientating overhead view of the library outside Athens. It was eerie. Jessica gaped, totally dazed by the sight of Carlo striding through the door, pouring himself a large drink and then throwing himself on that self-same sofa.

'Every reception-room and every corridor in my father's houses are protected by twenty-four-hour surveillance equipment. Only the bedrooms and the bathrooms are off limits,' Carlo informed her. 'You can see the date and the exact time displayed at the foot of the picture.'

'Yes,' she quavered.

'And now you can watch me fall asleep…really riveting stuff. Sunny makes her entrance in about half an hour—'

'Sunny,' she echoed weakly.

'I could have had the tapes cut to speed this up but I didn't want to spare you a single second of the entertainment.'

Swallowing hard, Jessica dutifully watched Carlo falling asleep, the most awful suspicion beginning to assail her. 'You can fast forward if you like,' she mumbled in a small voice.

'Are you sure?'

'Quite sure.'

With a sinking heart, Jessica watched Sunny creep in and stand gazing down at Carlo. A little while later, she curled up beside him and put her arms round him. A long while after that, Carlo shifted in his sleep and curved an arm round Sunny.

'I don't want to see any more,' Jessica told him, unable to meet his eyes.

'I insist,' Carlo said harshly. 'The sole highlight is entry of the betrayed wife.'

Her legs wouldn't hold her up any longer. She collapsed down on to the settee.

'We're on to the second tape before I wake up and chuck her out.'

'I don't need to watch it.'

He didn't switch it off. Through her straining fingers, Jessica caught a glimpse of her own entrance and it looked almost comic on camera, only the memory of how she had felt still cut into her painfully. Carlo had simply fallen asleep and Sunny had wrapped herself round him.

'I was exhausted that night. I slept like the dead.' Carlo uttered a sardonic laugh, his dark features tautening.

'How could I know that it was innocent?' Jessica

whispered. 'I thought that you wanted her. She was so sure that you did—'

'My father's leavings?' Carlo breathed with distaste.

Jessica lifted her silvery head in disbelief. His revulsion at the idea was unconcealed. 'But…but you said she was stunningly eye-catching—'

'So she is, but I have never found her sexually attractive. She reminded me of Bella. Vain, self-centred, thick as a brick apart from a certain greedy streak of native cunning when it comes to feathering her own nest—'

'Thick as a brick?' Jessica echoed, licking her dry lips in shock.

'Enjoy many scintillating conversations with her, did you?'

'Well…no, but you seemed so keen to keep her around; I thought—'

'You really expected me to chuck her out the day of the funeral?' Carlo enquired gently.

Jessica reddened. 'You should have told me how you felt about her.'

'I thought it was obvious…and you didn't ask,' Carlo reminded her drily. 'Until we had that stupid argument, I had no idea she even bothered you. You came at me out of the blue and I was in a bad mood.' Unusually, he hesitated, his sensual mouth twisting. 'I don't pay much attention to Sunny, I have to admit. I did think she'd given up on her aspiration to move from my father's bed to mine—'

'Like hell she had,' Jessica muttered feelingly.

'So I discovered. That night I woke up to find her wrapped round me like a boa constrictor, I was disgusted with her. I knew she wasn't in love with me. The first time Sunny looked at herself in a mirror she fell in love for the rest of her life,' Carlo drawled with an expressive grimace. 'I paid her off. The minute she got that cheque in her hand, she was off like a hare for pastures new.

She won't approach me again. She hates me like poison now. I don't think it had ever crossed Sunny's mind that a man *could* find her repulsive.'

That was music to Jessica's ears. Carlo had fulfilled what he felt to be his obligations to his former step-mother and if Jessica had only given him time, he would have done that while they were still living together. She knew then that she had to tell him what she had been forced to tolerate from Sunny.

His state of shock by the time she had finished speaking spoke for him. He had had no suspicion that Sunny was putting that much effort into undermining their relationship.

A disturbing silence fell then. Jessica began to wonder if Carlo had gone to all this trouble to force her to face him merely to prove that he had not been guilty of lusting after Sunny.

'I've also been thinking,' Carlo finally said heavily, 'about how much I allowed what happened with Bella to influence my attitude to you. Six years ago, I suspect you paid some of her dues for her. I was still pretty bitter. My ego was still smarting. I was determined that the next woman I wanted would come to me only on my terms. I didn't trust my own emotions. I wouldn't admit how strong my feelings for you were.'

'Strong?' Disturbed by the gravity of his mood, Jessica prompted him uncertainly.

'I was in love with you,' Carlo confessed harshly, and it was as if the admission had been tortured out of him.

'In love with me?' she whispered dazedly, and she couldn't even get excited by the revelation when he looked so grim about giving her that knowledge. She collided with shimmering golden eyes and sensed that for the very first time she was hearing the truth, not parts of it but *all* of it.

'Did you never ask yourself why I behaved as I did?

Do you really believe I would have gone to so much trouble merely to get you into bed?' Carlo prompted with a derisive twist to his strained mouth. 'It was my misfortune to fall for a woman on the brink of marrying another man. I wanted time with you and you wouldn't give me that time…and what was worst of all was knowing that you were fighting an attraction as strong as mine right from the beginning!'

'Yes,' she acknowledged unsteadily. 'But I didn't recognise that attraction for what it was. I was terrified of it.' She flushed unhappily and tried to laugh. 'I thought I was turning into a scarlet woman, but—'

'You hurt me as Bella never had the power to hurt me,' Carlo cut in flatly.

Hot moisture stung her eyes. She saw the truth of that statement in his expressive eyes. That was another first. He wasn't shielding his emotions from her. His guard was down.

'When I was informed that your father had been helping himself to company funds,' Carlo continued levelly, 'I was delighted. In fact, I was triumphant…'

'Yes,' she said painfully. 'I knew that.'

'And you were right, I didn't give a damn about Gerald. All I saw was a very useful weapon. I could have handled Sunny on my own if I'd needed to,' Carlo drawled half under his breath. 'What I really wanted more than anything was to get you flat on your back on the nearest bed and make you pay for walking out on me six years ago—'

'You wanted revenge. I kn-knew that,' she asserted shakily, moving away from him, no longer able to bear any form of proximity. It was over, wasn't that what he was telling her? He had dealt with Sunny; now it was *her* turn.

Carlo drove not quite steady fingers through his thick black hair, looking less in command of himself than was the norm. 'I'd be lying if I said I regretted it. I didn't...I don't,' he adjusted, seemingly bent on giving her the kind of honesty that only hurt her more. 'I didn't care what methods I had to use to get you back—'

'Tell me something I don't know!' Jessica condemned in a choked voice, desperately fighting off tears of pain and an increasing urge to show him the door.

There was a long silence and then, Carlo expelled his breath sharply. 'I still love you...'

There was an even longer silence while she stared back at him in shock, afraid to trust her own hearing.

'Still?' It was a whisper of awed hope. 'You still love me?'

'What the hell do you think I'm doing here with those tapes?' he demanded roughly.

'You were pretty objectionable when you came through the door—'

'You walked out on me—'

'And you thought of the last time.' With a look of remorse, she flung herself into his arms. 'Carlo...don't you know when you've won?'

He trembled against her. 'Won?' he repeated uncertainly.

'Don't you know that I love you?'

With a groan, he crushed her into a fevered embrace. 'We've been stalking each other like wary animals!' he vented furiously. 'How long have you loved me?'

'It feels like forever,' she mumbled truthfully. 'As if I woke up one day when I was twenty and there you were and I've never been free of you since—'

He muttered a driven imprecation, deciding that they were both talking too much, and swept her off her feet.

'The bed's through there,' she murmured helpfully.

His slashing sensual smile plunged her into an ecstasy of anticipation.

'Want me?' he breathed, standing over her, removing his clothes with far more haste than cool.

'Desperately.'

'No divorce.'

'Absolutely not.'

'Children?'

As he came down beside her, she laughed for pure joy. 'What is this?'

'The blueprint for the rest of our lives.' Rolling over, he pinned her beneath him, glittering golden eyes clinging to her delighted face. 'I am crazy about you—'

'I wish you had told me instead of my father!'

'I wanted you to say it first...how could you think I wanted a woman like Sunny?' he abruptly demanded.

'She kept on telling me you did.'

'And what about what I was telling you on our wedding-night?'

As he ran a possessive hand up to one pouting breast, she shivered deliciously and struggled to concentrate but really it was very difficult. 'We didn't get enough time together...I suppose I'll have to get used to that—'

'No. I don't want to live as Lukas did. I'm selling up...consolidating...delegating,' he enumerated raggedly, following every newly discovered curve of female flesh with positively compulsive intensity. 'Anything I can do within reason to avoid working a seven-day week. Unlike my father, I've been fortunate enough to find happiness with one woman and I don't intend to lose it again.'

'You couldn't lose me,' Jessica sighed ecstatically under the scorching heat of his hungry hands.

'I very nearly did,' Carlo breathed harshly. 'I should have told you I loved you.'

'I love you,' she said soothingly.

'I think we need a long vacation,' Carlo sighed, a very long time later after they had made love.

'No phone,' she said.

'An answering machine?' he bargained.

'And possibly…' Amethyst eyes rested on him hopefully. 'A lift?'

His darkly handsome features slashed with vibrant amusement. 'Definitely…a lift,' he agreed.

Catherine George was born in Wales, and early on developed a passion for reading which eventually fuelled her compulsion to write. Marriage to an engineer led to nine years in Brazil, but on his later travels the education of her son and daughter kept her in the UK. And instead of constant reading to pass her lonely evenings she began to write the first of her romantic novels, which was accepted by Mills & Boon® in 1982. When not writing and reading she loves to cook, listen to opera, browse in antiques shops and walk the Labrador.

THE RIGHT CHOICE
by
CATHERINE GEORGE

CHAPTER ONE

TAKE-OFF, the pilot explained with regret over the intercom, would be a little delayed. The plane bound for Pisa, full except for one aisle-seat halfway down the aircraft, rippled with a frisson of audible nerves from some of the passengers, and smart flight attendants circulated quickly to give reassurances. The delay was due to nothing more alarming than the late arrival of a passenger.

Georgia leaned across the man sandwiched between herself and her sister. 'And here he comes!' Charlotte, half-asleep from the tranquillisers she'd taken, eyed the commotion glumly from her window-seat as a tall, dark-haired man was installed with ceremony across the aisle from Georgia. Two of the female staff helped eagerly as he stowed his hand luggage away, and Georgia stifled a giggle as she listened to the voluble exchange in Italian.

'What's up?' said Tom in an undertone.

She leaned close to whisper in his ear. 'They're apologising for the accommodation. No room in first class. Shame!'

Tom relayed the news to his wife, but a wan smile was Charlotte's only response. Georgia knew that by this stage her sister wanted nothing more than to run from the plane and catch the next train home. The engines began to roar at last, the attendants moved to their places, Tom Hannay took his wife's icy hand and seconds later they were airborne.

Georgia sat back in her seat as the plane climbed above the clouds, unafflicted by the nerves her sister suffered. She turned to smile at Tom, relieved to see Charlotte's eyelids drooping. The pills were taking effect, and in minutes, as Georgia knew from experience, her sister would be fast asleep. Once the seatbelt light was off, the late arrival got to his feet and folded an expensive suede jacket into the overhead compartment. As he did so a slim leather wallet plummeted from it into Georgia's lap. She waited until he'd disposed his long legs to his satisfaction, then leaned across and handed back his property.

Gleaming blue eyes met hers with open admiration. '*Grazie!*' he said, smiling, in the deep, gravel-toned accents that Georgia had met often during her dealings with the Italian male. 'It fell from my jacket—I trust you are not hurt?'

'Not at all,' she said coolly.

'I regret I was late,' he went on, undeterred. 'Does the delay cause you inconvenience?'

'No, it doesn't,' she assured him, conscious that Tom was listening with amusement.

'You travel to Pisa only? Or do you go on to Florence?'

Georgia took the flight magazine from its pouch, hoping he'd take the hint. 'To Florence.'

'This is your first visit there?' said the Italian, settling back comfortably in his seat, so obviously prepared to chat that Georgia's hackles rose. Something about the man annoyed her. He was too good-looking, too confident of his own charms, too—everything.

'Yes, it is,' she said shortly, annoyed by his assumption that she was delighted to talk to him.

'You will enjoy it very much,' he stated, half-turned towards her, a hint of intimacy in his attitude which irritated her considerably. 'Firenze is an experience rather than just a town, you understand.'

She gave him a cool little smile, then looked up in relief as the rattle of trolleys put an end to the exchange. She let down her tray ready for the meal on its way to them, and out of the corner of her eye saw the Italian do the same, a wry little smile on his lips.

When the familiar plastic trays arrived Georgia slid a slice of cheese into the bread roll provided, tucked it into a napkin and put it aside. 'Charlotte's appetite usually wakes up when she does!' she murmured to Tom.

'I learned that early on,' he returned with feeling, doing the same. 'When we got to Paris on our wedding day my bride demanded a very late, very large meal via room service before the honeymoon could get off to a proper start.'

Georgia giggled, then frowned as she met the heavy-lidded blue gaze trained on her from across the aisle. She turned away quickly, annoyed to find her colour high, and grateful when a pretty flight attendant arrived to dispense coffee, wine, or anything else the handsome latecomer desired.

'You've made a hit there,' muttered Tom, grinning into his glass of wine.

Georgia sniffed. 'The passengers next to him are men. I was just the nearest female for his chat-up line. He must be a celebrity of some kind, the way the attendants are fluttering round him.'

'Face looks familiar,' he agreed, frowning. 'But I can't place it. Not an actor or something, is he?'

Georgia indulged in a bit of discreet peeping round the duty-free trolley, but the man's face was unfamiliar. 'Certainly got the profile for it,' she whispered. 'Complete with Roman nose.' She caught a glimpse of a long, slim foot in the kind of shoe that Italy was famous for, then the flash of a gold Rolex watch, worn loose on a muscular brown wrist, as the man accepted a refill of coffee. 'He looks used to the *dolce vita*, that's for sure—and to people dancing to his bidding.'

'Shut up, Georgie,' said Tom hastily. 'He'll hear you.'

But a glance at the aquiline profile reassured her. The heavy, black-lashed lids were closed.

The short flight to Pisa was soon over. As they made their descent Charlotte woke up right on cue, passionately grateful to find her ordeal almost over as she devoured the cheese rolls that her companions had saved for her.

The moment the plane touched down the elegant Italian was on his feet and ready for the off. He gave Georgia a dazzling smile and a slight, deliberate bow. '*Arrivederci*! Enjoy your visit.' He slung the suede jacket over one shoulder and made a swift exit from the plane to a send-off of farewells and good wishes from the aircraft attendants and a handshake from the pilot.

'Dear me,' said Charlotte as Tom retrieved their hand luggage. 'Who *was* that, Georgia? Someone important?'

'*He* thought he was,' retorted her sister, grinning.

Charlotte, a different person once the plane had landed, was jubilant as they waited for their baggage in the air terminal. 'Just look at this gorgeous sunshine!'

she exclaimed happily. 'And we've got two whole weeks of it, Tom.' She sighed as they made their way to the waiting train. 'A pity you aren't spending more than one night of it with us, Georgie.'

'A job's a job,' said Georgia blithely. 'Besides, Tom, angel though he is, can hardly want me tagging along.'

'Dead right,' said Tom bluntly, grinning to take the edge off his words. 'I love you madly, Georgia Fleming, but I want your sister all to myself.'

'Tom!' said Charlotte, shocked, as the train began to move off. 'What a thing to say.'

'It's true,' said her husband, unabashed.

'Thank you, darling.' They smiled at each other lovingly.

'Now don't go all sloppy on me, you two,' ordered Georgia sternly. 'Have a care for my youth and inexperience.'

Her sister hooted. 'I don't know about the last bit, but you're exactly eleven months younger than me. Mother never spares us grisly tales of her heroism in surviving two babies in nappies.'

Georgia pulled a face. 'Another reason for staying fancy-free a bit longer!'

'Don't you like children?' demanded Tom. 'If not, I pity the poor little beggars you teach.'

'Ah, but I can hand those back to their mothers when school's over for the day!' Georgia laughed. 'Of course I like children—I like babies too. It's the reproduction bit I'm not keen on. Why wasn't I born a man?'

Tom Hannay gave her a long, slow scrutiny. 'The answer to that's obvious.' He put an arm round his wife's waist and touched his lips to her cheek. 'Politically incorrect it may be, but the women in your family were all meant to be just that—women! Your mother included,' he added, with a grin.

They arrived at the hotel in a blaze of sunshine which turned the River Arno into a flowing ribbon of gold below Georgia's window. She leaned over the balcony in delight, moving aside tubs of flowers so that she could stretch to see the Ponte Vecchio in the distance and drink in the beauty and noise and sheer vitality of Florence in one great heady, intoxicating draught.

She'd been teaching English near Venice for a whole academic year already, but her love affair with Italy merely intensified as she grew to know the country better. Even the stress and strain of instilling English into reluctant little heads took none of the gilt off the gingerbread. She'd spent two working vacations at the Venice school's summer camp in her student days, before getting her English degree.

This, indirectly, was responsible for her presence here right now, in the summer, when the school year was over. One of her pupils had sung her praises so much that a friend of his parents had come to see her at the school to ask if she would give his little daughter English lessons during the summer vacation. At first Georgia had been reluctant to give up so much of her holiday. But in the end the thought of a summer in Tuscany had been too tempting to pass up and she accepted, after stipulating that she must spend a week at home first.

Georgia leaned on the parapet dreamily, her heartbeat in rhythm with the throb of traffic from the *autostrada* across the Arno as she gazed at the view. Venice had been the realisation of all her dreams of Italy. But

Florence, with its incredible wealth of Renaissance art, promised to surpass them.

Charlotte and Tom were spending a night of luxury here with her at the Lucchesi, then they were off to a Tuscan farmhouse for the rest of their holiday, to laze beside a pool and recharge their batteries before returning to London, where Charlotte, a legal secretary who'd married her boss, worked for her busy solicitor husband.

For Georgia tomorrow would be different. Signor Marco Sardi was sending someone to drive her to the Villa Toscana, where her duties as English teacher to young Alessandra Sardi would begin immediately.

Deciding that a bath was the next thing on the agenda, Georgia moved the flowerpots back in place, then looked up in surprise as Tom's anxious face appeared above the stone partition that divided her balcony from theirs.

'Georgia, come in here a minute, please!'

'Something wrong?'

'Charlotte's not feeling too good.'

Georgia raced next door in alarm.

'What's up?' she said urgently as Tom, wearing a hotel bathrobe only a shade paler than his worried face, let her in.

'She's throwing up in the bathroom,' he said. 'You speak the lingo, Georgie. I think we need a doctor.'

Georgia went into the bathroom where her sister was bent over the basin, sluicing cold water over her face.

'I just lost the cheese rolls,' gasped Charlotte, reaching blindly for a towel. 'Take no notice of Tom—I most definitely don't need a doctor. You know my stomach doesn't travel well. The taxi ride from the station was a bit too exciting for it.'

Georgia put her arms round her sister carefully and held her close. 'You're shivering,' she said sternly.

'You would be too, if you'd just lost the entire contents of your digestive system!'

Georgia led her back into the bedroom to a very worried Tom.

'Darling, I'm all right. Really I am,' said Charlotte as he took her in his arms. 'I just need a shower and some tea and dry biscuits or something. When I'm feeling braver I'll take some of that revolting stomach gloop Mother forced on me.'

'Thank God she did,' said Tom fervently as he drew the sheet over her.

Georgia gave the order to Room Service, made sure that there was nothing more she could do for Charlotte, then went back to her room to shower.

Later, in a brief, almond-pink dress, her heavy, sunstreaked hair framing a glowing, lightly tanned face, she joined Tom and Charlotte to find the latter still in bed, looking pale but less haggard, and triumphant at having retained the tea and toast that Georgia had ordered.

'Oh, Lord, Georgie, you look so *healthy*,' groaned Charlotte.

'And gorgeous to boot,' added Tom, with a leer. 'Now you're here, little sister, I'll take a shower.'

Charlotte eyed him in alarm. 'Darling, shower in Georgie's bathroom, would you? I might need ours in a hurry if I lose the toast.'

Tom Hannay assured his wife that he would do anything in the world for her, collected Georgia's key and took himself next door.

'I'm so sorry, Georgie,' said Charlotte in remorse as

her sister perched on the end of the bed. 'I've rather put a damper on things. I can't face the thought of dinner.'

'Of course you can't,' said Georgia cheerfully, and thrust a strand of gleaming hair behind her ear. 'We'll have a meal up here instead.'

Charlotte looked guiltier than ever. 'I can't face the thought of *your* dinner, either. I'd much rather you and Tom went down to the restaurant. I can doze a bit, and you and Tom can enjoy a proper meal.'

'But we can't just leave you here alone!'

'Oh, yes, you can.' Charlotte yawned and slid deeper in the bed. 'To be honest, I quite fancy a couple of hours' rest on my own. I need to recharge my batteries for tomorrow, and the drive through all this Tuscan scenery they rave about.' Her face lit with a smile as Tom came in, rubbing his wet hair with the sleeve of his robe. 'I was just telling Georgia you must both go down to dinner and leave me here for a bit to recover. Then she can order a snack for me when you come up later.'

Tom protested vigorously at first, but Charlotte won him over with the smile he could never resist. 'I hate leaving you alone, darling,' he told her, smoothing back her hair.

She held her face up for his kiss, smiling. 'Don't worry, Hannay, this is the only time in your life I let you dine with a gorgeous blonde!'

Georgia wrinkled her nose in protest. 'Gorgeous I like, but *not* the other bit, please. Just "fair" will do.'

'That's what they said about Helen of Troy—and look at the trouble she caused,' chuckled Tom. 'Anyway, my fair Miss Fleming, give me a minute then we'll go down. I could eat a horse.'

*　　*　　*

When they arrived in the dining room only two tables were still unoccupied. The maître d'hôtel led them to one near a window, expressed his regret that Signora Hannay would not be dining, provided them with menus, summoned a wine waiter, and left them alone to make their choice.

'Good thing you booked,' said Georgia later as they ate prosciutto with slices of perfect golden melon. She was halfway through grilled salmon served with a separate dish of tiny, buttery vegetables, when Tom let out a smothered chuckle as he poured Chianti Classico into her glass.

'Don't look now, Georgie, but guess who's sitting in state at the back of the room!'

'Who?' she said indistinctly, still too hungry to be curious about anything other than the contents of her plate.

'The chap who held us up on the plane.'

Georgia glanced up sharply, to find a pair of brilliant blue eyes staring into hers. But to her surprise they glittered with a hostility she could recognise right across the dining room.

'He seems very interested in you,' commented Tom, after a swift look. 'Perhaps he remembers you from the plane. Odd, though. Looks a touch unfriendly. Shall I stroll over and ask why he's glaring at you?'

'Certainly not,' snapped Georgia, then smiled in apology. 'Sorry, Tom. Maybe he thinks he knows me. Which he certainly does not.' She went on eating, her appetite unaffected. It would take more than a black look from some self-important stranger to spoil such a delicious meal for her.

'The waiters are pretty attentive—just like the girls on the plane,' observed Tom with interest.

'I wonder who he is?' she said idly, then laid down her fork at last, with a sigh. 'Mmm, wonderful.'

'Pudding?'

She sighed again regretfully. 'I'm tempted—but no, thanks, I won't. Let's get back to Charlotte.'

'Right.' Tom rose to pull out her chair. 'You can order coffee for three with Charlotte's supper.'

Georgia walked ahead of Tom through the dining room, tensing slightly as her path led past the man from the plane. Willing herself to ignore him, to her annoyance she found her eyes drawn like a magnet to his. Stiffening at the unveiled disapproval in the cold blue gaze, she reached for Tom's hand hastily and hurried from the room.

'I wouldn't have caused a scene,' he protested in the lift.

'Just making sure,' she retorted, still smarting from the experience. 'Signor Sardi's paying my bill, remember. I didn't want repairs to broken furniture on it.'

'No chance—the guy's bigger than me.' Tom ushered her out on the second floor. 'I gave him my best legal scowl. Never fails!'

'Oh, let's forget the wretched man,' said Georgia, secretly deeply dismayed by the disturbing little incident. 'I won't drink coffee with you, Tom. I'll just find out what Charlotte wants from Room Service, then I think I'll turn in. I'm tired.'

'Pity you couldn't have had a day's grace before going off to the job.'

'I know. Never mind. I've been waiting to see Michelangelo's *David* all my life. He won't walk out

of the Accademia before I get round to him,' said
Georgia brightly.

Charlotte was feeling very much better after a nap,
and full of enthusiasm for the soup and toasted sandwich that she asked Georgia to order for her. She chuckled when Tom told her that the impressive Italian from
the plane had been dining only a few tables away.

'And looking daggers at our Georgie, would you believe?' he added. 'I was all for confronting him, but she
dragged me from the dining room in case I made a fuss.'

'Good move,' approved his wife. 'As I remember it,
he was rather larger than you, darling.'

'All right, you two,' broke in Georgia, with a yawn.
'If there's nothing more I can do I'm off to bed.'

'Come and have breakfast with us on our balcony,'
suggested Charlotte, kissing her goodnight.

Georgia found an envelope on the floor when she
went into her room. It contained a terse message in
Italian, instructing her to be in the hotel foyer at eleven
the following morning, when she would be collected for
the drive to the Villa Toscana.

Georgia frowned. The writing was quite unlike that
of Marco Sardi, who had written to her twice during
the past few weeks, his style infinitely more courteous
than the brusque note in her hand. She shrugged and
dropped it in a waste bin. Maybe it was a phone message which had lost something in the transcribing.

She filled a glass with mineral water from the small
refrigerator, then went out on the balcony to sit for a
while at the table there to enjoy the moonlit night before
going to bed. She had lied to Tom about being tired.
She'd felt a sudden, familiar desire to be alone.

She stared moodily at the improbable golden moon

hanging over the Ponte Vecchio. Why had the blue eyes of the unknown Italian held such hostility? Perhaps he was allergic to blondes. Yet the Renaissance Florentine ideal had been fair hair not too different from her own, though with hazel eyes instead of her own uncompromising black. Georgia's eyes were a throwback to a Spanish great-grandmother, and the contrast with fair, Fleming hair was striking. Normally it appealed to men on sight. But not to the hostile Italian stranger, obviously. Not that it mattered. She was unlikely to meet him again.

She sat looking at the moon until it dipped out of sight beyond the edge of the balcony, then went reluctantly to bed to spend a restless night, her sleep troubled by blue-eyed monsters who stalked her through her dreams.

CHAPTER TWO

NEXT morning the sun woke Georgia early, and she had showered, dressed and packed long before Tom came knocking to announce that breakfast for three was waiting on the balcony next door.

To Georgia's relief she found Charlotte fully recovered and hungry for their breakfast of yoghurt and fresh rolls spread with preserves. When the two coffee-pots had been drained dry Georgia got up to go.

'You've got the phone number of Villa Toscana, so give me a ring before you go back,' she said as she kissed them both goodbye.

'We'll give you a ring tomorrow!' said Charlotte promptly. 'Just to make sure all's well.'

Georgia laughed, hugged her sister once more, then went off to join the luggage that a porter had already taken down to the foyer. No one, she was told pleasantly, had yet arrived to collect her. Georgia went into the big lounge, installed herself in a pink brocade chair alongside a tall palm, took a large pair of sunglasses from her bag and immersed herself in one of the magazines from the glass-topped table beside her. From time to time she glanced up from the latest offerings from the Italian couturiers, but no one seemed to be waiting for her.

She smiled at some of the excesses thought up by the designers, hoping that her own sartorial restraint would meet with Signor Sardi's approval. Georgia had long legs which she knew looked good in the sand-coloured linen trousers she'd finally chosen. With them she wore flat leather shoes the same gleaming chestnut as her large bag and a plain white cotton shirt tucked in neatly. Her hair was caught back at the nape of her neck with a silk scarf striped in shades of brown and gold.

A few moments later Georgia glanced across at the reception desk and stiffened. A familiar figure was talking to one of the receptionists. The hostile Italian himself, she thought angrily, and buried her nose in the magazine, hoping that he'd be well out of the way before she was collected for the trip to Villa Toscana.

'Signorina Fleming?' enquired a startlingly familiar voice, and Georgia looked up from the magazine in surprise. The man from the plane stood looking down at her, dressed in chalk-pale linen trousers of superb cut, and a shirt the exact colour of the unfriendly eyes that she'd found so hard to get out of her mind the night before.

She inclined her head graciously.

'Allow me to introduce myself,' said the man in rapid Italian. 'I am Gianluca Valori.'

The name had a familiar ring to it. Perhaps he was a footballer. He'd certainly announced it in a way which expected recognition. Georgia preserved a dignified silence, raising her eyes to his in mute enquiry through the dark lenses of her glasses.

'I am to drive you to the Villa Toscana, Miss Fleming,' he went on, plainly irritated by her lack of response. 'Marco Sardi is my brother-in-law. If you doubt me, the hotel manager will confirm my identity.'

Her heart sank. 'That won't be necessary, Signor Valori.' Georgia spoke his language fluently enough, but with a slight English accent that she knew most Italians found charming. This one, it was plain, did not. Nettled by his attitude, she rose to her feet, hefted her bag, and informed her escort that her luggage was waiting near the reception desk.

Gianluca Valori had only to approach, it became obvious, for any hotel staff available to swarm with offers of help, and Georgia's modest amount of luggage was borne off down the white linen runner laid fresh over the red-carpeted front steps each morning. She waited serenely while her escort settled her bill, bade farewells all round, then ushered her outside to the Lungarno della Zecca Vecchia where a long, crouching black panther of a car lay waiting.

Good grief, thought Georgia in alarm as she saw her luggage piled in the back. I'm travelling in *that*?

Her escort installed her in the passenger seat of the sports car with impersonal courtesy, then got behind the wheel and, within minutes, it seemed to Georgia, Florence was left behind and they were hurtling along the A11 *autostrada* at a speed which frightened her silly.

'You are afraid?' asked the driver eventually, glancing at her colourless face.

'Yes,' she said tersely. 'Could you slow down, please? Otherwise I shall be sick.'

He lifted one shoulder and reduced his speed slightly. 'There is no danger, Miss Fleming.' He smiled crookedly, the first sign of warmth that he'd displayed since his frank male interest on the plane. 'I am an experienced driver.'

'So am I,' she returned, her colour restored a little. 'But not at such speed, nor in a car like this.'

He thawed slightly. 'You like the Supremo? It is our finest achievement, I think.'

Georgia's eyes narrowed. Supremo? *Valori*? Of course. The firm of Valori was small, but it manufactured some of the most luxurious, speedy cars in the world, and the Supremo was the sports car every man dreamed of owning. Valori racing cars were a legend in the world of Grand Prix too…

She bit her lip in sudden dismay, casting a swift, embarrassed glance at her companion's forceful profile. Oh, dear, oh, dear. No wonder his name was familiar. Gianluca Valori had once been one of the most brilliant racing drivers Italy had ever produced. She'd even seen him on television, his teeth a flash of white below the visor of his peaked cap as he sprayed champagne in laughing triumph on the winners' rostrum.

'You feel ill, Miss Fleming?' he enquired, frowning at her.

'No. Thank you.' Just very, very stupid, she thought bitterly.

'We shall be there shortly,' he informed her. 'The villa is near Lucca, a mere thirty minutes from Florence.'

She nodded, tense, certain that the trip took normal drivers twice as long as Gianluca Valori in his Supremo. They bypassed the walled city of Lucca, then turned off at a more leisurely speed onto a narrow road along a valley through undulating hills, where from time to time a stand of cypress pointed dark fingers like exclamation marks on the horizon, calling attention to the unfolding vista. She caught glimpses of beautiful houses on some of the slopes, then a monastery, before the Supremo nosed carefully down a road which was little more than a track.

At the end of it Gianluca manoeuvred the Supremo through gates leading into a beautiful garden ablaze with flowers and tantalising glimpses of white statuary. And at last they drew up in front of a house very different from the daunting Palladian building that Georgia had half expected. The Villa Toscana was relatively small, a perfect example of architecture from the late eighteenth century, with a strong Napoleonic flavour about its hyacinth-blue walls and white-painted shutters.

'We have arrived,' said Signor Valori drily, eyeing her rapt face.

'Yes,' said Georgia hurriedly. 'Yes, of course.' She gave him a smile for the first time, taking off her glasses to see the colours of Villa Toscana in all their glory. She turned back to him, forgetting her animosity for a moment. 'What an exquisite house!'

He stared into her eyes for a few seconds, then lifted a shoulder and looked at the building, his face sombre.

'My sister had faultless taste. She oversaw the restoration of the villa at every stage.'

Georgia's eyes filled with compassion. So Marco Sardi's dead wife had been Gianluca Valori's sister.

Suddenly a small figure in a pink T-shirt and shorts came flying from the house, and Gianluca Valori leapt from the car to sweep the child up into his embrace, kissing her on both cheeks before tossing her up in the air then catching her again and setting her on her feet.

'Come, Alessa,' he said as Georgia got out of the car. 'Welcome Miss Fleming to your home.'

Blue eyes just like her uncle's surveyed Georgia from a small, pale face beneath glossy black hair braided into a thick plait tied with a pink ribbon. 'I don't know how in English, Luca,' she informed her uncle, eyeing Georgia with reserve.

Georgia smiled as Luca Valori explained that Italian would do, since Miss Fleming spoke their language very well.

'So until your lessons begin you may keep to Italian,' he added, smoothing a hand over the dark hair.

'Hello, Alessandra, I'm very happy to meet you,' said Georgia, holding out her hand.

The child took it with a dignity far beyond her years. 'Welcome to Villa Toscana, miss,' she said with touching formality.

'Thank you.'

A young man came to unload the car as Georgia walked with the child and her uncle into a ravishingly beautiful hall. Inlaid wood gleamed on the floor below half-panelled walls lined with green moiré silk. On one of them hung a great gilt mirror which reflected the vivid colours of flowers arranged in brass jardinières on a pair of marble-topped tables.

A smiling woman in a neat cotton dress came to welcome Luca Valori with a flood of voluble Italian so rapid and accented that Georgia was hard put to it to follow it.

'Slowly, Elsa,' he teased. 'Miss Fleming speaks our language well, but she will not understand if you speak like a river in spate!'

The woman laughed, and spoke more slowly, asking if Georgia would like to go to her room before taking coffee or tea in the conservatory.

'I would like to wash very much,' said Georgia gratefully, then turned to Luca Valori. 'Thank you for driving me here.'

He bowed formally. 'I regret I frightened you with my speed.'

'Did you go zoom-zoom, Luca?' demanded Alessa, eyes sparkling.

'I did. But Miss Fleming was frightened, so I could not zoom-zoom all the way. Which is why we took so long to get here,' he added, raising a sardonic eyebrow at Georgia.

'I'm sorry I delayed you. If you're in a hurry to get away I'll say goodbye now,' she added coolly, and held out her hand.

Alessa giggled and nestled close to her tall uncle. 'Luca lives here now—' Her face clouded suddenly and a strong arm drew her close.

Georgia dropped her hand, finding it difficult to hide her dismay.

'I stayed overnight in Florence to get some business done early this morning. And for the privilege of driving you here, of course.' Luca Valori's smile told her that he knew exactly how she felt. 'I was glad to save Marco the trouble of fetching you because he is busy today. Not,' he added softly, 'that a night in Florence is ever a penance. Last night, in particular, was most interesting.'

'Franco has taken your luggage to your room, miss,' said Elsa, to Georgia's relief. 'If you will follow me, please.'

The bedroom allotted to Georgia was on the top floor of the house. She exclaimed in delight when Elsa threw open the door of a room which was on two levels, the first a small sitting room, the second a bedroom reached by a flight of four gleaming mahogany steps. The entire room was papered in a riot of roses with leaves of a rich, vibrant green which was repeated in the plain carpet. Two armchairs upholstered in rose velvet flanked a writing table with a lamp, opposite a pair of white-shuttered windows. On the balustraded upper level a white crocheted spread covered a bed which lay alongside long windows framing yet another breathtaking view.

Elsa turned a small brass knob in one of the rose-covered walls and threw open a door to reveal wardrobe space and shelves, then climbed the steps and opened a second door. 'The bathroom, Miss Fleming,' she announced. 'When you are ready, please come down and I will take you to the conservatory.'

'Thank you,' said Georgia appreciatively, gazing round at her new quarters. 'This is utterly charming. Where does Alessandra sleep?'

'In the room next to yours, miss, and Pina, her nursemaid, in the room at the end.' Elsa went to the door, then turned. 'Everyone calls her Alessa, miss.' She smiled to soften any suggestion of rebuff and went out.

Georgia went to wash, admiring cream marble and gilt fittings. She brushed out her hair, retied it, then paused, frowning at her mirrored face for a moment as she wondered what there was about it to antagonise a complete stranger. She shrugged, added a touch of lipstick, then went down two flights of stairs to the hall to find Elsa, who emerged from the kitchen regions to take her through a formal sitting room where French windows opened into a short, glass-roofed corridor leading to a large conservatory with a more relaxed atmosphere. Cane furniture was scattered with bright cushions;

newspapers and magazines lay on the numerous tables and green plants were everywhere. There were shirred blinds masking part of the windows from the bright noon sunshine, but wide doors stood open to the gardens, where the sound of running water lent an illusion of coolness to the hot July day.

Luca Valori rose as Georgia joined him, but Alessa was nowhere to be seen. Elsa asked if the young lady would like tea, but Georgia requested the strong Italian coffee she'd become addicted to, and Elsa went off to fetch a fresh pot, leaving an awkward silence behind her.

'Please sit down,' said Luca at last.

Georgia chose one of the sofas, and Luca returned to his chair.

'Is your room to your taste?' he asked politely.

'Yes, indeed. It's charming,' Georgia assured him, feeling on safe ground with the subject of interior decorating until she remembered that everything at the Villa Toscana had been chosen by his dead sister. She turned to gaze through the half-veiled windows. 'The garden looks beautiful. Do I hear running water?'

'A trout stream runs through the grounds.' His mouth curled in a wry smile. 'How polite you are, Miss Fleming.'

She gave him a grave, considering look, and decided against an answer. 'Where is Alessa?'

'She is with Pina, the young nursemaid who has been with her since she was born. Alessa will join us for lunch.' He paused, eyeing her soberly. 'You will need patience. I must warn you that she has no wish to learn English. Nor to go to England with her father.'

'Then must she?' Georgia looked at him very directly. 'I know Signor Sardi wants her to learn English prior to a few months in London with him. But must she go with him? Surely Alessa could stay here, with relatives, perhaps, until he gets back?'

Luca Valori's eyes iced over, as though he resented her trespass into his family's concerns. 'Marco's sister would take Alessa willingly, but he cannot bear to be parted from his child for so long. Therefore she must go with him, and go to school in England for a while.' He hesitated. 'Marco thinks it will be good for her. I think so too.'

'I see.' Georgia saw only too clearly. Her job wouldn't be easy. So that she could instil a modicum of English to make life easier for his little daughter in London was why Marco Sardi had engaged her. But he had made it very plain that warmth and sympathy for his child were of far greater importance.

'You like children?' asked Luca, watching her closely.

'Yes. I've always wanted to teach.' Georgia looked up with a smile as Elsa came in bearing a tray. 'Thank you.'

The woman nodded pleasantly, then excused herself to oversee lunch.

Georgia poured strong black coffee from a silver pot into thin, flowered porcelain, handed a cup to Luca Valori, then added sugar and a dash of cream to her own and drank thirstily, making no further attempt at conversation.

'Was your lover sad to part with you?' Luca Valori said abruptly at last, the harsh question startling her so badly that the cup rocked perilously in the saucer.

Georgia laid it carefully on the table beside her then

looked up to meet the blue, dissecting gaze head-on. 'Forgive me; I think I misheard you, Signor Valori.'

He lifted one shoulder in the gesture that she was beginning to know. 'I think not. I asked if your lover objected to surrendering you into my care. Are you pretending he doesn't exist? You forget. I saw you with him on the plane, then again at dinner last night. I was surprised when I learned who you were. Marco told me the young lady he had engaged would be free all summer because her fiancé was serving in Cyprus with the British Army. Obviously he arranged some leave.'

Georgia controlled a rush of cold, undiluted rage. 'No, he did not,' she said stonily. 'My companion, both on the plane and at dinner last night, was my sister's husband. They were in the room next to mine.'

Luca Valori stared at her incredulously. 'Is this true?' he demanded.

'Of course it's true!'

His mouth tightened. 'Then I commiserate with the lady—both in her choice of husband, and her sister.' Eyes blazing with distaste, he leapt to his feet and, without a word, strode from the room.

Georgia stared after him, open-mouthed, too astonished for the moment to be angry. At this point Alessa finally put in an appearance, followed by a shy, dark-haired girl, and Georgia was forced to pull herself together.

Alessa marched towards her purposefully, her face screwed up in concentration. 'Miss Fleming, my uncle regrets. He—he—'

'Has urgent business,' prompted the maid lovingly.

Georgia was deeply glad of it, so relieved that her

smile was warm enough to dispel the girl's shyness. 'You must be Pina,' she said.

Pina nodded, smiling, then excused herself to go off to the kitchen.

'I wanted Luca to stay to lunch,' said Alessa, pouting, then fixed Georgia with a mutinous blue eye. 'Are you going to start lessons today, miss?'

'No, not today. I thought you might show me round your garden, perhaps your room and your toys too. So no lessons.' Georgia smiled gently at the little girl. 'And my name is Georgia. I prefer that to "miss".'

'Georgia,' repeated Alessa, frowning. 'Is that an English name?'

'I suppose so.' Georgia laughed. 'My father wanted boys, you see, so my sister's name is Charlotte instead of Charles—Carlo to you—and when I arrived I wasn't a boy either, so I am Georgia, instead of George or Giorgio—'

To her horror the small face crumpled and tears streamed down Alessa's face. She knuckled her eyes in misery and Georgia drew the child into a gentle embrace, making soothing, inarticulate noises of comfort until the sobs lessened.

'What is it, darling?' she asked gently. 'Can you tell me?'

'Mamma had—a boy baby—but they both—went to heaven.' Alessa sobbed, rigid and unyielding at first. But at last she abandoned herself to the embrace, seeking comfort like a little animal as she burrowed against Georgia's chest, her tears soaking through the white shirt. Georgia held her tightly, responding fiercely to the child's sorrow.

'Cry, darling,' she said huskily. 'Let it all out.' Se-

cretly she was horrified. Naturally no one had found it
necessary to tell her that Maddalena Sardi had died in
childbirth, nor, she realised with foreboding, how recently it had happened.

It was a long time before Alessa calmed down suf-
ficiently to detach herself, at which point both of them
were very damp and the small face was lobster-pink and
swollen.

'I think we'd better change our shirts, Alessa,' said
Georgia. 'Shall we find Pina, or can you take me to
your room and show me where your clothes are?'

Alessa thought it over at some length, then, with a
hiccuping little sob, agreed to take Georgia up to her
room. It was charming, painted pink and white, with
many educational toys and books, as well as the collec-
tion of soft dolls that Alessa showed her visitor with
pride.

'My clothes are here,' announced the child, opening
a white wardrobe with scenes from fairy tales stencilled
on the door. Georgia helped Alessa off with the damp
pink T-shirt, replaced it with a clean white one, helped
her wash her face in the adjoining pink and white bathroom, then asked her to come next door to her own
room.

'You may find a surprise in here,' she told the little
girl as they went in.

Alessa's face lit up. 'A surprise for me?'

'No one else!' Georgia opened one of her bags and
took out a large, gaily-wrapped box. 'There. All the way
from England for Signorina Sardi.'

Alessa knelt on the floor, tearing off the paper to
reveal a large cardboard box. She lifted the lid with
impatient hands, then put them to her mouth, her eyes

saucer-wide with delight. A large, soft doll lay inside, wearing a dress, socks and shoes, her golden hair arranged in two braids which hung to her waist, and tucked in beside her was a small suitcase.

'That's her wardrobe,' said Georgia, changing into a sleeveless blouse. 'You can take her clothes off and dress her in two different sets. Do you like her?'

Alessa nodded vigorously, clapping her hands. 'She is beautiful, miss—Georgia! You brought her all the way from England for me?'

'I certainly did. Shall we take her from the box?' Georgia smiled, relieved. It was pure bribery, of course, to give a six-year-old such an expensive present, but, given the limited time she'd have to get to know Alessa Sardi, it had seemed like a good idea. And the doll had banished all trace of the child's tears. It had been worth it for that alone, thought Georgia with compassion as they went downstairs. Alessa danced ahead to display her present to Elsa and Pina, then ran back to Georgia to say that lunch was ready in the conservatory.

'I shall call her Luisa, and she can have Luca's place,' announced Alessa, and frowned. 'He couldn't stay for lunch, Elsa,' she told the housekeeper as the first course was brought in.

Wouldn't stay, more likely, thought Georgia, condemning Luca Valori out of hand for disappointing his little niece. And if he'd been away why hadn't *he* brought Alessa a gift too?

But as they were beginning on plates of delicious pasta with mushrooms, the first of the ceps, or *porcini*, much prized in Italian cooking, they heard the sound of a car, and minutes later Luca Valori strode into the conservatory, telling his ecstatic niece that he'd changed his mind. Business could wait until tomorrow.

'I decided you were more important than any business,' he told Alessa, then looked across at Georgia, his blue eyes hard. 'I confused what is important and what is not. But only for a while.' Then he applied himself with appetite to the pasta swiftly brought to him, and greeted the chicken *cacciatora* which followed with equal enthusiasm. So did Georgia.

It would take more than Mr Hotshot Valori to put her off her food, she thought, especially when it was of the quality served at the Villa Toscana. And conversation was no problem because Alessa was so thrilled with her English doll that it was the main topic for the meal.

'You are very lucky,' remarked her uncle at one point. 'It is a very beautiful gift.' He smiled at the little girl, his eyes dancing. 'You have not asked me what *I* brought you.'

'Papa says I must not,' said Alessa virtuously, but curiosity overcame her good resolutions. 'What did you bring me, Luca? Is it a doll too?'

'No, it is not, and I think you shall wait until this evening to receive it, now you have such a beautiful gift from Miss Fleming already.'

'Her name is Georgia,' Alessa informed him importantly, and turned enquiringly. 'Shall Luca call you Georgia too?'

'Of course. If he wishes to,' added Georgia serenely, her smile saccharine as she turned it on Luca Valori.

'How kind,' he returned blandly, then turned to Alessa. 'What are you going to do this afternoon, little one?'

'Will you come with me in the pool, Luca?' she pleaded.

He patted her cheek regretfully. 'Alas, I am expecting a very important call from Milan soon. Perhaps later, darling.'

'I could take you in the pool, Alessa,' offered Georgia.

The little girl looked doubtful. The new teacher was obviously no substitute for the glamorous uncle. 'Can you swim, miss—Georgia?'

'I certainly can. Can you?'

Alessa shook her head.

'Then I can start teaching you. This very afternoon, if you like.'

Alessa clapped her hands in glee. 'Oh, *yes*—please,' she added belatedly, and picked up the doll. 'Come, Luisa, we must find Pina and change our clothes.'

As Georgia got up she gave Luca Valori a cool little smile. 'If you'll excuse us, then?'

'No doubt I'll see you later,' he said with rather chilling significance.

Not, she thought drily, if I see you first. But of course that was nonsense. If Luca Valori lived at the Villa Toscana there was no way that she could avoid seeing him.

She sighed. Too bad that the most attractive man she'd met in her entire life thought she was having an affair with her sister's husband. She'd have to put him right on that subject as soon as possible, and not just for her reputation's sake either, she realised, a militant gleam in her eye. Open hostility from any man, whatever his nationality, was a new experience, and surprisingly hard to take. Hurt pride, if nothing else, made it imperative to try and change his mind about her before she left the Villa Toscana.

CHAPTER THREE

THE afternoon was a great help in Georgia's campaign to win the heart of Alessa Sardi. The pool in the gardens was a large, kidney-shaped affair, deep enough at one end for Alessa to be prohibited from the water unless accompanied by an adult.

'So I can only go in the pool with Papa or Luca,' explained Alessa as she slid into the water into Georgia's embrace. She shrieked with delight as Georgia towed her by the hands across the shallow end.

'Now you hold onto the edge of the pool and kick with your legs, then I'll show you how to move both legs *and* arms,' said Georgia, and moved off through the water in the stylish breast-stroke she'd learned at school. 'There,' she said, thrusting her wet hair back as she stood up in the shallow end. 'Now I'll take your chin, Alessa, and you try to copy me. That's right, darling, relax—I shan't let you go.'

With Pina for an admiring audience, the swimming lesson proceeded very successfully, ending in a noisy splashing session and a game with a ball in the shallow end. When Georgia delivered the little girl up into Pina's waiting towel she tensed as she saw a tall, bronzed figure dive cleanly into the water at the far end, and, swimming with a powerful, easy crawl, Luca Valori was on his feet beside her in the shallow end within seconds. He smiled up at his excited little niece, then turned to Georgia.

'You did well, Miss Fleming. I watched the lesson from my bedroom window.'

Georgia, at close quarters to the spectacular body of Luca Valori, forgot any idea of charming him in her hurry to get away. 'Alessa loves the water fortunately. Please excuse me; I must shower and dry my hair.'

For answer he heaved himself up out of the pool in a single movement and leaned down to give her a helping hand. Georgia was forced to take it, and let him pull her from the water, glad that her plain black swimsuit was functional rather than alluring as she hurried to collect her robe and wrap herself in it.

'Pina says we have English tea for you, Georgia,' said Alessa from the folds of her towel as the maid slid sandals onto the child's feet. 'And Elsa has made little cakes.'

'Lovely!' Georgia smiled at her warmly. 'Then I shall hurry through my shower and meet you—where, Alessa?'

'In the garden, if you wish.' Luca Valori waved towards a table and chairs shielded by a large canvas umbrella.

'Alessa shall choose,' said Georgia lightly.

'The garden, the garden,' chanted the child, and smiled pleadingly at her uncle. 'You too, Luca.'

He bowed, laying a hand theatrically on his heart. 'I obey your command, princess.'

She laughed delightedly, then pulled at Georgia's hand. 'Hurry, then. Come *on*, Pina.'

Georgia followed Alessa and Pina upstairs, promising to be down in the garden as soon as her hair was dry. She stood under a hot shower, shampooed her hair and sat looking through the windows at the Tuscan hills afterwards, frowning as she wielded her hair-dryer. At some stage she would have to take the bull by the horns and ask Luca Valori what she'd done to offend him, why her explanation about Tom had merely made matters worse. He might complain to his brother-in-law. And the last thing she needed was Marco Sardi's disapproval. It wouldn't do her standing at the school in Venice any good if it was known that he'd dispensed with her services.

She grimaced at the thought as she put on a fresh yellow polo shirt with her linen trousers, slid her feet into thonged brown sandals and left her hair loose to finish drying in the afternoon sunshine. She smoothed moisturiser into her flushed face, added a touch of rose-brown lipstick, then went to open the door in answer to a peremptory knock. Alessa was outside, wearing a vividly printed sundress. The dark hair was tied in bunches above her ears, and her blue eyes were sparkling as she clutched the new doll, who was now wearing jeans and a T-shirt.

'Are you ready, Georgia?'

'I certainly am, Miss Sardi. Where's Pina?'

'Gone to tell Elsa we are ready.' Alessa slid a small hand into Georgia's as they went downstairs, chattering about how smart the doll Luisa looked, and how much she'd liked the swimming lesson. 'Can we swim every day?' she asked eagerly.

'Of course—once we've done our English lessons.'

'Oh.' The small mouth drooped.

'They will be fun, I promise,' said Georgia firmly.

In the garden the table was laid ready with a silver tea-service and a coffee-pot, plates of petits fours and almond biscuits. Pina stood hovering, waiting for them, and Luca Valori, now fully dressed, to Georgia's relief, waited to pull out chairs for both ladies, while Pina filled cups and passed plates.

'You enjoyed your swim, Miss Fleming?' enquired Luca, accepting a cup of coffee from Pina.

'Very much. It's a great luxury to have a pool at one's disposal,' she said politely.

'There was no pool at our other house,' said Alessa, drinking milk through a straw.

'The restoration of this house was completed only recently,' explained Luca, his face shadowed.

So Maddalena Sardi had been allowed very little time to enjoy the fruits of her labours.

'I wondered why Alessa couldn't swim,' Georgia said quietly.

'Little one, why not play ball with Pina for a while until Miss Fleming has finished her tea?' suggested Luca, smiling at his niece.

Alessa pouted for a moment, then nodded obediently. 'Will you come too, later?'

'Of course.' He watched as the child scampered away across the grass with Pina, his eyes sombre.

Georgia braced herself. 'Signor Valori, I need to avoid upsetting Alessa in any way. I've no wish to intrude, but would you be kind enough to let me know just a little about her mother, please?'

'Very well.' Luca held out his cup for more coffee. 'Maddalena died six months ago, only a short time after the move to Villa Toscana. She was ten years older than me, you understand, and stronger in mind and personality always than in body. Her physician was deeply concerned when she became pregnant again at the age of forty-three.' He paused, frowning. 'I am sure Marco will not mind my telling you this.'

'Alessa told me she went to heaven with a baby boy,' said Georgia, staring down at her clasped hands. 'It was—heartbreaking.'

'The exact word.' He cleared his throat. 'We were all heartbroken. Marco most of all, naturally. A husband cannot help but feel guilt in such circumstances.' His voice deepened and grew husky. 'My sister was determined to bear a son, but the result was tragedy.'

'I'm deeply sorry—' Georgia's voice failed. Tears stung behind her dark glasses, and she turned away from the surprised blue eyes to look across the garden to where Alessa was chasing a large coloured ball. The silence lengthened, broken only by the laughter of the child as Pina lost the ball in the shrubbery.

'Miss Fleming, I have decided to say nothing to Marco,' said Luca at last.

Georgia looked at him blankly. 'Would he object to my knowing the facts?'

'You mistake me. I meant that I would say nothing on the subject of your brother-in-law.'

She stiffened. 'Signor Valori, there is nothing *to* say on the subject.'

'You will forgive me if I disagree,' he said silkily, then looked up as Franco, the gardener, came to announce that the English lady was wanted on the telephone.

'Speak of the devil,' murmured Georgia, getting up.

Luca followed suit, eyeing her narrowly. 'Devil?'

'Nothing personal,' she assured him. 'Excuse me. Please tell Alessa I won't be long.'

Georgia hurried into the house as fast as her long legs

could carry her. Franco showed her into a small study at the back of the hall, then left her to talk in private.

As expected, Charlotte was on the line. 'Hurry up, slowcoach,' said her sister. 'What took you so long? This is costing me money!'

'I was in the gardens. You should see the place, love; it's a gem of a house, with a pool and its very own trout stream!' Georgia went on to astonish her sister with the identity of the man on the plane, described the terrifying drive from Florence to the Villa Toscana with a Formula One ace at the wheel, and, for the crowning touch, related Luca Valori's suspicions about Tom in the role of Georgia's lover.

'But didn't you enlighten him—tell him about James?' demanded Charlotte, when she'd stopped shrieking with laughter.

'Of course I did. But he already knew about James, and for some strange reason the fact that Tom's my brother-in-law seemed to make things worse! Anyway, enough about me. Are you better?'

Charlotte, it seemed, was feeling wonderful, the farmhouse was too romantic for words, Tom was standing at her elbow, demanding to hear the joke, and her phonecard was running out.

'Ring you again next week, before we go back,' said Charlotte, 'and, Georgia, make sure—'

The line went dead and Georgia went back to the garden, feeling suddenly homesick. To her relief only Alessa was waiting for her. Luca Valori was nowhere in sight.

'My uncle has writing to do,' announced the little girl. 'Who was on the phone?' she added inquisitively.

'My sister. She's on holiday here with her husband.

Well, not here, exactly, but not very far away. Now, how about a tour of the gardens? You can show me all your favourite places.'

Alessa assented eagerly, proud and happy to show Georgia the trout stream gurgling over the stones in its bed, and the kitchen garden, where all kinds of vegetables thrived under Franco's hand. Great camellia trees and other flowering species strange to Georgia gave pools of shade where a statue stood out palely here and there, and beds full of hydrangeas and geraniums blazed bright in the sunshine.

In the farthest corner of the gardens, out of sight of the house, a neglected old summer house stood high on tall supports, half-hidden among a stand of cypress. Alessa climbed the flight of rather perilous wooden steps eagerly and opened the door to reveal a hot room smelling of sun and dust, with battered wicker furniture and a view of the distant monastery from its windows.

'I love this little house,' said Alessa, throwing herself down on one of the chairs, 'but Papa says I must never come here alone.'

Georgia could see his point. 'We'll come here together. We could even do our lessons here sometimes, if you like.'

Alessa's expressive little face lit up. 'Can we? Papa thought you would want to use his study.'

'If he wants that, then of course we will. But if you'd prefer lessons in your room, or the conservatory, or here, we'll ask his permission, shall we?'

The child expressed delighted approval, to the point of taking Georgia's hand, unasked, as they went down the steps, her new doll clutched firmly in the other. As they went along the gravelled drive to the house

Georgia felt that she'd begun to make a reasonable start in winning the child's confidence. And Luca Valori, it seemed, had no intention of running to Marco Sardi with tales behind her back. Big of him, she thought as Alessa chattered like a little monkey. Not that there was anything to tell—something she'd make clear in words of one syllable at the first opportunity.

This came sooner than expected. Marco Sardi would be home late that night, Elsa announced to his daughter's intense disappointment when they got back to the house.

'He will come to see you in bed,' she assured Alessa, then smiled at Georgia. 'He asked me to welcome you to Villa Toscana, miss, and has requested Signor Luca to look after you at dinner. If he is late, he will see you in the morning before he leaves for the day.'

'Thank you, Elsa.' Georgia smiled rather ruefully. A dinner alone with a handsome man like Luca Valori should have been something to look forward to. But, with his disapproval for company, it was likely to be an ordeal. Wondering if she could possibly plead fatigue and ask for a tray in her room, she discarded the idea regretfully. Apparently it was taken for granted that the young English teacher would eat with the family—a privilege she had by no means been sure of. It would be churlish to give Elsa and her cohorts extra work. Besides, Luca Valori would think that she'd lost her bottle.

She grinned as she followed Alessa back to the garden for half an hour before the child's bathtime. None of her friends would ever believe that she'd had dinner with Gianluca Valori, the racing driver who, during his brief, shining hour of glory, had ranked with people like Mansell, Alesi, and the brilliant, doomed Ayrton Senna.

When Alessa pleaded with Georgia to supervise her bathtime, Georgia assented gladly, surprised when in return Pina offered to unpack Georgia's cases and put her clothes away for her.

Georgia agreed, delighted, far happier with a riotous half-hour in Alessa's bathroom than a session of unpacking. After several races with toy boats through the bubbles she helped wash Alessa's thick black hair, then swathed the child in a towel and cuddled her for a while before putting the diminutive nightie on her. Georgia brushed and dried the long, lustrous strands, her heart aching as the little girl leaned against her trustingly. Wealth and luxury were no substitute for a mother. The mere thought of losing her own mother gave Georgia a sharp, physical pain. And she was a grown woman of twenty-six. What it must be like for a child twenty years younger she shuddered to think, and hugged Alessa close.

'I'm sure you can read very well for yourself,' said Georgia diplomatically, 'but because this is our first day together, would you like me to read you a story before you go to bed?'

Alessa, her eyes heavy by this time, agreed readily. Her papa read to her when he came home early enough, she told Georgia, and ran to fetch an Italian translation of collected fairy tales from round the world. Georgia, beginning to feel slightly weary herself after a long day of speaking only Italian, summoned up her best dramatic style as she read *Puss-in-Boots* with a different voice for each character.

When Pina came to see if Alessa was ready for bed,

she stayed to listen, her eyes so loving as they rested on the child's face that Georgia felt reassured on one point: Alessa might have lost her mother, but she lacked nothing in the way of love from this girl, not to mention her father, uncle, and the brisk, dependable Elsa.

When the story was over Alessa made no demur when Pina said that it was time for bed. She thanked Georgia without being prompted, asked if she might have another story the following night, and climbed into bed with a sigh.

'I was cross with Papa about the English teacher. But I like you, Georgia. Do you like me?'

Georgia's eyes met Pina's over the glossy dark head, glad to see no hint of jealousy in the maid's indulgent smile. 'I like you very much indeed, Alessa. We shall get on well together.'

The small head nodded, then burrowed deeper into the pillow. 'Goodnight, Georgia.'

'Goodnight, darling. I'll see you in the morning.'

To Georgia's surprise she found her clothes not only unpacked and put away, but any crumpled garments neatly ironed.

'Pina, you're an angel,' she said out loud, and looked through the selection hanging in the wardrobe, wondering what was a suitable choice for dinner with a man who thought she was having an affair with her sister's husband. She grinned, picturing Tom's mirth when Charlotte passed the news on to him, then took down a plain black linen dress and held it against her, eyeing her reflection in the mirror-lined wardrobe. Just the thing. Drop pearl earrings and black linen pumps and she'd be suitably sober.

But dinner wasn't until eight. She would write to

James, then read until dinnertime. She ran a gloating eye along the row of books that Pina had unpacked from her holdall. At the school in Venice she taught one-to-one lessons to adults most evenings, and was usually too tired to do anything afterwards except watch television for a bit before falling asleep. Here at the villa she would have a rest after lunch, also this part of the day to herself, and she meant to make good use of both.

The letter to James was oddly difficult. He had disapproved of the vacation job in no uncertain terms in his last letter, which had irritated Georgia, and only spurred her on to accept, which made it a little difficult to describe her present location in the glowing terms it deserved. She bit her lip, trying to conjure up his face, but an ineluctably Latin face with blue, disapproving eyes, kept blotting out James's fair, Anglo-Saxon features. Georgia shooed it away irritably, feeling disloyal.

Not that she was officially engaged to James. She had described him as her fiancé to Marco Sardi mainly because she loathed the term boyfriend. But the fact that she wore no ring yet was her own fault, not James's. Her reluctance to become an army wife was the stumbling block. She wanted a career of her own first, to see some of the world independently. Which James found hard to swallow, but put up with because he was intent on making the army his entire career, and was willing to wait for Georgia until she was ready to settle down with him.

Georgia wrote a cheerful little letter at last, concentrating on the flight and the night in the hotel rather than on the glories of the Villa Toscana, and picked up her book afterwards with a sigh of rather guilty relief.

Georgia curled up in one of the chairs with Wilkie

Collins's *Woman in White*, and quickly became so enthralled that she shot out of the chair at last with only fifteen minutes to spare. She had to hurry to achieve an effect so impeccably restrained that Luca Valori would be forced to change his mind about her.

At eight precisely Georgia was ready. Perfumed and made up with great care—just the right dramatic emphasis for the eyes which looked so striking against the heavy, ash-fair hair she caught back with a black velvet ribbon. Other than her gold watch, the heavy *faux* pearl drops were her only ornament, and she eyed herself critically, feeling pleased with the result.

Like a general going into battle she descended the stairs, ready to take on the enemy, who appeared in the hall, right on cue, just as she reached it. Luca Valori was dressed in very much the same way as he had been in the morning, except that, tonight, shoes and trousers were black. The shirt, however, was the same shade of blue. Georgia smiled politely, wondering scornfully if he had all his shirts made for him in that precise shade to match his eyes. Poser!

'You look very elegant this evening, Miss Fleming.' He ushered her into the small, formal drawing room, where a tray of canapés and drinks waited on one of the marble-topped tables.

'Thank you,' she returned with composure.

He gestured towards the silver tray of bottles. 'What would you like?'

'Tonic water, please.'

His eyebrows rose. 'Can I not tempt you to an aperitif?'

'No, thank you. I rarely drink—other than a glass of wine with dinner.'

He shrugged. 'Then tonic water you must have.'

'Thank you.' Georgia accepted the drink and sat down, making no attempt at conversation.

'Are you always as silent?' he enquired at last, then smiled slowly. 'But of course you are not. I had evidence of that last night. With the fortunate brother-in-law you were very animated.'

'I've known Tom a long time.' She looked at him expressionlessly as he seated himself on the other side of the table.

'Evidently. But is your sister aware that your relationship with him is so very—*intimate*?' Luca gave her a caustic look, then drank half the glass of wine he'd poured for himself.

The open implication in his tone put paid to any explanations. Georgia seethed in silence, abandoning her plan to win Luca Valori round. Why should she justify her behaviour to a complete stranger? If Marco Sardi required enlightenment, fair enough. He was not only paying her wages, but was a kind, fatherly man whom she very much respected, from her short acquaintance with him. But Luca Valori, other than by his relationship with Alessa, had no right of any kind to sit in judgement.

She finished her drink and got to her feet briskly. 'Signor Valori, I'm sure you'll be relieved if I take myself off to my room rather than inflict my company on you at dinner. Perhaps you'd ask Elsa to send something to my room on a tray?'

Luca leapt to his feet, a hand out towards her in apology, then swung round in surprise as a quiet voice from the doorway said, 'I trust that will not be necessary, now I am here, Miss Fleming.'

Both protagonists turned sharply to confront the dark, tired man who stood watching them, one eyebrow raised.

'Marco! You are early,' exclaimed Luca with a smile, in no way discomfited by the arrival of his dead sister's husband—unlike Georgia, who blushed vividly in embarrassment.

Marco Sardi took her hand, looking amused. 'How do you do, Miss Fleming? I *had* hoped you were being treated well in my absence.'

Luca shrugged gracefully. 'A slight misunderstanding only, Marco.'

'I rejoice to hear it, Luca. Miss Fleming is our guest, and comes to us with the highest recommendations. It would be a great pity if she felt it necessary to catch the next flight from Pisa back to London.'

Georgia gazed at the drawn, clever face of Marco Sardi with gratitude. 'Ah, but I've made Alessa's acquaintance already, Signor Sardi. She is enchanting. Unless *you* ask me to go, I'd very much like to stay.'

'Good. I am most relieved.' His dark eyes rested on one face then the other. 'Please look after our guest, Luca, while I visit my daughter. Give me a few minutes to bathe before dinner and I will join you as swiftly as I can.'

Luca Valori smiled in reassurance at his brother-in-law, then turned with deliberate formality to Georgia. 'Miss Fleming, forgive me, I beg, or Marco will make my life hideous—Alessa also.'

Georgia inclined her head, deliberately gracious.

Marco Sardi looked from one to the other with an approving smile. 'Now, if you will excuse me, I shall be as swift as possible. I shall apologise to Elsa on my way for holding up dinner.'

CHAPTER FOUR

THE dining room at the Villa Toscana was used only for the most formal of meals, Georgia learned. Family dinner, just like lunch, was served in the conservatory. With an almost full moon lighting up the garden the view through the open doors was breathtaking and Luca Valori, to Georgia's surprise, suggested that she might care to stroll outside until Marco joined them.

She agreed cautiously. A walk across moonlit lawns was better than sitting inside together in fraught silence. And at first the silence continued as they walked, Georgia determined that Luca should be the first to break it.

'I wish,' he said at last, the deep, gravel-toned timbre of his voice more accentuated than usual, 'that I could turn the clock back to my first sight of you on the plane.'

'Oh?' said Georgia without encouragement.

He gave her a morose, sidelong look as they paced slowly. 'Before I realised you were not alone. That you were with a man.' He lifted a shoulder. 'How could you not be?'

'What does that mean?' she demanded hotly.

'You are very beautiful—I meant nothing more than that,' he said, equally heated.

'Oh.' Georgia subsided. No one had ever called her beautiful before. Not even James. Attractive, even striking sometimes, but not beautiful. Maybe the word gained something in translation.

'Do you intend to marry your fiancé soon?' he asked after a while, apparently forgetting about intrusion in her private concerns.

Georgia's instinct was to tell him to mind his own business, but, to keep the peace, she shook her head. 'No. We're in no hurry.' At least, I'm not, she amended silently. 'James is doing his six-month *roulement* in Cyprus with the British Army. From his letters it sounds like a lot of fun. James plays polo rather a lot.'

'Will you enjoy being a soldier's wife?'

'Probably.'

'You display little enthusiasm.' He gave her a brooding look as they strolled along the banks of the stream.

'James is a career soldier. In other words, the army is his life. I want to go on with my own career for a year or two before I turn into an army wife.'

Luca Valori gave his one-shouldered shrug. 'Or is the true reason a little different? Because the man you truly want is married already?'

Georgia's hands clenched into fists. 'Signor Valori, I am trying hard not to lose my temper. But can't you take my word for it that you're mistaken about my relationship with Tom?'

'As was agreed before,' he returned coldly, 'it is not my concern.'

She breathed in deeply. 'Right. Let's talk about something else—politics, religion, football; anything other than my love life!'

Luca stopped, and looked down into her upturned face, his eyes unfathomable in the moonlight. 'Perhaps we should begin again, erase everything before this moment in time.'

Georgia stood very still, hypnotised by the look in his heavy-lidded eyes, which were as dark as her own in the uncompromising black and white of the night. She blinked at last, and turned away, groping for the correct words with unaccustomed difficulty, and in the end lapsed into English to make her meaning clear. 'If you mean that for the short time I am here we can achieve some kind of—of civility, then yes, I agree.'

'*Civiltà*!' He gave an odd, brusque laugh. 'How very British!'

They walked in silence for a moment, then he gave her a wry, sidelong glance. 'But what I meant, Miss Georgia Fleming, was that we should continue our acquaintance rather more cordially. Come.' He turned, beckoning her towards the house. 'I suddenly have a great desire for my dinner.'

'So have I. My appetite is a family legend.'

'Good. I like to see a woman eat.'

'Your cuisine here is magical,' said Georgia, in an attempt at lightness. 'I've eaten everything put in front of me the entire year I've worked in Italy, yet I've lost weight!'

Luca laughed. 'I doubt that it is the same for everyone. Perhaps you work too hard.'

'They don't give me my money for nothing at the school,' agreed Georgia, warming to her attempt at friendliness. 'I was quite tired at the end of the academic year. To be honest, instead of coming here to teach Alessa, I wanted to stay home for a while with my parents.'

'Then why did you agree?'

'Signor Sardi's description of Alessa touched me, I suppose.' She smiled ruefully. 'I thought I might be able to help.'

'You were right—Georgia. Now that I am committed to this civility of yours, you permit my use of your name?'

'Yes.'

'You know my name is Luca.' He held out his hand.

Georgia hesitated, then put her hand in his, and he clasped it tightly, looking down at her in a way that made her uneasy, wondering if somewhere, somehow, she'd done something rash. She smiled, detached her hand, then went in to find Marco Sardi waiting at the table.

'Good,' he said with satisfaction, looking from one to the other. 'You have called a truce, I see. Now, let us apply ourselves to Elsa's miraculous cooking. It is a long time since lunch.'

Georgia found, to her relief, that dinner at the Villa Toscana was a surprisingly entertaining experience. In company with two cultured, intelligent men who drew her into the conversation on all topics, her attitude towards Luca Valori gradually changed. Both men were surprised when she said at one point that it was deeply refreshing to have her views consulted about matters some men thought totally beyond her grasp.

'But why?' said Marco Sardi, mystified.

'Because some men would not dream that intelligence lay behind such a face, I think,' said Luca, surprising her with his insight.

'But beauty such as Georgia's is only possible when

intelligence illuminates it,' said Marco, then smiled kindly. 'We are making our guest blush.'

But she wasn't really a guest, thought Georgia, merely someone he was paying to teach his daughter. Marco Sardi was a very courteous man.

'But then, Marco, you are used to the combination of brains and beauty,' Luca pointed out. 'Maddalena possessed both in abundance.'

Marco's face looked suddenly haggard. 'Very true. I miss her at the *fabbrica* as much as I miss her in every other way. Without you this past week, Luca, I have been hard pressed.'

'My sister and Marco handled the finances and sales of Fabbrica Valori together,' explained Luca. 'I am interested more in design and the mechanical side, but Marco is ruthless. He insists on sending me off on public-relations exercises. I was returning from one on the flight to Pisa.'

'His name and face sell more cars than any other sales promotion we can devise,' said Marco, making an obvious effort to throw off his melancholy. He looked at Georgia in enquiry. 'I assume you know Luca was expected to be world champion at one time?'

'No, I didn't know that,' said Georgia honestly. 'My father follows the sport avidly, but I'm not much of a Grand Prix fan myself. Though I remember seeing you on TV once, on the rostrum with the usual champagne bottle,' she added to Luca.

'That was before I yielded to Maddalena's urgings and retired to spend more time with the company.' Luca's face was sober. 'After the madness of the eighties, when the demand for our cars was so high that we had problems in meeting it, world recession hit our industry hard. We have always made luxury cars, you understand—sports models with style, built with loving care rather than by the robots of mass production.'

Marco leaned across and poured a little cognac into Luca's glass. 'But we weathered the storm, and others were rescued. Your British Aston Martin Lagonda, Georgia, was bought up by Ford, and Bugatti are now restoring Lotus fortunes, but the new Valori Supremo is outstripping all its rivals.' He laughed. 'Did you enjoy your ride in it with Luca?'

'Not a lot,' she confessed honestly. 'It was at that point I realised who he was. I was terrified!'

There was general laughter, then Luca lifted a shoulder in the now familiar gesture. 'My passenger's beautiful face turned green!'

At which Georgia's face turned pink. She got up, bringing both men to their feet with her. 'I think it's time I went to bed. You must both have a lot to discuss, and I must be bright and early for Alessa tomorrow. Perhaps you could give me your instructions about her lessons in the morning, Signor Sardi?'

'Of course, my dear.' He smiled at her kindly. 'I'm sure you will be good for my daughter. I need not tell you how much she means to me. I am selfish to insist on taking her to England with me, but I am required there when our London office opens, and must remain there until all is running smoothly.' His mouth twisted. 'I could not bear to be parted from her that long. Also Luca agrees with me, that the change of scene for a while will be good for both Alessa and myself.'

'I can understand that,' said Georgia with sympathy.

'At the moment Alessa is clinging to everything familiar,' said Luca.

'Which is why Luca is living here. She adores him,' said Marco simply, 'which is also part of the problem about England. She wants Luca to go too, and of course he is needed here.'

'I'll do my best to paint my homeland in glowing colours so she'll look forward to seeing it,' promised Georgia, then smiled at both men. 'Goodnight.'

'Goodnight, Georgia,' said Marco. 'Welcome to Villa Toscana. I hope you enjoy your stay here.'

'I'm sure I will. And I shall try hard to see Alessa enjoys my stay too.'

'I will see you to your room,' said Luca, and, afraid to wreck the fragile peace between them, Georgia made no protest. She walked with him through the drawing room and the dimly lit hall, making a note of the light switches he showed her on the way up both flights of stairs to her door.

'Thank you. Goodnight,' she said as they came to a halt.

'I came to learn whether you spoke the truth,' he said abruptly, and she stiffened.

'About *Tom*?'

He shook his glossy dark head impatiently. 'No! I refuse to discuss your sister's husband further.' He stopped dead, swallowed, then said gruffly, 'I mean your intention to keep to the truce between us. To observe these *civilities* of yours.'

She eyed him militantly. 'I rarely say things I don't mean. Contrary to your impression of me, I'm a pretty straightforward sort of person. The truce won't be broken by *me*—if only for Alessa's sake.'

Luca smiled. And Georgia was glad that she'd told him about James. When Luca Valori chose to exert it his charm was formidable. A fiancé in the background was an effective shield against it. 'Good,' he said softly. 'Life at the Villa Toscana will be more comfortable that way. For all of us.' He raised a slim black eyebrow. 'When you looked at me on the plane I thought you recognised me.'

'Your face was familiar,' Georgia admitted, then gave him a mischievous smile. 'I thought you were a movie star.'

Luca's wide, classically cut mouth twisted in mock disgust. 'No. Nothing so pretty. I like grease on my hands.'

'Were you sorry to give up racing?' she asked curiously.

He nodded. 'Yes, very much. I would lie if I denied it. But then when Ayrton Senna was killed I was devastated—glad I had left the world of the track behind. No one, I realised, is invincible.' He shrugged. 'Valori no longer build Formula-One cars for the Grand Prix circuit. We concentrate now on fast cars for the connoisseur.'

'Your family must be glad.'

His face shadowed. 'It pleased Maddalena. So that, at least, I was able to do for her before she died.'

Impulsively Georgia reached out a hand to him, and he took it. 'I—I'd better say goodnight and get my beauty sleep—' She stopped, biting her lip.

'You have no need of it,' he assured her promptly, and Georgia withdrew her hand, but Luca recaptured it, smiling. 'I think you are not accustomed to hearing your looks described so. Have you heard of Andrea della Robbia?'

She nodded. 'He was a sculptor during the Renaissance.'

'You could have been the model for some of his faces.'

'Then I'll have to go and look at his work, if only out of curiosity!'

'I am willing to be your guide, whenever you wish—if such a thing is allowed within the terms of this truce?'

'That depends on how much time off Signor Sardi allows me,' she said breathlessly. 'Goodnight.'

He reached for her hand, raised it to his lips and kissed it. 'Goodnight, Georgia.' He held onto the hand, his grasp tightening as he straightened to look down into her wary eyes. He moved closer involuntarily, his gaze falling to her mouth, and her heart gave a thump. Then her hand was free and she turned away swiftly into the safety of her room.

Georgia slept better than expected, all things considered, but woke early to keep her rendezvous with Marco Sardi at breakfast in the conservatory. The day was already hot, and the sunshine so bright that she discarded jeans in favour of a dress in thin black cotton dotted with yellow and white.

'Good morning,' said her employer, getting up at her approach. 'You look as though you slept well.'

'I did, indeed. Good morning, Signor Sardi.' Georgia sat down next to him, helping herself to coffee as he indicated. 'I heard Alessa go downstairs with Pina. Where is she?'

'Luca took her into the garden so that we might discuss her lessons in peace.' Marco Sardi held out his cup for more coffee. 'Naturally I will not presume to instruct you on your method of teaching, only to ask that you do not work her too hard, and give her a long rest after lunch. Alessa was far from pleased at the idea of more lessons now school is over for the summer.'

Georgia smiled. 'Understandable! But don't worry, Signor Sardi. The lessons will be short at first, and as much fun as possible, I promise.'

'Fun,' he repeated, with a wry smile. 'None of my teachers ever made lessons fun, as I remember. My friends, the Donatis in Venice, are deeply impressed by their son's progress in English now he is your pupil. But, far more important than that to me, they said you were kind, and loved children.'

'I shall try to be Alessa's friend as well as teacher,' promised Georgia quickly. 'A very easy task—she's an endearing child.'

'And the image of her mother.' He rose with a sigh, his face set in weary lines. 'And now I must leave. Thank you for rising so early for our talk, Georgia. You shall report on Alessa's progress at dinner tonight.'

'Papa, Papa,' called Alessa, running in from the garden. 'Look what Luca brought me from London!'

'Say good morning to Georgia,' admonished her father.

Alessa obeyed hastily, with a quick smile for Georgia, then thrust out her wrist, which was adorned by a small white watch with large numerals in luminous colours. Marco Sardi admired it with the requisite extravagance, caught his little daughter up in a hug and kissed her on both cheeks, then set her down as Luca, in a superb, handmade grey suit and the inevitable blue shirt, came strolling in.

'Good morning, Georgia,' he said, with a smile. 'You slept well?'

She returned the smile with reserve. 'Good morning. I slept very well, thank you.'

'Come, Luca, we must be at Valorino by nine,' said Marco.

'But first,' said Luca, 'have you arranged time off for Georgia?'

Marco Sardi clapped a hand to his forehead. 'No, I have not!' He turned to Georgia in apology. 'Weekends are yours, unless some crisis occurs at the *fabbrica*. If I am called away we shall come to some other arrangement.'

Georgia assured him that for the short time she would spend at the Villa Toscana she was quite willing to forgo any time off until the end of her stay. 'I thought I'd spend a short break in Florence afterwards before term starts in Venice.'

'You must have *some* time for yourself,' said Luca emphatically, then glanced at his watch. 'But we can discuss that this evening. Come, Marco, let me drive you—'

'No!' said his brother-in-law, completely without malice. 'We shall go separately, as always. A waste of petrol, but kinder to my nerves.'

When they had gone Alessa looked forlorn for a moment, until asked to share Georgia's breakfast.

'I shall ask Pina to bring more juice and coffee,' she said importantly, very much lady of the house, and soon they were eating fresh hot rolls spread with butter and preserves, washed down with fresh orange juice and strong black coffee diluted, for Alessa, with a great deal of hot milk.

'Good,' said Pina, when she came to clear away. 'You have eaten well today, Alessa.'

The child looked surprised, as though she hadn't noticed how much she'd eaten, then asked Georgia when they could go swimming again.

'After our morning lesson,' said Georgia firmly, steeling herself against the entreaty in the gentian-blue gaze.

'I thought we would start tomorrow,' said Alessa hopefully.

'Your papa wants you to start today,' said Georgia, taking the coward's way out. 'So after breakfast we'll do some lessons. Afterwards we'll go for a walk in the garden, and after that we'll have a swim before lunch.'

Alessa, as Georgia fully expected, proved to be a bright pupil. And, because Georgia produced several visual aids in the shape of photographs and her own brightly coloured drawings, Alessa enjoyed her first lesson. In a surprisingly short time she knew numbers and letters, and could introduce herself in English and say a short phrase or two. She was astonished when Georgia said that it was time to finish.

'Already? Can I speak Italian now?' she demanded as Georgia put her things away.

'Yes, of course. But English only during lessons, Signorina Sardi.'

The rest of the morning passed quickly. During the walk through the gardens, Alessa, intoxicated with her new expertise, demanded the names of the flowers and trees in English. 'I hope Papa comes home early tonight,' she said, skipping along. 'I shall talk to him in English, Georgia. He will be *very* pleased.'

Georgia, secretly very relieved that the lesson had

gone so well, agreed that Alessa's papa would be delighted.

'Luca too,' said the child with satisfaction, and held out her wrist to admire the watch. 'Anna and Chiara will be jealous.'

'Who are they?' enquired Georgia as they went indoors to change for swimming.

'My friends at school. They have uncles too, but not famous like Luca.' Alessa scampered off to the beckoning Pina, and Georgia went into her room with a wry smile. Luca Valori obviously gave reflected glory to his little niece.

There were no more lessons that day, other than a reprise of Alessa's new English vocabulary at bathtime. Pina listened with admiration as she bathed and dried her charge, while Georgia sat on a stool, prompting when Alessa faltered.

Afterwards Georgia read another fairy story, but this time Marco Sardi arrived before she'd finished, and Alessa hurled herself into her father's arms, smiled up into his loving face, and said very slowly in English, 'Good evening, Papa; how are you today?'

CHAPTER FIVE

THE pattern of the first day was repeated in almost every detail as others succeeded it. The weather was consistently hot and sunny, and each morning the English lesson was followed by a walk and then a swim, a long rest after lunch, then a game with a ball in the garden while Alessa recapped on the vocabulary she'd learned earlier. And each evening Marco Sardi and Luca Valori were regaled with Alessa's latest English conversation before Georgia went to her room to enjoy a breathing space before joining the men for dinner.

This, she acknowledged to herself as she dressed, was the best part of the day. She was rapidly growing deeply attached to Alessa, but the concentrated one-on-one style of teaching was surprisingly tiring, even with a long break in the middle of the day. Especially when she knew Marco Sardi wanted his daughter capable of the basic necessities in English by the time she left. After Alessa went to bed each evening Georgia was very grateful for the hour or two's grace before dinner, knowing that her work for the day was over.

And, she admitted secretly, each evening at dinner there was Luca Valori for company. Marco Sardi, who missed very little, Georgia knew, behaved as though he was entirely unaware of Luca's growing—and very open—predilection for their 'English guest', as he unfailingly referred to Georgia. As the days went by Luca made it plain that his earlier hostility to Georgia was a thing of the past, that he enjoyed her company, and was strongly attracted to her. Georgia was disturbed by the confidence in his blue eyes, as though Luca Valori had no doubt that she reciprocated whatever it was he felt.

Before coming to Italy, she had been assured by her principal that for a sensible young woman there would be admiration, but little danger from the Italian male of the species. And she had been right. Georgia's looks attracted admiration, but her dealings with Italian men had been mainly with very much married mature professional men, who needed English lessons for their work, or teenage male students who were appreciative but respectful, and never gave her cause for offence.

Luca Valori was something else entirely. For one thing, although their exchanges were always conducted in his own tongue, Georgia knew that he spoke English very well. Life on the international circuit of the racing track would have added to the English he'd probably learned at school, but for some reason he never made any attempt to speak to her in anything but his native tongue. Neither did Marco Sardi, though he, she knew very well, spoke fluent, Tuscan-flavoured English, since their first communications had all been made in her own language.

English was something kept solely for her lessons with Alessa. And Georgia knew that her command of Italian wasn't sufficient to ask Luca if he was just flirting with her, or whether—James or no James—he intended an all-out assault on her defences at some stage. In the light of his suspicions about Tom he might well consider her an easy target, even take it for granted that she'd accept him as a lover. She felt the blood rush to her face at the mere idea.

'You are tired this evening?' asked Marco Sardi as they lingered over coffee.

Georgia smiled, and shook her head. 'Not really. I wish all my pupils were as bright as Alessa.'

Luca turned his lambent blue gaze on her, his eyes moving over each feature of her face with an indolent relish that heightened the colour in her cheeks. 'You find the heat trying, Georgia?' he asked, her name sounding like a caress in the deep, husky voice.

'No,' she said briskly. 'I love the sun.'

'Which is evident. You glow!' He turned sharply at a slight sound from the man beside him. 'What is it, Marco?'

Marco breathed in carefully. 'Nothing,' he said, shrugging. 'I should eat less red meat. It gives me indigestion.'

'If anyone looks tired, Marco, it is you,' said Luca sternly. 'Take the day off tomorrow.'

'No, no,' protested the other man. 'I just need rest.' He rose to his feet, with a smile for Georgia. 'I shall submit to the weakness of age and indulge myself with an early night.'

'Goodnight.' Her smile was sympathetic. 'I hope you feel better by morning.'

'I feel better already,' he assured her, and smiled into Luca's searching eyes. 'Don't worry; I'll be up bright and early tomorrow.'

When he had gone Luca sat in the chair nearest to Georgia's sofa, staring out at the moonlit garden. 'Marco worries me,' he said, frowning.

'I can see that. Is he always so thin?'

'No. He is not. I shall persuade him to visit a doctor. He has been working too hard since Maddalena died.'

He lifted a shoulder. 'I understand why. He loved her very much. Theirs was a very passionate marriage, you understand. It is very hard for him in many ways without her.'

Georgia coloured as it dawned on her what he meant.

'I have embarrassed you,' said Luca, looking at her sharply. 'It was not my intention.'

'No, of course not.' She gave him a crooked little smile. 'Sometimes, when I'm tired, my brain slows down and it takes me longer to understand what's said to me. At the school there are other people who speak English. Here I function in Italian all day long, other than the lessons with Alessa.'

'I speak English,' he said abruptly. 'But not as well as you speak Italian, Georgia. And I prefer to talk with you in my own language because your accent charms me. And not only your accent. As you know well,' he added with emphasis.

Georgia rose to her feet precipitately. 'It's time I said goodnight.'

Luca got up more slowly, his eyes holding hers. 'Why? Are you afraid?'

'Not afraid exactly.' She held his gaze unwaveringly as she searched for the right word. 'Prudent? No, wary. That's it. I'm wary,' she went on slowly, digging deep into her vocabulary, 'of giving you, or anyone else, the wrong impression.'

Luca moved closer, the heavy lids veiling the gleam in his eyes. 'Are you saying that because of this soldier of yours you are immune to me? Or is Tom Hannay the real obstacle?'

Georgia's eyes flashed dark, resentful fire at him. 'Will you stop all this nonsense about Tom?'

'I know very well that it is not nonsense at all,' he assured her, in a way that set her teeth on edge. 'I also know I have the power to make you forget him. And all other men—this James of yours included.' And with a sudden movement he caught her in his arms and held her close, the thudding of his heart like a hammer against her breasts. 'Tell me you are indifferent to me— if you can!'

Georgia was quite unable to say anything, struck dumb from the mere fact of being in Luca Valori's arms and wanting so much to be kissed that she couldn't find any words at all, Italian or English.

Luca gave a smothered, exultant laugh and bent his head with tantalising slowness. She was trembling when his mouth met hers at last, with practised enticement. At the contact her lips parted involuntarily and Luca's polished skill vanished. Abruptly they were two breath-less, vibrating bodies fired with the same elemental need which surged through them both like an electric current, welding them together with its heat.

For the first time in her life Georgia felt every last scrap of reserve melt in the crucible of the sudden, over-whelming passion which obliterated everything else in the world until the shrill demand of the telephone broke the spell. Luca cursed wildly, and let her go, and Georgia returned to earth with a jolt, breathless and shaken and utterly astounded by the cataclysm that had overtaken her.

Luca snatched up his mobile phone from a nearby table and yanked out the aerial with a force which threatened to break it. 'Valori,' he snarled, listened for a moment, then his face suddenly set into grim, granite lines. To Georgia's surprise he spoke in husky, accented English.

'Of course. I will call her. A moment please.' He almost flung the instrument at Georgia. 'For you,' he snapped, and strode out into the moonlit garden.

Heaving in a deep, ragged breath, Georgia said 'hello' in a voice she hardly recognised as her own.

'Georgia? Is that you? Hi, gorgeous, it's Tom. Was that the hostile Italian?'

'Yes,' she said, resigned, and sat down in the nearest chair abruptly. 'It certainly was. How's Charlotte?'

'Right here at my elbow, panting to talk to you.'

'Out of the way, Tom,' said his wife impatiently. 'Georgie?'

'Hello, Charlotte.'

'Are you OK? You sound odd.'

'Couldn't be better,' lied Georgia. 'Have you stopped being sick?'

'Yes. And now I'm all tanned and brown like you, and blend in with the locals rather well. We actually stirred ourselves to go somewhere yesterday and took a drive to Siena. What a miraculous place! Tom climbed that tower and got dizzy with the view, but I chickened out. Have you had any time off yet?'

'No. I stayed here over last weekend because both Alessa's father and uncle were tied up in work with some crisis. But next weekend I hope to get to Florence.' Georgia listened to her sister enthusing over the marvels of Michelangelo's *David*, promised to queue for hours if necessary to get in to the Accademia to see him, then spoke swiftly, giving her sister messages for their parents before Charlotte's phonecard ran out.

Georgia pressed the off button, thrust the aerial home and put the phone back on the table, then hurried to the door. But her plan to escape Luca failed. He came racing from the garden to intercept her.

'Georgia!'

She turned reluctantly, her eyes questioning on his taut, unsmiling face.

'I ask your forgiveness,' he said harshly. 'It was not my intention to—to behave in such a way.'

Georgia felt suddenly very, very tired.

'You have nothing to say?' he demanded, coming closer.

'I'm too tired to speak Italian,' she said wearily in English. 'So I'll just say goodnight.'

'Please,' he replied in the same tongue. 'First you must understand I did not—did not wish to assault you.'

'I know that,' she said, surprised. 'It was hardly an assault.'

'Perhaps I do not use the right word,' he said, scowling.

'You just wanted to show me how irresistible you can be,' she said, without emotion, and smoothed back hair that had suffered considerably from his attentions.

He stood very erect. 'I wished to show you it is possible to—to make love with other men.'

'*Other* men?' she said, incensed.

'*Dio*! I meant,' he said in exasperation, 'a man who was not this Tom Hannay—nor this fiancé of yours.'

'His name is James. And before I get thoroughly offended I think we'd better revert to Italian,' said Georgia rapidly. 'So you can understand once and for all that to me Tom is just my sister's husband. I'm fond of him, but nothing more. James is—is the man I'm in love with,' she finished in a rush, appalled to find that she was lying.

'I do not believe you,' he said flatly.

Georgia's eyes flashed. 'Whether you believe me or not is irrelevant. Signor Sardi's opinion is the one that counts.'

Luca stared at her implacably. 'You think he would not mind if he knew the truth about your affair with your sister's husband?'

'There is no affair. But tell him if you like,' she said flatly, and turned on her heel, only to find her wrist caught in a grip that bruised as he swung her round to face him.

'And did you tell Tom Hannay that his call came at a most inconsiderate moment?' he demanded, his eyes blazing.

Georgia stared at him. '*Sconsiderato*?' she repeated blankly.

'The wrong moment, then,' he said impatiently, and seized her other hand. 'To feel such joy, such passion, then to be hurled to earth by the sound of the man's voice—' He gave his familiar, eloquent shrug, then pulled her against him, but Georgia stood rigid in his embrace.

'So this is also the wrong moment,' he said bitterly, and thrust her away.

Georgia glared at him. 'For a long list of reasons, there isn't going to be a right moment.'

'Why not?' he said imperiously. 'Can you deny that you responded to me, that you caught fire in my arms?'

'No. And I've no intention of losing my head in that way again. I'm here as an employee, paid to teach Alessa, so what happened was neither wise nor sensible.

And last, but not least, you won't believe me about Tom.' Her voice cracked. 'He's my sister's husband, for pity's sake! I object to your insinuations. Strongly. James would too.'

She glared at him, hoping that he couldn't tell her palms were wet and her mouth dry with the effort it was taking to convince him that he had no hope of breaching her defences again. 'Goodnight,' she said at last, and turned away, half hoping, half dreading that he would leap after her and take her in his arms. But Luca Valori stayed where he was, scowling, and Georgia walked from the room, her head high.

Next morning Marco Sardi was alone in the conservatory when Georgia and Alessa joined him for breakfast.

'Two letters for you, Georgia. Luca brought them in before he left. He wished to oversee some modification they are making to the new Supremo engine,' said Marco, and smiled at his daughter as she tucked into her breakfast. 'You are eating well, my darling,' he said lovingly.

Which was more than could be said for her father, thought Georgia with concern. She had little appetite herself this morning, but that would soon pass. It would take more than a quarrel with Luca Valori to put her off her food for long. But Marco Sardi had been eating very little for days, unless he consumed an enormous meal at some point during his working day. He was growing visibly thinner, and Georgia was uneasy about the greyish tinge to his face. Unable to ask personal questions, she asked instead whether he would be home over the weekend.

'I will indeed,' he said emphatically. 'You have been

here nearly two weeks, and so far you have had little time to yourself. Tomorrow is Saturday, and I shall take Alessa to spend the day with my sister and her family. Would you care to come with us? Or perhaps you could come as far as Lucca and do some exploring on your own.'

'Can I get a train or a bus there to Florence?' said Georgia eagerly.

'Can you drive?'

'Yes. I drive the minibus at the International School.'

He smiled. 'In that case you may have the keys to the car Franco uses for Elsa's marketing.'

Alessa, who expressed a strong wish to accompany Georgia to Florence next day, had to be propitiated by lessons in the summer house, which Georgia allowed now and then as a treat to vary routine. But the day was hotter than usual, with a sultry heaviness to the air, and Georgia cut the lesson short to bring the swimming lesson forward, sure that the weather was building up to a storm.

For the first time since she'd come here, the day dragged so much for Georgia that she greeted Marco Sardi's early arrival home with as much pleasure as Alessa. Thankful that she could go off for a bath with a clear conscience, Georgia left Alessa to her father and Pina and sought the comfort of cool, scented water, wondering if she could plead a headache to avoid a confrontation with Luca at dinner. Then she scowled at herself in the mirror. Coward! Of course she'd go down and behave as though nothing had happened. Nothing much *had* happened, anyway. With any other man a few kisses would have been totally unremarkable. Whereas one touch of Luca's mouth on hers and she'd lost her

wits. Her face flamed at the mere thought of it. A good
thing Tom had rung at that particular moment,
sconsiderato or not.

When she arrived downstairs at eight as usual Georgia
found that she had nothing to worry about. Luca was
not, it seemed, joining them for dinner. Furious at her
own disappointment, she did her best to talk normally
with Marco, and made no comment on Luca's absence.

Marco, though obliging enough to tell her that Luca
was dining with an old friend, omitted to say whether
the friend was male or female. Like the day, the meal
seemed endless to Georgia, and it was almost a relief
when she heard the first rumble of thunder over coffee.
Before long the rain was coming down in torrents, and
lightning lit up the conservatory with an almost constant
display of fireworks.

Although Alessa, she learned, had no fear of thunder-
storms Georgia went to bed early, mainly because she
was sure that Marco Sardi would consider it bad manners to retire before she did. She detected relief in his
weary eyes when she said that she was at the exciting
part of the novel she was reading, and took herself off
to her room to torture herself with the thoughts of what
Luca was doing.

The only fear the spectacular storm inspired was
worry over Luca's return through it in the Supremo. He
might stay where he was for the night, of course.
Georgia couldn't decide which option appealed to her
less, and got ready for bed in a state of nerves which
the rising crescendo of the storm did little to soothe.
She was used to the ferocity of the storms in this part

of the world, but this one was particularly melodramatic.

She heard Marco Sardi go into his daughter's room next door, as he did every night before he went to bed. In a lull in the thunder she heard his footsteps recede again, then lay on her bed watching the storm through the long windows beside her bed, hoping now that wherever he was, and whoever he was with, Luca would stay there, at least until this father and mother of storms was over.

She thought she heard a car at one point, but couldn't tell if it was Luca in the Supremo. As the storm receded Georgia forced herself to concentrate on the thriller she was reading, and eventually succeeded, mainly because she was about to discover the identity of the killer.

Georgia was so deep in the final denouement that the frantic knocking on the door brought her out of bed with a pounding heart. She threw open the door to find Pina there in her nightgown, her incoherent anguish so great that it took a moment for Georgia to understand the gist of her story. When she did she went white to the lips.

'No, Pina, Alessa is not with me. She must be with her father.'

The girl twisted her hands in utter misery. 'No. Signor Marco went back to Valorino to fetch some papers once the rain stopped. And she is not in his room. I looked.'

'Right.' Georgia pulled herself together and reached for her dressing gown. 'Go and put something on, Pina, then we'll start a proper search. She must be somewhere. Maybe she's gone down to the kitchen for something to eat.'

But Alessa was nowhere in the house. While Pina,

hysterical with anguish by this time, went to rouse Elsa and her son Franco, Georgia raced outside to the pool, dreading what she might find there. But the security lights which flashed on at her approach showed her at once that the pool was empty. She went back to join the others, demanding torches.

'It is possible Signor Marco took Alessa with him in the car,' said Franco hopefully.

Georgia, seriously doubting this, suggested that Elsa gave Pina something to calm her down, and put water to heat for hot drinks. Then she told Franco to search the vegetable garden, and all the grounds behind the house, while she covered the lawns and shrubberies and anywhere else she could think of. Suddenly inspiration struck her.

'The summer house!' she said to Franco.

'*Signorina*?'

Georgia gestured down the drive with her torch, searching desperately for the word. '*Il padiglione, il padiglione!*' she cried, and raced off to the remote corner of the grounds where, far beyond the range of the security lights, the summer house lay hidden, high in its copse of cypress.

Georgia hurled herself up the slippery, splintered wooden steps, Franco at her heels as she tried to open the door. 'Alessa!' she screamed, and heard a faint sound in response as she tried to open the door, which had jammed shut.

Franco put her aside, drew back his foot and kicked in the door, and next moment a sobbing, distraught Alessa was clasped fast in Georgia's arms.

'I shouted—but—no one came. I couldn't—open the door,' sobbed the terrified child, while Franco offered up fervent prayers of thankfulness and explained that the rain-swollen door must have slammed shut with a gust of wind, then refused to open again.

'Give her to me, miss,' he said tenderly. 'I will carry her down the steps.'

'Luisa! Luisa!' cried the child, and Georgia shone the torch to look for the doll. She pounced on it, cursing herself for having bought the thing for Alessa in the first place.

'Darling, you came back for her—you should have called me; I would have fetched her for you!' Georgia shone her torch for Franco to make his way safely to the ground with Alessa before trusting her own weight to the stairs, then heard a car roar in through the gates, looked up as she saw headlights, and lost her footing.

She grabbed the handrail, then screamed as the staircase disintegrated beneath her, her flailing hands met empty air and she hurtled to the ground in a welter of creaking, splintering wood. Her breath left her body as she hit the earth, something struck her head with a stunning blow, and Georgia knew no more.

CHAPTER SIX

GEORGIA opened her eyes on a room she'd never seen before. No rioting roses. The walls were covered in ivory watered silk. And she was lying in a tester bed with coral damask curtains caught back with tasselled gilt ropes. Her eyes widened, then shut again quickly against the throbbing pain in her head.

'Ah, you are awake,' said a man's voice in Italian.

Georgia, slow to translate, couldn't find the energy to reply. She nodded. And regretted it. She breathed in sharply, and a cool, dry hand held her wrist to check her pulse.

'Gently, Miss Fleming. Open your eyes, please.' She obeyed, and saw a slim, grey-haired man in a dark suit. He smiled at her encouragingly. 'Keep them open.' He shone a slim torch beam in each eye in turn, then asked if she felt sick.

Georgia thought about it. 'No,' she said doubtfully in English. 'Not really. But my head hurts.'

'A large piece of wood struck it,' he said matter-of-factly.

Georgia, blinded with swift recall of her fall, reared up in sudden alarm.

'Alessa!' she gasped. 'Is she all right? Where is she? Where am *I*?'

'Alessa is perfectly well, Miss Fleming. She is safely asleep in her own bed.' He smiled, easing her gently against the pillows. 'I am Dr Claudio Fassi, and this is merely another room in the Villa Toscana, on the ground floor. Luca brought you here rather than carry you up so many stairs to your own room.'

'Luca?' repeated Georgia faintly.

'Yes. He is waiting impatiently outside the door. Signor Sardi also.' Dr Fassi smiled soothingly. 'You gave everyone a great fright. However, I think you have not come to much harm. You have a lump on your head, and you have sprained an ankle, but you are not, I am certain, concussed. There is no need to convey you to the hospital, as Luca wished.'

Georgia's thinking processes were not at their best. It took her a long time to translate the precise Italian of the doctor, who appeared to understand English but not to speak it.

'You're sure Alessa is all right?' she asked anxiously. 'I remember now. She was shut in the summer house— *il padiglione*,' she added urgently.

Dr Fassi's eyes twinkled. 'She is well, I promise you, and you are improving, Miss Fleming—your Italian is coming back to you.'

She turned her head away in anguish. 'It was all my fault.'

'That the staircase collapsed? I think not! Signor Sardi is very angry with himself for leaving it in disrepair.'

'But it was the doll I brought Alessa which caused it all. She went back to fetch it and got shut in.' Tears trickled from her closed lids. 'Sorry,' she said, sniffing. 'I don't know why I'm crying.'

'You have suffered great anxiety, followed by trauma. A few tears will do you no harm.'

'Everyone says that here,' she said huskily, and

opened her eyes. '*Piangi*. Cry. The British say, "Don't cry."'

Dr Fassi smiled kindly. 'You also have a saying, do you not—when in Rome do as the Romans do? Now, my dear, I shall order a tray of weak tea for you, and leave some very mild painkillers for your headache. Two only tonight, please, and no further dose unless absolutely necessary.'

Georgia thanked him hoarsely, watched the door close behind him, then turned her head into the pillow and gave way to tears of weakness, until she heard a husky, familiar voice saying her name urgently.

She turned on her back to look up at Luca and Marco, who were standing by her bed, Luca's eyes burning like blue flames.

Marco Sardi, haggard with anxiety, grasped her hand tightly. 'Georgia, I beg your forgiveness. I knew the steps were unsafe, but I had forgotten them.'

'Please don't apologise. It was an accident.' She scrubbed at her eyes with a tissue from the box on the bedside table. 'You've had more to think about than the summer house lately.'

'You are a kind young lady. But it is no excuse,' he said with remorse. 'I was spared the horror of seeing you fall. It was Luca who arrived on the scene, to find Alessa screaming in the arms of Franco and you unconscious beneath a pile of wood.' He shuddered involuntarily, and Luca put a hand on his arm.

'Marco, enough. I am sure Georgia does not blame you.'

'Luca is right,' she said emphatically. 'I blame myself. I should have noticed when Alessa left the doll behind—'

'Nonsense,' said Luca roughly. 'Besides, who would have imagined that Alessa would have gone out alone into the night to fetch her doll? Pina is afraid of thunder, and the child thought you would be sleeping, Georgia, so she went to get the doll herself. She thinks of herself as the doll's mamma, you see. The person responsible.'

Marco thrust a hand through his silvered dark hair. 'I should be proud that my daughter was both brave and responsible, but all I can think of is that I should have stayed home, and not gone back to Valorino for some figures that could well have waited until Monday—'

'Please, Signor Sardi,' entreated Georgia, then smiled as Elsa appeared with a tray. 'Ah, my tea.'

The atmosphere changed abruptly. Elsa, formidable in a voluminous dark dressing gown, took charge, thrusting pillows behind Georgia and pulling the covers up under her chin with fierce propriety as she suggested that both men would do better to seek their own beds and leave Georgia in peace in hers.

'Here are your pills, my dear,' she said, handing the patient a glass of water. 'I have brought biscuits for you to eat before you drink the tea—on the doctor's instructions,' she added firmly, to quell any signs of insurrection.

Georgia felt too feeble to protest about anything. After both men bade her goodnight, under Elsa's eagle eye she swallowed the pills and nibbled listlessly on a biscuit while the older woman turned off all the lights except the one beside the bed.

'Is Alessa really all right?' Georgia asked anxiously.

'The doctor gave her a little something to make her sleep,' said Elsa soothingly. 'And in the morning, when she sees you are better, she will be very happy, I promise. Perhaps you would like her to eat breakfast with you?'

'Oh, yes, please.' Georgia drank some of her tea, taking in her surroundings as well as she could in the dim light. 'What room is this, Elsa?'

'It is the one kept for Alessa's great-grandmother. She cannot climb stairs, so Signora Sardi made this room specially for the visits of her grandmother.' Elsa stood by the bed, her hands clasped in front of her. 'When Signor Luca brought you in, soaked and unconscious in his arms, I told him to put you here. He was wild enough with fear without having to carry you up several flights of stairs!'

So Luca had been in a bit of a state, which was hardly surprising, considering the drama he'd found when he arrived home. Georgia lifted the covers to find that she was wearing a blush-pink silk nightgown quite unlike anything she owned, and bit her lip in dismay.

'No, no,' said Elsa quickly, misunderstanding. 'It was I who prepared you for bed.'

'Yes, of course. Thank you.' Georgia steeled herself. 'But Elsa, who does the nightgown belong to?'

'Signora Conte, the master's sister. She always leaves things behind when she stays here,' said Elsa, and smiled in reassurance. 'She will not mind.'

Neither did Georgia now. It would have been too painful for words for Alessa to see something once worn by her own mother.

Once she was alone Georgia turned out the light and tried to settle herself to sleep, but in the darkness she kept on reliving the moment when the stairs had given way and she'd hurtled into space. She shivered and reached out and turned on the light, like a child needing a candle in the dark.

Her head, she realised after a while, was better. The ache was receding, the throbbing less violent. She slid wary fingers into her hair to find the lump and grimaced. Either the thickness of her hair had protected her or she had a mortifyingly thick skull. She lay against piled, lace-edged pillows, suddenly depressed as a throb from her ankle warned her that she was unlikely to drive herself to Florence for a while, even less to explore it on foot.

A tap on the door interrupted her musings.

'Come in,' she called quietly, then stared, her eyes wide as Luca came into the room and closed the door softly behind him.

'I saw your light,' he said swiftly as he approached the bed. 'I knew you were awake. I could not sleep until I made sure all was well with you.'

Georgia's heart was beating so hard that she tugged the covers under her chin to hide it. 'I don't feel wonderful,' she said in English. 'I've had some pills, so my head doesn't hurt so much, but it refuses to muster my limited Italian vocabulary.'

He smiled wryly. 'I have no such excuse for my lack of English,' he replied in the same tongue.

It didn't really matter what language they spoke in, Georgia realised. Their eyes were communicating in a way which dispensed with words.

'You frightened me,' he said abruptly. 'For a moment I think—thought you were dead.'

Georgia raised a hand to her head, giving him a rueful little smile. 'It takes more than a block of wood to finish me off, apparently.'

Luca drew nearer, looking down at her in a way which accelerated Georgia's pulse. 'For a moment there in the rain and darkness I could think only that we parted in anger. Then I felt your heart and heard it beating—'

'It's beating now,' she whispered, staring up at him.

Luca bent forward involuntarily, then turned away abruptly. 'Forgive me,' he said in Italian. 'I should not have come here tonight. I told myself I wanted to make sure you had everything you needed, but I lied. To you and to myself.' He turned suddenly to face her, his eyes glowing like sapphires in his set face. 'When I carried you in here you were like a dead thing in my arms. Then Marco came, thank God, to comfort Alessa, but Elsa and Pina took you from me and shut me out. I could not sleep until I had—'

'Had what?' said Georgia gently.

He breathed out, eyes closed, then dropped to his knees beside the bed and slid his arms round her, his cheek against her hair. 'Until I had held you in my arms and felt you warm and alive to my touch,' he said, and raised his head to look down at her. His eyes darkened, and he bent his head to hers, their lips meeting with a mutual gasp of pleasure. Georgia locked her hands behind his head and surrendered herself to the engulfing heat of Luca's kiss, oblivious of throbbing head or any other hurts. She felt a shudder run through Luca's broad chest, and hugged him closer.

'Don't go yet,' she said as he raised his head.

'I don't want to go at all,' he groaned, his mouth against her throat. His lips moved upwards until they found hers, his arms cruelly tight, and Georgia gasped as her head gave a sudden, sickening throb.

Luca jumped up in alarm, looking down into her dilated eyes, which widened to circles of jet in her pale face. 'You feel ill?'

She tried to smile. 'My head just reminded me it hurts, that's all.'

'And I am a brute to behave so when you are still so fragile,' he said with passionate disgust. 'Shall I call Elsa?'

'Certainly not,' said Georgia tartly. 'How would you explain your presence in my room?'

'I had to come,' he said harshly.

'I'm very glad you did.' Her eyes glittered into his. 'I couldn't sleep either. It was a long, miserable day, Luca.'

'For me also.' He clasped her hand in his, his smile turning her bones to liquid.

'Are we friends again?'

'*Friends*?' He gave a smothered laugh. 'Ah, you English! How can you and I be friends, Georgia? You know very well I wish to be your lover.'

The transient glow faded from her face. 'That's out of the question.'

He scowled. 'Why?'

'I'll write out a list of reasons and give them to you tomorrow.'

Their eyes clashed for a moment, then Luca shrugged.

'Forgive me. You are tired and need rest. Tomorrow we will talk again.' His eyes caressed her possessively. 'We shall discuss all these reasons why I should not be your lover, and you will see that none of them will deter me. I want you, Georgia. I want you very, very much.'

'And you always get what you want?'

He nodded, confidence in every line of his tall, graceful body. 'Always!'

Georgia took a long time to get to sleep after the door closed on Luca Valori. The cards, she thought wearily, were well and truly on the table. But for the first time in his life Gianluca Valori would find that there was one thing he couldn't have.

She lay staring at the beautiful room despairingly. If he'd been someone else it would be different. Someone more ordinary. But Luca was the very embodiment of everything she'd ever wanted: looks, charm, intellect, and the ability to set her on fire at his merest touch. This was the stuff all lovers should be made of, thought Georgia bleakly. And he wanted her. But it was what he wanted her *for* that posed the problem.

Georgia lay listing the obstacles that stood in the way of any relationship with Luca Valori. It was out of the question for them to conduct a love affair under Marco Sardi's roof for a start. And once the period of coaching Alessa was over she was going back to her parents until the term began at the school near Venice. The contract for her second year there was already signed, and she had no intention of endangering it, not even for Luca Valori, whose great drawback was the fact that he was so well-known. Mrs Blanchard, the principal of the International School, had made it plain that she required employees with impeccable behaviour on her staff. Which ruled out any dalliance by one of her teachers with a man who had once won the adulation of all Italy for his exploits on the Formula-One circuit.

And there was James, she thought in sudden, horrified remorse. He should have been right at the head of the list. She bit her lip, thinking of the letter she'd received, telling her how much he missed her and how much he was looking forward to seeing her again, once his spell in Cyprus was over. But since she'd met Luca even her weekly letter to James had become a chore.

Burning with guilt and aching all over, unable to put Luca's kisses from her mind, Georgia wrestled with the problem of James, facing the fact that she'd never really been in love with him, and that this, not her career, was her real reason for putting off the wedding. It was a deeply disturbing discovery—one which left her sleepless for the entire, interminable night.

It was a heavy-eyed invalid who welcomed the arrival of Elsa. The brisk, sympathetic woman exclaimed over the rings under Georgia's eyes, helped her hop to the bathroom to save her injured ankle, then brushed the mass of thick fair hair, taking care to avoid the bump.

'You did not sleep well, my dear,' she stated as she settled Georgia back into a swiftly tidied bed.

'No. My head ached.' Georgia smiled gratefully. 'I'm very sorry to cause you more work.'

Elsa snorted. 'Nonsense. I will send Pina and Alessa in with your breakfast tray. But today you drink tea, not coffee,' she warned. 'Dr Fassi instructed me.'

Georgia gazed at the bright day outside, where the sun was shining as though the storm had never happened, then the door opened and Alessa shot across the room, her eyes big with anxiety.

'Georgia, are you better?' she entreated, and Georgia smiled, holding out her arms.

'Yes, I am. But come and give me a hug and I'll be better still!'

The child flung her arms round Georgia's neck and

clutched her tightly. 'You fell and hurt your head, and it was all my fault—'

'It was *not* your fault—I just missed my footing. And my head's fine!' said Georgia emphatically. 'Anyway, I should have noticed Luisa was missing and fetched her myself. Ah, look, darling, Pina's bringing our breakfast.'

The girl bade Georgia a shy 'good morning' as she put down a heavily laden tray, enquired after the invalid's health, then put a small table beside the bed and drew a chair up to it for Alessa. The child chattered like a magpie as Pina served the meal.

'If you have everything you want, miss, I shall help Elsa serve breakfast to the master and Signor Luca,' said the maid.

'I can give Georgia anything she needs,' said Alessa importantly, and Georgia chuckled.

'As you see, Pina, I lack for nothing!'

Much reassured by the sight of Georgia apparently little harmed by the adventures of the night, Alessa disposed of a good breakfast, touchingly adult in her efforts to see that the invalid was given every attention.

'I wish I wasn't going to Zia Claudia's today,' she said, once the meal was over. 'I'd rather stay home and look after you.'

'I'll be fine. I'll probably sleep all day.' Georgia smiled affectionately. 'You can impress your cousins with the English words you've learned.'

Alessa looked less than enthusiastic. 'The doctor says you are not to walk for two days,' she informed Georgia. 'You must stay in bed until he comes to see you again.'

'Oh, dear,' sighed Georgia, but secretly she wasn't

too unhappy to hear this. She was far from her usual self in more ways than one, and if Marco Sardi was taking his daughter out for the day a long rest in this beautiful bedroom held a very definite appeal. 'Then, if I have to stay here, Alessa, could you fetch some books from my room for me? I shall read so the time will pass quickly while you're away.'

Alessa ran off readily on her errand, and a moment later Marco Sardi arrived with Pina, to enquire after the invalid. He stayed only while Pina was collecting the breakfast things, expressing his regret once more for the faulty stairs, and his relief that Georgia was looking much better than the night before.

She assured him that once her ankle was pronounced fit to walk on she'd be up and about as usual.

'But you should have been driving to Florence today,' he said remorsefully, motioning Pina to remain.

'The museums will still be there when I finally make it,' she said philosophically.

It was mid-morning by the time Dr Fassi arrived. He restrapped Georgia's ankle, examined her thoroughly and pronounced her fit to get up as long as she put no weight on her foot for at least two days. Once Marco Sardi had received assurances from the doctor that the young English lady was a healthy young woman who had taken no lasting harm from her mishap, he brought Alessa in to bid Georgia a reluctant goodbye, then took his daughter off to visit her cousins. By this time it was noon, and Luca was the only one missing from Georgia's list of visitors.

Elsa came bustling in to help Georgia take a bath with one foot out of the water—a process which caused great hilarity and tired Georgia not a little by the time she was dry and cool in a thin pink cotton dress. She sat on the bed with her foot on a stool while Elsa tidied her hair, then looked up in surprise as Luca came in with a knock at the door and flipped her heart over in her chest with his smile.

'She is ready?' he said to Elsa.

'Yes. Lunch will be in half an hour.' The woman smiled, assured a grateful Georgia that it had been a pleasure to help, then went away to the kitchens.

Luca looked even more irresistible than usual to Georgia, in a dazzling white T-shirt and faded old jeans crafted by some master hand, with soft leather moccasins on his bare brown feet. He picked Georgia up in his arms and, ignoring her squeak of surprise, carried her swiftly to the conservatory, where he set her down on a sofa and hooked a stool into place.

'There,' he said, breathing hard. 'Rest your foot.'

Georgia, even more breathless than he, obeyed silently, her colour high as he sat beside her and took hold of her hand.

'How are you this morning?' he asked, in a husky tone caressing enough to ring alarm bells in her brain.

'I'm fine. In fact,' she added, 'I'm not an invalid. Surely there's a walking stick somewhere? You needn't have carried me!'

'You are wrong. I desperately needed to hold you in my arms,' he informed her smugly, so triumphant that she couldn't hold back a smile. 'To hold you close and breathe in the scent of you has taken my breath away. Ah, Georgia. You have such a beautiful smile.'

So do you, she thought silently, gazing at him. 'I was wondering where you were this morning,' she said, then could have bitten her tongue as the triumph deepened on his face.

'You missed me!' he said with satisfaction. 'I knew you would.'

'Is that why you didn't visit the invalid?' She narrowed her eyes at him and he looked pained.

'Of course not. I had to drive to Valorino first, to consult with one of the mechanics this morning. Just so I could devote the rest of the day to you.'

Georgia looked away. The whole day with Luca. Pure bliss—or pure insanity. 'It's very kind of you, but you're not obliged to keep me company,' she said austerely. 'I have books to read, letters to catch up on—which reminds me—may I ring my parents today, please?'

Luca frowned, his blue eyes astonished. 'You have no need to ask. Ring your parents any time you wish. Or anyone else,' he added reluctantly. 'Unless he writes so many letters you need no phone calls to your lover.'

'No point in worrying him. But I'd like to talk to my mother.' She smiled as she waved a hand at her foot. 'I think I'll gloss over last night's experience.'

'Which one?' he asked swiftly. 'Your fall, or the time spent in my arms?'

She glared at him. 'I shan't mention either! Because both of them were isolated occurrences. Neither will happen again.'

Luca leaned back in the corner of the sofa, his long legs stretched out in front of him. He looked at her for a long time in silence, then shook his head slowly. 'It is useless to struggle, Georgia. Fate has brought us together. We are meant to be lovers.'

'No, we are not!' She felt like a sitting duck, marooned on the sofa with no chance of getting away. 'Even if I—I wanted to I wouldn't dream of repaying Signor Sardi's kindness by behaving so badly under his roof. He hired me to teach his daughter, remember. Which is all academic anyway. You've forgotten about James.'

'I have not,' he said grimly. 'Nor Tom Hannay.'

Georgia glowered at him. 'Will you *please* forget Tom?'

'Promise to do the same and I will.'

At which point Pina arrived to lay the table for lunch, and all hostilities were temporarily suspended. By the time Elsa arrived, with *crostini* for their first course, and bade Luca carry Georgia to the table, both of them had cooled down somewhat, and Georgia was able to enjoy the paté-spread toast more than she'd expected to in the circumstances.

They were obliged to talk of impersonal subjects while Pina cleared plates and brought wine and mineral water, then returned with plates of *arrosta*, rosemary-flavoured roast pork, served with artichokes drizzled with the matchless local olive oil.

The meal had been cleared away, Georgia had drunk the tea the doctor advised, Luca had downed several cups of black coffee, and she had been lulled into believing that he meant to drop the subject, when he resumed their conversation as though there had been no break in it at all.

'We *shall* become lovers,' he said conversationally, startling her. 'I believe fate has brought us together for just this purpose, Georgia.'

'This isn't fair,' she said with sudden passion. 'For

the moment I can't even walk, let alone run away from you.'

He gazed at her in surprise. 'Why should you run away from me?'

She sighed in exasperation. 'Can't I make you understand? Just because you want something doesn't mean you can have it. I don't *want* to be your lover, Luca Valori.'

'You lie,' he said, unmoved, and picked her up, holding her high against his chest. 'See? It is you who are breathless.' He bent his head and kissed her mouth before she could turn away. 'What would you like to do now? Shall I take you back to your room for a rest?'

'Yes, please,' she said in a stifled voice. She kept her head turned away from him as he carried her back through the hall and along the corridor that led to his grandmother's room. He laid her on the bed, propped pillows behind her and bent until his lips rested on hers, light but sure, and very possessive. He raised his head to gaze down into her dark, wary eyes. 'I will come back for you later, when the sun is less fierce. We shall have tea together in the garden. I shall call Elsa now, and she will help you to bed.'

Georgia, helpless against the rock-solid wall of his assurance, hated the sensation, yet when he bent his head to kiss her again she couldn't resist him, and he knew it. She had to clench her hands to stop them locking round his neck. Luca raised his head at last, breathing raggedly, his eyes molten as they clashed with hers. He stood up slowly, his mouth curving in a smile of such intimacy that she flushed scarlet. 'Sleep,' he said, in the deep, caressing voice which was a seduction in itself, then he went swiftly from the room.

Sleep! Georgia sat upright and gingerly put one foot on the floor, then looked up in alarm as the door opened again. But it was Elsa who came in.

'Don't put weight on that foot,' scolded the house-keeper. 'Come. I shall help you to the bathroom, then you must rest.'

Later, cool in the exquisite satin nightgown, and tucked neatly beneath a fresh linen sheet, Georgia lay against the pillows feeling as though a lot more than a flight of steps had fallen on top of her.

Luca Valori wanted her, and was accustomed to victory in more ways than on the racing track, it was obvious. It was going to be very difficult to hold out against him. Mainly because every instinct yearned to give in. And he knew it. But it just wasn't possible. Luca was a dream lover. Unfortunately a dream lover of enough substance to make her almost forget James. She tried to conjure up James's fair, angular face, but it was blurred and indistinct, like an old photograph, quickly superimposed by the imperious features of Gianluca Valori.

Luca Valori's intentions, of course, had nothing to do with marriage or any other kind of commitment. And, to do him justice, he'd never tried to mislead her that they were. A love affair with Alessa's English teacher would be nothing more than a little diversion for him before he settled down to perpetuate the Valori dynasty with some suitable Tuscan beauty.

CHAPTER SEVEN

THE thought was surprisingly hard to bear, to the point of causing unwanted tears to slide down Georgia's cheeks. She scrubbed them away fiercely, assuring herself that they were perfectly natural—just the aftermath of the episode the night before. She thrust all thought of Luca away, and did her best to relax, but, although Elsa had closed the blinds firmly, to encourage sleep, it was some time before Georgia drifted at last into an uneasy doze.

She woke from it with a start to find someone bending over her, and uttered a cry which was stifled by a warm, seeking mouth that ignited a stab of involuntary response before she woke fully, panicking, and tried to push Luca away. He overcame her resistance with ease, as though he'd expected it and was having no nonsense with any opposition. She shivered as it dawned on her that he'd made his declaration of intent at lunch and now he was here to follow it up.

'Do not worry, *carissima*,' he said, the mixture of English and Italian strangely seductive in the deep, caressing voice. 'You are half-asleep still, so we shall use your language—until the time for talking is over.'

At this Georgia, very much awake, renewed her struggles in earnest, but he laughed, restraining her effortlessly.

'Stop it!' she panted. 'I meant what I said. I won't—you can't—'

'I can and I will,' he assured her, and returned his mouth to hers, stifling her protests with lips which caressed and cajoled as he drew her up into a powerful embrace, one arm holding her close while his free hand smoothed and soothed, running down her spine with a practised, delicate touch that she felt like a trickle of fire through the thin, borrowed silk. For a few throbbing, breathless moments Georgia yielded mindlessly to him, then from somewhere summoned up the fast-evaporating will to push him away.

'Elsa!' she choked.

Luca pushed her against the pillows, and lay down, his arms locked around her. 'Franco has driven Pina and Elsa into Lucca for the shopping,' he said in a voice hoarse with desire. 'We shall not be disturbed, *tesoro*.'

To her dismay Georgia found herself trembling violently, assailed by a mixture of so many emotions that it was hard to separate one from the other. 'I—can't—believe this!' she panted.

'That I desire you?' he whispered, and bent his head to touch his tongue to the places his hands laid bare. Hot darts of response shot through her, performing the double feat of turning her both liquid with desire and tense with fury at her own uncontrollable response.

'No—*aah.*' Her breath left her in a groan of anguish as his clever hands wrought such exquisite havoc that she could scarcely endure it. 'Luca, please—'

'Ah, *carissima*, you are so beautiful, so perfect in my arms—I want you so desperately; do not fight me!' His voice was so deep and husky with desire that it struck an answering chord deep inside her. She tried to ignore it, to protest, but Luca silenced her with his mouth and hands, caressing her to a fever pitch of response until she was overwhelmed by so great a tide of longing that when at last Luca took possession of her, with such ease and mastery, she gasped for an instant at the sudden, thrilling shock of it before the reality of what was happening revitalised her into frantic, futile opposition.

But it was too late. His superbly fit body was programmed for conquest and release, and all too soon Luca gasped in the climactic throes of the passion which rendered him blind and deaf to her entreaties.

Then it was over. Georgia pushed him away with hands that shook. Luca Valori sat up, still breathing hard, his colour high and his eyes glittering as they met the bitter resentment in hers. He slid from the bed, pulling on the clothes she'd never even noticed him take off. She averted her head, pulling the sheet up under her chin.

'*Carissima*—' he said urgently.

'Just go,' she said, in a voice so quietly bitter that he leaned over her and took her hand. She snatched it away, and dark colour rose in his face.

'We must talk,' he pressed. 'You are angry that this has happened, but I was so sure—'

'Sure of what?' she snapped.

'That you felt the same desire for me as I do for you,' he said simply, buttoning his shirt. 'Your words said no, but your body said yes. Admit it, Georgia. Because,' he added softly, his eyes meeting hers, 'it would not have been physically possible to take possession of you with such rapture if you had felt no desire for me.'

Georgia bit her lip in mortification. He was right, of course. She *had* wanted him. 'I just didn't think you'd really take advantage of the fact,' she said hoarsely. 'I wanted you to kiss me, and touch me, but not—not—'

She swallowed convulsively, her free hand to her head as the colour drained suddenly from her face.

Luca leapt to her side. *'Che cosa—?'*

'My head.' She thrust a hand into her tangled hair. 'Go away, please. *Now*!'

Georgia felt his hand on her hair and flinched away, heard him mutter a muffled oath. At last the door closed behind him, and she threw the sheet back and got out of bed, clutching at the bedpost for support. Hopping and limping in turn, she made it to the bathroom, turned on the hot water, then lay in it as hot as she could bear it, wishing that she could stay where she was for the foreseeable future.

When she struggled out at last, wrapped in a bath-towel, she hobbled to the doorway, then paused, bristling with hostility as she found Luca waiting for her, showered and immaculate in pale linen trousers and one of his inevitable blue shirts. Without a word he picked her up and carried her to the chaise longue at the foot of the bed.

'You took the bandage off,' he said, eyeing the bruised, swollen ankle.

'I had a very necessary bath,' she returned bitterly.

'I will send Elsa—'

'No!'

'Yes. She has returned.' His eyes met hers. 'When I left you Elsa was escorting my grandmother into the house. Nonna saw me leave this room and asked why I was there. It is her room when she stays here, you understand. Elsa explained about you. My grandmother demanded my reasons for being alone with you in your room, and drew her own conclusions. She was—not pleased.'

Georgia closed her eyes in despair. 'You didn't tell her what happened?'

'No. You think I am a fool?' Luca's mouth twisted. 'But of course—you do. I told her very little. But I fear she assumes much.'

She groaned in horror. 'Then I must leave at once.'

'You cannot!' he said fiercely. 'In your condition—'

'You ignored my *condition* earlier on!' Georgia flung at him. Luca flinched, then turned on his heel and strode from the room. A moment later Elsa came in with an armful of clothes, put them down on a chest, took one look at Georgia and folded her in a firm embrace.

'Cry,' she commanded.

Georgia, much heartened by this treatment, obeyed for a moment or two then found she didn't want to cry any more. Elsa smoothed the tumbled fair hair back from Georgia's face. 'Come. I am to help you dress, then you are to take tea in the conservatory with Signora Valori.'

'Oh, *no!*' Georgia shuddered, but knew that there was no way of avoiding the interview with Luca's grandmother.

She let Elsa bind her ankle again, then put on fresh underwear and the demure pink dress. She sat still meekly while her hair was brushed, then requested her handbag from the bedside table and made a few repairs to her face—to Elsa's disapproval.

'After such an experience why tire yourself with such things?'

'I need it to boost my morale,' said Georgia.

'Signora Valori is a very kind lady. You need not fear her.'

Georgia gave a wry smile. 'I'm not frightened. Just embarrassed. I wish I could run away and hide.'

Elsa made soothing noises, then went from the room to fetch Luca. He came quickly, grimly silent after a look at Georgia's cold, withdrawn face. He bent down and scooped her up in his arms and carried her, still in silence, to the conservatory where Emilia Valori sat enthroned behind a silver tray.

The elegant old lady stared in surprise as Luca carried his burden in and set her down on a chair by the table, then pulled out a stool for Georgia's foot. 'Nonna, this is the young lady engaged to give Alessa English lessons.'

'How do you do, *signora*?' said Georgia, flushing. 'I sprained my ankle.'

At the look on his grandmother's face Luca's handsome mouth compressed. 'She did so last night, in the accident I described to you, Nonna,' he said harshly. 'Not as a result of my attentions.'

'I am deeply relieved to hear it. Now present us properly, please.'

Georgia felt as though she was living through some surreal dream as Luca Valori presented her to his grandmother with formality, for all the world as though this were a tea-party where the two women had only just met.

'You speak our language well, Miss Fleming,' said Signora Valori, and gestured at the tray. 'Will you take tea or coffee?'

'She is forbidden coffee,' put in Luca.

'I'd love some coffee,' Georgia said flatly, ignoring him, and the other woman smiled and filled a cup with strong black liquid, then, without consulting Georgia, added a spoonful of sugar.

'It will do you good,' she said firmly, and fixed her tall, grim grandson with a look. 'I think it best if you leave us, Luca.'

'Nonna—' he began urgently, but the small, elegantly dressed head shook in refusal.

'You are in no position to object.'

Luca paused in front of Georgia. 'This is not my idea, you understand.'

She looked up at him in frozen silence, and with the usual lift of his shoulder he gave a brief, unsmiling bow to each lady and strode out into the garden.

'And now he will drive that dangerous machine along the *autostrada* and try to channel all his anger and shame into speed.' Signora Valori shook her head, and fixed Georgia with a commanding blue eye. 'Now then, Miss Fleming, I met my grandson emerging from the room you are occupying since your accident. No one was in the house at the time, so, tell me, did you invite him there?'

'No, I did not,' said Georgia expressionlessly.

Signora Valori eyed Georgia thoughtfully. 'Tell me, did you give Gianluca cause to believe his advances might be welcome?'

It took a moment or two for her meaning to sink in. Georgia's chin lifted. 'If you mean was I attracted to your grandson, then the answer is yes.' She sighed deeply. 'After my fall my common sense deserted me, I admit. We were both shocked and—and upset by the accident, and we exchanged a few kisses. If that is what you mean by encouragement, then I suppose I am partly to blame. He was quite frank about wanting—wanting to be my lover.' She bit her lip miserably. 'I made the mistake of saying that it was impossible, never dreaming that he'd take it as a challenge. That it would lead to what happened just now.'

'Then he did make love to you,' said Signora Valori quietly.

Georgia stared at her in dismay. 'Didn't he tell you that?'

'No. He refused to give his reasons for being in your room. You have merely confirmed my suspicions.' The old lady sighed. 'So, Miss Fleming, may I ask what you want from Gianluca by way of reparation?'

'Nothing whatsoever—thank you,' added Georgia belatedly. 'Unless you could persuade him to move out of the Villa Toscana until I leave for England.'

'I am sure that could be arranged.' Signora Valori frowned. 'But when you have time to think, my dear, you may find you need more than that.'

Georgia put down her coffee-cup with a hand which shook.

'Forgive me,' went on her inquisitor relentlessly, 'but may I ask how old you are, Miss Fleming? Were you a virgin before meeting with Luca?'

'I'm twenty-six,' said Georgia, and smiled bitterly. 'And this was not, as you so rightly suspect, my first experience of—of sex. I am virtually engaged to James Astin, who is a captain in the British Army. I've been in no hurry to marry him, because I wanted a career of my own before settling down to be an army wife.'

'And in the meantime you met my grandson.' The old lady sighed. 'Did Luca know you were not indifferent to him?'

'Yes.' Georgia flushed. 'He knew. But I told him that

any relationship of the kind he wanted was out of the question.'

'Why?' asked Signora Valori.

Georgia stared at her blankly. 'I would have thought that was obvious. I won't lie to you. I was deeply tempted. But I couldn't throw away the prospect of a perfectly suitable marriage just because Gianluca Valori wanted me for a—a playmate for a while. Also I have a job at a school near Venice. The principal is a strict lady. She would probably dispense with my services if she knew I was mad enough to have an affair with any man during my employment—let alone a man idolised nationwide for his exploits on the Grand Prix circuit.'

'I see,' said the other woman thoughtfully, her slim black brows drawn together below her coiled white hair. 'And are you wondering if such a fiasco could have consequences?'

Georgia nodded miserably, and Signora Valori raised a shoulder in a familiar mannerism.

'Who knows? Nature can be very cruel, bestowing children on those who do not wish for them and depriving others who want them desperately. But I trust,' she added with emphasis, 'that if a child should result from Luca's attentions you will inform him.'

Panic rose in Georgia at the mere thought of it. She didn't want a child. Not now, not like this. 'There's probably no cause for concern,' she said firmly, then smiled at Signora Valori. 'I'm sure you'll be interested to learn how well Alessa's doing with her English.'

'By which I am to take it the subject is closed,' said the old lady wryly. 'Very well, Miss Georgia Fleming, we shall say no more. For the moment.' She opened a small handbag and took out a card to hand to Georgia.

'Here is my telephone number and address. Contact me at any time. Should you need to.'

She sighed heavily. 'Incidentally, my dear, believe it best for all concerned if Marco knows nothing of this afternoon's incident. He cannot remedy it, and he is very attached to Luca. It would merely add to his burden of grief over my Maddalena.' For a moment the autocratic little face looked old and weary. 'Do you agree?'

'Wholeheartedly,' Georgia assured her.

Emilia Valori nodded in approval, sat even more erect, and gave Georgia a determined smile. 'Now I shall do as you so obviously want, and discuss my great-granddaughter. Is she as clever as Marco believes?'

There was much activity in the villa that evening as Elsa prepared a special dinner in honour of Signora Valori, served earlier than usual so that Alessa could stay up for it.

'I had not meant to remain here longer than an hour or so,' the old lady told Georgia, 'because I am *en route* to Siena to stay with my sister. However, I think it best I stay to see Alessa. Also I would like another word with Luca. I have rung Vittoria to explain and will arrive in Siena after dinner instead of before.'

'I'm glad,' said Georgia gratefully. 'Will *you* ask Luca not to tell Signor Sardi about—about this afternoon?'

'At first I thought to give him orders on the subject.' The blue eyes twinkled. 'But I will make it a request. Luca does not take orders kindly. Will you ring the bell for Pina, my dear? I have something you may find very useful for a day or two.'

Pina was sent to ask Signora Valori's chauffeur for the spare ebony walking stick always kept in the car.

'Thank you,' said Georgia with fervour. 'Now I shan't feel so helpless.'

When she returned to the ground-floor room Georgia found that the bed had been stripped and remade, even to a fresh counterpane. Her clothes had been brought downstairs and hung in the wardrobe, and after the rest recommended by Signora Valori she changed into the black dress worn for her first night.

The effect was somewhat marred by wearing only one black linen pump, but Georgia shrugged philo-sophically, made up her face with great care, then gin-gerly brushed her hair into a smooth, shining coil which she secured with an onyx and gilt clasp. As she laid down the brush she heard cars drive up and then Alessa shouting 'Bisnonna!' at the top of her voice as she rushed to the conservatory to greet her great-grand-mother.

Georgia threaded her pearl drops through her ears, then stiffened as she heard a tap on the door. But it was Pina who put a head round it, smiling shyly.

'Signor Luca is asking when you wish to be carried to dinner, Signorina.'

So Luca was back.

Georgia flourished the ebony stick, smiling brightly. 'Tell him I can manage on my own now, thank you, Pina.'

Determined to suffer the tortures of the damned rather than accept help from Luca, Georgia limped slowly across the hall, leaning heavily on the stick, her teeth sunk in her bottom lip with effort as she negotiated the gleaming wood floor.

'*Stupidità*!' said a voice roughly, and without ceremony Luca tossed the stick on a long crimson sofa and scooped her up in his arms. 'You are prepared to risk further damage to your ankle rather than let me help you?' he demanded, glaring into her stormy eyes.

'Yes,' she snapped.

'We need to talk,' he stated grimly as he strode with her along the passageway to the conservatory.

'No, we don't. There's nothing to be said.' She turned her head away, then all further private conversation was suspended as Alessa came running to meet them, her face blazing with excitement because she was allowed to stay up to dinner.

'Are you better, Georgia?' she asked anxiously as Luca set his unwilling burden down on a chair near Signora Valori.

'Darling, I'm fine. It's just this silly foot. I'll be running around as fast as you in a day or two.' Georgia kissed the flushed little cheek, then gave a belated greeting to Signora Valori and Marco Sardi.

'Did you enjoy the peace and quiet this afternoon?' asked Marco kindly.

'Yes, indeed,' said Georgia in a strangled tone, and bent to examine her foot in embarrassment.

'Give her some champagne, Luca,' said his grandmother quickly. 'It is my weakness,' she added as Georgia straightened. 'I allow myself one glass a week. Tonight I may even have two.'

'Is this a celebration of some kind, Emilia?' asked Marco, amused.

'It's not often you have an English guest,' she returned blandly, and smiled at Georgia. 'We spent a very interesting afternoon together.'

'So your peace and quiet was short-lived,' he said to Georgia, who was beginning to wish she'd stayed in her room.

Fortunately the presence of Alessa prevented any lasting awkwardness, since she sat on Luca's knee and gave him a blow-by-blow account of her visit to her cousins, boasting of their amazement at her prowess in their swimming pool.

'You have done well, Georgia,' said Signora Valori in an undertone. 'Alessa is a different child.'

Luca glanced up sharply at the hint of familiarity between the two women, and Georgia turned her head away quickly, stiff with resentment at the mere sight of those brilliant blue eyes.

'Are you sure you feel well?' asked Marco, frowning. 'You look very flushed, Georgia.'

She smiled brightly. 'It's the champagne.'

Georgia was seated between Marco Sardi and Alessa at dinner, with Luca opposite, beside his grandmother. Each time she looked up she found his eyes trained on her, and to avoid them she engrossed herself in Alessa's account of her day, which had included impressing her cousins with the tale of her adventure in the storm.

'I told them I cried and cried when the stairs fell on you,' said Alessa, too excited to eat more than a few mouthfuls of the food put in front of her.

'It is lucky Georgia has only a sprained ankle,' said Luca abrasively. 'I had no idea those stairs were so unsafe.'

'It was always my intention to have them repaired,'

said Marco remorsefully. 'But lately—' He broke off, shrugging, and Signora Valori smiled at him kindly.

'Luckily there was no harm done, Marco.'

Georgia glared at Luca for adding to the lines on Marco Sardi's face. 'It was my fault for forgetting the doll,' she said with emphasis.

Luca said very little from that point on—something which, by his puzzled look, Marco Sardi was very much aware of as he noted the tension on his brother-in-law's handsome face. It was left to Signora Valori to keep the conversation flowing, and only Alessa commented on her uncle's silence.

'Are you all right, Luca?' she asked anxiously, and he smiled with genuine warmth at his niece, his eyes tender.

'I am very well, thank you, my darling,' he assured her. 'And, because Georgia has hurt her foot, tomorrow *I* shall take you swimming in the pool.'

Alessa was so pleased with this promise that she made no objection when Pina came to collect her to put her to bed. She bestowed kisses on everyone, asked her great-grandmother to come again soon, then went off with the maid, leaving the others to their coffee.

'In a few minutes I must leave,' said Signora Valori, looking suddenly weary. 'It is quite wonderful to see Alessa so animated and cheerful again, Marco.'

He nodded gravely. 'I am grateful to Georgia. She has been very good for my little one.'

'Alessa will miss her,' agreed the old lady, getting to her feet.

'We shall all miss her,' said Luca as he leapt to assist her.

'Then perhaps she will stay a little longer, if everyone

is very kind to her,' said Emilia Valori with significance. She bent over Georgia and kissed her on both cheeks. 'Goodbye, my dear. Remember what I said.'

Georgia was left alone at the table, feeling suddenly weary and homesick and in great need of her mother. Her ankle throbbed in unison with the bump on her head, and she looked up in appeal as Elsa came to clear away.

'What is it?' said the woman quickly. 'Do you need the bathroom?'

'I need to go to bed,' said Georgia thickly. 'Could you fetch my stick, please, Elsa?'

'Of course, of course. I shall help you—and tell Signor Sardi you were tired.'

In minutes Georgia was lying in the wide, cool bed, propped up on pillows with her hair brushed loose, a tray with tea and cold drinks beside her and a book in her lap. Released from the effort to smile and make conversation, slowly she began to relax, to put the events of the day into perspective. It was, she decided, impossible to erase the episode with Luca from her mind. She would go over it dispassionately instead, rather than let it assume nightmare proportions in some locked mental compartment.

For the first time Georgia let herself dwell on what had happened, to view the episode with Luca objectively. Because, although Luca had taken her by surprise, at a time when she was half-asleep and in a vulnerable state after the accident, it was useless to deny her ultimate response to him—a response she'd never felt before, certainly not on the relatively few occasions that she'd shared a bed with James, she realised, depressed.

What made one man's lovemaking so different from another's? Chemistry, presumably. But the biggest surprise had been her utter helplessness against the driving force of a man determined to be her lover. It showed very graphically how lucky she'd been never to have run up against it before.

Admittedly the sprained ankle had been a contributing factor in her lack of defence. But there was more to it than that. In Luca's arms she'd experienced rapture as well as resentment at male domination and his utter confidence in her willingness. And, she thought wearily, she'd learned something else too. Even if she never laid eyes on Gianluca Valori in her life again, marriage with James was no longer possible.

The realisation banished sleep altogether. Despite her headache and deep reluctance for the task, she forced herself to write to James immediately to tell him so. The letter took a long time, with a lot of discarded notepaper before she finally made it clear to James, as tactfully and gently as possible, that she could never be his wife.

Utterly exhausted afterwards, feeling like a murderer, Georgia picked up her book and tried to read, half her attention on the sounds of a household retiring to bed. Elsa and Pina, she knew, retired early on Saturday nights to go to church early on Sunday mornings. Luca's whereabouts she refused to dwell on.

After another hobbling, painful trip to the bathroom Georgia returned to bed, to read again in an attempt to woo sleep, but it was impossible. Guilt over James, not least because she kept thinking of Luca instead, kept her wide awake. Would Luca leave the villa as she'd asked? He must have another home somewhere, because it was obvious that he'd only moved into the Villa Toscana after his sister died. If it weren't for Alessa, of course, the simplest solution would be to leave the villa herself. She thought about it at length, but couldn't bear the thought of hurting Alessa by leaving earlier than arranged. As it was, the parting would be hard enough when the time came.

It was an hour after midnight when Georgia stretched out her hand to turn off the lamp, then froze as she saw the door open. She held her breath, her heart hammering as Luca came into the room and shut the door noiselessly behind him.

CHAPTER EIGHT

'I WILL not harm you further, I swear,' said Luca harshly. 'But I must talk to you.'

Georgia gave him a hostile stare. 'Then please speak English. I'm too tired to struggle with a foreign language tonight. Besides, there's nothing to say.'

His jaw tightened. 'There is much to say,' he replied, switching to English, his accent marked as he searched for the right words. 'I begin by expressing my regret for what happened. It was a mistake.'

'A *mistake*?' she said, incensed.

He shrugged impatiently. 'If you insist on English I may not use the right words. Yes, it was a mistake. But you must understand—you possess for me something I have not met before in a woman. It drove me to madness today. Perhaps the accident last night sent me crazy. Suddenly it was agony to think of you with this James of yours—Tom Hannay also. I wanted—*needed*—to show you what love could be like between you and me, that I could make you forget both of them in my arms. And when you yielded to my kisses so—so ravishingly I thought—I believed—'

'I would welcome you into my bed with open arms once everyone was out of the way today,' she said brutally, and had the satisfaction of seeing dark colour rush into his face.

Luca turned away, but only to fetch a chair. 'You permit?' he said formally, and at her shrug of indiffer-

ence seated himself as if prepared for a long discussion.
'I know that in your country customs are different,' he
began slowly. 'Your religion, certain attitudes—'

'Towards sex, you mean,' she said without emotion.
'You thought that because I'm twenty-six years old,
with a reasonable face and figure, and independent
enough to take a job in a foreign country, I was sure to
have a string of lovers as well as James. One more, you
thought, would make very little difference.'

'That is not true,' he said hotly, and leaned forward,
his eyes blazing into hers. 'I believed only one lover,
though I also suspected your *cognato*, this Tom Hannay.
I desired to make you forget all men but me. It was not
my intention to—' He stopped, and breathed in deeply.
'Please believe me, Georgia! I wanted you badly. *Dio*,
I still do. You had kissed me, here in this room after
the accident; I held you in my arms and you responded
to me; my need for you was like fire in my blood. I
thought—'

'In Grand Prix terms you thought you were in pole
position,' she said scathingly, and turned her head on
the pillow wearily. 'It's all right, Gianluca Valori. I ab-
solve you of guilt. After the accident I suppose I wasn't
quite sane myself. You took me by surprise when you
kissed me here last night.' Georgia turned back to him
with a sardonic little smile. 'But it never occurred to
me that you'd actually follow the kisses up right here
under your brother-in-law's roof. Heavens above, Luca,
I've got a sprained ankle, a bump on my head *and* I'm
in your grandmother's bed.'

'I know, I know,' he threw back at her, scowling
blackly. He raked a hand through his thick dark hair.
'But last night I thought at first you were dead. Then I

found you were not.' He drew in a deep, unsteady breath, his eyes brilliant as they locked with hers. 'From the moment I first saw you on the plane I desired you, then today, to have you helpless in my arms—' He shrugged morosely. 'I lost my head.'

'Don't worry, I shan't sue,' she said bleakly.

'Sue? What is that?'

Georgia thought for a moment. *'Citare in giudizio?'*

'You have no need for the law!' he retorted, and sprang to his feet, his face dark with offence. 'I am a Valori. We pay our debts. Tell me what you want of me and it is yours.'

She looked at him in silence, then smiled faintly. 'Anything?'

Luca Valori stood like a man facing a firing-squad. 'Anything.'

'Then I think I have the right to demand—' Georgia paused tantalisingly, enjoying the tension in his face '—your absence.'

He looked thunderstruck. *'Cosa?'*

'Your absence,' she repeated patiently. 'I want you to leave the Villa Toscana and stay away until I go home in three weeks' time. You can visit Alessa on my days off,' she added. 'Elsa can ring you to let you know when I go out.'

'But Alessa wants me here. You will not be so cruel to the child,' he added, with such triumph that Georgia could have hit him.

'With me here she won't mind so much. And you did say "anything",' she reminded him. 'Are you going back on your word?'

'No, I am not!' Gianluca Valori gave her a fulminating look and strode to the door. He opened it, then turned to look at her. 'My grandmother told me you wanted me to go, but I did not believe her. She told me I was fortunate. That some women would be demanding money, or, worse, even marriage, in the circumstances.'

'I've already got a bridegroom, just waiting for me to name the day,' Georgia said, fingers crossed under the sheet. That once James received her letter this would no longer be true was nothing at all to do with Luca.

'So?' He smiled sceptically. 'If *I* proposed marriage I think you might send this soldier of yours away.'

Georgia went white with rage. 'You can think what you like! Nevertheless, I don't want you for a husband, nor do I want any money from you. I can earn my own. So goodbye.'

'Goodbye?' He stared at her incredulously. 'You mean this?'

'Yes.'

He came back to the bed, looking down at her flushed face, at the mass of fair, tumbled hair, and suddenly his eyes flamed. Before she realised his intention he reached down and pulled her up into his arms, his mouth bruising hers with a punitive, angry kiss. Georgia lay limp against him. Instinct told her that resistance was unwise. If she fought, Luca might decide to carry on where he'd left off, and one way and another that would be a very bad idea.

'No,' he said harshly, reading her mind. 'I will not add to my crime. But if this is goodbye I will make sure you remember me.'

He bent his head and kissed her again, but this time with such passionate enticement that she failed to control a shiver of response, and he caught her close against him in the crook of one arm while his free hand slid over the satin covering her breasts. She gasped and he made a smothered sound deep in his throat, his kiss deepening until her senses reeled and she would have given her soul to throw her arms round his neck and repeat the experience of the afternoon. But pride and sanity kept her rigid in his embrace, and after a moment Luca laid her against the pillows, his breathing hurried as he straightened to stare down at her.

'Very well, English teacher. I will go tomorrow. It goes hard with me to submit so tamely. But I gave my word.' He waited for a moment, then, when she said nothing, he lifted a shoulder in his usual, negligent shrug and strode from the room.

Next morning Pina arrived alone with the breakfast tray, to report that Alessa would be in later. She was break-fasting with her father and uncle, because Signor Luca was going away for a while.

'Really?' said Georgia lightly. 'A business trip?'

'No, miss. He is going to his house. Some building repairs are needed there.'

'Oh.' Georgia fought with her curiosity and lost. 'Where does he live?'

'In the hills a few kilometres from here.' Pina poured tea, then began tidying the room. 'The house was a farm once. Signor Luca has done a lot of work on it.'

Georgia asked no more questions, much as she'd have liked to, and when Alessa came running to see her she had managed to shower and dress and was ready to hobble to the conservatory with the aid of her stick. Marco Sardi was waiting for her to enquire how she was, and Georgia assured him that she was almost fully recovered.

'Even so, do not overdo things today,' he advised. 'Dr Fassi will call this afternoon. By the way,' he added, 'Luca sends his good wishes for your recovery, but he will be away for a time. His house needs attention, he says.'

'So Pina told me.' Georgia sat down on a sofa, smiling gratefully as Alessa rushed to place a stool under the injured foot. 'Thank you, darling.'

'I will look after Georgia, Papa,' she assured her father. 'And I will be very good.'

Marco Sardi laughed indulgently, and kissed his child lovingly. 'Then I may go to Valorino with a light heart!'

Having demanded Luca's absence, Georgia found that she missed him quite desperately. Without his company to look forward to in the evenings life was suddenly flat. Her main consolation was the rapid improvement in her ankle. By the end of the week she was walking without a stick, but the doctor advised against a return to her old room, saying improvement would be swifter without several trips a day up two flights of stairs.

Georgia was sorry. To remain in the bed where Luca had held her naked in his arms was no help in putting the incident from her mind. And to her deep dismay she went on missing him more and more as each day passed. Marco Sardi came home each night, scrupulously passing on good wishes for her health from Luca, and Georgia accepted them politely, hoping that he couldn't tell that the very mention of Luca's name made her pulse race and her appetite decrease.

Since Marco Sardi seemed to eat less and less each day, and Georgia was little better, Elsa became quite voluble on the subject and demanded to know if there was something wrong with her cooking. Assured that her food was superlative, as always, she confided to Georgia next day that the master was worrying her.

'He is still grieving,' she said darkly. 'Without the *signora* he is like a lost soul. Only Alessa keeps him alive, I think.'

Even allowing for a touch of Latin drama, Georgia could see that Elsa had good cause for worry, and assured her employer that she was quite happy to remain at the villa over the weekend if he needed rest instead of spending the time with Alessa.

'No, my dear. Certainly not. You must go on your postponed trip to Florence. I enjoy time spent with my daughter; also Luca is joining us for lunch. You can leave us alone with a clear conscience.' His eyes twinkled. 'When you go for good we shall have to manage without you, remember.'

'Yes, of course,' she said automatically, her enthusiasm for Florence diminished by the prospect of missing Luca.

'Georgia,' he went on, stirring sugar into his coffee. 'You would tell me if there was something wrong, I hope.'

She looked at him, startled. 'Wrong?'

He shrugged. 'You eat less than I these days, and Luca is irritable and withdrawn and working like a man possessed at the *fabbrica*. I have no wish to intrude on your private concerns, but while you are under my roof I naturally feel responsible for your welfare. I know Luca is attracted to you. Then suddenly he says he must go. That his house needs his attention. I do not believe it. I think you had a quarrel. And if you have been offended in any way I wish to know.'

'There's nothing wrong, I assure you,' said Georgia, feeling utterly wretched at the lie. 'And my lack of appetite stems from lack of exercise. I'm now good as new and shortly I'll be eating like a horse again.'

Marco Sardi looked unconvinced. 'Very well, my dear. If you say so. Now let us talk of arrangements for tomorrow. Unfortunately Franco needs the car. But he will take you to the station and you can go by train to Florence. Then either he or I will pick you up again when you return.'

'I'd prefer that,' said Georgia truthfully. 'Dr Fassi advised against driving for another week, so the train will be fine. I've got maps and a guidebook, so Florence, here I come!'

Georgia was up at the crack of dawn next day, bade an affectionate farewell to a sleepy Alessa, then went off with Franco to catch the train to Florence in the gold heat haze of a Tuscan summer morning.

She enjoyed the journey and got off the train at Stazione Santa Maria Novella in Florence. Guidebook in hand, she hurried off among the other passengers, but slowed down as she reached the tempting windows of expensive shops set in the Renaissance buildings and *palazzi* of the Via Tornabuoni. Then, after consultation with her map, she made her way to the great Piazza della Signoria, and the Uffizi, the treasure house of Florentine Renaissance art. Though here in Florence, thought Georgia as she joined the queue waiting to get in, she really should think of it as the Rinascimento, since she was in the place where it all began.

Surrounded by tourists and students talking every language under the sun, Georgia waited patiently, watching the waiters who moved among the tables in the outdoor restaurants. She would have dearly liked a cappuccino, but not enough to yield her place in a line which was already snaking in a double row as the time to open approached.

At last Georgia paid her lire and ascended the great stone Vasari staircase to the gallery where the paintings, she found, were arranged by centuries, so that the art lover could feed on a banquet of art laid out in strict chronological order from the thirteenth to the eighteenth century.

If the outing had been planned as a welcome diversion to take her mind off Luca Valori, it failed. As Georgia moved from one famous painting to another she found her delight in the visual feast marred by a quite violent longing to have him beside her to share it. She had managed to persuade herself these past few days that she'd done rather well in expelling him from her life. It was daunting to find herself so wrong.

But her depression lifted gradually as Georgia, daughter of a surveyor, gazed on paintings which displayed the Renaissance skill and fascination with perspective. And the exquisite paganism of the maidens in Botticelli's *Primavera*, when she managed to find space enough in the crowd to gaze at them, was just as enchanting as she'd expected.

It was a couple of hours later, feeling almost dazed by such an overdose of visual pleasure, that Georgia emerged from the gallery near the Loggia dei Lanzi, and managed to find a free table in a crowded outdoor café. She ordered a much needed cappuccino and a pastry, and settled down to write the postcards she'd bought in the Uffizi, deeply remorseful at posting James her goodbye letter instead of the views of Florence sent to her parents and Charlotte and Tom.

She sighed and ordered another cappuccino then went off to tackle the wait to get into the Bargello, which her guidebook stated had once been the prison where the bell tolled for every execution. These days, she read, it was to sculpture what the Uffizi was to paintings.

Georgia paid her bill, then threaded her way through the crowd, past the great square fortress of the Palazzo Vecchio with its high off-centre tower, and with the aid of her map quickly reached the Bargello to see the great achievements of Michelangelo and Donatello, who'd lived to be eighty, she read as she waited in line, and was never short of commissions. When Georgia finally saw the latter's long-haired *David* in bronze in the Great Hall on the first floor she could see why.

The Bargello was about to close by the time she'd paid the various works of Michelangelo and his contemporaries the necessary respect. Her ankle had begun to throb, her head ached a little, and Georgia decided to skip lunch and call it a day.

She caught a train back as soon as she got to the station, and abandoned any idea of ringing Franco to fetch her, as arranged. She was much earlier than intended, and Franco might not even be there, which might force Marco Sardi to collect her. For once, she thought, yawning in the crowded train, she would forget the expense and take a taxi from Lucca to the villa.

When Georgia finally arrived at the house she found it in uproar. Alessa came running to her and flung herself into Georgia's arms, crying bitterly, followed by a distraught Pina.

'It is the master,' said Pina, red-eyed. 'He has been taken ill. Signor Luca has driven him to the hospital.'

'Hospital?' asked Georgia, going cold. Her arms tightened round Alessa. 'There, there, darling, don't cry so hard.'

'Papa's ill!' sobbed Alessa, and looked up at Georgia in appeal. 'Will he go to heaven like Mamma?'

'Of course not, darling,' said Georgia firmly, devoutly hoping that she was right.

'But Papa had a pain and Dr Fassi said he must go to the hospital so they could make the pain go away.' The child burrowed her head into Georgia's shoulder. 'Dr Fassi made your pain go away here, at home!'

'I think you should let Pina wash your face, while I go and talk to Elsa,' said Georgia lovingly. 'Then perhaps you and I could have tea together in the conservatory, darling.'

With utmost reluctance Alessa went upstairs with Pina while Georgia raced to the kitchen to talk with Elsa.

'It looked like a heart attack,' said the housekeeper, confirming Georgia's worst fears. She sighed, her face lined with worry. 'Thank the good Lord you came back early. Fortunately Signor Luca was here and took charge.'

'I should have been here,' said Georgia wretchedly. 'I could have gone to Florence any time. Signor Sardi insisted I took time off, but—'

'My dear, you're here now.' Elsa managed a smile as Alessa came back with Pina. 'Now you shall have some tea—perhaps something to eat. Are you hungry?'

Georgia shook her head and put an arm round the

little girl. 'Just some tea, and perhaps some of your delicious biscuits, Elsa. Come on, darling.'

As soon as they reached the conservatory Alessa climbed onto Georgia's lap. 'I want to see Papa,' she said forlornly.

'The moment the doctor says you can, you shall,' promised Georgia, and coaxed her to eat some of the biscuits that Elsa brought in herself with the tea, Pina following close behind.

'It is good you are back,' said Elsa, watching the child relax in Georgia's arms.

'I'll move back upstairs, next to Alessa,' said Georgia with decision, and Pina hurried off to move Georgia's belongings, plainly glad to have occupation.

Alessa, worn out with tears and shock, was already half-asleep against Georgia's shoulder as Elsa confided in an undertone that she had been worried about the master for some time.

'So have I,' agreed Georgia softly, smoothing the child's ruffled dark curls. 'He's eaten very little for the past week or two.'

Elsa nodded, looking worried. 'Thank God Luca was here. He is a tower of strength in emergency.' She gave Georgia a wry little smile. 'The only time I've seen him lose his head was the night he came in with you unconscious in his arms.'

Georgia flushed, but met the woman's eyes squarely. 'He will move back here now, of course.'

Elsa nodded. 'He has no choice. Alessa needs him.'

So do I, thought Georgia. 'Elsa,' she said quickly, 'does Signora Valori know?'

The woman shook her head. 'She is old. Signor Luca thought it best to wait a little until—'

'Until you have better news to give her,' said Georgia firmly, shifting the sleeping child more comfortably on her lap.

Elsa nodded, brightening. 'True. Now I shall take away the tray and make a start on dinner.'

Alessa slept for a while, then woke with a start. The relief on her face when she found herself with Georgia was deeply moving, and won her a hug and a kiss.

'Papa?' said the child hopefully.

'No news yet, poppet,' said Georgia, getting to her feet. She held out her hand to the child. 'Come on, let's find Pina and get you bathed and in your nightgown. Then I'll read to you, and as a treat maybe you can have a snack in bed for once.'

The programme met with tearful approval and Alessa went off with Georgia obediently, calling for Pina as they went through the hall. Bathtime was as protracted and time-consuming as Georgia could make it, made joyful in the end when a panting Elsa burst in, beaming all over her face.

'Signor Luca has telephoned to say your Papa is better, little one. He sends his love and tells you to be a good girl.'

The joy on Alessa's face was so radiant that Georgia had to swallow hard.

'Now I am hungry!' announced Alessa, and Elsa took Pina off at once, promising to send her up with a special supper by way of celebration.

It was after nine by the time Alessa was sleeping peacefully and Georgia felt free to take a swift bath. Surprised to realise that she was hungry too, she brushed her hair dry as quickly as possible, dressed swiftly in the almond-pink dress and went to check on

Alessa. By the light of a small lamp she found the child fast asleep and Pina dozing in a chair beside the bed. Relieved, she went downstairs to find Elsa crossing the hall.

'I will bring dinner to the conservatory in a few minutes,' said the woman, plainly in a hurry to get back to the kitchen, and Georgia, armed with a book, went along the corridor to the conservatory, happy to read for a while until the meal arrived.

But Luca Valori had arrived before her. He rose to his feet, elegant as always, but his face weary below hair still damp from a shower.

'Elsa tells me you know I must stay here while Marco is in hospital,' he said without preliminaries. 'I have no choice.'

'But of course!' Georgia bit her lip. 'I had no right to ask you to go. Not that any of that is the least important now. How is Signor Sardi?'

Luca pulled out a chair for her and resumed his own. 'He is better. It was not a heart attack, as we all feared. He was in great pain, but it was due to what the consultant in Pisa diagnosed as an inflamed gullet, not a problem with his heart.'

Georgia let out a great sigh of relief. 'Thank heavens! I know all about that, as it happens. My father suffered from it a year or so back before he retired. It's the preliminary stage to—to—' She searched for the word and Luca smiled.

'Ulcers,' he supplied. 'Brought on by stress, of which Marco has had more than his share since Maddalena died.'

Georgia gave him a smile of such radiant relief that his eyes lit in swift response.

'He was obliged to swallow a camera!' he said, grimacing, and Georgia nodded.

'I don't know what you call it, but in English it's an endoscopy. My father had that done. It highlights the problem and shows it up on a television screen. In Dad's case it meant a careful diet and a course of pills and medicine, and now, unless he's careless, he has no problem at all.'

'Good. I trust it will be the same for Marco—' Luca leapt to his feet suddenly. 'Forgive me, I did not offer you a drink. I thought we might celebrate with champagne.'

'I ought to eat something before I have a drink,' said Georgia apologetically. 'Since breakfast two cappuccinos are all I've had all day except some tea when I came home.'

Luca gave her a sharp look, then smiled slowly. 'I'm glad.'

'That I haven't eaten anything?'

He shook his head. 'That you can think of the Villa Toscana as home—in the circumstances.'

CHAPTER NINE

OVER dinner that night Georgia did her best to keep the atmosphere light, and in the main Luca co-operated. In their mutual relief that Marco Sardi's illness was not a heart attack after all, they ate an excellent dinner of Elsa's famed *bistecca fiorentina,* accompanied by a Chianti Classico of such excellence that Georgia rashly cast caution to the winds and drank two glasses of it as well as the celebratory glass of vintage champagne.

During the meal they discussed the paintings and sculpture that Georgia had seen earlier, the redecoration in train at Luca's house in the hills and the new orders crowding in for the Supremo, talking together like two civilised people as though the incident in the ground-floor bedroom had never happened.

As they drank coffee together later Luca smiled at Georgia teasingly.

'So you have been to Florence without seeing Michelangelo's *David*!'

Georgia nodded ruefully. 'I left him for the crowning touch to the day, but after the visit to the Bargello I was tired and my ankle hurt, so I caught the next train back instead.'

'It must have been a shock to arrive home to the news of Marco.'

'It was.' She shivered. 'Poor little Alessa was in a terrible state, convinced he was going to die like her mamma.'

He stared into his cup, his eyes sombre. 'He was in such pain that I confess I shared her fears.' He looked up with a smile. 'They were unfounded, thank God, and we can all sleep in peace tonight.'

Georgia nodded. 'And I shall hear if Alessa wakes.'

'Then you have moved back to the room next to hers,' he said, with a scowl.

'Yes.'

'You could not bear to stay in the other one?'

She eyed his averted profile with hostility. 'Nothing of the sort. On Dr Fassi's advice I did stay there until today. But I thought I'd sleep near Alessa in the circumstances, in case she might need me in the night.'

'It is a coincidence, then, that you moved once you knew I was coming back to the villa to stay?'

'Entirely.'

He lifted a sardonic eyebrow, and thrust out his cup for more coffee.

Georgia refilled it with a commendably steady hand. 'Should you drink so much coffee late at night?'

'I sleep badly lately whether I drink coffee or not,' he said with sudden violence, and drained the cup.

Georgia rose to her feet hurriedly. 'It's late—time I went to bed. Goodnight. I'm glad Signor Sardi is not in danger.'

Luca stood up, looking down at her broodingly. 'I shall take Alessa to Pisa to visit him tomorrow. Take advantage of her absence and rest, Georgia. You look tired.'

'It's been quite a day,' she returned lightly.

'Very true.' He gave her a formal little bow. 'Goodnight. I think it best I deny myself the pleasure of escorting you to your room.'

She bit her lip, then on impulse held out her hand. 'Luca, couldn't we forget everything that happened before today? Go on from here as—as friends for the rest of my stay, for Alessa's sake?'

He lifted her hand to his lips and kissed it. 'Very well, Georgia. If that is what you wish.' He smiled into her eyes. 'Only a fool would refuse friendship offered by a beautiful woman. And I may be many things but I am not a fool.' His mouth twisted. 'Except on a certain recent occasion, of course.'

Georgia withdrew her hand. 'I repeat, Luca, let's forget all that. Goodnight.'

Next morning Luca was waiting at the breakfast table when Georgia arrived with Alessa. He brought a beaming smile to the child's face by telling her that he'd rung the hospital, that Papa was much better and looking forward to her visit that afternoon.

Alessa was so overjoyed that the meal was a very happy one, with no constraint possible between the two adults as the child chattered nineteen to the dozen. Later all three of them spent time in the pool, and afterwards shared a cold lunch in the garden.

'Luca says you must rest while we are away this afternoon,' ordered Alessa, and Georgia smiled.

'Then of course I will,' she said demurely, and Luca laughed.

'Because you feel inclined to do so, no doubt, not from any obedience to my wishes!'

'You understand me very well,' she said as Alessa went off with Pina to tidy herself for the outing.

'If only that were true!'

'I'm a very uncomplicated person.'

'So am I.'

'In that case life should be peaceful for the rest of my stay.'

'It is a possibility, of course.' Luca smiled. 'But I think you should know that I meant every word, Georgia.'

She fixed him with a dark, suspicious gaze. 'Which word in particular?'

'I am merely making it clear that although I have agreed to this friendship you propose I still want to be your lover. Even more now than before.'

Georgia frowned. 'What do you mean?'

He stared at her, swinging car keys from a long, slim forefinger. 'I am obsessed with the desire to teach you the full glory of what love can be between a man and a woman.' His eyes kindled. 'I found your surprising lack of expertise in such circumstances very seductive. I yearn to further your education, English teacher. It is *that*, not the coffee, which keeps me awake at night.'

A great tide of colour rushed into her face, her angry retort stifled by the return of Alessa in all the glory of a new blue dress.

'I'm ready, I'm ready,' cried the child, running towards them. She held up her face for Georgia's kiss, then took Luca by the hand. 'See you later, Georgia.'

'Yes, darling,' said Georgia with difficulty. 'My best wishes to your father.'

Luca smiled at Georgia, his eyes brilliant with laughter at her barely contained outrage. 'Make sure you rest,' he said softly, with such false solicitude that her teeth ground together as he took his little niece off to the waiting car.

Left to herself, Georgia lay in a garden chair under

an umbrella, in no mood to take herself off to bed as Elsa strongly advised. She needed to be in the open air, too restless to cage herself up in her room after Luca's parting shot. In a way, she conceded when she'd calmed down a little, it was flattering that he still wanted to make love to her after the embarrassing sequel to the first time. But that was it, of course—a simple matter of image. Gianluca Valori wanted her to remember him as the greatest lover of all time. Which, unfortunately, he was, as far as she was concerned.

Not that it mattered, Georgia promised herself. No way would it happen again. And not solely because it would be incredibly stupid on her part either. She found Luca Valori irresistible in almost every way, and she'd be lying to herself if she tried to deny it. His kisses and caresses set her on fire as no other man's had ever come near to doing. Georgia's heart beat faster and her pulse raced at the mere thought of his lovemaking and she buried herself in her book, forcing her attention on the story in an attempt to erase him from her mind.

When Pina brought a tea-tray out later she reported that Signor Luca had rung to say that he would be later than expected in returning because he was taking Alessa to her aunt's house near Lucca on the way home, to report to Signor Sardi's sister.

Georgia was glad of the respite. She had a leisurely swim as the heat lessened, then went indoors to laze in the bath and finish her book before making her weekly call to her parents. After talking to her mother she felt restless and a little homesick as usual, and, to get over it, spent a lot of time fussing with her hair and going through her limited wardrobe for something to wear to dinner. Although she refused to become Luca Valori's latest playmate, she was human enough to want to look her best for the meal that they would share alone in Marco Sardi's absence.

But Franco was obliged to fetch Alessa home from her aunt's house. Luca had been called away to some crisis at Valorino.

On a Sunday evening? A likely story, thought Georgia scathingly as she listened to Alessa's account of her visit to the hospital. No doubt he had a very different kind of call to make, on some lady more complaisant than Alessa's English teacher.

'The doctor says Papa needs rest,' reported Alessa, 'so he must stay at the hospital for a little while. But he is much better, Georgia. Oh, I forgot. Zia Claudia said I must tell you she was sorry not to bring me home herself. She drove to Pisa to see Papa instead.'

Having taken such care with her appearance, Georgia couldn't bring herself to plead a headache and ask Elsa for a tray in her room. Once Alessa was settled for the night Georgia was obliged to eat in solitary splendour in the conservatory, her dinner utterly ruined by speculation on where Luca was eating his, and with whom.

Furious at her irrational jealousy, Georgia forced herself to linger with the tea-tray that Elsa insisted on providing, then went for a stroll in the garden before taking herself to bed. As she wandered restlessly under the velvety, starlit sky she heard a car turn in at the gate and her heart leapt as she recognised the distinctive throaty growl of the Supremo.

Luca was a lot earlier than expected. Georgia hurried into the house, then slowed deliberately to a walk on her way to the hall, where she found Luca on his way to the stairs. To her astonishment he was filthy.

'There *was* a crisis, then?' she said, and could have bitten her tongue at the gleam of white teeth in Luca's dirty face.

'You doubted it?' he said mockingly.

Georgia shrugged. 'On a Sunday night it seemed— unusual.'

'There was a fire in one of the outbuildings at the *fabbrica*. Nothing serious. I helped put it out,' he said without drama.

'No fire brigade?'

'Oh, yes, they came. But by that time the flames were under control—we are prepared for such accidents.' He scowled. 'Someone disregarded the "no smoking" signs.'

Elsa came hurrying into the hall, and gave a screech at the sight of him. 'Luca! What happened?'

He explained, and she went hurrying off to prepare a meal, telling him to get out of his filthy clothes at once and take a bath.

Luca smiled wryly. 'You must find my relationship with our servants strange.'

'No.' Georgia grinned. 'We don't have any at home to have a relationship with.'

'Elsa was with the family before I was born. She is fiercely independent in many ways, yet her loyalty to us all is unswerving, always.'

'Just as well, when you come home at this hour on a Sunday night expecting dinner!'

'It would be useless to tell her not to bother. Besides,' added Luca, 'I am starving. Forgive me, I must take a shower.' Halfway to the stairs he turned. 'Will you stay to talk to me while I eat? Or are you too tired?'

Georgia knew she could easily say that she'd been

on her way to bed. But in two weeks' time she would be saying goodbye to Luca Valori for good. 'No,' she said before she could change her mind.

'No, you will not stay, or no, you are not too tired?'

'I'm not tired,' she said with perfect truth. 'If you want I'll keep you company.'

'Thank you,' he said gravely. 'I will be ten minutes.'

Georgia watched him leaping up the stairs, then turned to make her way back to the conservatory, feeling pensive. She might not want a love affair with Luca Valori, but it was very hard to refuse herself the pleasure of his company while she still had the chance.

Luca, hair still wet, joined her in less than ten minutes, and downed a large quantity of mineral water before he allowed himself a glass of wine. 'It was thirsty work tonight, but no harm done, thank God. No one was hurt.'

'You feel great responsibility for your employees, I take it,' said Georgia.

'Our workforce is not very big, and most of them have been with us for years and send their sons for training to take their places.' Luca smiled. 'Naturally I feel responsible, as my father did before me. Sadly he died when I was in school, so it was left to Maddalena to take responsibility until I was of an age to do so myself.'

'And your mother?' said Georgia hesitantly. 'I don't wish to pry, but did she die young too?'

'At my birth,' he said tersely. 'As did Maddalena when her son was born.'

Georgia looked stricken. 'I'm so sorry—I shouldn't have asked!'

'Why not? It is no secret.' Luca looked up in relief

as Elsa came in with a laden tray. 'Wonderful. I could eat a horse.'

'You will eat veal and artichokes, as Georgia did. A good thing I kept some back for you,' said Elsa severely. 'Why can't you leave the dirty work to others, Luca?'

'Because I like it too much,' he said, seizing a knife and fork. 'Now leave me in peace to eat, woman. I'm too old for your scolding.'

Elsa snorted, directed a look of pure love at his sleek dark head and went back to fetch more tea for Georgia.

'Do you never tire of all this tea?' demanded Luca, his mouth full, and Georgia giggled.

'Actually I do, sometimes, but Elsa is convinced the British drink nothing else, so I haven't the heart to disillusion her. Tell me,' she added, 'is Signor Sardi really well enough to leave hospital soon, as Alessa said?'

Luca assured her that after a few days' complete rest, which Marco was already bored with, he would be fit enough to come home. 'Along with a course of medication and a strict diet for a while, just as you said. No wine or spirits, no coffee, no vinegar in salad dressings, no citrus fruits.'

Georgia nodded. 'Nothing to aggravate acidity.'

Luca pulled a face. 'I pity him. Marco loves wine and coffee with equal passion. However, as I pointed out to him, it will be worth it to spare Alessa another fright like that. It was a powerful argument.'

When Luca had finished his meal he proposed a walk in the gardens. 'To clear the smoke from my lungs,' he said, coughing a little.

Georgia went with him gladly. 'The stars here look

so enormous,' she commented as they strolled across the manicured grass.

'It is more southerly here than your country, Georgia.' Luca breathed in deeply. 'At my house it is cooler, because it is higher up in the hills. Will you visit me there before you leave, Georgia? Bring Alessa to chaperon if you wish!'

'Then I will. Is the work nearly finished there?'

He shrugged. 'It was only a few repairs to a wall, and a new coat of paint in my bedroom. It is very different from this house. Not so civilised. It was a farm once. I want to preserve its identity.'

'It sounds interesting. Charlotte and Tom stayed at a farmhouse somewhere...' Georgia trailed into silence, wishing that she'd had the sense to keep quiet on the subject, and Luca caught her by the arm, bringing her to a halt beyond the shrubbery which lined the lawns near the house. The trout stream rushed by, giving its illusion of coolness, and Georgia stood very still, conscious in every nerve of the heat in Luca's hand, of the scent of grass and flowers in the air, of the knowledge that this moment would never come again.

'Tell me that you are not in love with this James of yours,' commanded Luca abruptly, and Georgia sighed, unable to lie.

'I suppose I'm not,' she admitted reluctantly. 'At least, not in the way that you mean.'

'There is only one way,' he whispered. 'This way.' He drew her into his arms and kissed her, and Georgia yielded to the pressure of a long hand at her waist as he slid the other into her hair to hold her face still. Luca's mouth settled on hers with a coaxing delicacy that seduced her far more effectively than a bruising kiss of passion. With a sigh she slid her arms round his neck and felt a tremor run through the body that felt so natural, so utterly right against her own. The quality of the kiss altered and their breathing quickened, and suddenly his arms were cracking her ribs and her fingers were digging into his shoulders, and with a muffled sound he buried his face against her hair.

'I want you, Georgia,' he said, so quietly that she sensed his words rather than heard them.

'I know.'

'Do you want me?'

She was so long in answering that he raised his head and put a finger under her chin to lift her face to his. 'Is your silence my answer?' he demanded. 'Are you telling me you feel nothing for me, when I know very well that you do? I *know* when a woman trembles to my touch, when her lips open to me like a flower—'

'Yes, I know you know,' she said flatly. 'And that's the trouble.'

'Trouble?' He thrust her away from him to stare down at her in the dim light. 'I cannot read your face out here in the dark,' he said, and tightened his grip on her arms. 'What do you mean?'

'You know far too much about women. Which isn't surprising with your looks and reputation—'

'Reputation?' he demanded, incensed.

'As a racing driver,' Georgia said quickly. 'You must have had lots of adulation in your time, Gianluca Valori. And a great many women must have wanted you, for your looks, for your body, and for something else that some men have and some men don't—charisma, sex appeal, call it what you like.'

'Whatever it is, you are obviously immune to it,' he said bitterly, and dropped his hands.

'No, I'm not,' she sighed. 'I wish I was. But in a fortnight I'll be gone from here, and soon after that I'm returning to my job at the school near Venice.' Suddenly she reverted to English, needing the exact words to hammer home her point. 'You can't be my lover for the simple reason that, even if there were no James and I was willing, here in Italy you're too well-known. I'd lose my job if I became another of your playmates, Luca.'

'Playmates?' he said with distaste.

'Whatever you like to call your ladies,' she said bluntly. 'I'm not denying that I find you attractive. Out here under these big Italian stars of yours I'd have to be a nun not to respond to you. But I'm not going to because you and I inhabit different worlds. I'm not getting involved with you, Luca. You agreed to be friends, remember. Are you going back on your word?'

Luca breathed in deeply, shaking his head. 'No,' he said wearily. 'I will not go back on my word. You win, Georgia. If it is friendship you want, then I shall never touch you again.' He thrust a hand through his hair. 'And I shall keep to it because just to touch you drives me mad. I have never wanted a woman the way I desire you.'

'Only because you can't have me, Luca,' she said gently, and turned away and went back alone through the gardens, wincing at the glare of the security lights as she broke into a run in her hurry to get in the house. Breathless and oddly desolate, she snatched up her book and hurried up the stairs to her room, haunted by the feeling that she'd just made some fateful, irreparable mistake.

CHAPTER TEN

GEORGIA saw very little of Luca after that. Due to Marco's absence from the *fabbrica* Luca spent so much time there that sometimes a brief half-hour in the late evening was all the contact they had. There were no more dinners for two, nor moonlit strolls in the garden. Which made things easier all round, Georgia told herself firmly. And when Marco Sardi came home there were only a few days left of her stay at the Villa Toscana.

Luca drove Marco to the villa during the afternoon, stayed for a while at Alessa's request, then returned to Valorino with nothing more personal for Georgia than his white, public smile in farewell.

Marco Sardi looked so much better that Alessa was ecstatic, and pleaded to stay up for the evening meal as a special treat. Her father consented indulgently, telling her that Signora Valori would be joining them.

'She likes to eat early, so it will suit everyone,' he declared. 'Other than Luca, of course, who likes to eat late. But he will not be joining us tonight. He is attending a business dinner in my place, as representative of Fabbrica Valori.'

Georgia went off to help Alessa choose a dress to wear for dinner, feeling tense. The prospect of Signora Valori at the dinner table was daunting, particularly since Luca would be absent from it.

When Georgia was dressing Pina knocked at the door

to say that Signor Marco would like a word with her in his study before dinner. Georgia tied back her hair with a black velvet ribbon, tucked her cream silk shirt into the waistband of her narrow black linen skirt, then went downstairs. She knocked at the study door and went in, a questioning smile on her face.

'You wished to see me, Signor Sardi?'

He was dressed informally, in a light linen suit with a silk shirt open at the collar, and looked rested and a lot younger after his enforced rest in hospital. He smiled at her and waved her to a seat in front of his desk, then took the chair behind it.

'Georgia, I wish to thank you for all your good services to Alessa. Knowing she had you, as well as Elsa and Pina, made my time in hospital easier to bear.'

'You're very kind,' murmured Georgia.

Marco Sardi regarded her with speculation. 'And now I'm going to presume on *your* kindness and ask a great favour.'

'If I can help in any way I'll be glad to,' she said promptly.

'Would you consider prolonging your stay?' He smiled wryly. 'If you would stay here with us until Alessa goes back to school I would be deeply grateful.'

'But I thought you were leaving for England at the end of August,' she said, surprised.

'My doctors have forbidden that for the time being. The opening of the London office has been postponed until the New Year.'

'I see.' Georgia looked down at her clasped hands. 'I had rather hoped to spend time with my parents—'

'Of course, of course.' His smile was kind. 'Since my doctor says I may not return to the *fabbrica* for a few days, why not fly home this weekend to visit your family? I have already contacted Signora Blanchard at the school in Venice, and she gives you leave for the first week of term, so that you may visit your parents again before you begin the new academic year.' Marco Sardi smiled in wry apology. 'I thought it best to gain official permission before laying my plan before you.'

Georgia hadn't the heart to refuse. 'Then, yes. If you really want me to I'll stay.'

He rose to his feet, holding out his hand. 'You have my grateful thanks, Georgia. Now join us in the conservatory. Emilia has already arrived.'

The meeting with Signora Valori passed off with no awkwardness at all, to Georgia's relief. Elsa surpassed herself with the meal, and Alessa's joy in having her father home invested the evening with an air of festivity not even Luca's absence could spoil.

'Alessa has been talking to me in English,' observed the elegant old lady in approval. 'I am not fluent in your language, Georgia, but speak enough to know Alessa has made splendid progress.'

'Thank you, *signora*.' Georgia smiled at the little girl. 'We work well together, don't we, poppet?'

Alessa nodded happily. 'Lessons with Georgia are fun!'

'Then you will be pleased to know Georgia has consented to stay with us until you return to school,' said her father, and Alessa's eyes opened wide in delight.

'You will really stay, Georgia?'

Georgia nodded, any doubts about the idea not only dispelled by the child's reaction, but by Signora Valori's approval later. After Alessa went to bed the two women were left together while Marco strolled in the garden to smoke the one cigar a day that he was allowed.

'It is good to see the child so happy, Georgia. You are kind to give up more of your time.'

'It's not exactly a hardship to stay on in this beautiful house to teach a bright little pupil like Alessa,' said Georgia with truth.

'I know, my dear.' The astute blue eyes locked with Georgia's. 'But after the incident with Luca—which it is better to discuss than leave festering in secret—I thought perhaps you would have wished to leave the moment your time here was over.'

Georgia's eyes never wavered. 'There was no real harm done, *signora*. As I said at the time, it was a misunderstanding. Which has been cleared up. Luca and I have agreed to be friends.'

'Friends?' said Emilia Valori drily. 'Luca has really agreed to this?'

Georgia smiled rather mischievously. 'More or less.'

'In my experience, my dear, pure friendship is surprisingly difficult between a beautiful woman and a red-blooded man. If only on one side there is usually a desire for something warmer eventually.' The blue eyes twinkled. 'You feel no desire at all for my grandson?'

'Of course I do.' Georgia smiled ruefully. 'But I have no intention of giving in to it. There are too many differences between us. Background, culture—all kinds of things.'

'Including religion, I imagine,' said the old lady thoughtfully.

'Actually, no. I'm not as devout as my parents would like, but I'm a Catholic just the same.'

'I see. Does Luca know this?'

'No. I've seen no reason to tell him—or anyone else except you, *signora*.'

'Because respect for my great age forbids you to tell me to mind my own business!' The old lady laughed, and Marco strolled in to join them, pleased to see them enjoying each other's company.

Georgia enjoyed her brief holiday at home. The time passed swiftly, though Georgia did little more than walk the dog, help her mother with the cooking, do a little weeding with her father and stay in bed late each morning to make up for her irritating insomnia at night.

Charlotte and Tom joined them for Sunday lunch, which meant a lot of good-natured teasing about the hostile Italian, but the subject was dropped the moment Charlotte, beaming, informed her family that she was pregnant.

'It wasn't a stomach upset at all!' she said as Georgia hugged her. 'I rather suspected as much, but I wouldn't say a word in case I was mistaken.'

Georgia turned to Tom, laughing. 'So it's all your fault, then.'

He grinned like a Cheshire cat. 'It had better be!'

The parting from her family was surprisingly hard when the time came to leave them at Heathrow. If it hadn't been for Alessa Georgia would have got back in the car and given up all thought of ever returning to the Villa Toscana, and thus stayed safely out of Luca's orbit for good. She would have avoided mentioning him to her parents at all if her father hadn't discovered, via Tom, that he was actually Gianluca Valori, well-known to fans of Formula-One Grand Prix racing.

'We shan't see you now until September, then,' said her mother, hugging her, and Georgia nodded, feeling oddly tearful.

'I'll come home for a week before I start school,' she promised, and tore herself away to go through to the flight-departure lounge to wait for the plane to Pisa. This time Franco would be waiting for her at the airport with the car, instead of her having to take the train to Florence.

When the plane landed Georgia collected her luggage, made her way through Customs then stopped dead, her pulse racing as she saw a familiar dark head above the crowd.

Luca craned his neck, then his eyes met hers, lit up, and he pushed his way towards her and took her bag. 'Welcome back, Georgia. I had business in Pisa, so I relieved Franco of the task of meeting you. You enjoyed your weekend?'

'Yes,' she said breathlessly, appalled by how pleased she was to see him. 'So much I almost didn't come back.'

Luca frowned as they went to the car park. 'You did not wish to return to us?'

'Yes, of course. I wouldn't hurt Alessa for the world—'

'But you had no care for my feelings!' he threw at her, and unlocked the gleaming black Supremo. He tossed her bag in the back, then helped her into the passenger seat and got in behind the wheel. He turned to look at her, and Georgia swallowed, suddenly overcome by the sheer force of his physical presence in the confines of the car.

She could see the faint blue shadow along his newly

shaved jaw, smell the faint citrus scent of something he'd used afterwards, and as he flung a familiar suede jacket onto the back seat his hand brushed against her shoulder and the contact sent a stab of fire through her. So much for friendship, she thought bitterly as he started the engine. Her instincts had been right. She should never have come back.

They chatted politely, like two acquaintances, until they reached the road to the villa, then Luca turned a molten sidelong look on her. 'I missed you, Georgia.'

'But you're hardly ever at home!'

'Then you missed me also,' he stated in triumph, grinning through the windscreen.

'Of course. Everyone at Villa Toscana misses you when you're not there,' she said prosaically, but Luca's grin only widened as he turned the car into the familiar driveway.

Georgia had barely time to get out of the car before a small figure came hurtling from the house into her arms, hugging her in a frenzy of delighted welcome, crying her name over and over again, and Georgia knew that if only for Alessa's sake she'd had no choice about coming back.

Alessa clutched her hand as the three of them went into the house, and said in triumphant, careful English, 'Welcome home, Georgia. I have missed you very much.'

'What a clever girl!' crowed Georgia, and entered the hall to such enthusiastic greetings from Elsa and Pina that she could have been away for five years instead of five days—a comment made with dry amusement by Marco Sardi as he came strolling from the study to add to Georgia's welcome.

Georgia dismissed her qualms as she dressed for dinner that evening, deciding that now she was back she would take each day as it came and enjoy it to the full—something to look back on with pleasure when she left the villa for good to get on with the rest of her life. Fine words, she told her reflection drily, now you're here. But afterwards you may feel different, my girl.

It was good to dine in company with the two men again, to laugh at Marco Sardi's grumbling when Elsa served a dinner tailored to his new diet rather than to his preferences. Georgia listened with avidity as the two men discussed the latest political crisis, and contributed her own account of the televised Puccini opera seen during her stay at home.

'Your family is well?' enquired Marco, and Georgia nodded.

'Very well; particularly my sister. We all had lunch together on Sunday, and Charlotte announced she is expecting a baby—' She bit her lip, and Marco shook his head at her reassuringly.

'Georgia, life goes on and babies arrive. I trust your brother-in-law is very happy at the news?'

Georgia nodded, avoiding Luca's eyes. 'So is my mother!'

After dinner Marco excused himself to retire to bed early.

'I am still under orders, you understand,' he said wryly. 'Luca is a stern taskmaster. He says I may not return to Valorino if I break the rules.'

Luca nodded, grinning. 'I promised Dr Fassi I would make you keep to your diet and get plenty of rest. So goodnight, Marco; sleep well.'

'The weather has broken,' said Luca after he'd gone.

'So tonight there is no walk in the garden. Sit here with me for a while. It is too early to go to bed.'

Georgia curled up in the corner of a sofa, listening to the rain drumming on the glass roof. For a moment Luca stood looking at her, as though he took pleasure at the mere sight of her, then he sat beside her, took her hand and looked into her eyes.

'Does it trouble you, this baby of your sister's?'

Oddly enough, it did in a way, thought Georgia, but only because she felt a totally surprising envy. At the memory of Tom's euphoria she smiled involuntarily.

'Not in the least,' she said cheerfully. 'Charlotte was quite ill when we first arrived in Florence. I'm only too pleased that her stomach upset was due to nothing more serious than pregnancy.'

Luca's fingers smoothed the back of her hand delicately. 'I hope all goes well with her.'

'There's no reason why it shouldn't,' said Georgia, surprised.

'It is not always so.' He gave her a sombre look. 'Have you never wondered why I am not married?'

'Often.'

'Because, if I marry, everyone will expect a Valori heir to carry on the name.' His grasp tightened cruelly. 'You know what happened to my mother and Maddalena. I will put no woman at such risk.'

Georgia gazed at him, astonished. 'But surely you want a family of your own?'

'I have Alessa.' His eyes lit with a glow which rang alarm bells in Georgia's brain. 'And I have no intention of denying myself the pleasures that all men crave. I need *you*, Georgia. I invented the appointment in Pisa today just so that I could meet your plane. Because I could not endure another moment without you. Can you look at me with those beautiful black eyes and tell me that you care nothing for me?'

'No,' she said baldly, 'I can't.'

'Then why must we keep to this ludicrous idea of friendship?' he said hoarsely. 'I would not offend your principles by suggesting you share my bed here in Marco's house. But I have a house of my own—'

'Are you suggesting we sneak off at weekends to your place?' she demanded, incensed.

'No!' He caught the hands she wrenched away. 'Listen, Georgia. Do not go back to the school in Venice. Come to me at the farm—'

'Why?' she demanded scornfully. 'You don't need English lessons.'

'No. I need *this*.' Luca caught her in his arms and kissed her, but she twisted away.

'I knew I shouldn't have come back,' she said bitterly, and jumped to her feet, but Luca leapt to bar her way.

'Why?' he demanded, his eyes glittering into hers. 'You wished to stay with this James of yours, who writes to you so much? He was there, in England?'

'No. I told you—he's in Cyprus,' she said wearily. 'I didn't see him.'

'Good!' Luca relaxed, a look in his eyes that, with wrath, she identified as satisfaction. 'It is no use to fight, Georgia. We were meant to be lovers. You know it.'

'I know nothing of the kind.' Georgia pushed him aside, but he caught her in his arms, holding her close. She stiffened, but Luca shook his head.

'It is no use,' he repeated softly. 'Your body tells me what you refuse to admit.'

'Possibly,' she said hotly. 'You're a very sexy man, and I'm a normal, healthy female, but that's as far as it goes. When I leave here we'll never—'

The rest of her protest was smothered by his mouth, which took possession of hers with such flagrant ownership that she thrust at him with impotent hands, only to have them caught in one of his as he raised his head to look down into her eyes.

'Never is a long time,' he whispered. 'In the night I wake thinking of how you felt beneath me that day, of the silken feel of your skin...'

Georgia tried to close her ears to the deep voice which whispered such liquid, mellifluous seduction that her traitorous body responded to it even as her brain told her to drag herself away while she still could. Her breathing grew ragged and chills ran down her spine as he slid his mouth to her throat, then she pulled herself together and pushed him away, meeting the heat in his eyes with a look so bright and cold that he scowled blackly.

'What is it?'

'Luca, listen to me. I'm not going to live with you. If—if there were no James, perhaps if you were someone more—more ordinary, my own nationality, even, I might consider it. With you it's different.'

He stood back, his face suddenly hard. 'You mean I must marry you before I am granted the delights of your bed?'

'Good heavens, no,' she said, so genuinely surprised that she spoke in English. 'It never occurred to me.'

'I find that very hard to believe,' he replied silkily, in accented, but perfectly plain English. 'Are you saying that if I asked you to be my wife you would refuse?'

He shook his head, smiling cynically. 'I do not think so.'

'You must believe what you choose, of course,' she said very quietly, 'but it's the truth. I don't want to marry you, or anyone else at this particular moment in time. Not even James. I like my life the way it is. And James is willing to wait until I'm ready to settle down.'

'You are lucky to have so tame a lover,' sneered Luca, a pulse throbbing beside his set mouth. 'If you were mine—'

'But I'm not,' she said coolly. 'Goodnight.'

Georgia arrived in her room a few moments later, feeling so weary that she could have scaled the north face of the Eiger rather than climbed two flights of stairs. She got ready for bed slowly, her movements oddly uncoordinated, then for comfort got out her diary to note the date of her return flight the following month. If Luca went on trying to get his own way, she thought grimly, four whole weeks of holding out against him would take every bit of will-power she possessed.

Georgia sighed, stuck the little pencil back in the slot, then frowned and opened the diary again. Her pupils dilated as she saw an entry in entirely the wrong place. She leafed through a few pages, stared at the entry again, then sagged against the pillows, an arm over her eyes in despair.

CHAPTER ELEVEN

AFTER Marco Sardi returned to his responsibilities at Valorino, Luca Valori was able to spend more time at the Villa Toscana—a circumstance which Georgia reacted to with varying emotions. Far from being daunted by her refusal he seemed spurred on by it, and drove her mad by trying to engineer time alone with her. Marco Sardi was amused. And, Georgia knew, approving. It pleased him to see that the more obvious his charismatic brother-in-law made his pursuit, the farther Georgia retreated.

She kept busy by teaching Alessa, and asked Marco Sardi's permission to drive the child to visit the house where the composer Puccini had lived and some of the other beautiful old houses open to the public in the area. Together she and Alessa looked at fabulous paintings and furniture, and wandered through gardens of breathtaking loveliness, the child happy to do whatever Georgia suggested, even to the point of talking English during the expeditions.

'I don't want to go back to school,' said Alessa mutinously one day.

'Why not?'

'Because when I do you must go away.'

'I'll come and visit you sometimes,' promised Georgia, hoping that she could keep her word. 'Venice

isn't very far away. Perhaps your father will bring you
to visit me too.'

'Or Luca,' said Alessa eagerly. 'He likes you,
Georgia.'

'Like' seemed hardly the word sometimes, thought
Georgia drily when she excused herself to go to bed
immediately after dinner. As both men rose to their feet
the look Luca gave her should have turned her to stone
on the spot. His eyes were like discs of blue ice as she
said her goodnights and pre-empted any plan that he
might have had to speak to her alone.

At the weekends she avoided him by continuing with
her exploration of Florence, driving herself there in the
Fiat instead of accepting the lift he offered.

Two weeks later, when she returned from a Saturday
spent gazing at the paintings in the Pitti Palace, Georgia
dined alone with Marco Sardi. Luca, it seemed, had
finally given up on her and resumed his normal social
life.

'Emilia rang today while you were out,' announced
Marco. 'She would be very pleased if you would lunch
with her tomorrow, and suggests she send a car for you
at noon unless she hears otherwise.'

'How very kind of her,' said Georgia, surprised.

'She knows I am taking Alessa to spend Sunday with
my sister and her family, and thought you might like to
keep her company.'

Georgia liked the idea a lot, but when Emilia Valori's
stately limousine came to collect Georgia the next day
the owner was sitting in the back, a rather mischievous
smile on her patrician features. The chauffeur jumped
out to hand Georgia in beside his mistress, and Emilia
patted Georgia's hand.

'I thought it would be more interesting to go out for lunch. Gianni shall drive us through parts of Tuscany you may not have seen yet, and then we shall stop for a meal at a place I think you will like.'

Georgia shrugged, smiling. 'Whatever you say, *signora*. It's very kind of you to invite me.'

The sharp blue eyes subjected her to a prolonged scrutiny. 'You look tired, my dear. Is Alessa wearing you out?'

'No. It's just the weather. We northerners find it hard to sleep in heat like this.'

Emilia nodded thoughtfully, then turned away to wave a hand at a Palladian mansion perched on a hillside in the distance. She continued to point out various features of her much loved Tuscany as they drove through blinding sunshine which made Georgia glad of the car's efficient air-conditioning.

Eventually Gianni nosed the gleaming black car up a hillside track, negotiated a few hairpin bends with panache and came to a halt in front of a house with slanting, asymmetric roofs and a rustic, arcaded façade which blended well into its setting of hillside vineyards. Rust-red curtains fluttered in the open arches, and a veil of greenery softened the rough creamy stone of the walls.

'Quite an out-of-the-way place for a restaurant,' commented Georgia as she turned to help Emilia Valori out of the car.

'It is not a restaurant, my dear,' confessed the old lady, with no trace of remorse. 'This is La Casupola, the home of my grandson. And here comes Luca himself, to spare me your reproaches.'

Georgia stared, unsmiling, as Luca appeared round the side of the house at a run, dressed in white denims

and a blue shirt, his bare feet thrust into faded espadrilles. His hair was wet, and he was buttoning the shirt
as he came, and had obviously just taken a bath. He
gave both ladies an encompassing smile, kissed his
grandmother on both cheeks, then lifted Georgia's rigid
hand to his lips.

'Forgive me. I was helping Vito tune the engine of
his truck. Welcome to my home, Georgia. And forgive
my grandmother also. The deception was mine. You
would not have consented to come here any other way,
so—' he shrugged '—this was my solution to the problem.'

Georgia gave him a tight, dangerous smile, angry
with him because he knew that there was no way she'd
make a scene in front of the lady watching the exchange
with open enjoyment. 'Why should there be anything
to forgive? It's my day off, the sun is shining, and
Signora Valori has taken me on a tour of parts of
Tuscany I might otherwise never have seen.'

'You are not angry, then,' he commented, standing
aside for them to enter.

Georgia avoided an answer by commenting with
pleasure on the rustic charm of La Casupola, which, she
learned, meant hovel and was Luca's little joke for a
home which, if not as sophisticated and luxurious as the
Villa Toscana, was much more to her own personal
taste.

The house was sparsely furnished with sturdy dark
old pieces that Luca had collected together over the
years. Old-fashioned mattresses covered in bleached
linen cushioned the settles pushed against most of the
walls, and hangings everywhere were the rust-red of
those which wafted gently in the open arches of the

terrace, adding a note of warmth to the stone walls and floors and making a frame for the breathtaking view visible from every window.

Luca installed his grandmother on one of the upright chairs at the table and provided his guests with sparkling white wine, grown, he said, with a look at Georgia, from his own vines. He pulled out a chair for her, then seated himself on the ledge of one of the arches, fit and brown and so good to look at that Georgia felt a pang of something very akin to pain as Luca waved a proprietorial hand at the vista spread out below.

'Do you like my view, Georgia?'

'How could I not?' she said with truth. 'This is the most idyllic bit of Tuscany I've seen so far.'

'You find it quiet after the noisier pleasures of Florence yesterday?' asked Emilia, sipping her wine.

'Peaceful rather than quiet.' Georgia smiled. 'I went to the Pitti Palace to look at all the pictures, and after that I finally managed a visit to David.'

'David?' said the old lady.

'Michelangelo's *David*, Nonna,' said Luca, grinning. 'And were you disappointed?'

Georgia shook her head vigorously. 'No. How could I be? I just stood there for ages in awe. What a masterpiece!'

The meal was brought in by a plump little woman who greeted Emilia Valori with great deference as she brought plates of simple, perfect pasta in a savoury, basil-flavoured tomato sauce.

'Rosa's cooking has not deteriorated, I see,' commented the old lady as she ate sparingly.

'I have not been here very much since Maddalena

died,' said Luca, 'but Rosa keeps the place immaculate, and never complains when I arrive unexpectedly. Her husband and son tend the vines,' he added to Georgia, then looked up with a smile as Rosa came in with a streaming tureen, to serve them with dark, strongly flavoured meat in a sauce that Georgia found oddly sweet.

Halfway through the meal she laid down her fork in defeat. 'I shouldn't have eaten so much pasta,' she said apologetically.

'The dish is not to everyone's taste,' agreed Emilia. 'The sauce is made with vinegar, sugar, and chocolate—a local way of preparing hare.'

Hare? Georgia felt her stomach lurch and drank deeply of her glass of mineral water, averting her eyes from her plate.

'Forgive me—I asked Rosa to make a true Tuscan speciality. You would like something else?' said Luca quickly, and she shook her head.

'No, thank you. Just some water, please.'

When the meal was over Emilia Valori announced her intention of a nap on one of the padded settles. Luca piled cushions behind her, kissed her cheek, then looked at Georgia in enquiry.

'Would you like to rest too? Or would you prefer a tour of my home, then a walk outside once the sun is less fierce?'

Georgia nodded, still troubled by memories of the Tuscan way with hare, and followed him up wide stone stairs to the upper floor, where the same russet curtains hung at windows in rooms painted to harmonise with the stone of the house. A pair of vibrant oils of local scenery lit up a wall of a room which was obviously Luca's inner sanctum. Books were piled on tables beside deep leather chairs and couches, and as well as the expected television and video recorder there was a stereo, a fax machine and a computer.

'So you can keep in touch with the outside world even as you relax,' commented Georgia. In deference to what she'd believed was a visit to Emilia Valori she wore a dark blue dress of cotton voile dotted in white. The filmy material floated slightly in the breeze from the open windows as she examined compact discs on a shelf near the stereo system, her profile turned to the man who stood leaning against a wall, arms folded, his eyes on her face.

'Why are you so remote?' he asked abruptly, in a voice so harsh and yet so musical that Georgia had to steel herself against its appeal. 'I thought we agreed to be friends,' he added, moving from the wall. 'But you are no longer friendly, Georgia, and there is so little time before you go away.'

She turned very deliberately and met the brilliant blue gaze with eyes as black and expressionless as jet. 'I'll be honest, Luca. You are a very attractive man. In many more ways than looks,' she added, and held up a hand as he started towards her. 'No. Please don't touch me, because we both know what will happen if you do. And I can't let it happen, for reasons we've already discussed. So, for the time left to me at the Villa Toscana, will you leave me alone, please?'

'I cannot leave you alone! I never thought to say the words to any woman in my life, but it is no use. I am in love with you!' he said rapidly, swallowing hard as though the words had choked him. 'How can you look at me so coldly, like a woman made of marble?'

Since Georgia felt very hot, and beads of perspiration

were standing out on her upper lip, this was a very strange question, she thought in a detached, dazed kind of way. She moved towards him in sudden appeal. 'Luca—bathroom—please?' she said in hoarse, peremptory English.

Her urgency galvanised him into action, and seconds later Georgia was alone in a cool, white-tiled bathroom, parting with the hare and the pasta and what seemed like everything she'd eaten for several days. Afterwards she staggered outside to find Luca waiting for her on the landing.

'Georgia—you look like a ghost!' he exclaimed, keeping to English. 'Come, *cara*, lie down on my bed for a while.'

'But your grandmother—' she protested feebly.

Luca swept her objections aside. 'She will understand. And I shall leave you alone,' he added bitterly. 'You need fear no further assault on your virtue, I swear.'

Georgia's virtue—old-fashioned word, she thought muzzily—was her last concern at the moment. She let Luca lead her to a large, cool room with curtains drawn against the afternoon sunlight. He sat her gently on a wide bed with a carved wood headboard, then disappeared through a door. She heard water running and then felt a cool, damp cloth on her forehead as he bathed away the perspiration.

'Rest now,' he said as he laid her against the pillows. 'I shall return later. Sleep, *carissima*.'

Georgia obeyed gratefully, and woke later from a deep, dreamless sleep to find Luca standing at the edge of the bed. She sat up with a jerk, then moaned, putting a hand to her head as it reeled, and Luca leapt to lay her back against the pillows, his face strangely stern.

'Signora Valori—' began Georgia, but Luca laid a finger on her lips.

'She begs your forgiveness, but was obliged to return home for an appointment with a friend for dinner—'

'But I should have gone with her—'

'No.' Luca stood looking down at her in a way which did very little to improve Georgia's well-being. 'We must talk, you and I. And talk here, away from Marco and Alessa and all interruption, until certain matters are cleared between us.'

'I can't see why,' she returned, shivering a little despite the heat.

'You soon will. When you are ready, come downstairs and Rosa will bring tea. I have brought your handbag. It is here alongside the bed.'

As the door closed behind him Georgia sat up experimentally. This time the room stayed still; she got to her feet carefully, and found her legs steady enough to carry her to Luca's austere, functional bathroom. Nothing of the sybarite here, she thought as she dashed her face with cold water. A few minutes later, feeling better, she touched her mouth with lipstick, brushed her hair and went from the room to descend the shallow stone stairs to the ground floor. Luca rose from the table as she reached the terrace.

'Sit down, please, Georgia,' he said, pulling out a chair.

She obeyed, eyeing him warily. This was a very different Luca from the passionate, persuasive man of only an hour or so before. Well, two hours, she amended, after a glance at her watch. Her sleep had been longer than she'd thought. She was about to ask what was wrong when a concerned, anxious Rosa brought a tea-tray and begged the *signorina* to say if there was anything she wished to accompany the tea.

'No, nothing, thank you,' replied Georgia, with a grateful smile. 'Just tea will be wonderful.'

There was an awkward silence after Rosa had gone. Georgia asked if Luca would like tea, but he shook his head, and she sipped thirstily, wishing miserably that Signora Valori could have waited for her.

'I had a talk with my grandmother while you were sleeping,' said Luca at last. 'It was very instructive. It showed me what a stupid fool I've been.'

Georgia frowned. 'A fool?'

He nodded, his face sombre. 'First because, as Nonna said, only a fool would have tried to seduce someone we, as a family, were responsible for.'

It was fortunate for Georgia that for once he was speaking slowly and deliberately, instead of the usual liquid, rapid Italian that sometimes left her grasping for nuances of meaning. She poured herself another cup of tea, and drank a little of it as Luca went on speaking.

'I had no excuse for what I did,' he said tonelessly. 'I knew about this James of yours, also your sister's husband. But it was this very knowledge which drove me to show you that as a lover I could make you forget both of them. I was so sure that once you were in my arms you would discover this, but when we were to-gether at last, alone, your body against mine—' His mouth twisted. 'For the first time in my life I lost con-trol, I ignored your protests, blind to everything other than my desire for you.'

Georgia eyed him uneasily, experiencing a sinking feeling nothing to do with the hare.

Suddenly his head lifted and the blue, searching eyes held hers relentlessly. 'My grandmother pointed out to me this afternoon that you could be expecting my child.'

Since, for the past two weeks, Georgia had been tortured by the same suspicions, she found nothing to say, and the colour drained from Luca's face.

'You *are* pregnant?' he demanded hoarsely, and she shrugged miserably.

'I don't know—'

'But nature is giving you warning that you might be,' he said with tact.

She breathed in deeply. 'I'm afraid so. It's never happened—or *not* happened before, so I suppose it's possible I may be. It seems so *unfair*,' she added with sudden passion.

Luca winced, and passed a hand over his face. He took a handkerchief from his pocket and mopped his brow, looking as sick as Georgia had felt earlier. 'I will arrange a visit to Dr Fassi. It is important that we know as soon as possible.'

'Why?' she said stonily.

He glared at her, outraged. 'Why? Surely that is obvious!'

'If I'm pregnant,' she said in English, just to make sure she made it clear, 'I shall deal with the problem myself. I want nothing from you.'

Luca sprang up, pulling her from her chair. 'What is this "deal with the problem"?' he demanded. '*Un aborto*? Is this what you intend?'

Whereupon Georgia slapped his incensed face as hard

as she could and bent to pick up her bag. 'Drive me back to the villa, please,' she ordered, her voice shaking with fury.

'Not until you tell me what you mean to do,' he said roughly, catching both her hands in his.

'All right,' she said through her teeth. 'I intend to go back to England in two weeks, after which I hope never to see you again in my life.'

'Then your hopes will not be realised,' he spat back. 'If you are carrying my child I will marry you.'

'I don't *want* you to marry me!'

He shrugged indifferently. 'So? You will marry me nevertheless. A Valori honours his debts. I am to blame for your—your condition. Therefore I will make reparation.'

'But you can't!' she said breathlessly. 'If we marry we're stuck with each other for life. It's the reason I've never got involved before. I'm a Catholic, just like you.'

'Ah, I see,' he said, enlightened. 'This is why you struck me when I mentioned abortion.'

'No, it's *not*,' she flung at him, even more enraged. 'It wouldn't matter if I was a Hindu or a Seventh-day Adventist or any other religion you care to name. I resented your assumption. Anyway, the solution to my little problem—'

'*Our* problem,' he corrected.

Georgia pulled her hands from his. 'No, Luca,' she said wearily. 'The problem's mine. I have no intention of marrying you. A single parent is no novelty in England. I'll cope with *my* problem the way I think fit. And it certainly doesn't include marrying someone who doesn't want to marry anyone at all, let alone me.'

Luca thrust a hand through his hair, scowling blackly at her. 'That was before I knew—'

'We don't know yet,' she interrupted, though deep down inside she did. Somehow.

'Then why were you so ill this afternoon?'

'It was the hare.'

'I don't think so.'

'Think what you like,' she snapped. 'Now please take me back to the villa. And don't you dare breathe a word of this to Signor Sardi.'

'You think I wish to broadcast my stupidity?' he demanded, and stalked ahead of her to where the Supremo lay waiting beside the house.

Georgia eyed the car reluctantly, pushing the heavy hair back from her face. 'For once,' she said wearily in English, 'will you drive slowly, please? I still feel a bit fragile.'

Luca stared at her in resentment for a moment, then his face changed dramatically and he took her in his arms, holding her gingerly as though she were an invalid. 'Forgive me, Georgia—I have no right to be angry. The blame is mine. I shall make sure everyone knows that.'

Georgia leaned against him for a moment, then stepped back, squaring her shoulders. 'No need for that,' she said briskly. 'Once I'm back in England no one here need know a thing about it.'

'*I* know,' he threw back at her, opening the car door. 'So does my grandmother—and Elsa. It is a secret no longer. One more, in the person of Dr Fassi, can hardly make any difference.'

'I have no intention of seeing Dr Fassi,' retorted

Georgia, and closed her eyes quickly as Luca began the tortuous descent to the road.

Her protests were in vain. Next morning Dr Fassi came to see her before lessons began, after Marco Sardi and Luca had left for Valorino.

'Luca says you were ill yesterday at the farm,' he said, smiling at her scarlet face. 'So Elsa will come with us to your room. I shall take a look at you to make sure all is well.'

A day or two later Dr Fassi called again, took Georgia aside and told her that the tests he'd done were positive.

'Don't look so tragic, my dear,' he said gently. 'Luca says you will be married as soon as possible.'

'You've already told *Luca*?' said Georgia, shattered.

'He instructed me to do so.'

It was pointless to lose her temper with Dr Fassi, Georgia reminded herself, and managed a smile as he took his farewell.

She moved through the day with the smile pinned to her dazed face, in an attempt to allay Alessa's anxiety. The little girl was very worried by two visits from Dr Fassi, and had to be reassured by mention of a stomach bug which was now better.

'I am glad to see you recovered,' said Marco Sardi at dinner that night, which to Georgia's mingled dismay and relief they ate alone. Luca was away for a few days on a business trip again, she was told, and gave herself a scathing lecture because she felt abandoned. After dinner that evening Georgia was called to the telephone to speak to Signora Valori.

'You will forgive an old woman for her interference,'

was the lady's opening gambit. 'It was necessary for Luca to know the damage he had done.'

'How did you know there was any damage?' asked Georgia faintly.

'Call it womanly intuition, or anxiety, or anything you like, but the moment I saw you on Sunday I was convinced I was right. Your reaction to the hare only confirmed my suspicions. I thought Luca should share them. He tells me I am right.'

'Yes,' said Georgia miserably.

'Do not upset yourself, my child. Luca will marry you as soon as you wish.'

'But I don't want him to. It isn't necessary these days. Times have changed. I don't want a husband.'

'They are very useful in certain circumstances,' said Emilia Valori drily. 'And in this one I think you will find you have no choice.'

She was right. When Luca returned to the villa two evenings later he sent Pina up to Georgia's room to demand her presence in the garden before dinner. She went down a few minutes later to find him by the pool, staring into the water. When her reflection appeared beside his he turned sharply.

'How are you?' he demanded, taking her hands in his.

Georgia tugged them away, her face stony. 'You know how I am.'

'I have just returned from a visit to your parents,' he said abruptly, taking her breath away. 'I have told them exactly what happened.'

'You did *what*?' Georgia stared at him, appalled.

'You had no business to talk to them before I did. How dare you?'

He ignored her, speaking rapidly—so rapidly that it was difficult for her to follow him. 'I confessed all, then I asked for your hand in marriage, and after a while, when your charming parents had recovered from so great a shock, they agreed that this was the only solution possible—for both of us.'

'And if I don't fall in with all this?' she said wrathfully.

'But you will,' he said with sudden authority. 'It is not what either of us would have wished. I admit it freely. But, since you are to bear my child, you have no choice. You will marry me, Georgia, as soon as it can be arranged. Afterwards the way you choose to conduct our marriage will be up to you. The child, of course, will be my concern.'

'It will not! I may be pregnant by accident, but one thing you can be very sure of, Luca Valori—my child will be *my* concern.' She glanced up at him, her eyes flashing in the sunset light, and Luca shrugged.

'Then you have no choice. My son—or my daughter—must be born here in Tuscany, to grow up here as a Valori.'

'You mean that if I refuse to be parted from my child I must do the same,' she said wearily.

'Is it so great a sacrifice?' he said softly, taking her hand. 'We agreed to be friends, remember. We can be husband and wife and still remain friends, Georgia.'

'Have you any idea,' she began slowly, choosing the words with care, 'what it will be like for me, knowing you are chained to me in a marriage you don't want?'

Luca's face set, adding years suddenly to his finely

chiselled good looks. 'I was blind to all except my own desires that afternoon. I took what you were not willing to give, and the gods have a saying, do they not? Take what you want, and then pay for it.'

CHAPTER TWELVE

STARS hung like diamonds in a black velvet sky as Luca turned the Supremo up the private road to La Casupola on the evening of Georgia's wedding day. Lights were burning in all the windows as Rosa and her husband, Vito, came out to welcome their young master home with his bride.

Luca, to the delight of everyone except his wife, picked Georgia up and carried her over the threshold, then set her down and turned to shake Vito's hand and receive a kiss from Rosa, a look from her bridegroom prompting Georgia to do the same.

When Rosa was sure that Georgia lacked nothing for her comfort, and Vito had taken the luggage upstairs, the couple left to retire to their own home in the village a mile away and the newly-weds were left alone.

Georgia stood in the middle of the room feeling lonely and alien. The light from two rose-shaded bronze lamps flanking the stone fireplace merely seemed to emphasise the dark shadows beyond their radius.

'Rosa has left us a cold supper,' said Luca quietly. 'Would you like a rest before eating, or a bath?'

Georgia nodded silently, and he waved her before him up the wide, shallow stairs. She hesitated on the threshold of Luca's bedroom. Nothing had been discussed about sleeping arrangements. Vito, naturally, had placed all the luggage in the master bedroom.

Luca took her by the hand and led her inside. 'The

bed is large. And we shall both share it. I shall not touch you.'

'Surely there's another bedroom,' said Georgia coldly.

'There are two.'

'Then I shall sleep in one of them.'

Luca barred her way to the door. 'No, you will not. You are my bride. And Rosa looks after this house. I do not wish it known that you refuse to sleep with me. But sleep,' he added grimly, 'is the only thing required of you. I forced you once. I shall not do so again.' He took off his tie and threw his jacket on a chair on his way to the door. 'Please come downstairs when you are ready to eat.'

Georgia watched him go, feeling strangely detached, as though the events of the day had happened to someone else. A brief ceremony in London early that morning had joined her in marriage to Gianluca Valori, since nothing he or her parents could say would persuade her to the full church ceremony with nuptial mass. It had been strange to stand before the priest with only Marco Sardi and an ecstatic Alessa to witness it, alone with her parents and Tom and Charlotte, all of whom, she knew very well, were still reeling secretly from the surprise of it all.

John Fleming had insisted on paying for a wedding breakfast at the Ritz, to gild his younger daughter's wedding day with at least a little glamour, and surprisingly enough it had been a very festive meal. For her parents' sake Georgia did her best to smile and join in, purely to reassure her family that she was happy with the future that Luca had mapped out for her so relentlessly.

Though, to be fair, she thought as she undressed, the bride-to-be had taken so little interest in the wedding that in the end Luca had lost patience, his only consultations made with her mother and father, who were rather happier about the whole thing than she was. Her parents had always been rather lukewarm about her relationship with James Astin, and made no secret of being very much taken with Luca. They made it plain to their daughter that they admired his impeccable reaction to the situation. Even Charlotte and Tom had obviously liked him more than anticipated.

Luca had been stiffly courteous at first, but, after the relaxing effect of the vintage champagne they were served, unbent to Tom, who took Luca's initial reserve as awkwardness with the situation rather than anything personal. Alessa, of course, was a big hit with everyone. Anne Fleming was entranced with the child's careful English, and deeply touched by Alessa's joy at having Georgia for her very own aunt now that she was married to Luca.

'And when I live in England, will you visit us?' asked Alessa eagerly, and was assured that all Georgia's family would be only too delighted to visit the Sardi home and welcomed both Alessa and her father to theirs whenever they wished.

In fact, thought Georgia, yawning, everybody loved everybody except the bride and groom, who had barely exchanged two words on the flight to Pisa, and very few more on the drive from the airport to La Casupola. The time before the wedding had been a dream-like, unreal period to Georgia, who had hoped against hope, right up to the last minute, that somehow a miracle would happen to prevent it. But nothing had, and here she was, Signora Valori no less, with a few ordeals stretching in front of her as Luca planned to take her to meet not only his relations but Marco Sardi's as well.

She had flatly refused a conventional honeymoon, and the only concession made to it was Luca's absence from Valorino for the first two weeks of his marriage. To display to the world at large, he'd said to Georgia, in one of their rare moments of privacy before she flew back to England to prepare for the wedding, that their marriage was as normal as possible. She could call it face-saving on his part, hypocrisy, or anything else she liked, but a honeymoon of sorts she would have, whether she wanted it or not.

The other reason for Georgia's feeling of unreality was her health. The hare, it seemed, had been the real culprit for her stomach upset after all on her last visit to La Casupola. The baby was causing her no problems at all, either with her digestion or her shape. If anything, she was thinner in places than usual, which she wouldn't have noticed if her mother hadn't commented on it when the oyster silk suit bought for the wedding had been a little on the loose side when the time came to wear it.

Secretly Georgia had hoped that Dr Fassi's tests were wrong, and once back in England bought herself a pregnancy testing kit and did her own tests. But there was no mistake. One brief sexual encounter with Luca Valori had been all it took to turn her entire life upside down.

Once out of the bath Georgia brushed out her hair, which had been twisted up in a sophisticated coiffeur to complement the wickedly expensive hat that her mother had insisted she buy.

'Either that or you wear some flowers in your hair,' Anne Fleming had said, and Georgia, rejecting anything as bridal as flowers, had worn a straw tricorne tilted low on her forehead, with a wide-meshed veil to hide the reluctance in her eyes during the brief ceremony. But in the end her refusal of flowers had been useless after all. When she arrived at the church a radiant, excited Alessa had been waiting with two posies of creamy rosebuds—a small one for herself and a larger one for the bride. And during the ceremony Luca had slid a circlet of gold encrusted with rubies on her finger instead of the expected plain gold band, and afterwards kissed her squarely on the mouth before yielding her to the usual barrage of kissing from the rest of the party.

Georgia swathed herself in a bathtowel and went out into the bedroom to search in a suitcase for something to wear, hesitated, then with a wry little smile took out the amber satin nightgown and peignoir that Charlotte had bought her.

'I'd look terrible in that colour, but with your hair and eyes you'll look good enough to eat,' had been her sister's verdict, and Georgia slid the nightgown over her head, then examined herself in the long cheval-glass which she rather thought was new since her last visit to Luca's bedroom. The nightgown was in her usual size, but showed rather more of her breasts than she would have liked. She leaned forward in surprise as she saw that they were visibly fuller. She might be thinner as yet in her lower half, but the rest of her was definitely burgeoning.

Georgia wrapped herself hurriedly in the peignoir, tied the sash tightly, slid her feet into satin mules rather more glamorous than her usual scruffy espadrilles and, with a last, doubtful look in the mirror, left the room and went noiselessly downstairs. The stairs led directly into the living room, and halfway down she paused to look at Luca, who was sitting on one of the padded settles, his legs stretched out in front of him and a glass of what looked like whisky in one hand as he stared into space with an air of depression that no self-respecting bridegroom should have worn. She sighed and his head went up, his eyes meeting hers as she went slowly down the last few steps to the room.

'I wasn't sure if you were here or in your room upstairs,' she said awkwardly as he rose to his feet, her face hot at the look his lids fell like shutters to hide.

'After we have eaten we can drink coffee there—or some of your famous tea, if you prefer,' said Luca. 'How do you feel?'

'A little tired from the travelling. Otherwise very well.'

'*Bene.*' He smiled. 'Have you noticed how good I am?'

'Good?' She smiled back involuntarily.

'I have spoken only English all day,' he pointed out.

Georgia chuckled. 'So you have.'

'Just for this day, you understand, in deference to my English bride.' Luca waved a hand towards the trio of shallow steps that led to the dining room. 'Come. Our wedding breakfast was a long time ago.'

'You should have eaten something on the plane,' said Georgia as he held the door open for her; then she exclaimed in delight at the lighted candles and the posy of flowers that Rosa had arranged with such loving care. 'How lovely!'

Luca pulled out a chair and bowed ceremoniously. 'Sit. For tonight only I will wait on you.'

Feeling a great deal better in more ways than her physical health, Georgia watched in pretended amazement as Luca fetched a series of dishes from the refrigerator in the kitchen, laughing as he served her with mock formality and with his own hands dressed her salad with the celebrated local olive oil.

'Rosa wished to serve us,' said Luca as he attacked his meal with appetite. 'But she understood when I told her I wanted to be alone with my bride.'

'Why did you?' said Georgia bluntly, buttering a thick slice of *ciabatta* bread.

'I thought my bride would prefer it.' Luca gave her a brilliant blue look. 'This way no pretence is necessary, and we can dine like the friends we have agreed to be. Let us toast the agreement in this excellent Brunello.'

'You speak very good English,' she commented. 'I don't know why you make me speak Italian all the time.'

He laughed and filled her glass with ruby-coloured wine. 'Because your accent charms me, and the mistakes you make are very—' he frowned in thought '—*accattivante*?'

'Endearing,' said Georgia, flushing again.

Luca smiled. 'I hope you feel the same about my mistakes, *tesoro*.' His face darkened abruptly. 'Except for one, of course. That I think you will never forgive.'

Georgia laid down her knife and fork. 'Luca, let's put our cards on the table—be very honest with each other,' she added as he raised an enquiring eyebrow. 'I know it sounds odd, but right up to the moment we were married I hoped, by some miracle, it wouldn't be necessary—'

'You hoped to lose the baby?' he shot at her, eyes glittering.

'No!' She stared at him, startled. 'No. I didn't want that.'

'Then what miracle were you hoping for?' he demanded. 'That I would change my mind about wanting to bring up my own child?'

Georgia's shoulders sagged. 'Put like that, it does sound rather silly. Anyway, what I'm trying to say is, now that we *are* married I'll try to make the best of it.'

'*Va bene*—so shall I.' He reached out a long, slim hand and Georgia put hers into it, giving him a smile which turned into a yawn.

'Sorry, Luca. I think the day finally caught up with me.'

'*Allora*—come to bed. Leave all these things to Rosa in the morning.' He stood up, holding her eyes with his. 'I made no mistake of English tenses when I said, Come. If I leave you to go to bed alone you will lie wakeful and tense waiting for me to join you. So we shall prepare for the night together, and talk like the friends we have decided to be, and you will not feel awkward and nervous. You have nothing to fear from me, Georgia.'

'I know.' She gave him a rather shy smile. 'You'll have to make allowances. I've never shared a room with a man before.'

He grinned in response. 'Neither have I!'

Georgia woke in the night to a feeling of strangeness which she realised came not only from her surroundings but from the fact that she was sharing a bed with someone who took up a great deal of room. Luca Valori, accustomed to sleeping alone in his huge bed, was lying diagonally across it.

She lay curled up, quiet as a mouse, afraid to disturb him by trying to shove him over. They had survived the slight awkwardness of getting ready for bed very well, and for a while had lain talking over their wedding day before, to her intense astonishment, Georgia realised that she couldn't keep awake. She smiled in the darkness. If someone had told her this morning that she'd share a bed with her elegant, rather remote bridegroom and fall asleep very happily in the process, she would have laughed them to scorn. But Luca was right. It was better to start as they meant to go on. Or as Luca meant them to go on.

'You are awake,' said a deep, husky voice in the darkness, and the long legs retreated, giving her more room. 'Forgive me, Georgia, I have almost pushed you out of bed.'

She chuckled. 'I didn't like to push you back—'

'In case you woke me,' he interrupted, resigned. 'I gave you my word, Georgia. You can sleep in peace.'

Which had rather too much of a churchyard flavour, she thought, pulling a face. 'I know that. I was just being polite.'

Luca gave a smothered chuckle, and turned on the lamp beside his bed. He raised himself on an elbow to look at her. 'I am thirsty. Would you like something?'

Georgia nodded. 'Fruit juice?'

'Whatever you want.' He stood up, gave a stretch which threatened the silk pyjama trousers tied round his narrow hips, wrapped himself in a dark robe and went from the room.

While he was away Georgia paid a visit to the bathroom, brushed her hair, laughed at herself for doing so, and was back in the wide, carved bed, propped up against the pillows, when Luca returned with wine, fruit juice and glasses on a tray which he put down on the table beside him.

'Would you care for some champagne in your orange juice?' he said, shrugging off his robe. 'I think it can do little harm.'

'At three in the morning?' said Georgia, laughing to hide a frisson of response to the muscular beauty of his torso. 'A bit decadent.'

Lifting a negligent shoulder, Luca handed her a glass, filled one for himself, then slid in beside her and leaned back, relaxed, against the pale, carved wood of the bedhead. 'But tonight is a special occasion, Georgia.' He glanced sideways at her, his eyes softening. 'Is it so very difficult for you, *innamorata*, to think of yourself as my wife?'

When he called her 'sweetheart' it was remarkably easy. Georgia gave him a look from beneath her lashes. 'No. Now that it's signed and sealed it's easier to cope with, somehow.'

'Then you do not hate me any more?'

'I've never hated you, Luca!'

'But you would not allow yourself to fall in love with me.' He stared down into his glass. 'I wish that I had such iron British control over my own emotions,' he added suddenly in his own swift, melodic tongue. 'I need to confess, Georgia.'

'Confess?' she asked, wondering if she understood him properly.

'When I said you must sleep here with me it was nothing to do with Rosa, or anyone other than myself. I had a feeling here—' he struck himself in the chest '—that if we began to sleep apart from the first night our marriage would have no hope of success.' He turned his head and looked down into her intent eyes. 'Also I am human. You are beautiful and my wife, and I wanted to share a bed with you.'

Georgia drained her glass and held it out for more, smiling mischievously. 'I know you did.'

Luca leaned over to fill her glass and handed it back to her. 'You made no protest,' he said, in a tone which made her pulse quicken.

'No. It—it seemed only fair.' She drank from the glass, then looked up at him accusingly. 'You forgot the orange juice!'

'No. I did not forget. I am trying to seduce you with champagne—and patience,' he said candidly, his smile doing so much for his cause that Georgia, conscious of a glow that had nothing to do with the wine, smiled back, shaking her head.

'You said I could conduct our marriage any way I liked,' she reminded him.

'Have I tried to impose my will?' he returned, his eyes glittering under lowered lids.

'I rather think that's what you're doing right now!' Georgia finished the wine and handed him the glass.

Luca set both their glasses on the tray, then turned casually and drew her into his arms so that she lay against his chest with her face turned up to his. 'This friendship of ours should allow a little contact, Georgia.'

Relaxed by the exquisite wine, comfortable in the embrace of arms which held her loosely rather than constricting her, she nodded casually. 'Yes.'

'Good. Because now we are married there is one question I must ask.'

She frowned, tilting her head back to see his face more clearly. 'What is it?'

'Today I met Tom Hannay, and liked him more than I believed possible,' said Luca gruffly. 'But that night—'

'Which night?'

'At the Lucchesi in Florence. My room was on the same floor as yours, Georgia. I had asked after you at Reception because I wished to speak with you on the phone, to introduce myself and make arrangements for the next day.'

She stirred restlessly, but his arms tightened.

'Let me finish.' He breathed in deeply. 'As I went up to dress for dinner that evening I saw Tom Hannay come out of your room, obviously naked under his bath-robe.'

'So *that's* why you thought he was my lover!' Georgia shook with laughter against his bare chest. 'You thought he was sneaking back to his wife after a session in my bed?'

'You may think it funny, but I did not,' he said rapidly, holding her tightly. 'I had already seen you on the plane. I thought fortune was smiling on me when I discovered that my beautiful fellow passenger was the teacher Marco had engaged for Alessa. Then I saw Tom leave your room and—'

'Thought the worst,' she said, resigned. 'I wasn't even *in* the room, Luca. Charlotte was sick when we got to the hotel. I stayed with her while Tom had a shower in my bathroom. Charlotte asked him to in case she needed theirs in a hurry again.'

Luca stared down into her eyes in astonishment. 'You mean I have tortured myself all these weeks for nothing?' His eyes narrowed suddenly. 'But there is still this James of yours.' He shook her gently. 'I hoped you would invite him to the wedding so that he could watch as we became man and wife.'

'Oh, did you? James would have hated it.' Georgia sighed. 'I feel guilty because I rather made use of James, used him as a sort of barrier to try to keep you at a distance.' She sighed ruefully. 'Before I met you I'd found your countrymen appreciative but very respectful. You—well, you were different.'

'I was different because I fell in love with you,' he said with heat. 'You know very well that I wanted you from the first. And when you had the accident I was out of my mind for a while, enough to believe that if I made love to you I would erase these lovers of yours from your mind and you would fall in love with me. But my plan failed.'

'Not really,' muttered Georgia against his chest, and felt him tense.

He held her away from him. 'Say what you mean!' he commanded.

'I was already in love with you anyway,' she said unevenly. 'I tried so hard not to be, Luca, but it was no use. I wasn't *forced* to marry you. This isn't the Middle Ages. If I'd really wanted to bring up my child alone nothing could have stopped me. I married you because, deep down, I wanted to.'

'You love me?' he demanded imperiously.

'I suppose I must do.'

He let out an explosive sigh and bent his head to hers in a kiss which went on so long that both were breathless and shaking when he raised his head.

'*Carissima*,' he breathed, and with unsteady hands began to caress the full, ripe curves only partially veiled in amber silk. Suddenly he closed his eyes in anguish and pulled away.

'*Dio*—I forgot!'

'Forgot what?' she said crossly.

'The child—'

'He won't mind.'

'Are you sure?' Luca held her close, rubbing his cheek against her hair. 'I am on fire for you, Georgia. You can feel that I am.'

Her cheeks flamed as he splayed a long-fingered hand at the base of her spine to pull her hard against him. 'It *is* our wedding night,' she said breathlessly, and tilted her head back to look into his eyes, her own so brilliant with promise that Luca let out a great, unsteady sigh, and slowly, delicately, taking undisguised pleasure in the task, took off the nightgown and laid her flat on the bed, his eyes moving over her in a caress so arousing that she stirred restlessly and held up her arms to him in an invitation he accepted with triumph.

He smiled into her glittering, heavy eyes and began, with patience, and all the skill and subtlety at his command, to erase all memory of their previous encounter. He made love to her with such self-control that she was helpless and pleading before he surrendered to his own need and took her to dizzying heights of pleasure, all the while telling her how beautiful, how exquisite she was and how much he loved her, the liquid Italian love words interspersed with English so that the brand new Signora Valori was left in no possible doubt about how much she meant to the man she'd married only hours before.

Afterwards they lay entwined in the warm darkness as their heartbeats slowed, and Luca laid a hand on her stomach, his fingers caressing.

'It is hard to believe,' he whispered.

Georgia stretched luxuriously, putting her hand on his to keep it in place. 'I know. Charlotte's sick all the time, but so far I just get a bit sleepy in the evenings.'

'A very desirable habit for a bride,' chuckled Luca against her throat.

Georgia reached up to smooth his untidy hair. 'I wasn't being awkward about a honeymoon, darling. I really did want to start our marriage here, in your home.'

'Our home,' he contradicted, kissing her. 'And I am glad. Here at La Casupola we are not required to do anything. We can stay exactly where we are as long as we want. But there is a pool behind the house if you wish to swim, and we can go to Lucca or Florence to dine whenever you like.'

'You may be glad to in a day or two,' said Georgia, hoping she wasn't right. 'I might bore you.'

Luca rolled over to capture her beneath him, easing his weight on one hip with such practised expertise that Georgia noted it wryly. 'You will never bore me.'

'If I do I can always get a job, go back to the school and teach,' she teased.

'You can if you wish,' he said, surprising her, then spoilt the effect by caressing her in a way which sent everything out of her head but her body's responses to his touch. 'But I hope very much you will not, *innamorata*. I must find a way to persuade you to spend your time here. With me.'

Dawn was lighting up the Tuscan hills before they slept, and it was some time later in the morning, when they were sharing the breakfast brought to the terrace by a beaming Rosa, before Luca raised a quizzical eyebrow at his wife.

'So, Georgia. This marriage of ours. It is better than you expected?'

She put down her cup of coffee and gave the matter due consideration. 'If you mean the bed part, yes. Thank you for your patience in making it so beautiful for me.'

'I wished to atone for the other time,' he said soberly. 'Also I was afraid at first to harm you in any way.'

Georgia smiled mischievously. 'You forgot about that after a while.'

'I know.' The sombre look remained. 'Georgia, I want a promise from you.'

'I made a few in church yesterday,' she pointed out.

'I want you to promise to tell me if you feel in the least ill at any time—until the baby arrives,' he added, his eyes shadowed.

Georgia's face softened. 'Ah, I see. Of course I promise. Though I feel on top of the world right now.' She thought for a moment, trying to think of some way to reassure him, then her eyes lit with inspiration. 'Luca, do you think I look like my mother?'

He looked surprised. 'Why, yes, I do. Your mother is a beautiful woman.'

'And strong as a horse.' Georgia shot a look at him. 'You know that my father's the Catholic? Mother isn't anything in particular.'

'You are trying to tell me something, *carissima*?' he asked, frowning.

'There are precisely eleven months between Charlotte and me, and Charlotte was born exactly nine months from my parents' wedding day. Both of us took only a few hours to arrive, with no complications. But after that Mother decided to take matters into her own hands to avoid having a baby every year. Otherwise,' added Georgia, with a grin, 'heaven knows how many sisters and brothers I might have had. But the point is that, just like Mother, I'm not sick in the mornings, I feel even better than usual, and my only problem lately has been the feeling that you were trapped into a marriage you would never have dreamed of making otherwise.'

'Whereas to have you belong to me is a dream come true,' stated Luca with emphasis. 'The mere thought of losing you changed my mind about marriage.'

Georgia gave him such an incandescent smile that he leapt to his feet and took her in his arms, kissing her with a fervour she responded to in kind.

'So no more worrying,' she said when she could speak.

'I will try,' he promised.

She smiled up at him. 'Luca, I know it's our honeymoon, but could we go and see your grandmother today, since she didn't feel up to coming to the wedding? I want to tell her how much I like being another Signora

Valori. And how grateful I am for what she insists on calling her "interference"!'

On a bright, windy Palm Sunday the following year Georgia and Gianluca Valori joined with the crowds in the black and white marble beauty of the Duomo in Siena to hear mass, their blue-eyed son gazing up at the bright lights and crowing at the music from the safety of his father's arms.

As they moved slowly to the door afterwards, through the tourists massed at the back to watch the service, Luca obtained three palms in the shape of olive branches, one of which he presented to his wife, who thanked him with a kiss. He put one into the tiny, clutching fist of his son, then tucked the third into his jacket pocket, and smiled at Georgia as they emerged into bright, dazzling sunshine.

'I've got one too,' said Alessa, who was following behind with her father and great-grandmother. She hurried to gaze adoringly at the baby. 'He was so good, Georgia; he didn't cry.'

'No,' said Georgia, chuckling. 'He's fine out in company. He prefers to demand attention at night.'

'He is male,' muttered Luca in an undertone, enjoying the colour which rose in his wife's cheeks as she met the look in his eyes.

'This was a very charming idea of yours, Luca,' said Emilia Valori, joining in with her own share of baby-worship. 'Thank you for bringing me here today.'

'I wished to give thanks for the safe arrival of my son, and the well-being of my wife,' he said simply, 'and Georgia is very drawn to Siena, so here we are.'

'You look very well, Georgia,' commented Marco

Sardi as they walked towards the great, fanshaped square.

'I feel well. I did all along.' Georgia gave her husband a grin. 'It was Luca who suffered, not me.'

'She assured me that in her family such things happen with the minimum of fuss,' agreed Luca, surrendering the baby to Georgia. He pulled a face. 'Nevertheless, I was glad when it was all over.'

'So, no doubt, was Georgia.' said his grandmother drily. 'And how is Charlotte's little one?'

'She's so cute,' said Alessa, who had become a regular visitor to the Hannay household since her move to London, a factor which had done much to reconcile her to her temporary stay in England. 'Her name is Flora, Bisnonna. But little Carlo is more beautiful, I think.'

'Since he has his mother's hair and his father's eyes he can hardly fail to be,' said Emilia Valori with satisfaction.

The family party enjoyed lunch together then separated afterwards to go their different ways—Signora Valori to her home in Lucca, Alessa and Marco to the Villa Toscana—while Luca drove his wife and son home to Rosa, who suffered withdrawal symptoms if the baby was out of her sight for long.

When the baby had been fed and changed and put down for a nap Georgia sat with Luca in his *studio* upstairs, so that they could hear if Carlo cried. Luca drew his wife down beside him on one of the sofas, and held her close in his arms as he rubbed his cheek against the thick, coiled hair, then began pulling the pins from it so that it fell to her shoulders in the way he liked best.

'You look too cool, too perfect with your hair up,'

he said, and ran his hands through the heavy strands before kissing Georgia's willing mouth. He smiled as he raised his head.

'What is it?' she whispered, curling against him.

'I was just remembering last Easter. I had no idea then that in less than a year I would be a husband and a father, and very, very happy with the arrangement.'

Georgia smiled. 'That makes two of us.' She tipped her head back to look at him. 'Do I take it that your views on marriage have undergone a change, then?'

'Now that Carlo is here and you are safe and well in my arms marriage is everything I could wish for,' he assured her. 'Is it the same for you, my heart?'

'Yes, darling, it is.' Georgia pulled away a little to look at him rather warily. 'Though sometimes I shiver at how close I came to rejecting it all.'

Luca frowned. 'I do not understand.'

'I didn't have to marry you,' she said, her eyes falling.

'No,' he said grimly. 'I know that. You were prepared to bring our child up alone.'

'I wouldn't have had to do that, either. After—after you made love to me that day I wrote to James immediately, ending our relationship. He refused to accept it, so once I knew I was expecting your baby I wrote telling him so. But James still wanted to marry me, even offered to help me bring up the child—'

'*Cosa*?' Luca stared at her in outrage. 'He wanted to steal you *and* my son?'

'If there was any stealing, Luca Valori, it was the other way round,' said Georgia severely. 'And it was very good of James.'

Luca said something violent and extremely rude

about James Astin, glaring at his wife, who smiled at him, unmoved.

'You've missed the point, Luca. I'm trying to tell you I *chose* to marry you.'

Luca pulled her to him with sudden ferocity, his mouth bruising hers with a kiss of such possession that Georgia pushed at him in protest until his arms slackened and his mouth softened, and then she returned the kiss with the response only he could ignite in her.

'It is well you chose me,' he said raggedly, when he raised his head. 'I would not have rested until you became my wife, Georgia.'

'I didn't really *choose* you. From the moment I first saw you there was never really any choice at all,' she said, burying her face against his shoulder.

'Then why did you fight me that afternoon?' he demanded, incensed.

'Because you obviously wanted me for another playmate. And I wanted so much more than that.' Her head tipped back and she raised a wry eyebrow at him. 'Which I got, well and truly, didn't I?'

'Are you sorry?' he asked imperiously.

'No. You know I'm not,' she whispered, kissing him.

'Then let us go to bed before Carlo wakes to demand his mother. It has been so long, my darling. I need you so much more than he does at this moment.' Luca stood up, holding out his hand. 'Come. I would carry you, but—'

'I'm not as sylph-like as I once was,' said Georgia, smothering a laugh as they went to peep at their son, who lay sleeping like an angel, the afternoon sunlight haloing his small, blond head.

'Very true,' Luca whispered, and drew her along the

landing to their room, where he drew the russet curtains, enclosing the room in a warm, intimate glow. 'Also I wish to conserve all my energies for more fulfilling activities.' He sat down on the edge of the bed, pulling her between his knees so that he could bury his face between the ripe curves of her breasts.

Georgia's head went back, her eyes closed to savour the exquisite sensation of his lips; then they were locked in each other's arms on the bed, feverish in their need of each other.

'I want you so much, *carissima*,' groaned Luca, then gazed into her brilliant eyes. 'This is truly allowed now? The consultant made this plain to you?'

'Yes—yes—yes!' Georgia yielded exultantly as Luca began kissing her with a lack of restraint made fiercer by the abstinence of the last months, both of them catching fire so quickly that long before either of them had intended they were engulfed in the white heat of physical reunion without any preliminaries other than their intense need of each other.

Afterwards, still holding her cruelly tight in his arms, Luca raised his head and looked down into his wife's dark, dazed eyes.

'I feel sorry for this James Astin of yours.'

She smiled sleepily. 'I don't believe you.'

He ran the tip of his tongue over her bruised mouth. 'I mean it. To lose such joy as this—he is to be pitied.'

'You can't lose what you've never had!' Georgia smoothed his hair back from his damp forehead. 'There was never anything like this with James or anyone else. The "joy", as you put it, only happens with you, Luca.'

His eyes gleamed in triumph. 'This is true?'

'Yes.' Georgia eyed him quizzically. 'For you, of course, it's different.'

'Yes. It is. Utterly different.' He smiled, his fingers playing with a lock of her hair. 'I have made love to women before. You know that. But no one has ever brought me to such desperation of longing as you. And the others I just slept with and played with, Georgia. You are my life.'

For a moment she was speechless, her throat thickened with tears at the passionate sincerity of his declaration. She sniffed, blinked the tears away and smiled up into the brilliant blue gaze with the mischievous grin she knew he adored. 'I'm glad to hear it, Luca Valori.'

He smiled back. 'Why? It is so good to know you have tamed me so well?'

Georgia gave a hoot of laughter. '*Tame* you—that'll be the day!'

'Then why are you glad?'

'Because you're *my* life too,' she assured him, and melted into a crushing embrace which only slackened when an imperious, unmistakable cry came from the next room. 'Oh, dear, the other Valori male demanding attention! I'll be back soon—don't go away.'

Luca lay with his hands behind his head, watching her wrap herself in the white towelling robe she wore these days instead of the amber silk peignoir. 'Bring him in here. I love to watch you nurse him.'

Georgia blew him a kiss then raced off to see to her roaring son, who quieted a little as she changed him, his blue eyes so much like his father's that she hugged him tenderly as she carried him back to the other room.

Luca took the baby from her, waited until Georgia was settled comfortably against the pillows, then handed Carlo back, guiding him to the source of nourishment with a loving hand which lingered a little on the full, satiny curve before leaving the field clear for his son.

'That's a very thoughtful look,' said Georgia softly after a while, and he smiled at her.

'It just occurred to me that at one time my only ambition was to be world champion. At times I suppose I risked my life for it, yet now it seems so unimportant.'

She gave a little shiver. 'I'm glad I didn't know you then.'

'Why? Because of all my adoring fans?' he teased.

'No.' Georgia flipped her son up on her shoulder and patted his back. 'Because I love you so much, Luca Valori, I'd be in agony every time you were on the track.' She breathed in deeply and cradled the baby to her breast again. 'I can't bear to think of it.'

Luca reached over the downy fair head to kiss her. '*Dio*, how lucky I am. I took what I wanted that fateful afternoon with you—'

'Ah, but look what you had to pay for it!' she teased, returning the kiss.

He smiled triumphantly. 'My hand, my heart—my life, *tesoro*. A small price to pay for such a prized possession!'

Cathy Williams is Trinidadian and was brought up on the twin islands of Trinidad and Tobago. She was awarded a scholarship to study in Britain, and came to Exeter University in 1975 to continue her studies into the great loves of her life: languages and literature. It was there that Cathy met her husband, Richard. Since they married Cathy has lived in England, originally in the Thames Valley but now in the Midlands. Cathy and Richard have two daughters.

VENGEFUL SEDUCTION
by
CATHY WILLIAMS

CHAPTER ONE

WHITE was a dreadful colour. Isobel stared at her reflection in the dressing-table mirror and thought that she would probably never wear it again. It would forever conjure up a feeling of despair.

She began brushing her hair, long dark hair, almost black, which fell down her back in small waves. Sooner or later, she knew, she would have to stop brushing it. She had been up here in her bedroom for well over two hours now, getting dressed, but in reality dodging the inevitable which would be progressing now downstairs.

There was a knock on the door and her mother pushed it open and came inside, smiling. Isobel smiled back. The muscles in her jaw ached from the effort but she had no choice. Brides were supposed to be radiant. It was their hallmark. Whoever heard of a depressed bride?

'I'm nearly ready,' Isobel said, turning around and hearing the rustle of her dress under her. The sleeves felt too tight, restricting almost, and the neckline was too low, but then she had only herself to blame. Her input in choosing the thing had been next to nil. She had allowed her mother to pick the design from a magazine without even glancing at it. It had a top fitted to the waist, from where it fell in a series of chiffon layers down to her calves. She had been measured for it, had tried it on, had nodded at her mother and the seamstress, and she had hardly seen it at all.

Now she realised that she hated it, but then, she thought, she would have hated any bridal dress.

'How do I look?' she asked, standing up, and her mother's smile broadened.

'A picture, darling,' her mother said, with a sheen in her eyes, and Isobel said quickly, firmly,

'No tears—you promised.' Cry, she thought, and I shall burst into tears, and as well as being a depressed bride I shall end up being a depressed bride with mascara streaming down my face. Not an attractive sight.

'But where has my little girl gone?' Mrs Chandler held her daughter's hands and Isobel looked back at her with great love and a growing lump in her throat.

'I'm still here, Mum,' she said. 'You're not losing a daughter; you're gaining a son.' That took quite a bit of doing, and saying it made her feel ever so slightly sick.

'Of course I am, darling,' Mrs Chandler agreed, 'but your dad and I...well... Where have all the years gone? One minute you're a toddler, and now here you are getting married.'

'I had to grow up some time.' It was important to keep her voice light, carefree. It wouldn't do at all to have her parents suspect, even for a moment, that all was not well in Bride City. They would immediately start asking questions, and Isobel couldn't afford for that to happen. She loved them both far too much. She had been the much longed for and only child of a couple who had given up hope of ever having children, and from the day of her birth she had been showered with parental adoration. They had both taken an inordinate delight in everything she had done, said, thought, and Isobel had returned their joy with the same deep love.

'And how do I look?' Mrs Chandler gave a small twirl and Isobel grinned broadly.

'Spectacular.' She did, too. Mrs Chandler was as tall as her daughter was, but fair where Isobel was dark, although they both had the same shade of violet-blue eyes and the same long, thick eyelashes. She was sixty now, but her face was still beautiful, with that amazing bone-structure and that clear, faultless complexion. Parkinson's disease might have tainted her movements, slowed her speech, but it had not diminished her lustre.

'Dad's a lucky man,' Isobel said, and when she thought of her father she had another one of those awful lumps in the back of her throat again.

Mrs Chandler laughed. 'If you could have seen him an hour ago,' she said, 'you wouldn't have described him as a man toppling over under the weight of his good luck. He was scowling rather heavily and trying to squeeze into a dinner-jacket. He insisted that he could still get into the one he wore when we married, and of course he can't. The odd button at the bottom will have to be left undone, but I don't think anyone will notice, do you? All eyes will be on you today, my darling.'

That made Isobel feel almost as sick as she had felt when she had told her mother about not losing a daughter but gaining a son, but she smiled again and tried to look terribly radiant at the thought of that.

'How are the preparations going?' she asked, changing the subject. 'I'm sorry, I should have been helping, but...'

'But nothing. You can't be scurrying around a marquee in your gown, making sure that everything is all right! I know you're nervous—I was awfully nervous on my wedding-day—but there are enough hands downstairs making sure that nothing goes horribly wrong. The caterers have been wonderful, the food looks delicious and the guests have now started trickling in. Your father's holding the fort with Aunt Emma and your cousins. Telling his usual jokes. You know.' She was smiling, her eyes distant and full of affection.

The perfect family unit, Isobel thought. Except nothing was perfect, was it? As she had discovered to her cost.

'Has Jeremy arrived yet?' The question almost strangled her, but she kept right on smiling and looking happy.

'Due shortly.' Mrs Chandler started moving towards the door slowly. 'Darling, I shall have to go and help your father. He'll come and fetch you in a short while, when everything's about to start.' She paused by the door. 'I'm so happy for you, my dear. I know we both said—' she spoke carefully, seriously '—that we were a little disappointed that you didn't finish your university education, but I'm sure, seeing you now, that it's all for the best, and you knew what you were doing.'

She left and Isobel sat on the bed. Now that there was no one in the room, she felt free to stop smiling. She wished that her mother had not brought up the subject of university. She had had to swallow many bitter pills for this marriage, and that had been one of them.

She sighed, and across the room her eyes caught her image looking back at her from the full-length antique pine mirror in the corner of the room. Never mind the years slipping past; that didn't worry her. What worried her was the prospect of the future hurtling towards her.

She slipped on her high, satin shoes. They felt uncomfortable. She was a tall girl and accustomed to wearing flat shoes, but this dress needed high ones. They completed the image, and there was no doubt that the image was a remarkably beautiful one.

Her mother had once told her, rather proudly, that she had been striking even as a baby, and Isobel had never had any reason to doubt that. She only had to look in the nearest mirror to see that those striking looks had never abandoned her.

Her waist-long hair was like finely spun silk, black

silk; her skin was ivory-white and her features were perfect. From a very young child she had known admiration, and over the years she had become accustomed to it, even though she felt that her beauty had been a blessing, but in the end it was an irrelevance. Beauty, after all, was transitory, and sometimes, quite frankly, it could be a terrific disadvantage. It opened doors, but the reception waiting at the other end was not always the one you had hoped for.

She walked across to the window and stared down into the huge back garden which her parents had diligently cultivated ever since they had moved into the house. In a few years' time they would have to get a gardener to help them out, or else convert some of the land into pasture, if that were possible, but of course they would defer that until the last possible moment. Her mother had been told at the onset of her illness that her condition would worsen, but Isobel knew that she would continue to tend her garden, lovingly if not as thoroughly.

From here she couldn't see the arriving guests. They would be entering through the front door. Relatives, some of whom she had not seen for a long time; her university friends, who would probably gape and feel dwarfed by the dimensions of her parents' house, because she had never let on just how wealthy her background was; and of course schoolfriends, hers and Jeremy's, shared friends whom they had known from the year dot—just as they had known each other from the year dot.

She gazed down into the garden and attempted to speculate on their reactions to this marriage. Most, she supposed, would see it as a sort of natural conclusion, something expected, but some, her closest friends, had already expressed their horror at the match. She had always been the high achiever, the girl with everything, and they had told her, with varying degrees of tact, just how amazed they were that she was throwing it all away, throwing away a medical degree, for God's sake, to settle down and get married. Naturally she had said nothing. How could she?

Her parents had been disappointed as well, even though they had taken great pains not to condemn her choice. The fact was that they had instilled in her from day one the importance of education, and they had been bewildered when she had arrived home six months previously, sat them down and tonelessly announced her decision to marry Jeremy Baker.

Their immediate concern was that she was pregnant, which, Isobel had thought at the time, had been the only amusing thing about the whole sorry affair.

'It's just that it's all so sudden, darling,' her mother had said, frowning and trying to make sense of the impossible. 'I didn't even think that you and Jeremy were that close. I thought...'

Isobel had known what she had thought, and she had cut in hurriedly, with some nonsense about deciding at last where her heart lay.

'But can't it wait?' her father had asked in a concerned voice, and she hadn't been able to meet his eyes.

'We feel that this is the best way for us,' she had mumbled, and later, when they had gently asked her about her medical degree, she had fudged and muttered something about blood and guts not really being up her street after all.

In the end, they had left it, and her mother had embarked on the wedding preparations with zeal.

Her father was an influential man in the community and strings had been pulled so that everything fell into place with the perfection of an event that could have taken years in the making. Nothing was too small or too great for their daughter, and from the sidelines Isobel had watched and choked back the sickening misery that had threatened to overwhelm her at every turn.

She was consulted on the design for the wedding-invitations, the serviettes, the colours of the flowers which hung in profusion downstairs in the marquee, every conceivable shade of yellow because, her mother had decided, spring was yellow and so the flowers would all represent spring. Frankly, winter would have been more appropriate but she had bitten back the caustic observation and gone along with the general flow.

She began pacing about the room, glancing at the reminders of her childhood which still clung here and there: adventure books which she had devoured in her youth, before biology texts became much more fascinating, a doll which she could remember being given to her as a birthday present from her parents when she was five, a picture of her family which she had done when she was four and which her parents had proudly framed—three figures with odd shapes and stick-like fingers. Her parents had been immensely proud of that picture, but in fact art had been just about the only thing that had eluded her. She had a mind more attuned to the logical.

Ironic, she thought now, that her life, which had been cheerfully pacing towards the most logical conclusion in the world—a degree in the subject she had adored, a career helping people—had petered out into the most irrational ending.

That made her think of Jeremy, and she swallowed down the bitter resentment rising up her throat.

In less than one hour's time she would be his wife, and there was little point in constantly whipping herself with the insanity of it when there was nothing she could possibly do to remedy the situation.

She heard another knock on the door and stiffened in alarm. Surely not her father. Surely not yet. She looked at her watch, which showed that she still had at least forty-five minutes left of freedom, and said, 'Yes? Come in!'

If was probably her mother with some detail that needed sorting out, or else Abigail, the least tactful but closest of her childhood friends, who would no doubt launch into another lecture on the stupidity of the marriage.

'Fine,' she had said when Isobel had told her about Jeremy. 'Throw your life away on that worm! Throw away your hopes of being a doctor! And while you're about it, why don't you fling yourself under the nearest bus as well?' Abigail was studying drama and had cultivated a theatrical way of talking. 'I shall never mention another syllable on the subject again!' But she had continued to expound on the theme whenever they had met, and Isobel assumed that she was about to recommence.

It wasn't Abigail. It wasn't her mother. It was the last person in the world she wanted to face, but face him she did, defiantly across the length of the room.

'So,' he said, strolling into the room and shutting the door behind him, 'the bride is ready.' His voice was sneering, his expression hard and contemptuous.

'What are you doing here?' Isobel asked. Her heart was beating quickly, making her feel giddy and deprived of air. He had always had this sort of dramatic effect on her, as if his presence threw her system into some weird kind of overdrive.

'Didn't you think that I'd turn up?' Lorenzo smiled humourlessly. 'Why, Isobel, my dearest, I'm the best man.'

'Yes.' She licked her dry lips. 'But you should be downstairs, with everyone else.'

What she really meant was that he should be anywhere else, but not here, not in her room. She couldn't bear this game of cruelty he had played ever since he had found out about Jeremy, even though she could understand it.

'I never thought you'd do it,' he bit out, advancing towards her. 'When you told me five months ago what you were planning, I thought that it was a joke, some kind of mad joke.'

'No joke, Lorenzo.'

His hands shot out, grasping her arms, and she winced in pain.

'Why? Why, damn you!'

'I told you…'

'You told me nothing!' He flung her away and walked towards the dressing-table, resting on it with clenched fists.

Isobel followed him, stared at his back, the downbent head, and struggled not to put her arms around him.

Presently he turned around and faced her, his face dark and savage.

'Why are you doing this, Isobel? You're not in love with Jeremy Baker.' There was a sneer in his voice and she answered quickly, to avoid the subject of love.

'How can you speak about him in that tone of voice? I thought he was your friend!'

'We both know him,' Lorenzo bit out. 'He's unstable, reckless. You told me so yourself. Wasn't that one of the reasons that you stopped seeing him, even as a friend, after he went to work for your father? He frightened you. You were glad to be at university.'

'You frighten me too,' she said, 'when you're like this.' They stared at each other. He was furious and his fury, she knew, was given edge by his frustrated bewilderment at the situation. She looked at him, at the whip-hard strength of his body, the dark, sexy good looks which had turned every girl's head at school when he had joined years ago. He had only been sixteen at the time, but already his face had held promise of the powerfully striking man he was to become.

'I am trying to be reasonable, Isobel,' he said in a voice that didn't sound reasonable at all. 'I am trying to work out whether there's something here I'm missing or whether you need to be carted off to the nearest asylum in a strait-jacket.'

His eyes narrowed on her, curiously light eyes that were especially striking given the darkness of his hair and the olive tint of his skin. He was Italian, the son of emigrants who had settled in England, choosing their spot carefully so that their brilliant and gifted only son could be sent to one of the finest private schools in the country. He had easily gained a place on a scholarship and had landed among the students, bright enough but mostly with rich backgrounds, like a leopard in a flock of sheep.

He was different from them all, and he had never seemed to give a damn. He hadn't needed to. His brains were enough to guarantee respect. At sixteen, he possessed a formidable intellect that, it was whispered, outranked some of the professors. His mind was brilliant and creative, and his drive to succeed was formidable. Nothing since had changed.

'I know what I'm doing, Lorenzo,' she whispered, looking away to her hands which were clasped in front of her.

'You damn well don't!' he roared, and she glanced nervously at him and then at the door.

'You'll bring everyone rushing up to see what's going on!'

'And I'll tell them exactly what I'm telling you now! That you've gone off your rocker!'

'You don't understand!' she retaliated, and he moved towards her.

'What don't I understand?' He stood in front of her, staring down.

For a second she didn't have a clue what to say. From the start there had been a thread of suspicion underneath his anger at her decision and she realised that her words, spontaneously spoken, had tightened the thread. She couldn't afford for that to happen. He was too clever by half for him to be allowed a glimpse of the truth behind the black farce.

'I care about Jeremy,' she said, not meeting his eyes, and he tilted her chin up in a rough gesture.

'Like hell you do.' His hand moved from her chin to coil into her hair so that she was forced into looking at him. 'There's only one person you care about. Would you like me to prove it to you?' His mouth twisted into a smile but there was nothing gentle in it.

'Lorenzo, don't!'

'Why? Are you frightened?'

'No, of course I'm not frightened!' She tried to laugh but it came out as a choked sound. 'I am going to marry him,' she said, placing her palms on his chest and feeling his masculine energy whip into her like an electric current. 'You may not like the idea, but it's a fact of life and there's no point in trying to do anything about it.'

'You were my lover,' he said in a low, rough voice. 'Were you playing games behind my back with him? Is that it?'

'No!'

'You hardly saw him when you were at university.

You hardly went home and weekends were with me.'
His brain was ticking, thinking it through, applying the
same ruthless intelligence to the enigma as he applied to
any problem. 'He could hardly have come up to see you
during the week. He wouldn't have been able to wangle
the time off from his job.'

'He wrote,' she admitted. It was a small concession
and it was true. Jeremy had written.

'You arranged a wedding courtesy of written corre-
spondence?' Lorenzo sneered, and his grasp on her hair
tightened. 'Don't make me laugh. You went out with the
boy for one term when you were sixteen, yet you set a
wedding-date by virtue of a few letters?'

'This is pointless,' she whispered, and anger flooded
his face.

'You,' he said grimly, 'have been mine since you
were sixteen. You are twenty now and we have been
lovers for over a year. Jeremy has never been a part of
that picture. You have always belonged to me.'

The words invaded her mind and threw up images of
Lorenzo, his strong arms wrapped around her, his mouth
exploring her body. He had been her first and only lover.

'I belong to myself,' she muttered, trying to wriggle
free.

'Tell me that you're in love with him,' Lorenzo murmured savagely in her ear. 'Let me hear you say it.'

He was so close to her that she could feel his heart
beating, smell the rough sweetness of his skin. Ever
since she had known that she would marry Jeremy, she
had avoided Lorenzo Cicolla like the plague, because
his proximity was the one thing she had feared most and,
standing here, she knew that she had been right.

'You can't, can you?' he taunted. 'Then why? Has he
threatened you? Answer me!'

'Of course not,' she heard herself say quickly, too

quickly. 'I've known him since we were children. We played together. We had the same set of friends.'

'I played marbles with a girl called Francesca when I was ten but that didn't automatically mean that we were destined for each other, for God's sake! Anyway, you're talking in the past tense. The past tense is history.'

'History makes us!'

'You forget, I know him well too. Well enough to know that he can be dangerous. He has always taken risks, stupid risks, and the only reason he's got away with them is because his parents have had the money to bail him out every time.'

'He holds down a job!'

'That means nothing.'

'Why are you his best man if you hate him so much?' she asked bitterly. Why are you? Why did you have to be here?

'Don't you know? He offered it as a challenge, Isobel, and I never refuse a challenge.'

'You're as bad as he is.'

'My intelligence outstrips his,' he said in a hard, controlled voice. 'Any risks I take are born from cool calculation. Jeremy saw me as a threat the minute I set foot in that school and when he discovered that I couldn't be bullied into taking his orders, he did the next best thing. He decided to befriend me, and frankly I didn't care one way or the other. But don't you know that underneath the friendship there has always been an undercurrent of envy and resentment?'

'I know,' Isobel muttered. 'But he did like you.'

'He respected me.' Lorenzo said this without a trace of vanity. 'When he asked me to be his best man, we both knew the reason. The reason was you.'

She turned away, not wanting to hear any more. Everything he said was tearing her apart.

'You were the prize draw,' he mocked. 'You have always been the prize draw. In this little, tight-knit community, you were the light that outshone the rest. You dazzled everyone. You were the greatest trophy.'

'Where is this getting us, Lorenzo?' she asked, doing her utmost to keep the misery out of her voice.

'You're catapulting yourself headlong into disaster,' he grated, a dull red flush spreading over his cheeks. 'There is still time to get out of its path.'

This, she knew, was the closest he would ever get to begging, and it made every bone in her body ache with the craving to do just what he asked.

Everything he had said about Jeremy was true. Jeremy had been obsessed with her. He had singled her out and it had never really occurred to him that his privileged background, which had bought him everything, couldn't similarly buy him her. He had proposed to her when she was sixteen, still at school, while he had been at university, four years her senior. She had laughed. Now the joke was on her.

'I will marry Jeremy—' she looked at her watch '—in less than thirty minutes' time,' she said in a whisper, 'and that's all there is to it.'

His lips tightened and his expression changed subtly from anger to contempt. She didn't know which she hated more.

'I never took you for a coward or a fool, Isobel Chandler, but I'm rapidly revising my opinion.'

'People are more complex than you give them credit for,' she said in a low voice.

'What are you trying to say to me?' His eyes glinted and the sun, streaming in behind him through the large bay window, gave him a brooding, dangerous air that frightened and excited her. He had always frightened and excited her, she realised. He had walked into that school and she had been open-mouthed. She and every other girl in the class. They had been a group hesitatingly crossing the dividing line between childhood and adulthood, realising with an uncertain thrill that boys were not quite as uninteresting as they had once assumed. Lorenzo Cicolla with his bronzed skin and his black hair, four years older but vastly more mature than the other boys of his own age, had captivated their imagination. They had giggled from the sidelines, observed him from the distance with the blushing innocence of youth.

The fact that he had not looked at her, at any of them, even with the mildest of curiosity, had only added to his appeal. In fact, it was only when she was sixteen, ironically through Jeremy, that they had struck up a tentative friendship and he had admitted, with amusement at her reaction, that he had always noticed her. He might have been young, but he had already cultivated the dark, intense composure that had hardened as he got older.

'I'm not trying to say anything.'

'No? Why do I get the impression that you're talking in riddles?'

'I have no idea.' She shrugged but her hands were trembling, and she quickly stuck them behind her back and clasped them together.

'What did those letters say?'

She gave him a blank look, and then realised what he was talking about. She might have guessed that he would not have left for too long her unwary admission that Jeremy had written to her. There had only been one letter, but she wasn't going to tell him that.

'This and that,' she muttered uncomfortably. 'Why are we going through this?'

'Be more specific.'

'I can't. I don't remember.'

'Ah.' His face cleared and he shot her a cruel, cold

look. 'You can't remember what was said in those letters, yet you still decided to marry the man.'

'No! You don't understand! You're putting words into
my mouth,' she said in confusion.

'Can you blame me, dammit?' He gripped her and his
eyes were so ferocious that she was terrified that he
would do something awful, shake her until she came
apart. She opened her mouth to protest and his lips met
hers in a kiss that was fuelled by anger.

Isobel whimpered and pushed at him and eventually
he stood back and stared down at her.

'What's the matter, Isobel?' he asked, his mouth twisting. 'Can't you bear to bid a fond farewell to your
lover?'

'Stop it!' she moaned. She felt close to tears. When
she had first told him about Jeremy, he had been angry,
but proud. Too proud to question. He had stormed out
of her university flat and had not returned. Time had
obviously worked on his fury, stoking it. It was a
strange, back-handed compliment to her, but one she
would rather have avoided.

'Why?' he snarled.

'You know why! I belong to Jeremy now. It's just the
way it is.'

He turned away abruptly, but not before she caught
the hatred that her remark had aroused. She realised,
because she knew him so well, that she had not phrased
her heated reply in the most tactful way possible, but
just then, with her passions threatening to soar out of
control, she had had to say something that would deflect
him from realising how powerful his effect on her still
was.

She made a stilted move towards him, then there was
a knock on the door and she sprang back as though she
had been burned.

It was her father. He came into the room and gave them a puzzled look, in answer to which Lorenzo said, in a normal voice, as though nothing had happened between them, 'Just wishing the bride good luck. I doubt I shall see much of her once the wedding is under way, and we've known each other for so long and—' he faced her with a smile even though his eyes were as hard as diamonds '—so well, that I thought a private last farewell would be in order.'

Her father came into the room, oblivious to the undercurrents, and nodded with genial understanding.

'Quite understand, my dear fellow,' he said warmly. He had always liked Lorenzo. 'Lucky chap, getting this beautiful daughter of mine.'

Lorenzo looked at her with icy courtesy. 'I don't know whether luck had a great part to play in it. Love, perhaps, wouldn't you say, Isobel?'

'Yes, of course,' she said, reaching out to hold her father's hand. She couldn't look at Lorenzo. That would have been a Herculean feat quite beyond her just at that moment.

'Well, dear girl, luck or love doesn't change the fact that your time has come.' Her father cleared his throat and patted her hand and she thought how true his unwitting choice of expression was. 'I hope you're not feeling too dicky. I need your support or else I might just collapse with nerves before we make it to the altar.' He turned to Lorenzo with a grin. 'Wait until you're my age and your daughter is about to marry. You'll soon discover what nerves are all about. I've addressed enough roomfuls of people, but I've never felt this fraught before.' He rested his hand on his stomach. 'Viola says that it's indigestion caused by trying to fit my frame into this outfit. Mothers! Don't know a thing.' His voice held the same level of tender affection when he spoke of his wife as hers did when she spoke of him.

'Try telling them that,' Lorenzo said drily. 'My mama has always maintained that she rules the roost, which, of course, she does.' They both laughed at this and Isobel forced her lips into a mimicry of a smile.

'Well, my dear, shall we go down and make our grand entrance?' He looked at Lorenzo. 'Jeremy has been looking for you. Told him I didn't know whether you'd arrived or not. Didn't know that you were up here, paying your last respects, so to speak.' He had moved towards the door, his mind already on the task ahead, and he missed their various reactions to Jeremy's name.

Isobel clutched his hand and they stood aside so that Lorenzo could leave first, which he did, taking the steps two at a time. She heard his footsteps fading along the marble hallway and felt a dreadful sense of resignation, as if she had aged fifty years in the space of half an hour.

The wedding-ceremony and the reception were both being held in the massive yellow and white marquee, which had been connected to the back doors. She wouldn't even have the impersonal, imposing view of the inside of a church to fall back on. No, in the marquee they would all be standing close together, too close. Her mother had thought it a wonderful idea, and with cheerful apathy Isobel had agreed. Now she wished that she hadn't.

She and her father walked sedately down the winding staircase, through the hallway, into the grand apricot and green drawing-room, which had efficiently been cleared of empty glasses and full ashtrays by some of the hired help, and finally through the open French doors and into the marquee, and the further they progressed, the stiffer Isobel felt.

By the time they reached the marquee, and all eyes swivelled in their direction, she felt dead inside. She stared straight ahead, not meeting anyone's eye, least of all her dissenting clique of friends who had all, naturally, convened in the front row. Out of the corner of her eye she spotted Abigail—straight blonde hair, firm features, disapproving eyes.

Ahead she saw Lorenzo, dark and deadly and staring at her with a veiled contempt which only she would recognise. And beyond him Jeremy, dear, obsessed Jeremy, whose fate would now be entwined with hers forever.

CHAPTER TWO

THE accountant was saying something. Isobel looked at
him and tried to focus her mind on what was happening.
Next to her, her mother sat like a statue on the flowered
upright chair, leaning forward slightly, her body stiff as
board, her face set in lines of pain. She had been like
this for the past three months. Her body moved, her
mouth spoke, but the soul had gone out of her.

'It'll take time,' Richard Adams had told Isobel in the
privacy of the surgery. 'She'll go through all those emotions of anger, despair, shock, disbelief, but she's strong
enough to pull through. In time.'

Isobel looked at the unmoving figure with distress,
and wondered whether her mother's strength hadn't been
over-exaggerated.

'I advise you strongly to sell,' the accountant was saying, flicking through his paperwork.

'Sell?' Isobel shot him a dazed look, and he shook his
head impatiently. He was a small man, balding, with
quick, darting eyes and a manner that implied constant
nervous movement. He was efficient, though. He and his
team of two had run through her father's accounts like
torpedoes—dispassionately, ruthlessly.

'Your father's company has its head above water at
the moment,' Mr Clark said, his fingers twitching over
the paperwork. 'But only just. There has been some
shocking mismanagement over the past few years. Not,'
he added hurriedly, seeing Mrs Chandler's face turn towards him in sad, pained accusation, 'because of anything Mr Chandler did. After all, he had virtually re-

24

signed by the time… Yes, well, we often find that this is a problem in family firms. They employ friends, and there's altogether too much trust and too little ruthlessness. It shows in the company accounts eventually.' He sat back, crossed his legs, linked his fingers together on his lap, and fixed them with what was, for him, a relatively serene stare.

'The fact of the matter is that the company has been left jointly to you both, but it would be madness to continue running it keeping on some of the management who are currently employed there. In no time at all it would cease to be a going concern, and then if you did decide to sell it would fetch you next to nothing. It would become the victim of a predator looking for a dying company to dissect. Simple as that.'

Isobel looked at her mother and said gently, 'You go, Mum. You look tired.'

Mrs Chandler forced a smile on to her face. 'No, of course not, darling. After all, this affects me as well.' She made a small, despairing gesture with her hands and lapsed back into silence.

'I have a prospective buyer already,' Mr Clark said bluntly, 'and I suggest that you give very serious thought to selling to him. He has offered an absurdly generous price. You and your mother could retire millionaires.'

That was not a well-chosen remark. Mrs Chandler looked away with tear-filled eyes and said in a choked voice, 'The money means nothing at all to me, to us. It won't bring David back, will it? Or…' She couldn't go on. She began to sob quietly, resting her forehead in her hands, and Isobel hurried over to her side and wrapped her arms around her. She had hardly had time herself to grieve. She had had to carry her mother through her grief; she had had to be strong for her.

She made a silent, brushing gesture over her mother's

head to Mr Clark, who awkwardly rose to his feet, cleared his throat and muttered a belated, red-faced apology.

'Wait in the hall for me, Mr Clark,' Isobel said briefly, and he nodded and left noiselessly through the drawing-room door.

'I'm sorry, my darling,' Mrs Chandler said, 'I know I should be pulling myself together.' She raised her red eyes to Isobel, who tried to maintain a strong, reassuring face when she felt like breaking up inside. 'You poor love.' She managed a watery smile which made Isobel feel worse. 'I've been no comfort to you, have I?'

'You always are. Whatever you do.'

'Your loss has been double,' she sighed, and then said finally, 'Run along, darling, see what Mr Clark suggests. I'll leave it all to you.'

Isobel hesitated, but only for a moment. Things needed to be sorted out. The issues which Mr Clark had raised left no time for grief. Life continued to march on, demanding involvement. It had no respect for death.

Mr Clark was waiting patiently in the hall when Isobel went out to join him. She ushered him through to the kitchen, poured him some coffee, which he accepted with alacrity, and then took the chair facing him across the kitchen table.

'Who is the buyer, Mr Clark?' she asked, coming to the point, and he relaxed. Displays of emotion, she suspected, made him uneasy. He was only at home when discussing work.

'I have been dealing with a Mr Squires from London,' he said, sipping his coffee. 'There have, in fact, been several poachers waiting on the sidelines. Your father's business may have been mismanaged, but it still has considerable potential and an impressive client portfolio.'

'That being the case, what is there to stop me from running the business myself?'

'Knowledge.' He carefully placed the cup on the saucer, fixed her with those quick eyes, and said with clipped certainty, 'Good intentions won't make a success out of a business. Most of the hierarchy in your father's firm will have to be sacked. Many of them are friends of the family. Could you do that? Your training, if you don't mind my pointing it out, is not financial. Of course, I can only advise, but keeping the company going under your own auspices, merely for sentimental reasons, is not going to do much good. In the end, if it dissolves, you will see the loss of a great many more jobs than those which will be lost should you sell now.'

Isobel thought about that. What he said made sense. Everything he had said over the past few weeks made sense. Mr Clark, it had to be faced, was an eminently sensible man.

'When,' she asked, 'will you need my answer?'

'The sooner the better.'

She nodded and stood up, and he followed suit, collecting his various files and stacking them into his briefcase. He had come well-prepared. Statistics had been shown her, profit and loss columns had been methodically pointed out, budgets analysed, and he had been right: she knew very little about finance. In time, she was sure, she could get to grips with it, but 'in time' might not be soon enough, and she knew that it would have broken her father's heart to witness the dissolution of his beloved company. Better for it to carry on in a different form. Wasn't it?

She showed Mr Clark out, looked in on her mother, who had fallen into a fitful sleep on the chair, and then retreated to the library to think.

It was so hard being strong, she thought wearily. Decisions had to be made and her mother, she knew, was in no fit state to make them.

Isobel sat back in the leather swivel chair and closed her eyes. Memories were the worst. Her father sitting her on his knee when she was a child, going for walks with her, patiently telling her about the various plants and trees in the garden.

She didn't sob like her mother. The tears squeezed themselves out, but she didn't brush them away. They fell on to her hands, on her lap, her dress.

That dreamlike feeling of unreality which had first dogged her had gone. Now she could think of the policeman at the door, breaking the news to them that there had been a car accident, that both occupants had been killed outright, without trying to convince herself that she would wake up at any moment and find that it had only been a terrible nightmare.

Jeremy had been at the wheel of the Jaguar. He had been overtaking another car and had been hit by an oncoming lorry. He had been over the limit.

She had tried very hard, but bitterness towards him had overlaid any pain she might have felt. He had ruined her life.

The following morning she telephoned Mr Clark and told him to go ahead with the sale of the company.

'You have my trust in this matter, Mr Clark,' she said down the line. 'I will sign whatever needs signing, but I want no involvement beyond that.'

Her mother was out for the day, taken under wing by Jeremy's mother, who had been distraught at the funeral but over the past weeks had been a source of strength to Mrs Chandler. They were going to have tea in one of the coffee-shops in the village.

That left Isobel on her own, and she made her way

back to her own house. Ever since the accident she had been living with her mother, and it had been something of a relief.

The house she had shared with Jeremy, even after four years of marriage, had never felt like a home. She had looked after the gardens, arranged flowers in vases, hung paintings, but it had still remained a stiff, empty shell. A house could never become a home without love to fill it, and love was something that had been conspicuous by its absence.

She pushed open the front door, stooped down to collect the dribs and drabs of mail, and then, unemotionally, she resumed her sporadic job of packing Jeremy's clothes into boxes which she had retrieved from the attic. She should have done it sooner, weeks ago, but time had flown past so quickly.

Suits, ties, trousers, jumpers, shirts. She would give them all to charity.

It had all been so pointless. She could remember being twenty, being in love, Lorenzo. Her throat constricted. Of course that had been another life, and she had got over him. Time healed everything; that much was true.

She hadn't even had the reminder of his mother, because Mrs Cicolla had emigrated to America to be with her son three years previously.

She could still remember that dead, sickly feeling that had spread over her when he had announced at the wedding, not to her but to her parents, that he had decided to emigrate.

'Within a fortnight,' he had said casually, his hand in his pocket, his eyes not looking at her at all, eliminating her from his life in one fell swoop. Ex-lover with another man's ring on her finger. No longer worth so much as token politeness.

That had been four years ago, but the memory was as

clear as if it had been only yesterday, only a few hours ago.

She heard the buzz of the doorbell and ran down the stairs to answer it. Abigail. Isobel's face broke into a smile of pure joy. She hadn't seen Abigail, apart from briefly at the funeral three months ago.

'I tried your mum's house first,' Abigail said, coming inside, 'and when there was no reply, I thought that you might be here.' She looked sympathetically at Isobel. 'Do you need a hand with anything?'

They went upstairs and continued boxing the clothes, chatting. Abigail's status, in the space of only a few years, had reached mammoth proportions. She was in the newspapers all the time, her movements shadowed and faithfully, or unfaithfully, reported back on.

'How's your mum coping?' she asked casually, and Isobel paused to look at her.

'Not very well,' she answered truthfully. 'She seems to have retreated into herself.'

'It's understandable.'

'She doesn't even venture out into the garden. She says every blade of grass reminds her of him.'

Abigail didn't say anything for a while. 'And you, Izzy?' She looked away and busied herself with stuffing more clothes into boxes. Jeremy had had a lot of clothes. He had liked dressing the part of the wealthy landowner.

'He's in my mind,' Isobel said in a low voice.

'And Jeremy?'

Isobel stood up, dusted herself down and replied shortly, 'You know that he caused the accident. The coroner told me that in privacy. I asked him if he could withhold the information from his parents, and from Mum.'

'You always hated him, didn't you?'

'No.' Isobel thought about it, for the first time putting

into words what had never been said before. 'He trapped me into marriage, and please don't ask me how or why.' Those papers. She frowned. Where were they? He must have hidden them somewhere. They could not have vanished into thin air. Oh, no. He would never have been so careless as to misplace them—after all, they were the stick to be waved over her if ever she thought of desertion. 'Of course I hated him to start with, but you can't hate forever. It's too tiring. After a while, the instinct for self-preservation takes over or else you would just go mad.' She shrugged and they went down to the kitchen to have some coffee.

It helped having someone to talk to. It made her co-ordinate her thoughts, and Isobel found herself telling Abigail about Mr Clark's offer, what she intended to do with her house, her job.

'I might even contemplate finding out whether I can't complete some kind of medical course, take it up,' she said, blushing. 'Richard thinks it's a good idea.'

'Richard?' Abigail's eyebrows quirked. 'Dr Adams, you mean?'

'He's very encouraging.'

'And, so that's how the land lies.'

'Of course not!' Isobel laughed. 'You and that dramatic mind of yours! Richard and I are simply good friends. He's been kind to me over the years.'

And they left it at that. Abigail departed late that evening and Isobel returned to find her mother in better spirits than she had been for weeks.

'Emily is helping me to put everything in perspective, the dear woman,' she said, sipping tea and picking bits of salad from her plate like a choosy bird deliberating over which morsels to consume. 'David is gone, and hiding myself away isn't going to change that. I've spent too long hiding. I want to start thinking about tomorrow. What did Mr Clark say?'

So Isobel told her, and the following morning, by some uncanny coincidence, he telephoned to inform her that the purchaser had arrived and would she come down to his offices on the High Street to sign some bits of paper.

Isobel dressed carefully for the occasion. A sober grey wool suit, because the chill of autumn was in the air, her pearls, cream-coloured shoes.

She looked in the mirror and saw the reflection of a twenty-four-year-old woman, nearly twenty-five, who, in the midst of loss, now found herself on the brink of freedom for the first time in four long years.

She smiled, and the image smiled back, showing her what she hadn't seen for a very long time. The same stunning face, but with the black hair trimmed to a bob, a tall, lithe body, eyes that were a little sad, as though they had seen too much.

She swept out of the house, feeling better than she had done for a while, and arrived at Mr Clark's offices well in time.

Mr Squires wasn't there. Isobel drank coffee, made small talk to the accountant, and began to feel slightly annoyed that she was being kept waiting. Hadn't this man heard of common politeness?

She glanced at her watch and caught Mr Clark's eye. He was looking worriedly at his own watch. Presently he stood up, and said that he would go and have a look to see what had happened to the gentleman in question.

'Perhaps he's lost,' he volunteered politely, to which she was tempted to point out that he could only have found himself lost in a town the size of theirs if he was a mental incompetent, in which case was she really doing the right thing by selling him her father's company?

He vanished out of the room and ten minutes later, having quietly convinced herself that Mr Squires, the invisible man, was definitely not in the running as a prospective buyer for the company, she heard the door being pushed open.

She automatically looked around.

The shock she felt on seeing Lorenzo Cicolla standing in the doorway was as great as if she had looked out of the window and casually seen a mushroom cloud hanging over the town, announcing nuclear war.

He strolled into the room, not taking his eyes off her face, and she stood up, drained of colour. She was shaking, trembling like a leaf, like someone who had seen a ghost. Her mind felt as though it was being bombarded by so many images, so many feelings, that any minute it would shut down from overload.

'Lorenzo Cicolla! What are you doing here? I'm expecting a Mr Squires—he should be here any moment. You're not Mr Squires,' was all she managed to get out, which was an achievement since her vocal cords appeared to have deserted her.

She had never expected to see Lorenzo Cicolla again. He had been the stick of dynamite thrown into her young life, blowing it to pieces, and those pieces had never successfully been put together again. But still, she had relegated him to the past. She had locked that haunting image into a safe room and she had tried damned hard never to open the door.

What was he doing here?

'No,' Lorenzo agreed smoothly, unsmiling, his pale eyes assessing her with arrogant thoroughness. 'I'm not, am I?'

He sat down in the chair next to her and crossed his legs, and she wished desperately that she could stop staring but she couldn't. It had been a long time.

The passage of time showed itself in the tiny lines by
his eyes and mouth, the hardness of his features, but
apart from that she might have been staring at the
Lorenzo of old. He had the same terrifying sex-appeal,
the same dark, brooding good looks.

'I apologise for staring,' Isobel said stiltedly, 'but I
can't believe that it's really you, sitting there.' She threw
him a tentative smile which met with a blank wall.

'I was sorry to hear about your father,' he said
abruptly, looking away. 'I'm afraid the news was rather
late in reaching me.'

'Thank you. Yes. It was a tragic accident.' Platitudes
were becoming easier to mouth. No one felt comfortable
with raw emotion and she had learned to control her
responses to the polite condolences of neighbours and
people in the village.

'And of course, Jeremy.'

'Thank you. Of course.'

'What exactly happened?'

She shrugged and her fingers nervously plucked her
wool skirt. 'The car went out of control. There was a
lorry coming in the opposite direction. Jeremy was killed
outright. My father—' she paused and took a deep, sta-
bilising breath '—died in the ambulance.'

'How is your mother coping with it?'

'Why are you here?' It was easier to ask that now that
she had recovered some of her self-control.

He smiled coolly, and she could see dislike and contempt lurking beneath the surface. It made her blood run
cold. 'Surely we aren't yet finished with the preliminaries, are we, Isobel? It's been years—four years to
be precise.'

'Yes. I know. You left this town without a backward
glance, Lorenzo.' Her heart was still beating irregularly
and she had the strangest feeling of having stepped into

a mad, nonsensical world, like Alice in Wonderland. One blink and it would all disappear. She blinked but nothing disappeared, not even the breathless tension gripping her lungs, making breathing laborious and difficult.

He shrugged. 'I always knew that I would return, when the time was right.'

'And why is the time right now?'

'Because, my dear, I am about to buy your father's company.'

'You!' She looked at him in stunned silence. 'But Mr Clark said... He told me...'

'That Mr Squires was interested. Yes. Mr Squires was interested, on my behalf.'

She stood up and began pacing the room, while Lorenzo remained where he was, watching her, his face revealing nothing.

'You can't be serious,' she said at last, standing in front of him but not too close, because something about him was vaguely menacing. Had this been the same man who had fired her passions once upon a time? Surely not!

'I have never been more serious about anything in my entire life.'

'But why?'

His lips thinned. 'Because I like the beauty of the wheel that turns full circle.'

'Revenge, Lorenzo?' she whispered incredulously.

'Oh, revenge is too strong a word.'

'Then why my father's company?'

'It poses an interesting challenge,' he drawled, but the lazy cruelty was still there in his voice and in the rigid lines of his face.

'And the fact that my father owned it has nothing to do with it?'

'A little, I suppose.' He shrugged dismissively, although his eyes never left her face, not for a second. 'Besides, I've become tired of city life. Chicago has lost its appeal. It will be nice returning here for a while.'

'You'll be coming back *here* to live?'

'But of course. What else did you expect?'

Not that. Anything but that, Isobel thought. Four years ago they had parted in anger and bitterness. Words had been spoken, things said… She stifled the memory of her disastrous wedding-day, that awful confrontation in the garden, before he had walked out of her life forever. Had he simply been biding his time until an opportunity such as this arose, or had the death of Jeremy and her father rekindled buried feelings of anger?

'You don't look too thrilled with the prospect,' he said, eyebrows raised, his mouth curling with a hint of cynicism.

'Of course, it will be nice to see you…' Her voice trailed off.

'Don't lie, Isobel. Your face is too transparent.'

She flushed angrily. 'What do you want me to say? You walk back into town after four years and announce that you plan on settling here, but there's nothing pleasant about the announcement, is there? You're not planning on settling here for the good of the community. You're planning on settling here because you have a chance to settle old scores.' She looked at him bitterly. 'Aren't we both too old for this?'

He banged his fist on the table with such force that Isobel jumped and looked at him warily. He wasn't going to get violent, was he? Then she laughed nervously to herself. Of course not. How could he in such a public place? Besides, she knew Lorenzo. He had never been a man given to displays of violence.

You don't know him now, though, a little voice

warned. People change. The face she was staring at with apprehension was the face of a stranger, a dark, menacing stranger.

'Too old?' he sneered. 'Too old to forget the past, Isobel?'

'What happened happened a long time ago...' She glanced at the door and he followed the line of her eyes with a cold smile.

'Mr Clark has been told to wait until I am ready.'

'What?'

'I informed him that there were things I wanted to discuss with you in private.'

'The sale of my father's business isn't a private matter,' she began, but that wasn't the object of his discussion, was it? 'Can't we put the past behind us? We can be friends...'

'Friends?' He almost laughed at that, his eyebrows shooting up in an expression of contempt that made her burn. 'I'm sure you'd like nothing better, Isobel.'

'What does that mean?'

'Oh, only that I'm here, rich and successful—the two prerequisites, if I remember correctly, for any man to be worthwhile in your eyes.'

'That's not true!' More memories flooded back and she felt faint.

'No?' He relaxed back in the swivel chair and folded his hands on his lap. 'Then pray tell me why you married Jeremy, and why you stayed married to him for four long years? Your precious status quo. You needed it so badly that you sacrificed your life for it.'

Isobel stood up, trembling, white. 'I don't have to remain here and listen to this,' she said curtly, turning towards the door.

'Sit back down!'

She looked at him over her shoulder. 'You don't give me orders, Lorenzo Cicolla!'

'Sit back down!' he roared, and she hastily sat back down, wondering whether his bellow wouldn't bring Mr Clark scurrying back into his office. But no one came.

'Now you listen to me,' he said, and his voice was the voice of a man with steel running through his veins. He leaned forward. 'Your father's company needs a buyer if it's to survive in one piece.'

'I can choose my buyer,' she said coldly, and he laughed under his breath.

'Really?'

'Mr Clark told me that there are several offers in the pipeline.'

'No offers, Isobel.'

'But...'

'I am the only bidder. Without me, your father's company will quickly fall into ruin. It's a wonder that it hasn't before now. If it falls into ruin, my darling, it will be sold off in bits and pieces to the highest bidders and you will watch your father's handiwork go down the drain. Do you want that?'

Isobel looked at him with dislike. He was enjoying this. He was enjoying her discomfort, enjoying watching her in a position of helpless subservience. How could she ever have felt love for this man? He was a sadist.

She could, she knew, explain, after all these years, why she had married Jeremy, but if he was hell-bent on revenge, then might not that confession give him the ammunition he needed? It was a chance she could not take. Her father was dead. He was beyond pain. But her mother was still alive, ill, vulnerable, and already buffeted by enough misfortune.

Besides, and she might as well face it, the Lorenzo Cicolla she had known, the man who had once, so long ago that she could scarcely recall, made love to her, laughed with her, was gone. This was someone else. Someone she no longer understood.

'What do you gain from all this, Lorenzo?' she asked with quiet desperation.

'Passing satisfaction,' he said, his lips twisting, and she clenched her fists uselessly at her sides.

'At my expense.'

'Is that so difficult to understand?' He smiled with sarcasm.

'Why fight when we can—?'

'Make love?'

Colour swept into her face. She could feel it burning through her, making her perspire lightly, and the hairs on the back of her neck stand on end.

'When we can be friends…' she whispered.

He was looking at her, his eyes roving insolently over her body. 'A tempting thought,' he said silkily. 'You're still a beautiful woman. More so. Time has put character into your face. But no, I think I can resist you.' He was smiling again, that cool smile that made her want to hit him. 'I don't think I could stomach the thought that your friendship had only been offered because I am now rich enough to pay the right price.'

'You're despicable.'

That brought an angry flush to his face. 'Your marriage to Jeremy Baker was hardly what I would call a noble gesture, Isobel. Or perhaps it's simply my peasant mind that persists in thinking in such inconvenient black and white terms.'

Isobel looked at him from under her lashes. Peasant? Hardly. He might have come from the wrong side of the tracks, as Jeremy had been fond of saying whenever his name cropped up, but no one looking at him would ever have guessed that. Sitting there, in his expensive tailored suit, he looked what he was: wealthy, sophisticated, ruthless.

'Why didn't you stay in America?' It was more the agonised voicing of a private thought than a question demanding an answer.

'I told you. I lost interest in the bright lights.'

She doubted that. He had not 'lost interest' in the bright lights. He had merely decided that there was a bigger, more fulfilling challenge waiting for him here.

He would initially have been drawn to her father's company because it probably fell into the realms of what he was accustomed to dealing with. The actual ownership was, she suspected, added spice.

'How did you find out about…?'

'It was reported in the financial news,' Lorenzo answered. 'Bob Squires, my man in London, faxed me the article. He thought that I might find the coincidence amusing as well as a possibility for take-over. Of course, he doesn't know a great deal about my personal life, but he did know where I had lived in my youth.'

'I see. And does anyone know much about your personal life, Lorenzo?' she asked bitterly, and was rewarded with a look of angry discomfort. It only lasted seconds but in that time she had a fleeting glimpse of something lying beneath the cold, arrogant exterior.

'I dislike people who try to pry into what's no business of theirs.' He stood up abruptly and gazed out of the window, his back to her.

'What a lonely life you must have led all these years,' she murmured, and he spun around to face her, his eyes savage and mocking.

'I hardly think that you're someone qualified to pass judgement on the quality of other people's lives,' he said tersely. 'Marriage for money, quite frankly, makes me sick. Were you *ever* happy, Isobel? When the socialising was over and there were just the two of you left in your big, expensive, empty house?'

She looked away, agitated, and said nothing.

'I thought not.' He had regained his composure but he didn't sit back down. He prowled restlessly around the room, staring at her, and she felt like a trapped rabbit, knowing that whatever he said she would lose because she was incapable of justifying her past.

'If you want me to sign papers,' she said stiffly, 'I shall do so. If not, I'm leaving.'

'You'll leave when I'm ready for you to leave.'

She met his cool grey eyes with anger. 'I don't work for you, Lorenzo. You're not my boss! I'm prepared to sell my father's company to you because the move was recommended by Mr Clark, but beyond that I want nothing to do with you!'

'Now there's a thought,' he murmured, moving behind her and resting his hands on either side of her chair. Her body froze. She wanted nothing to do with him but his sexuality, which had held her in its snare all those years ago, was as powerful as ever. She could feel it emanating from him, from those strong arms only inches away from her.

'What are you talking about?' she asked, licking her lips nervously.

'You could,' he murmured, 'always work for me. Wouldn't that be fun?'

'No,' Isobel muttered in a strangled voice. She wanted badly to move but she was afraid, she realised, of touching him.

'No,' he agreed, 'perhaps it wouldn't be. Or perhaps it wouldn't be enough.' The grey eyes swept over her, the eyes of a predator that had trapped its quarry and was lazily contemplating what course of action to take next.

'What do you mean? What are you talking about?' Her voice had risen a pitch higher.

'The fate of your father's company is in my hands, Isobel. Without me, everything he spent a lifetime working for will vanish like a puff of smoke.' He smiled as though the thought afforded him immense satisfaction.

Isobel looked at him in frozen shock.

'Another buyer can be found,' she persisted weakly.

'I think not.' Another smile, and she felt a quiver of confused alarm.

'No…' He strolled lazily to the window, his hands in his pockets, and turned to face her. 'I have returned, Isobel, and this time I am calling the shots. I will have you, Isobel Chandler, and then, when I tire of you, I shall cast you aside.'

'And you said that you didn't want revenge?' There was a dangerous electricity in the air.

He contemplated her coldly.

'Revenge. Such a basic word. But maybe you're right. Maybe revenge is the only thing that can satisfy me. I will put a ring on your finger and you will be mine for however long I want you. In return, I will salvage your father's company.'

CHAPTER THREE

'NEVER!' Shock made her start back and she found that her hands were gripping the arms of the chair. 'You're mad!'

'Why?' His voice was controlled, but whip-hard, and his eyes pierced into her with a venom that made her cringe.

'I can't believe that you would go to such lengths, Lorenzo… The past is over and done with…'

'It is *never* over and done with. Do you understand me? It has festered inside me and now that I have my opportunity to do something about it, I damn well will.'

'I will never marry you!' He hated her. It was as simple as that. Dislike, contempt, wounded male pride, those were never strong enough to describe what he felt towards her. She could see that now, and she knew with utmost finality that she could never unburden her secret to him. If he was prepared to marry her simply to sate his desire for revenge, then how could she ever trust him?

'You will do precisely what I say, Isobel, because you have no choice.'

'Never! Do you understand, Lorenzo Cicolla? Never, never, never!' She stood up because she was too agitated to sit down, but she didn't walk towards the door. Something in the room kept her rooted to the spot.

'Why ever not, my dear?' he asked with aggravatingly exaggerated politeness. He was standing behind the desk, towering over her. 'In fact, I have no idea how you could resist such a charming proposition. After all, you'll be able to maintain your status quo; you'll have your wealthy lifestyle. If I recall correctly, those were the things that meant so much more to you than I ever did.' There was no fondness in his voice as he recalled their shared past, no softening in his features. If anything his face hardened, and she shivered.

'Believe what you will,' she muttered, looking away, and he moved around the desk so swiftly that before she realised it he was standing next to her. He curled his fingers into her hair and dragged her face to his.

Her heart began to beat, to pound, and she licked her lips nervously. She would never marry him, but some primitive response to his masculinity unfurled deep within her and her eyes widened in shock and an instinctive response to retreat as quickly as she could.

But retreat was impossible. His grip was like a vice. She stood completely still and tried to stifle the treacherous warmth rushing through her.

'Believe what I will, Isobel?' he asked, his lips curling. 'Surely you mean, believe what you told me? Told me four years ago?'

She didn't answer. Was there a way to answer the unanswerable?

The memories sprang up at her like monsters rushing out from the dark. The wedding-day, gloriously sunny, a still, fine spring day that had felt more like summer. Jeremy, looking at her with satisfaction, knowing that he now owned her.

She had been surprised and taken aback when Lorenzo had remained for the reception. She had thought that he would take the first opportunity to leave a situation which he despised, but a part of her realised that he would remain because to leave would be to throw in his hand; it would have been running away, tail between legs, admitting defeat. It would have been what Jeremy wanted. But it would not have been the Italian way: there would have been no retreat without honour.

She had mixed with friends and relatives and she had watched Lorenzo out of the corner of her eye.

In retrospect, she could see that the explosion had been only a matter of time.

Jeremy had spent the afternoon showing her off, baiting his bitter rival. Little snide remarks scattered here and there, and then more often.

Isobel could remember gritting her teeth in frustrated anger at Jeremy's game-playing. He had always been fond of displaying his parents' wealth to Lorenzo.

Money. It had always been the one thing that had separated Lorenzo from the rest of them. His parents had come to England with very little, and although his father had held down a responsible job at one of the engineering companies, he had always had what had amounted, in comparison with the rest of them, a minuscule income. Lorenzo's school uniforms had been bought from the second-hand sales at the school, and text-books were never bought at all; they were borrowed from the library.

'Thinking about it, Isobel?' The smooth, cruel voice brought her back to the present, and she blinked and looked at him, disorientated.

'Thinking about what?' He had always had an amazing ability to read her mind, but she preferred to plead ignorance rather than to admit that he was spot on.

'Your glorious, happy wedding-day. So many people milling around, all the pillars of the little community, elaborately turned out for the affair of the year.'

'That's not fair!'

He continued as if she hadn't spoken. 'And of course you looked the part—you did your parents proud, Isobel, my dear.'

Isobel closed her eyes. She remembered the compliments. She had looked exquisite. She had been told that over and over again, and she had smiled prettily every single time. Her mouth had ached by the end of the evening.

'"Lucky Jeremy Baker." I could see the thought running through more than one envious male mind.' The dislike was thick in his voice and she kept her eyes lowered and her hands clenched in front of her. 'Lucky Jeremy Baker, netting the biggest fish in the sea. He paled next to you, but then everyone did, didn't they, Isobel?' he asked softly. 'Everyone except me.'

Her heartbeat quickened. She pictured them together, making love, his bronzed body wrapped against her flawless ivory one.

The thought flashed with startling clarity through her mind, and she shoved it back with a certain amount of disturbed confusion.

She remembered Jeremy. Slim, blond-haired, blue eyed, with that brand of good looks that were always charming in young children but in men were hardly ever sexy.

She had never found him particularly attractive. There was something in him that was vaguely unsettling, but they had always belonged to the same group of friends, drifting apart at one stage because of their age difference, but then drifting back again because in a town the size of theirs it was inevitable that they would. Their friends were all offspring of parents who, in their tiny community, knew each other very well.

'Why are we going over old ground?' she whispered helplessly, not daring to raise her eyes to meet his. Breathing in his masculinity was making her head spin. Losing herself in those terrible, mesmeric eyes would only make the condition worse.

'Isn't that what old friends do?' he mocked harshly. 'Reminisce?'

'Old friends...?' The question hung in the air with a certain amount of pathetic sadness clinging to it, and he flung her aside abruptly, turning away to resume his position behind the desk. As if he owned it. As if he owned the entire office.

She hazarded a glance at him through lowered lashes. This situation was bizarre, ridiculous. If she had any sense at all, she would gather her wits about her, toss him a cool smile and walk out. Instead she listened to the silence, thick as lead, and sat back down in the chair.

Other unwanted memories of that wedding-day came back to her, relieved to be out at last from their exile in the furthest reaches of her mind—Abigail telling her with brutal frankness that she supposed congratulations were in order.

'Only if you really think so,' Isobel had replied, shoving the sleeves of the hateful wedding-dress up as far as they would go.

'You'll wreck your dress doing that.'

'Who cares?' she had answered, and had received a shrewd look in return.

'You should,' her friend had said. 'This should be neatly dry-cleaned and then carefully placed into storage somewhere for the line of little Jeremy Bakers you'll no doubt be producing over the next few years.'

'Never!'

Well, she thought now, at least that much had proved true. A child would have been the ultimate madness and she had never, not even once, been tempted, although all around her friends and acquaintances were having children and trying to persuade her that it was the next step.

'You've changed.' The observation, spoken without

thinking, took her by surprise. She hadn't meant to say that. She had meant to inform him that she would be on her way now that he would no longer be buying her father's firm, because marriage as a condition was out of the question.

He sat back in the black swivel chair and looked at her with a shuttered expression.

'Yes, Isobel, I'm now wealthy and successful.'

'That's not what I meant.'

He shot her an angry look which would have driven her into silence if she had let it, but she was damned if she would be at the receiving end of all the blows.

'I'm not interested in hearing your thoughts on the matter,' he grated, tapping restlessly on the blotting-pad with his finger.

'Why not?' she flung at him bitterly. 'And besides, why should I care whether you're interested in hearing what I have to say or not? You patently don't give a damn about me!'

'Hurt, Isobel?' he threw back at her, and his eyes glittered like silver. 'Disappointed that I wasn't prepared to pick up the pieces of our relationship from where you ditched it on the roadside four years ago?'

'Of course not.'

'You over-estimate your charm. You might turn any number of heads here, but you forget that America is not entirely devoid of its share of lovely women.'

He was watching her closely, like a scientist observing a live specimen, waiting to see how it would react to various stimuli.

Isobel maintained her calm with effort.

'I do not "over-estimate" my charm, as you put it, nor am I aware of any amount of head-turning going on here, and I'm quite sure that America is bursting with lovely women—whatever that remark is supposed to mean.'

His lips tightened and she could tell he wasn't impressed with her retort. Did he really expect her to surrender in this war without a fight? Had he expected to waltz back here and make her dance to his tune without a murmur? She was sick to death of dancing to other people's tunes. She smiled guilelessly at him.

'I take it you've wined and dined your fair share of lovely women? Is that what you're trying to say to me?' She didn't like the thought of that and, more than that, she didn't like the thought that he could still provoke this level of wild jealousy inside her.

'What makes you think that I did the wining and dining?' he asked with a certain amount of mockery. 'Equality is rampant over there.'

That, she knew, was a lie. She couldn't see him allowing any woman to pay her way. It wasn't his style at all. With all her immense family wealth, he had never once allowed her to pay for a single meal. Instead they had eaten out at cheap bistros or else made do with bread and cheese on the bed. Followed by love. Her body warmed at the thought of that and she looked at him furtively, then glanced down at her entwined fingers.

No, Lorenzo Cicolla was Italian through and through. No amount of expensive American tailoring could ever change that.

She remembered how she had reacted on her wedding-day to his announcement that he would be leaving the country.

After the initial shock had worn off slightly, she had murmured to him in a low voice, 'You never told me that you were thinking of going to America.' Around them various voices were arguing, debating the pros and cons of starting life without any financial help, an argument initiated by the revelation of his trip abroad to play the options market.

'Would it have made the slightest difference?' he had asked cuttingly, and she had remained silent.

The silences between them were the things that she remembered most clearly about that torturous time, the things which she could not reveal, the words she could never say.

'I thought not,' he had said in an icy voice, and her eyes had pleaded with him for some understanding but had hit a blank wall of hostility. 'My post-grad results will be excellent but I don't think I'll return to this little hot-bed of intrigue to wait for them. No, I've already booked my flight.'

Then she had asked, in a dull voice, 'Where will you stay?'

'In a slum, I expect.' He had smiled a cool smile. 'As we both know, penthouse apartments are out of the question for someone who hasn't got parents rich enough to lend a convenient hand.'

Her face burned now as she thought back to her answer to that.

'I could give you—' she had begun and he had snarled savagely.

'Don't even say it. Charity is something I find repellent.'

Charity, she thought, looking at him, was clearly not an emotion he had assiduously cultivated in America. Oh, no. Charity couldn't be further from his mind in this demonic deal he wanted to cut.

'You'll be bored to tears within a month of living here,' she said, thinking prosaic thoughts so that the tingling in her blood could subside and return to its rightful place in a past which was no longer relevant.

'Oh, I think the element of novelty should keep me going for a while.'

She knew what he was referring to. The novelty would be her. When he tired, he would leave. They looked at each other, thinking the same thought—enemies on the same wavelength.

'In that case, you'll have to make do without the novelty of my father's company, because there is no way that your condition for buying the firm will be met.'

She stood and he said softly, 'Sit back down. I've already made it clear to you that you don't leave this office until I'm through.'

'And I've already made it clear to you that you don't run my life.'

'Hasn't Mr Clark told you what you can expect if I *don't* buy the company?' he said idly, clasping his hands behind his head and surveying her through narrowed eyes.

'He said that the company has great potential and a large client portfolio,' she replied, siphoning off most of what he had, in fact, told her.

'It's struggling to make ends meet. In less than a year its potential will be a nostalgic memory and its large client portfolio will be a thing of the past.'

'A year is a long time,' Isobel interjected mutinously. 'Anything can happen in a year.'

'For instance?' He appeared no more than mildly interested in her answer, which infuriated her more than if he had retaliated with some scathing, pithy observation.

'For instance,' she snapped, racking her brains to think of a few intelligent and probable for-instances, 'I could find someone to run the company on my behalf!'

'Who?'

'Well, if I had someone in mind, I wouldn't be here, would I?' she said heatedly. 'Humiliating myself.'

His eyebrows rose. 'Humiliating yourself?' he asked, as though the thought of her humiliation had not crossed his mind in any way, shape or form. 'Sure that's the emotion you had in mind?'

He stood up and strolled over to her, and she looked at his approaching figure with growing alarm.

'What are you talking about?' she asked, in such a breathless voice that she felt obliged to clear her throat and say as normally as she could, 'I don't know what you're talking about.'

He was close to her, staring down at her, and she looked up at him with impotent frustration.

Why couldn't he have stayed put? Why couldn't he have obliged and become a distant memory? Memories could be painful but they could also be dealt with. His presence here was altogether more intrusive and not one that she had ever bargained for.

Living with Jeremy had done wonders for her self-control. She had built a fortress around herself, a protective moat which no one could cross, and behind that moat she had concealed herself.

Now Lorenzo Cicolla had come back and already she was beginning to find cracks in her armour.

He raised his hand and ran one long finger along her cheek in a gesture so unexpected that for a second her heart seemed to stop beating.

'Ever since you laid eyes upon me, your colour's been a little on the hectic side,' he said softly, with a trace of cool mockery in his voice.

'Anger does that to a person,' she muttered as his finger trailed along her neck. 'Will you please remove your hand?'

'Why?'

'Because it makes me feel acutely uncomfortable.'

'Why does it?'

'Because,' she said, trying to sound controlled, 'I don't relish being touched by a man who hates me.'

'Are you quite sure, Isobel? Your mouth says one thing but your body is telling me something altogether different.'

He reached down without taking his eyes off hers, and she felt his hand cup the swell of her breast, neatly encased in its expensive grey wool suit.

There was nothing neat about her reaction, though. She had an instant of feeling that everything had plummeted out of control. Her breast seemed to enlarge, and her nipple hardened, longing for that touch to go further.

Her breath caught sharply in her throat and she pulled away.

'How dare you?' she said, choked and furious, with herself and with him. 'How dare you?' She was running the risk of spluttering now, so she fell into silence and made do with looking at him with icy hostility.

She had forgotten what a man's touch felt like. Her body had lapsed into a self-imposed celibacy and she had told herself that making love was something she didn't need. How wrong she had been. Lorenzo's brief caress, which stemmed from no more than a cruel need to prove his point, had aroused her to a pitch which she had never imagined possible.

She folded her arms around her, warding off any more potential invasion of her privacy, and glared at him.

'You were saying?' he prompted, as though the little interlude had not occurred.

Isobel looked at him and wondered dazedly what he was talking about now.

'About your grand ideas for saving your father's company?' he continued, walking across to the window and peering down with his back to her.

It was hardly reassuring talking to a back. She got the distinct impression that reassurance was the one thing he did not intend to extend to her, and he was making the point perfectly clear without uttering a word.

'I have no one specific in mind to run the company,' she said in a glacial voice, while he continued to lavish his attention on what was, she knew, hardly a spectacular view. 'But I'm sure it would be no problem finding someone.'

'From where?' he asked, not bothering to turn around. 'Off the street?'

'There are such things as employment agencies.'

He slowly turned around, reluctant, no doubt, she thought sourly, to abandon his fascination with the view of a half-empty pavement.

'What sort of person would you ask them to trot along to you?' he asked. He lounged indolently against the window-frame and appeared to find her thoughts on the matter vaguely amusing.

'Someone qualified,' she informed him.

'Qualified in what?'

'In triple by-pass surgery,' Isobel snapped, which appeared to amuse him still further. 'In running a company, of course.'

'Ah.' He paused, then asked with a frown, 'How do you know that he would be any good?'

'I'm not a moron. I would use my instinct.'

'Speaking as an ex-medical student? I'm impressed. And what would you do with the existing members of the board? Put them out to pasture? You know all of them personally. Can you really afford to make yourself unpopular in a town of this size?'

His logic infuriated her. 'I'd keep them on,' she snapped.

'And lose money even faster. What a shrewd business brain you're displaying here.'

'I'll take my chances. I'd rather do that than get myself involved in any sort of alliance with you.'

The cool amusement left his face as though it had never been there.

'You've become very self-righteous over the years,' he said with icy dislike. 'I don't recall such an attack of primness four years ago when you threw your lot in with Jeremy Baker. You never loved him but that certainly didn't stand in the way of progress, did it? How did you manage to justify that to yourself, Isobel? Did you grin and bear it and think of England? Was the union of two such illustrious families worth it?'

'You're hateful!'

'That's rich coming from you.'

'You can't buy me, Lorenzo.' Even as she said it she knew how ridiculous it sounded. To all intents and purposes, she had been bought four years ago. She tasted the bitter truth on her tongue and fought it back.

She remembered some of Jeremy's choice remarks at the wedding-reception.

'You might have had a lot going for you, Lorenzo,' he had said at one point, after he had consumed too much alcohol, and his tongue, already too loose, had loosened still further. The three of them had been sitting alone at the main table. She could still remember how embarrassing it had been. 'But,' he had continued in a slurred, resentful voice, 'money was the one thing that you never had. For God's sake, your mother used to work in some of our houses!' He had laughed then, as though he had made some particularly amusing observation, but neither of them had joined in.

'Money buys everything,' Lorenzo now said scathingly, 'and you are no exception.'

'Money can't buy happiness. It can't buy love. It can't buy respect. It can't buy health.'

Lorenzo looked away. 'How philosophical,' he commented sarcastically, and she sighed, weary with the whole damned thing.

'Please don't do this,' she said evenly. 'I know that you were upset when I married Jeremy...'

'Upset! You English! Yes, I was *upset*.'

'Not so upset that you didn't vanish to America without a backward glance; not so upset that you didn't cavort with God knows how many "lovely women"!'

'Did you expect me to keep in touch with you, Isobel? Write you pining letters so that you could wisely try and mend a broken heart from across the Atlantic?'

'You haven't got a heart.'

His face hardened. 'I'm a lucky man, in that case.' He paused, then asked in a voice that was edged with contempt, 'Was that what you wanted? To have me keep in touch even though you were married? Carry on being lovers while you and Jeremy played the perfect couple to one and all?'

'That's disgusting!' Colour rushed to her face.

'There are more disgusting things,' he said harshly, and she wished desperately that she could find the strength to walk away from this dark stranger who wanted to hold her life in his hands so that he could crumble it in his fist whenever he chose.

He was casting his mind back. She could see it. She knew what he was thinking. It was a memory that had haunted her for four years. The memory she had tried hardest to kill. But like all bad memories it had planted roots and refused to go.

'Don't tell me that you've forgotten that pretty little

scene in your parents' garden four years ago?' His face was set in lines of bitter hatred.

'It's stupid delving back into the past,' she mumbled in a woolly attempt to avoid the unavoidable.

'I was in the garden. Jeremy followed me. He hadn't yet got his fill and I was actually beginning to regret my decision to stick out the damned thing when the most sensible thing would have been to decline his best man invitation and to face the fact that some challenges to one's honour had to be surrendered.'

'He had had too much to drink.' Her voice was a whisper.

'Always had been over-fond of the bottle, hadn't he, our dear Jeremy? He followed me into the garden and took up where he had left off.'

She remembered. She had been chatting to her mother while out of the corner of her eye she had noticed their departure from the marquee. She could recall thinking, Well, at least any argument wouldn't be overheard. She might not have wanted the wedding, but on the other hand she hadn't particularly wanted to see it degenerate into an all-out fight between the bridegroom and the best man.

As soon as she possibly could, she had followed them both. At first she hadn't seen them. It was a very large garden, landscaped, with quite a few trees and clumps of rhododendron. It had been designed with a view to being informal but arresting, and she had had to peer around a bit before she saw the two figures by one of the trees.

They had been arguing, that much was clear from the stance of their bodies. Jeremy had been gesticulating rather a lot, but Lorenzo's body had been rigidly still and, as she had approached she had seen that his expression was one of tightly controlled anger.

'Always money, wasn't it, Isobel?' Lorenzo asked tightly. 'The great insurmountable divide.'

'No.' The monosyllabic answer was a weak denial. It hadn't been money, not with her, never with her, but how could she explain that to him without revealing the secret which she was forced to clutch to herself?

He was pushing her into confronting things which she would be unable to defend, even now. She looked into his eyes and read the relentless fury there, still burning after all this time.

'No? You must have an extremely short memory, in that case.' His voice was cool and silky, but his expression wasn't. There was a tautness about his dark features that sent a shiver through her.

'Stop,' she said, and he gave a short laugh.

'If I recall, money was all that mattered to you, wasn't it?'

Isobel didn't answer. Her mind flew back to that scene in the garden when she had been called upon to defend Jeremy, to agree by her silence that money had mattered, that it had been the one thing which Lorenzo could never give her and the one thing that had severed their relationship.

'My darling wife,' Jeremy had said, with a smile of sly triumph, 'told me that you weren't good enough for her. She said that poverty was all right for a while, that it could be quite bohemian in a way, but that in the end it would be just too uncomfortable for her.'

And she had not been able to defend herself. Her hands had been tied.

Lorenzo had looked at her with bitter contempt, the same way that he was looking at her now, the same way that he had looked at her the minute he had set foot in Mr Clark's office. He had forgotten nothing and he was not prepared to forgive. He would never be prepared to forgive. He would extract every ounce of blood from her and he would use whatever method came to hand to do it.

She felt the mounting despair of someone caught in a long, dark tunnel with no light at the end of it.

Jeremy's death should have brought her release, but instead she had jumped out of the frying-pan into the fire.

'Here's your big chance to set the record straight, Isobel. No Jeremy around now.' He gave her a long, leisurely, cool look. 'I'm waiting with bated breath for your version of what was said. I'm waiting for you to tell me that it was all a terrible mistake, an error of judgement on my part.'

'Why should I tell you anything?' she answered, and a look of savagery flashed across his face, quickly replaced by cold, bored mockery. 'You wouldn't believe a word I said anyway. You wouldn't want to. You came back here because, unexpectedly, circumstance has opened up an opportunity for you to make me suffer. I have no intention of throwing myself on your mercy. I'm not a fool.'

'You've always been a fool, Isobel Chandler,' he said in a voice that could have cut glass. 'You were a fool to become involved with me in the first place. I attracted you because I was from the wrong side of the tracks, and that sort of thing can hold quite a bit of appeal to a girl of your impeccable upbringing, can't it? But you made a grave mistake, my darling. You're right. Circumstance has thrown me a lifebelt, and I have every intention of using it.'

'I won't allow this,' she said, confused and frightened by the intent in his eyes. He had always been single-minded; he had always possessed the sort of personality that gauged a situation, assessed the outcome and then went for it. His ferocious drive had amused and bewitched her once because she had seen it through the eyes of a girl in love. Now she wasn't amused or bewitched. She was standing in its path, and all she could see was herself being rollercoastered into bits.

'I have nothing further to say to you,' she informed him. 'I won't sell my father's company to you, whatever you offer.'

'Oh, I shall have control of it, Isobel, just as I shall have control of you. There's no point fighting. It's only a matter of time.'

He walked across to the office door, opened it, and within minutes Mr Clark was hurrying in.

Isobel looked at him and should have felt a feeling of relief, but she didn't. All she felt was dread at the dark threat behind Lorenzo's words.

'All sorted out, I hope?' Mr Clark bustled to his desk, his eyes busily glancing at the two of them and apparently not registering anything amiss in the atmosphere.

'Not quite.' Lorenzo sat down on the chair opposite the desk and crossed his legs elegantly.

'Ah.' That obviously stumped Mr Clark. 'What appears to be the problem?'

'I won't sell.' Isobel spoke calmly but firmly. In the chair next to her she could feel Lorenzo. Some weird sixth sense seemed to register his presence so that every pore of her being was in a state of tense awareness. It was a feeling she hated because she had not felt vulnerable for a long time; she had learned to hide within herself, and to depend on that carefully cultivated talent for self-control.

'She'll sell,' Lorenzo said smoothly. 'There are just a few rough edges to work through. A few terms and conditions to be agreed upon.'

She didn't need to see his face to imagine the utter

confidence written there. Mr Clark was clearly convinced. He looked relieved and settled back comfortably
in his chair. Things would progress as normal. Never
mind her objections. They were technicalities.

She badly wanted to protest but she didn't.

This was neither the time nor the place to indulge in
a debate on the subject. But Lorenzo Cicolla was not
going to have his way. If he wanted war, then she would
fight.

CHAPTER FOUR

'How absolutely delightful for you, darling.' Mrs Chandler looked at her daughter with a smile, but Isobel refused to smile back. It was all of a week since she had set eyes on Lorenzo, and that week had been ample time in which to feed her growing panic at the prospect of his moving back to England to live.

He hated her. That had been evident in the cold, contemptuous slant of his eyes every time he had looked at her in Mr Clark's office, in the curl of his lips, in the well-chosen cruelty of his words. And now, four years on, he had the wherewithal to make her feel his hatred.

She looked at her mother, now frowning, and said as tactfully as she could, 'Mum, he's changed. He's not the man you used to know.'

'People don't change overnight, Isobel.'

'Four years is hardly what I would call overnight!' She stood up and began clearing away the dishes, and her mother began helping her. Isobel took this as a good sign. For the past few months she had been too lethargic, too wrapped up in her unhappiness to do anything, but recently, over the past couple of weeks, Isobel had noticed little changes in her mother.

'What I mean, darling, is that *fundamentally* people don't change. Oh, their fortunes may go up or down, their lifestyles may alter, but basically, they always remain the same.'

'Your theory falls down when it comes to Lorenzo Cicolla,' Isobel informed her, not wanting to prolong the conversation, but not quite knowing how to terminate it.

'He's become cold and ruthless. Why do you think that I have reservations about selling to him?' Start, she had thought, with the *reservations* ploy, so that when downright denial became inevitable her mother would find it easier to accept. As it was, it had taken quite some doing to convince her mother that selling immediately wouldn't have been the best option. After all, they both *knew* Lorenzo, didn't they? They both *knew* him for an honourable man who would see that everything was handled in a thoughtful and fair manner, didn't they?

They had cleared the table and Isobel turned on the tap, running the water until it was the right temperature, then filling the sink and piling the plates and cutlery in.

'Darling, I do think you're exaggerating a little.' Mrs Chandler picked up a tea-towel and began drying. 'You probably felt a little awkward with him because you used to go out with him.'

Now *that*, Isobel thought resentfully, was definitely not on the conversation agenda. So much water had flowed under the bridge since that time that whole landscapes had changed in the process.

'What are you planning to do tomorrow?' Isobel asked, adopting diversion tactics, and received a sly, amused glance from her mother.

'Of course,' Mrs Chandler said, 'I shall have to meet him. It's only polite, after all.'

'I have no idea where he is, and anyway why on earth do you have to meet him?' Isobel retorted, keeping her face steadfastly averted. 'It's hardly as though the deal has gone through. It's hardly as though he *owns* the company. We don't owe him a debt of gratitude.' Strong stuff, Isobel thought, biting back the urge to carry on for several hours in the same vein.

'Whatever went on between the two of you in Mr Clark's office?' her mother asked curiously.

'Nothing. Money and power's gone to his head, that's all,' Isobel muttered. 'There. Dishes done. Coffee?' She poured them both a cup and they retired to the sitting-room.

Outside, the autumn evening was drawing in and the light was deep and gold. It filtered through the trees in the garden and skirted across the well-maintained lawns. Isobel had arranged for two of the local lads to do the garden twice a week and, despite a few feeble protests, Mrs Chandler had been quite relieved.

'Darling, I know that you're handling this business, but any decisions must finally be taken with my agreement, mustn't they?' Mrs Chandler picked up the conversation as though there had been no lapse in between. 'It would seem very odd, don't you think? Having nothing to do with him when he is thinking of buying the company and, more to the point, when he is, after all, a family friend?'

'No.'

Isobel sprawled back in the chair and tried to look sleepy in the hope that it might deflect her mother's temporarily one-track thought processes. Lorenzo's return, she realised, had coincided with her mother's re-entry into day-to-day living, and it was providing her with a great deal of fodder with which to take her mind off her own personal worries.

'You're being difficult, Isobel.'

'No, I'm not,' Isobel said, and she heard the sulky petulance in her voice with irritated amusement. 'It's just,' she continued in a crisper tone, 'that I don't see the point of making a fuss over Lorenzo Cicolla just because he's decided to return to Deadsville, Yorkshire, as he no doubt sees us here, or even because he thinks he's going to buy Chandlers and have the opportunity to lord it over us. Why should we?'

'Because you were very fond of him at one stage, and of course, dear, I remember him quite clearly as a young boy, and I'd like to see how he is now!'

Isobel sighed in frustration and then shrugged.

'Well, I'm sure something can be arranged if he re-surfaces,' she added. 'Quite likely immediate lack of success in getting what he wants has put him off and he's taken himself elsewhere.' Never in a million years would she admit it, but, for the past week, she had found herself looking out for him, even though she hated herself for doing so.

'Perhaps you could check for me,' Mrs Chandler suggested, and Isobel gave her a horrified stare.

'Check?' she asked. 'Check? *Me*? After everything I've just said?'

'Yes,' her mother answered serenely. 'Would you object, darling? I do think it would be a nice gesture if we had him over to dinner. Just something light, of course. Apart from everything else, I'd like to discuss any hold-ups to the sale of the company. I'm convinced something can be worked out.'

'Dinner? Discussions? *Work things out*?' She sounded strangled and quickly swallowed some of the coffee.

'What else?' Mrs Chandler stood up. 'I think I shall retire now.' She moved towards Isobel and kissed her on the top of her head. 'It should be easy to trace him, though I'm sure he'll be in touch soon to resume dis-cussions. Let me know just as soon as a day has been fixed. You and I can prepare something.' She smiled wistfully. 'Do you know, I shall never forget those won-derful parties your father and I used to throw. All the neighbours,' she sighed. 'I don't expect I shall ever do that again. But it will be nice seeing a different face, and Lorenzo was always such a charmer.' She sighed again and Isobel followed her slow walk to the door

before falling back into the chair with a little depressed
groan.

Damn Lorenzo Cicolla. She would have been happy
to put the past behind her; there were so many questions
she had been dying to ask him, but he had made his
hostility clear from the start, and if she had felt any
warmth for him, it had been killed before it could take
root.

She stood up, collected the empty cups and took them
into the kitchen.

Of course, she had no choice but to ask him to dinner.
Her mother already thought it peculiar that she had been
so antagonistic in her reactions to him when to her, as
to any outsider, he would appear an old friend.

She spent the following two days wondering whether she
could convincingly develop temporary amnesia on the
subject of Lorenzo Cicolla, whether she should make a
token effort to find out where he was staying, perhaps a
quick phone call to the least likely place for him to be,
or whether she should simply make do with nothing under cover of reassuringly agreeing with whatever her
mother suggested.

As it turned out she was spared having to do anything
at all because she bumped into him quite by chance as
she was cycling back from the surgery after work. Or
rather he cornered her in his car, pulling up against the
kerb so that she was hedged in and forced to dismount.

'I thought it was you,' he said coolly, stepping out of
the Jaguar, and Isobel reluctantly stood facing him, her
hands gripping the handlebars.

He was wearing dark trousers and a white shirt rolled
to the elbows, even though there was quite a cool feel
to the air.

'Lorenzo,' she said woodenly. 'What a surprise. I

thought you might have changed your mind about coming back here now that you no longer have any reasons to remain.' Her heartbeat had unobligingly gone into overdrive and she tried to ignore that disastrous sensuality which he exuded without having to try.

'You didn't really think that,' he inserted with equal cool politeness. 'You knew that I'd be back.'

'How would I know that when you weren't around?'

'You mean that you've been looking out for me, Isobel? How flattering.'

Trust him, she thought sourly, to misconstrue an entirely innocuous remark. She looked at him with dislike and said, 'It's rather crowded here, and I'm late home, so if you don't mind...' That damned dinner invitation would just have to wait. She knew that her mother had a valid point, that decisions to do with the company had to be taken with her approval, but right now she felt unsettled and in no mood to prolong their conversation.

That wonderful sexual excitement which he used to induce in her all those years ago had now been replaced by feelings of muted panic and unease and a stupid stirring in her blood which, she told herself, irritated her more than anything else.

He didn't get back into his car. He remained staring at her, then he said, with a cursory glance around him, 'You're right, it is crowded here. Everyone leaving work.' He slammed shut the door and locked it.

'I won't keep you. My answer still stands.' She began to cycle off but he moved around the car with something approaching the speed of light and gripped the handlebars so that she was forced to stop.

'What do you think you're doing?' she asked furiously, looking up into those light, mesmerising eyes and feeling even more unsteady.

'So why don't we adjourn to the coffee-shop?'

'What for?' Her heart was racing but she continued to look straight at him.

'Now, now, is that any way for two old friends to treat one another?'

'The coffee-shop will be closed,' Isobel informed him bluntly, 'so I'm afraid we'll have to postpone the friendly chat for some other time.'

'In that case there must be a café or a wine bar within striking distance.'

'I have plans for this evening, Lorenzo,' she lied.

'What plans?'

'That's none of your business.'

'Come along. I want to talk to you.'

'I am not "coming along" anywhere. And, believe it or not, I have nothing to say to you. You made your position perfectly clear the last time we met! I was prepared to meet you in friendship and instead you chose warfare.'

'And were you upset, Isobel darling?' he drawled, and the colour shot into her face.

'I am too indifferent towards you to be upset by anything you say or do,' she replied quickly, and he gave her a slow, disbelieving smile.

'I'm cut to the quick,' he murmured.

She was, she discovered, feeling more flustered by the minute. 'What do you want, Lorenzo?' she asked in a low, hurried voice. 'There's nothing further to discuss about my father's company. You hate me and I understand that...'

His hand shot out to grip her arm. 'How very sympathetic of you.'

'These confrontations aren't going to get either of us anywhere.'

'Is that pub still open? The one old Wilkins used to run?' The snarl was no longer on his face. The coolness was back. The cat was once again toying with the mouse.

'Sam Wilkins died two years ago,' Isobel said. 'Not that I intend to stay here and run through life histories with you.'

The sarcasm was lost on him. He slipped his arm around her waist and before she could struggle had removed her bodily from the bicycle. Isobel sprang back from him, shaking from head to toe. The suddenness of the action had unnerved her, and the feel of his hands on her had been an electric shock to her system. It reminded her too dramatically of how she had felt in that office when he had touched her.

'Stop looking so wide-eyed, Isobel,' he said with a slight sneer. 'We both know that you're not sweet sixteen and never been kissed. We both know that you sold yourself to the highest bidder, so spare me the outraged expression.'

'Get lost, Lorenzo Cicolla,' she snapped, but keeping her voice down because she didn't need rumours spreading like wildfire through the town.

His mouth tightened. 'In a minute, one of these kind passers-by is going to step over and ask whether everything is all right. Isn't it easier just to come with me?'

'So that I can be insulted?'

'How,' he asked smoothly, 'can I possibly insult you when you claim to be so indifferent to me?'

She glared at him and he gave a bark of laughter, but he won, because when he turned away she found herself walking alongside him, her fingers wrapped so tightly around the handlebars that they hurt.

The pub, which was the very last building on the High Street, was fairly empty. The landlord, Sam Wilkins's son, whom she could remember as an overweight adolescent a few years older than she was, smiled at her, but his attention was on Lorenzo.

'Good to see you after all this time.' He nodded curtly, pouring them their drinks. 'Heard that you were going to be taking over Chandlers. News round here spreads faster on the grapevine than on a radio.' He placed their drinks in front of them. He was tall, rather florid in the face, and possessed a forthright tongue that had no respect for tact or diplomacy. 'Plan on staying long?'

'Long enough,' Lorenzo said, his eyes hooded.

Long enough, Isobel would have liked to add, to make my life a living hell. She took her drink and asked after Tom's wife and children.

'Town could do with some fresh blood,' Tom said, having confirmed the status of his wife and children and refusing to have his attention distracted by domestic chit-chat. He eyed both of them. 'And of course, with Jeremy gone…'

'Leave it alone, Tom!' Isobel said warningly, but Lorenzo laughed, with real amusement on his face.

'With Jeremy gone, what do you suggest, Tom?' he asked lazily, and Tom shrugged with a sheepish expression.

'Women aren't meant to be alone,' he stated, to which Isobel replied tartly,

'How very twentieth-century and forward-thinking of you, Tom.' Actually she was beginning to feel rather embarrassed, especially since she could feel Lorenzo's eyes on her.

They walked across to one of the circular oak tables by the fireside, and Isobel said crossly, 'Tom Wilkins should watch what he says. There's such a thing as an excess of honesty.' She sat down, crossed her legs and gave him a 'well, now that you've dragged me here, what do you want to talk to me about?' expression.

Lorenzo settled back in his chair, raised his glass to his lips and surveyed her over the rim.

'Makes a refreshing change from the hypocrisy I've encountered over the past four years out there in the concrete jungle.'

'You would soon get sick of it, were you to remain,' Isobel said coolly, and he raised his eyebrows.

'Is that wishful thinking on your part, or have you taken up amateur psychology in your spare time?'

'Hilarious,' she said, watching him. 'Now, what exactly would you like to talk about?' She looked at her watch meaningfully, which appeared to have the opposite effect of making him prolong his silence, while he contemplated her with something bordering on insolence.

'Actually, I thought you might be interested in what I had planned for your father's company.'

'You won't be taking over my father's company.'

'Nothing stands in my way when I've made up my mind. Another drink?' he asked, and she shook her head, furious at his arrogance.

'Some re-organisation,' he continued, as though she had not uttered a word. 'Do you know much about your father's business?'

'I told you, you won't be—'

'I will be taking over Chandlers, Isobel,' he grated, leaning forward, 'and I will be taking it over on my terms. Now, answer me: do you know anything about your father's company?'

'No,' she said tightly, deciding to humour him rather than sit through his relentlessness.

'Nothing at *all*?'

'No,' she snapped. 'Not that this line of conversation is relevant.'

'Good God, Isobel, what on earth have you been doing with yourself for four years?'

'I don't see what that has to do with anything!' she retorted hotly, flushing. He made her life seem so *trivial*. 'I work at the local surgery and it's a pretty full-time job. I hardly saw the need to take up a second career looking over my father's shoulder! Anyway, this is ridiculous. You might think that you can do what you want, that I'll give in to your bizarre conditions, but you're wrong!'

'I intend to streamline the whole operation. It's a bit like an octopus at the moment, with tentacles stretching here, there and everywhere, and very few of them reaping much by way of profit.'

'Those tentacles provide jobs,' Isobel hissed, temporarily side-tracked, and he looked at her with a hooded expression.

'I'll bear that in mind when I decide to make it a registered charity,' he said. 'Until then, the business has to shrink.'

'And to hell with the livelihoods that will be swept down the drain?' This seemed as good an area as any for letting off steam. Isobel took a deep breath. 'Some of the people there have worked in my father's company from the year dot. What do you intend to do with them when your great streamlining project gets under way? Throw them a few rueful platitudes about recession and pat them on the head?'

She expected him to get angry with her—in fact, if she was honest with herself, she quite wanted it because she dearly would have liked to release some of that pent-up, confused, alarming feeling that swept through her every time she saw him in a good raging argument. But he stared at her, then said in a low voice, 'So you do recognise that I plan on coming back here?'

'No.' She spoke sharply, reddening when she realised that she had been persuaded into an argument which had weakened her position.

'I lied when I said that I could resist you.' It was a statement of fact and there was no tenderness on his face when he spoke. 'You're as exquisite as you always were and I still want you.'

A dark excitement coursed through her and she looked away, alarmed.

His voice was husky, sexy. It made her senses spin and she had to force herself to say in a final tone, 'You can't expect me to sign myself over to you. I already...' She stopped, confused, and he moved forward, reaching out to hold her chin, to force her face to his.

'Made that mistake? Is that it, Isobel? Dammit, talk to me, woman!'

'There's nothing to discuss.'

'You betrayed me and I want to know why.'

His intensity unsteadied her and she made a heroic effort to regain her composure.

'Why won't you just let me be? Have my father's company. I'll sell it to you, but leave me alone.'

'Never,' he bit out, releasing her in an angry gesture.

There was a tense silence and she seemed to hear the workings of her body, the anxious, desperate beating of her heart, the mad flow of blood through her veins, the heavy thud of her pulse.

'Your plans for the company... What would you do with the people you laid off?'

'I'll allow you to change the subject for now,' he rasped, 'but only for now.'

It no longer mattered that he was going to tell her about plans which would never materialise. She would have welcomed any change of conversation. She would have gladly encouraged him to hold forth on metaphysics and its place in the kitchen if it had meant not having to withstand that terrible assault on her senses.

Besides, she told herself practically, she might gain an idea or two from what he had to say. Who knew, his suggestions might serve her well if it came to having to work things out for herself. *When*, she amended to herself, *when* it came to having to work things out for herself. She felt better now she could reason that one out, and she smiled encouragingly.

'I have an excellent redundancy package worked out, which will amount to early retirement for some of the older members of staff, all of whom will eagerly accept.'

'How do you know that?'

'Experience,' he answered with utter assurance. 'It's a misconception that most people want to devote as much of their lives as they can to working in an office. The majority would quite happily take early retirement and relax on the proceeds.'

Yes, she thought, that made sense.

'And who would you volunteer for early retirement? Hypothetically speaking, of course.'

Lorenzo was watching her through narrowed eyes and she wondered whether he was trying to gauge her sudden interest in a topic which she had only minutes before proclaimed to be a waste of her vocal cords. She hoped desperately that he would find nothing revealing on her face. Living with Jeremy had done a great deal to sharpen her powers of concealment. He had always enjoyed the hold that he had over her, and she had learned very early on that the more sensitive she appeared, the more he relished it, so in the end she had learned to disguise her emotions under a wall of blankness. Like all things, it had gradually become a second skin. Time could work wonders.

'Greg Thompson, Vic Richards, old McGraw—all of

whom are doing the company no good at all. They lack the drive that they no doubt had in their younger days.' He paused. 'Of course, there would have to be some reshuffling, but strings would be pulled to help those men who suddenly find themselves out of work to pick up the pieces and carry on.'

'Greg Thompson,' Isobel murmured. 'Vic Richards, Ronnie McGraw.' Shame, she thought, that she didn't have a notebook.

'Any more questions?' he asked, raising his eyebrows. 'Sure you can remember the helpful hints?'

'Helpful hints?'

'You won't get the chance, Isobel, so forget it. No one touches that company but me. I'll make sure of that.' He smiled coolly and she wondered what it would feel like to tip the remainder of her drink over his head.

'I told you. You can have the company.'

'You're part of the deal.'

'Why?' she asked with a feeling of dreadful apprehension. 'Why marriage?'

'Because running your father's company isn't going to be a hobby for me. Of course, I have other businesses, some in America, and that will involve travel, but I also have men who can run them efficiently in my absence. No, I plan on settling down here and this is the sort of town where respectability is essential.' He looked at her through hooded eyes. 'Would you have agreed to be my woman on the side?'

Colour crawled into her face. 'Of course not.'

'I want you, Isobel, and I intend to have you. Marriage is a bonus for you.'

'And fidelity?' she asked bitterly. 'Love?'

'Since when has the absence of love held you back?' he asked softly.

She stared at him, dry-mouthed. It shocked her that

he was prepared to go to such lengths to wreak his revenge. He didn't love her but he would marry her because he knew that marrying her was the one thing she wanted least.

Simply owning her father's firm would not be enough.

'And fidelity?' she asked, skirting round his question, which she could not answer without tying herself up in knots.

'What about it?'

'I see.' She did too. She saw that fidelity would mean absolutely nothing to him. 'You would feel free to indulge yourself whenever you wanted,' she observed bitterly.

'You see that, do you?'

The question hung in the air, tantalisingly asking for a response.

'I must go.' She stood up, half expecting him to prolong the conversation, relieved when he stood up as well.

'What's it like working with Adams?' he asked casually as they moved towards the door, and she threw him a surprised look.

'You told me that you worked at the surgery. There's only one.'

'Oh, yes.'

'Not that it mattered. I had you checked out before I came back anyway.'

'You had me what?'

She stopped by the door and stared at him in angry astonishment.

'Checked out,' he repeated calmly, as if they were discussing nothing more important than the weather. 'I thought that I might as well find out about you. I knew where you worked and for whom.'

'You had a detective trailing me?'

'Tom Wilkins will begin to get very interested if he sees us engaged in earnest conversation here.'

'Some seedy man in an overcoat, peering through binoculars?' she asked, aghast.

'Hardly. I asked Clark to find out about the family background, about you.'

'On what pretext?' The simmering phase was fast reaching a rolling boil. He pulled open the door and shoved her out and she turned on him angrily. 'That's the most despicable thing I've ever heard in my life!'

'You must have led a very sheltered life these past four years, in that case,' he said, unmoved.

'You had no right!'

'I was planning to spend quite some money buying your father's firm. I felt I had the right. Besides, I was curious.'

'You were curious. Well, that makes it all right then, doesn't it?'

They were walking along slowly and she made sure that she kept a very safe distance from him.

'Adams isn't married, is he?' Lorenzo asked in a casual voice.

'No.'

'What's he like? I remember him as looking like a giraffe. All limbs.'

'He's grown into a very attractive young man,' Isobel said stiffly. 'Not that it's any of your business.'

'Everything that has to do with you is my business.' He wasn't looking at her as he said that. He was staring straight ahead. Isobel glanced at him, at the hard profile, the lean, muscular body with its peculiarly graceful stride.

Abigail had once told her that she thought Lorenzo was remarkable, the sexiest man she had ever laid eyes on.

'He could go far in my line of business,' she had commented. 'He would make an imposing actor. He has the presence. He doesn't even need to open his mouth.'

Why hadn't he stayed put? Isobel wondered. Why hadn't he had the good manners to stay a memory, lurking at the back of her mind? Why did he have to bring his imposing presence back into her life? She had never recovered from him, but at least recovery would have been possible in the end if she was denied proximity.

Her only chance rested in his departing once again for distant shores.

She would never marry him; she would never give him his opportunity to wreak revenge, and perhaps, once he saw that, he would give up any attempt to persuade her.

'Cosy for you,' he said softly, next to her, 'working with a single, attractive man.'

'Yes.' Isobel turned to face him. 'We have a very good relationship.' She could have inserted 'working', but then why should she?

'And how did Jeremy feel about that?'

'Is this a question and answer session?' she asked politely as they reached her bike, and she grabbed hold of it and began walking along the pavement. 'Anyway, I'm surprised you didn't get your spy to fill you in on all these details. Lapse of yours.' She wished that he would vanish into thin air.

'Were you having an affair with him?' He reached out and gripped one of the handlebars.

'You can take it however you like,' she answered, and his mouth hardened.

'So you had an open marriage. I don't suppose I should be too surprised at that. Was Jeremy that nondescript in bed or did you feel that, once you had established your status quo, there was no need to pretend to feel anything for him? Or were you sleeping with both men at the same time, Isobel? If I recall, you always were a passionate little thing.'

Isobel's hands tightened on the handlebars until her fingers were white. She would have slapped him if she could, but little towns were not places for public fights, and she knew that he was deliberately playing with her anyway.

'I really must be going, Lorenzo,' she said, without looking at him, and his hand slid up to grip her arm.

'Not until you've answered my questions.'

Her response to that was to yank at her bike, and he let her, walking alongside her until they approached his car, at which point he held on to the bike and said, with the same semblance of politeness which didn't fool her for a minute, 'I'll drive you to your house.'

Isobel looked at him. In the gathering gloom of night-fall his face was all shadows and angles. A hard, powerful face, the face of a man who seldom, if ever, yielded to resistance.

'I want to meet your mother,' he said, his mouth twisting. In the darkness the grey eyes glittered with casual menace. 'After all, it won't be long before I shall know her very well indeed, will it, Isobel?'

CHAPTER FIVE

THEY drove the short distance to the house in silence. She could remember how much they had talked, years ago, planned, laughed, when any silences between them were filled with warmth. This silence was heavy with foreboding.

As soon as the car pulled up outside the house Isobel shot out, followed lazily by Lorenzo.

In a stroke of monumentally bad luck, as far as Isobel was concerned, her mother was at the door as it was pushed open.

She saw Lorenzo, and Isobel watched with a sinking heart the expression of warm delight on her mother's face, the exchange of greetings.

'How wonderful to see you, Lorenzo.'

Oh, God, Isobel thought. This had the makings of more than a five-minute chat on the doorstep.

'I suppose my daughter has arranged the dinner date with you? Naughty of her not to have phoned and warned me.' Her mother gave one of her throaty, relaxed laughs.

'No, as a matter of fact, she hasn't.'

'I forgot,' Isobel said. She stepped into the hall, blocking the entrance with her body, and said coolly, 'You must drop round some time for a meal, Lorenzo. Though I'm sure you'll be far too busy to accept in a hurry.'

'I should love to come round for dinner,' he replied, looking at her tight-lipped face with amusement.

'Why not now?' Mrs Chandler peered over Isobel's shoulder. 'There's a casserole in the oven—nothing terribly fancy, I'm afraid—and some vegetables from the garden.'

'I can't think of anything nicer,' he said with an infuriating smile, and he stepped past Isobel into the hall.

Her mother was right. Lorenzo Cicolla had great charm, an abundance of it. Hatred for her, she thought, had hidden it, but it was in full force now, and bowling her mother over by the second.

Both her parents had been very fond of him. She was tempted to point out the ruthlessness, the arrogance, the obliterating single-mindedness which rubbed shoulders with the dark, persuasive smile and the easy, sophisticated banter, but she held her tongue. Meeting her mother was a waste of time. He would discover that in due course.

They went to the sitting-room, with Isobel trailing behind them, listening to the warm exchange of two people who frankly liked each other and wishing that she could think up a suitable ailment that would spare her from what threatened to be a very uncomfortable evening ahead.

'Now,' Mrs Chandler said, after she had poured them all a drink, 'shall we get the uncomfortable part of this evening out of the way?'

Lorenzo raised his eyebrows in a question and Isobel felt her spirits sink a little lower. She swallowed her glass of wine in record time, helped herself to another to steady her nerves, and sat back.

'Sounds ominous,' Lorenzo drawled.

'I was absolutely delighted when Isobel told me the prospective buyer of David's company,' Mrs Chandler began, looking suitably delighted. 'It came as a great shock when Mr Clark told us that we would have to sell Chandlers. You see, it was David's great love building that company. I dreaded the thought of a stranger coming along, maybe taking it to pieces. Someone with no history in the community, commuting from another town, seeing the firm as something to make a profit.'

Lorenzo nodded. Isobel eyed him sceptically from under her lashes and wondered how much of that sympathetic air was real and how much feigned.

'I understand,' he murmured.

'Do you?' Isobel shot him an innocent look of raised eyebrows and curved lips. 'Then I take it you approached every company you took over as a sympathetic friend and not as an investor wanting to see his investment make money?'

Lorenzo frowned at her. 'I have always been fair in my take-overs.'

'Oh, how reassuring,' she murmured with a sweet smile.

'I told Isobel,' Mrs Chandler said hurriedly, giving her daughter a reproving, sidelong look, 'that I couldn't possibly foresee what the hitches might be. Perhaps you feel the company, on closer inspection, is not worth what you're prepared to pay? You can be quite honest with us, Lorenzo. After all, we go back a long way.'

'Businessmen are never honest, Mum,' Isobel said. 'They're diplomatic. Like politicians and salesmen.'

'Your father was honest.'

Isobel looked away at that. She thought of Jeremy, she thought of her marriage, she thought of sacrifices made before she was even old enough to enjoy life to the fullest.

'The price has nothing to do with it, Mrs Chandler,' Lorenzo said abruptly into the silence. He leaned forward, deposited his glass on the table in front of him and relaxed back on the sofa. 'You say that you want honesty, so I'll be blunt. This deal would have been wrapped up over a week ago, but I felt that I lacked the necessary co-operation from your daughter.'

'Isobel?'

Lorenzo glanced across to where Isobel was trying to conceal an expression of stony anger, and continued in an unhurried voice, 'I feel that in a town of this size it's imperative that I have every backing from the family members of the firm. Perhaps if I had been an outsider it would have mattered less, but everyone knows that Isobel and I know one another, and most people know that we were…involved at one point.'

'What does that have to do with it?' Isobel asked sharply, feeling her colour mount.

'Quite a bit. You see, if I take over Chandlers without the backing of your daughter, Mrs Chandler, it won't be long before tongues begin to wag. People will begin to wonder whether it was perhaps a hostile take-over, whether you had been forced to sell against your will. It would only be a short step before they began to have suspicions about me as a person. After all, Chandler has been a name in this town for as long as I can remember. Business would suffer because it would be impossible to operate successfully here with hostility in the air.'

'Don't you think you're exaggerating a little?' Isobel asked, recognising a trap and wriggling to squirm out of it.

He shook his head. 'In a big city you're anonymous. In a town like this you're not. There's a constant process of symbiosis at work. You think what would happen if Tom Wilkins sold his pub to someone who wasn't accepted. How long would it be before the pub began having trouble attracting customers? How long would it be before it was forced to close down completely?'

Mrs Chandler was nodding in slow agreement.

'I am perfectly willing to sell Father's company to

him,' Isobel muttered, feeling guilty and then angry that she should when she had absolutely nothing to feel guilty about.

Was it her fault that he had laid down conditions which were impossible to meet? Was it her fault that he had returned with only one thing on his mind: revenge?

'You haven't been very enthusiastic though, darling, have you?' Mrs Chandler asked with gentle reproof, which made Isobel redden even more.

'Not enthusiastic at all,' Lorenzo murmured, in a disappointed voice, sliding his eyes across to her and only just managing to contain his amusement.

'Darling.' Mrs Chandler stood up and her voice was very firm. 'I hope you'll think very carefully about this; I hope you will do everything in your power to convince Lorenzo that he has your full backing. I shall go and see to the food and let you two discuss it between yourselves.'

'You…! You…! Words fail me, Lorenzo Cicolla!' she said as soon as the door closed behind her mother.

He smiled.

'Your mother *did* say that she wanted honesty.'

Isobel helped herself to another glass of wine, because her nerves needed further bracing, and tried to formulate a suitably scathing reply to that.

'You have to admit that what I said made sense,' Lorenzo carried on, before she could think of her scathing reply.

'I have to admit nothing of the sort!'

'Your mother agrees with me.'

'You talked your way around her,' Isobel muttered darkly. 'That lecturer of yours was right. You should have studied law. You have a mind devious enough.'

'Is that a compliment?' He looked perfectly relaxed, his mouth curved into an amused smile.

'No, but I'm sure you'll take it as one. How could you turn my mother against me?'

'I wasn't doing anything of the sort. I was simply pointing out that I needed your co-operation if this venture was to succeed the way I'd like it to.'

'Your idea of co-operation and my mother's idea of co-operation aren't exactly the same though, are they?' Isobel asked with sarcasm. 'What do you think she would say if I told her the truth? That what you had in mind wasn't along the lines of the occasional invitation to dinner and cheery greetings on the street, but a ring on my finger.'

'Who knows? She might be thrilled.'

'And if I told her that the only reason you wanted my so-called co-operation was for motives that had nothing to do with the company?'

'She probably wouldn't believe you.'

Their eyes met and Isobel felt her head spin. Too much wine. She hardly ever drank. She should have fortified her nerves with mineral water or orange juice.

She half closed her eyes and said, 'I feel giddy.'

'My poor darling,' he murmured, with a low, sexy laugh. 'Is that because you're overwhelmed at the realisation that you're going to marry me, like it or not, or because you've had too much to drink?'

'I haven't had too much to drink.'

'Three glasses.'

'I hate people who count how much other people have had to drink. And I'm not going to marry you.' She should be feeling angry, *furious*, in fact, but she really did feel light-headed, and somehow she couldn't summon up the energy for an argument.

When her mother returned and announced that dinner would be ready shortly, Isobel stood up, hoped that she would be able to walk a straight line across the room, and announced that she needed to go and change.

Under a stream of lukewarm water she tried to get her muddled thoughts into some kind of coherent order, and in the end abandoned the unequal struggle.

Lorenzo, who from of old could run rings round most people, had succeeded very thoroughly in running rings around her.

She wasn't going to give in, she knew that, but she felt too relaxed to think about how she was going to stop him without incurring her mother's disapproval.

When she emerged fifteen minutes later, in a pair of jeans and a jade-green jumper, she could hear her mother's laughter and Lorenzo's low, deep voice wafting from the sitting-room.

They both looked around as she walked in, and her mother, still smiling, said, 'No more shop talk tonight. Lorenzo's been telling me all about America. I've always wanted to visit there.'

'No, you haven't,' Isobel said, wondering whether she dared indulge in one last glass of wine—after all, the evening was hardly over—and deciding that she would. She felt much better after her shower. Not so languorous and floaty. 'You and Dad hated having holidays outside England. The few times you went to Europe you always came back looking exhausted.'

'True,' Mrs Chandler conceded with grace. 'But Lorenzo makes it sound terribly exciting.'

Lorenzo, Isobel wanted to point out, could make sitting in a room and watching paint dry sound terribly exciting.

She frowned. Of course that was a long time ago, before she discovered that she hated him. Or was it, she thought confusedly, and if it wasn't, then what did that mean?

'Did you know that he now owns several companies, darling?' her mother asked.

'Really?' Isobel tried to invest her voice with interest. 'Staggering. I'm deeply impressed.'

'It must have been terribly hard work,' Mrs Chandler said thoughtfully, turning her attention back to Lorenzo. 'I have heard that America is a very competitive place. Is it?'

'Highly.' He had helped himself to another glass of wine and he took a mouthful of it. 'For the first year I was there, I think I must have had two hours' sleep every night. I was working crazy hours. Not that I minded.' He laughed and Mrs Chandler laughed with him. When he decided to be charming, Isobel thought, there were very few people who could resist him, least of all members of the opposite sex.

'I was living in such a hell-hole,' he continued, 'that the office was palatial in comparison.'

'How awful for you,' Mrs Chandler said, looking at her daughter for some contribution to the conversation.

Isobel murmured obligingly, 'How horrendous. However did you cope?' She had worked it all out. If she were seen to be co-operating with him, at least in front of her mother, then, when the deal fell through, well, no blame could be laid on her doorstep, could it?'

Lorenzo was looking at her, his eyes narrowed and serious. 'I coped, Isobel, with thoughts of returning here in due course. I had gone to America to find success, and success was precisely what I intended to bring back here with me.'

'Very single-minded.' Her mother approved, apparently. She had married a man who had been ambitious as well. It was an ethos which she could understand. 'I do so hope that you'll buy David's company.' Her eyes lost some of their unreserved sparkle. 'I know it will be in safe hands with you.' She turned to Isobel. 'You do see, don't you, darling?'

'If you want me to,' Isobel muttered, which met with a disapproving frown from her mother, and she quickly amended her remark, adding, 'I'm sure Lorenzo would make sure that it was firing on all cylinders in no time at all.' *Be seen to co-operate*, she thought.

Her mother was nodding. 'David was worried about it for quite some time before he died,' she said, which made Isobel look at her in surprise. Her father had been worried about the company? He had never let on!

'Why?' Lorenzo asked, and Isobel could see his ears pricking up.

Mrs Chandler shrugged sadly. 'He knew that there were loopholes in the management, but he was desperately against firing old friends, and of course quite a few of the hierarchy in the company *were* old friends.' She glanced at Lorenzo. 'You know what it's like here. We all know one another.'

'A dangerous situation.'

'It can be, but also a comforting one. David spent so much time trying to work out a solution. The only other time I have ever known him to be worried to that extent was years ago. He never told me what was wrong and eventually, whatever it was, he sorted it out.' She stood up. 'Well, so much for memory lane. I shall go and see to that casserole. I'll call you when everything's ready.'

Which, of course, was Isobel's cue to jump up and offer to do it instead, but her mother shook her head and murmured, 'No, darling, you stay here and entertain Lorenzo. You haven't seen each other for such a long time.' She looked at him with affection and Isobel felt very much like telling her that she would do better to expend her affection on a swarm of killer bees.

'And remember, you two, no shop talk!'

As soon as Mrs Chandler had left the room, Lorenzo looked at Isobel, his eyes veiled.

'Still feeling giddy?' he asked. He sounded amused and she scowled at him.

'Not in the slightest,' she said airily.

'You soon will if you finish that glass of wine. Four was always your limit.'

Isobel blushed and finished the glass of wine. 'I'm surprised you remember that,' she remarked. 'With only two hours' sleep every night, for years on end, you'd think that your powers of recall might have dulled a bit.'

He laughed, and it was the laugh she had known years ago, that wicked, amused laugh that made her bones go funny. Or was it her imagination?

'Don't think that you're going to get your way just because I'm not arguing with you,' she rushed in, uncomfortably aware that the room was too hot, or too small, or too *something*, because she was feeling awfully conscious of his presence there on the sofa, semisprawled, his trousers contouring his muscular legs in a way that she found quite fascinating.

'Perish the thought.'

'You're enjoying this, aren't you?' Isobel asked, with less bitterness than she might have normally. 'You're enjoying watching my discomfort.'

'I have always enjoyed watching you, Isobel,' he said ambiguously, which made her go red. She stood up agitatedly and began pacing through the room, her body as tense as a coiled spring because she knew that his eyes were on her, following her.

'Oh, for goodness' sake, stop prowling,' he ordered, and she gave him a wry look.

'You've become very fond of giving commands, Lorenzo,' she said silkily, pausing next to his chair to look down at him.

With a swift gesture his fingers circled her wrist, and he pulled her down on to the arm of the chair. Only some instinctive sense of balance saved her from falling on to his lap, but the suddenness of the action winded her and she looked at him in angry embarrassment.

'That's better,' he said comfortably, still gripping her so that she had no option but to remain where she was or else initiate a struggle which she knew she would lose. He was a strong man. Right now he was pinning her down with ease, as effortlessly as a tiger pinning a mouse under its paw.

'You may think that the only reason I'm here is because I get some sort of vicarious thrill in putting your nose out of joint, but as a matter of fact I'm here because I wanted to see your mother, believe it or not. It's been a long time.' His voice was deep and velvety, and altogether hypnotising. Isobel looked at the dark, chiselled contours of his face and tried very hard not to betray her confused awareness of him.

'How is her illness?' he asked quietly, and she lowered her eyes.

'She copes with it. She always has.'

'She's always been a strong woman.'

'That's what Richard says.'

His eyes sharpened at that, as did his grip on her wrist.

'Ah. Dr Adams. We hadn't finished our little discussion on him, had we? Does he say that during working hours or out of them? Were you fooling around with the single, attractive Dr Adams? You haven't answered me that.'

'We're friends,' she informed him. Was he jealous? Her heart gave a swoop of pleasure at the thought of that, but the pleasure didn't last long. If he was jealous, it had nothing to do with emotional reasons. If he was jealous it would be because a man in her life would detract from her vulnerability and he wanted her vulnerable, he wanted her in a position where he could hurt her the way she had hurt him four years ago.

No amount of wine should relax her into forgetting that, she thought to herself.

Besides, she decided, why should it matter what he feels for me? She looked at that dark, handsome face and, somewhere at the back of her mind, an answer to that began to take shape. She shoved it aside quickly, though.

'She took Dad's death very badly,' Isobel heard herself saying in a hurried, nervous voice. 'They had been together for such a long time, I suppose, and, of course, she was always very dependent on him. He took care of everything. She had no idea how to manage the most basic of her finances.'

Was he listening to her? He was staring at her but he didn't appear to be taking in a word she was saying. She began to feel more addled.

'Can I have permission to return to my chair now?' she asked, clearing her throat.

His voice, when he answered was husky. 'No. I rather like you here.'

'And how is your mother?' Isobel stammered, clearing her throat again. She sounded breathless and a little choked. Would he believe her if she said that she had been suffering from a sore throat? Would he let her go if she told him that she was in dire need of a couple of throat lozenges? Perhaps she could mention her giddiness again, although right now she felt too rigidly tense to be giddy.

'Fine. Looking forward to the possibility of moving back here.' He idly crossed his legs and relaxed back in the chair. 'She's in Italy at the moment. She'll probably be there for a couple of months, until things are more settled here with me.' He absentmindedly began stroking the inside of her wrist with his thumb and her body began feeling feverish. 'Tell me what's been happening around here for the past four years,' he murmured softly, coaxingly. 'In a calm, non-argumentative fashion, because you're supposed to be co-operating with me, aren't you?'

'It would take too long.' She fidgeted on the arm of the chair. 'Besides, I'm very uncomfortable in this position.'

'Are you?' he asked with a wicked smile, then he pulled her down so that she tumbled in an undignified heap on to his lap, and she began to struggle uselessly.

'What the hell do you think you're up to?' she said, out of breath. He had one arm around her neck, and the other resting on her thighs. She wriggled again, and the arm moved from her thighs to her chest, so that his hand was spread just beneath her breastbone. She wasn't wearing a bra, and under her jumper she could feel her breasts grow heavy and painful, she could feel her nipples hard, aching, erect with excited longing.

'My mother,' she said, enunciating as carefully as she could, 'will have a heart attack if she walks into this room and finds us like this.' She was so close to him that she could see the little flecks of deeper grey in his irises, the fine lines around his eyes. She knew that if she wasn't careful his nearness would go to her head like incense, and—and what? she wondered with an inward shudder.

'It might force us to tell her that I intend to be her son-in-law. Besides, she's safely ensconced in the kitchen, taking care of dinner,' he murmured.

'There's just so much time someone can spend on preparing vegetables and setting a kitchen table,' Isobel said, ignoring his suggestion, even though it stirred something in her, something treacherous, a reluctant fire waiting to be rekindled. Keep it calm, she told herself shakily, pretend that his hand isn't inches away from your breast, that his mouth isn't inches away from yours, and you'll be all right.

Lorenzo ignored that. 'When you married him,' he muttered, 'I spent so long going quietly mad at the thought that you would be making love to him.' His hand moved to cup her breast and he groaned slightly as though surprised and dismayed by an involuntary reflex action over which he had no control.

Isobel gasped. Her breathing was forced and erratic and she had a terrible feeling that if she closed her eyes she would never resurface back to reality. She kept her eyes wide open and reminded herself that this was a man who felt nothing for her but fury and dislike. The fact that her body was longing to respond to his touch was a temporary heat against which she knew she had to fight because if she gave in to him, even momentarily, she would never be able to live with herself again. It was the wine. She should never have had that fourth glass. He had been right.

'Let me go,' she said, in as normal a voice as she could muster. 'I don't want to talk about him or about my marriage. I don't want you to touch me.'

'Don't you?' he whispered. 'You want me as much as I want you.'

'No.' She moved but it was a weak gesture. Her limbs felt like lead. She wanted to move, to run away, but her body was no longer functioning. It had decided to stay put.

He looked at her, and his finger moved to toy with her nipple until she wanted to scream out in frustrated longing. She clenched her fists into balls and tried to breathe steadily.

'Don't do that. I don't want you to do that, Lorenzo. The time for that has long gone.' Her voice had sunk to a breathless whisper.

'Don't lie. You're enjoying this.' He raised her jumper and exposed her breast, covering the taut nipple with his mouth. She shuddered. She thought dazedly, We're enemies, but nothing was responding to reason.

She pressed his head against her and arched back as his mouth suckling against her breast sent volts of electricity through her body, through every nerve-ending.

'Tell me,' he murmured hoarsely, 'tell me about him. I need to know. Jeremy is dead and the past can no longer haunt you.'

'There's nothing to tell.' She pulled herself away, mortified at what had just happened as reality reasserted itself, and he drew back with a gesture of angry rejection.

'Damn you, Isobel,' he bit out, and she sprang off him, taking two steps backwards on shaky legs.

'You don't care about me, Lorenzo. What makes you think that I would ever confide in you? What makes you think that I would ever tell you about the past four years?' She laughed bitterly, hating him for arousing her and hating herself for her treacherous body.

'Oh, keep your bloody little secrets!' he said harshly, standing up, and she took a couple more steps backwards. He looked as though he was about to say more, his eyes like flint, his powerful body tensed with self-imposed control. But whatever more he had to say she didn't find out, because they both heard Mrs Chandler approaching and, in an automatic reaction, they both turned away from each other.

Isobel dragged a smile on to her face just as her mother walked through the door, but she still made sure that she didn't look at Lorenzo.

She was so overcome that she felt sick. Sick and giddy. As if she were suffering from some dreadful tropical disease that had infiltrated her whole system and left her incapable of coherent thought or action.

Wine had nothing to do with what had just taken place. It was as if a dam had burst and yearnings which she had spent years denying had surfaced, filling her and taking her over.

'All ready.' Her mother looked bright and alive. She took Lorenzo's arm, pressing him to tell her more about America, more about what he had been doing there. Isobel glanced at him from under her lashes and wondered whether his body was still throbbing the way that hers was, or whether his passion had died the minute she had pushed him away, the minute reality had shown him the face of the woman he now hated.

He said he wanted her and he did, but his hatred was more powerful than his desire. By marrying her he would satisfy both.

No one would think now, though, that he had anything on his mind other than an evening ahead of pleasant company and invigorating conversation.

The man, she thought, was an actor of the first order. He had always, even as a teenager, had the ability to conceal deep feeling, and that ability had obviously been honed to perfection over the years.

Isobel trailed behind them, feeling like a sulky schoolgirl at an adult gathering.

Her mother had laid the kitchen table, apologising in case Lorenzo thought it too informal, knowing that he would laugh warmly and make the right noises of appreciation. He did, and he really seemed to mean it.

Mrs Chandler had brought out a bottle of wine from the wine cellar and she handed it to Lorenzo, who opened it quickly and efficiently.

'Isobel hardly drinks at all, do you, darling? Tonight is the first time that I've seen her have more than one forced, polite glass of wine,' her mother said conversationally as he poured them each a glass, and Lorenzo raised his eyes in a question.

Immediately, and for no reason whatsoever, she felt on the defensive.

'I prefer not to,' she admitted carefully, sitting down and indulging in another sulky schoolgirl mannerism of toying with the cutlery. This was not like her at all. She had become cool, contained, virtually unflappable over the years. Where, she wondered, was all that now?

Lorenzo was looking at her; she could feel his eyes boring into her head, waiting for an elaboration on that statement. She had never been a heavy drinker when she knew him, but on the other hand she had not been averse to a glass of wine. In fact, she could think of countless times when they had cracked open a bottle and lain back, talking about nothing and everything, and she was quite certain that he remembered those occasions as well. He seemed to remember everything else.

'Jeremy—' her mother began, and Isobel cut in sharply.

'Mother!' He already knew, of course, that her marriage had not been a roaring success, but for some reason she was loath to confirm the depth of its failure. She didn't think that she could stand his pity as well as his contempt.

'He was fond of the odd glass now and then...?' Lorenzo pressed as he helped himself to a generous serving of chicken.

'More than the odd glass,' Mrs Chandler reflected, glancing quickly at her daughter.

'The vegetables,' Isobel stated in an over-loud voice, 'are home-grown.' There was no way that she wanted her mother to launch into the subject of Jeremy and his drinking. She knew that both her parents had been appalled and worried at his habit, which had steadily worsened over the years. At first they had made attempts to discuss it with both of them, then with her, since Jeremy became tight-lipped and defensive the minute it was mentioned as a problem, but she had laughingly joked the matter away, and after a while they had fallen silent on the subject. But she would have to have been blind not to notice their anxious glances at one another whenever she and Jeremy were around. They had found his behaviour distasteful, as she had. They had found *him* distasteful, but were too polite ever to mention it. But it had been there in their eyes, in glances caught when they thought that their daughter's attention was elsewhere.

No doubt her mother now thought that Lorenzo, as an old friend, was entitled to confidences on the subject, but Isobel was not about to fall into any such way of thinking.

'Mum,' she continued firmly, 'still maintains the vegetable plot at the back of the garden.' She concentrated heavily on the chicken on her plate. 'We have all kinds of herbs, green beans, potatoes. In summer the strawberries are marvellous.'

'In fact—' her mother was looking at Lorenzo and her face was sheepish but wistful '—and, darling, don't take this the wrong way, but just between the three of us, David and I had always hoped—' she paused and Isobel stared at her, horrified at some unformulated suspicion of what was to come '—had always thought that you two…that you two would perhaps…who knows…? Silly of us, wasn't it?' She smiled and so did Lorenzo, a smile of triumph meant for Isobel's eyes only.

The smile of the victor.

CHAPTER SIX

THE subject was dropped as gracefully as it had arisen, but throughout the light-hearted chat about gardens Isobel could feel her head swimming with the desperate implications of her mother's remarks.

She had never, not once, mentioned any such thoughts to *her*. What on earth had possessed her to mention them now? In front of Lorenzo?

She looked at him, a sideways look, and wondered whether it was her imagination, or was a smile of satisfaction hovering on his lips?

She poured herself another glass of wine, throwing him a defiant look which met with an amused curve of his mouth, and only considered it safe to resurface back into the conversation when, inevitably, they began discussing old friends.

'Isobel tells me that Richard Adams is doing rather well,' Lorenzo murmured casually.

Probing, Isobel thought sourly. Did he want to find out from another source whether there was anything more to their relationship than she had told him? Did he think that they had carried on a torrid, clandestine affair behind Jeremy's back? She wouldn't have put it past him. In fact, there wasn't much she wouldn't put past him.

'What a nice young man,' Mrs Chandler said warmly. She looked at her daughter. 'You rather enjoy working with him, don't you, Isobel?'

'Immensely.' She noticed the slight frown on

Lorenzo's face and smiled. 'He's bright, he's sympathetic, he's thoughtful.'

'A paragon, in other words,' Lorenzo said with an edge of coolness in his voice. 'How odd that he never married.'

'Waiting for the right woman,' Mrs Chandler said.

'How odd that *you* never married, Lorenzo,' Isobel said brightly. She sipped her wine and looked at him over the rim of her glass.

'Why?'

'Because you're free, single and, I suppose, quite eligible.'

'You think so?' he asked in that lazy, charming voice of his. He sat back and gave her the full brunt of his attention.

'I'm sure there are some women who would find you appealing,' Isobel replied, lowering her eyes. 'Especially in America. Don't women outnumber men over there?'

'Do they? I wasn't aware of that statistic.' He threw Mrs Chandler a semi-offended smile and said, reverting his attention back to Isobel, 'I'm not sure I like your back-handed compliment, that I'm only eligible because there's a surplus of women waiting to trap an unsuspecting man.'

Mrs Chandler laughed, which she was meant to, but there was a certain gentle calculation in her eyes that Isobel didn't care for.

'Anyway, I won't pry into your personal life, Lorenzo,' Isobel said briskly.

'Feel free. What would you like to know?'

'Nothing.'

'I find that difficult to believe. Surely you must be curious about me after four years.'

Mrs Chandler was watching them closely, with the amused half-smile of an adult watching the antics of two children, but that didn't fool Isobel. She knew her mother too well to be taken in by that bland, pleasant expression.

'No,' she said, hastily retreating from the conversation, and he shrugged, willing to let it go for the moment.

They had managed to proceed through the main course, and her mother now brought dessert to the table. An apple pie which, she felt compelled to admit, was left over from the day before.

They began chatting about Abigail—lustrous Abigail and her soaring career—and Isobel gradually relaxed. She was tremendously proud of her friend. She had done some plays on Broadway and Isobel grew voluble on the subject, comparing notes with Lorenzo, who had seen them both, laughing as the wine resumed its effect and they went over old times.

Talking over old times was safe, just so long as those old times didn't involve memories of Lorenzo, and they didn't.

He could be disarmingly witty and, by the time the apple pie had been consumed, any electricity in the atmosphere had evaporated.

Her mother began clearing away the dishes, and Lorenzo insisted that she relax in the sitting-room while he and Isobel tidied up the kitchen.

'The chef never washes,' he informed her, and she bustled away obligingly, leaving them alone in the kitchen.

'I feel as though I've drunk a case of wine,' Isobel said as she began washing. It felt good being here with him, in the warm, mellow kitchen with the blinds down and the chill autumn air blowing outside. Her caution seemed to have vanished.

'It agrees with you,' he said smoothly. 'You don't

look as though you're permanently sharpening your weapons for a fight.'

'I'm not too sure I like that picture of myself,' she answered, laughing. 'You make me sound like a battle-axe.'

'Do I?' he asked softly from next to her. 'You're too damned beautiful ever to be described as a battle-axe. Battle-axes have iron-grey hair pinned into buns and enough wrinkles to tell the world just how dissatisfied they are with life.'

'Really?' She grinned to herself, and thought in a muddled way that she shouldn't be feeling happy, not here, not with him. 'I can't think that you've had much to do with grey-haired, wrinkled women who are dissatisfied with life.'

'What sort of women do you think I've had to do with?'

She plunged her hands into the soapy water and thought, at the back of her mind, that there was something dangerously exciting about this conversation.

'I have no idea.'

'Oh yes, you have,' he whispered huskily.

'Good-looking women, I suppose. Women who look stunning when they're draped on your arm.'

'I'm not interested in women as ornaments. I never have been. You of all people should know that.'

'Should I? Why?' She was so aware of him that she didn't dare lift her eyes to his.

'Do you consider yourself ornamental?'

She laughed nervously.

'This is not a conversation to have when I'm feeling light-headed,' she said, turning around with her back to the kitchen sink, and he dropped the tea-cloth and faced her, leaning to rest his hands on either side of her.

'What kind of conversation would you like?' he

asked. 'Shall we talk about horticulture? Politics? The mating habits of the beaver?'

She stared down at his hands and was aware that quite a bit of her light-headedness was not due to the wine. Her heart was beating fast, so fast that she felt as though she were suffocating.

She looked at his strong hands, at the fine dark hair curling over the watch-strap. She followed them up, her eyes dwelling on the curve of his neck, the breadth of his shoulders, and by the time they reached his face she found that she was breathing quickly, gasping for air.

'Or shall we talk about something else, Isobel? Shall we talk about Jeremy?'

'No. There's nothing to talk about. My life,' she added in a whisper, 'has been nothing to talk about.'

Lorenzo didn't answer. He folded his arms around her and drew her to him. She could hear the steady beat of his heart as she rested her head against his chest and bit back the sudden urge to cry.

'Oh, Isobel,' he murmured, stroking her hair. 'Was it dreadful?'

She liked him stroking her hair like that. She so badly wanted to be comforted.

'I miss my father dreadfully,' she whispered, inconsequentially, and he didn't say anything. He didn't have to. He understood. She knew he did.

'Why won't you talk to me about it?' he asked roughly, and she squeezed her eyes tightly shut. She heard him sigh under his breath, but there wasn't the usual reaction of fury. He just continued stroking her hair. Friends, she thought, for the moment.

Except... She felt a quiver of real alarm. Except she didn't want his friendship, did she? It would be an impossible friendship anyway, because two people could never really reach each other when underneath there was an undercurrent of contempt and mistrust. Right now her defences had been lowered, she recognised that, and so, quite possibly, had his. He had, after all, had a few glasses of wine himself.

She drew back and looked straight into his face, and the realisation that she was looking at a man whom she still loved, whom she had never stopped loving, rocked her to her foundations.

She made a weak attempt to herself to rationalise that this stupid reaction was simply something born from unusual circumstances. Jeremy was no longer around, her father was no longer around—her dear father whom she had loved so much—but suddenly Lorenzo was, and nostalgia was playing its part in dictating emotions which, when she sat down and thought about them, didn't really exist.

But it was only a weak argument. She closed her eyes and knew that her heart had only ever belonged to one man. She had thrown away her chances with him because of necessity, and now there were no chances left because, at the end of the day, he hated her.

She took a deep, steadying breath and pushed past him.

She would have to be doubly careful now, she thought. If Lorenzo wanted to hurt her then he really wouldn't have to try very hard if he knew how she still felt about him.

Wouldn't that be the sweetest of poetic justice? she thought bitterly.

She fetched three cups from the cupboard, knowing that he was watching her.

'I take it that means that you don't want to talk to me about your marriage?'

'I told you,' Isobel mumbled, with her back to him, 'there's nothing to talk about.'

'In that case, why the secrecy?'

'Why can't you forget about what happened?' she asked. She heard the give-away desperation in her voice and covered it up by making a great fuss with the coffee-machine.

'He had something over you, didn't he?'

'What makes you say that?'

'You never loved him. No one who knew you seriously expected you to marry him. Abigail thought that for some reason you married him because you had to, you were compelled to—'

'Abigail?' She faced him swiftly. 'When were you talking to Abigail about me?'

'I went out to dinner with her after one of her plays.'

'She never told me. Why were you discussing me behind my back?'

'We weren't discussing you,' he answered tightly. 'There's no need to feel paranoid. We were talking about the past and you cropped up in the general conversation.'

'Oh, really?' Her voice was laden with scepticism. What had he been doing with Abigail? She felt a twinge of jealousy at the thought of the two of them, sitting in some cosy restaurant, smiling and exchanging confidences.

Abigail had never mentioned having seen him. Why? Had she had a fling with him and decided that discretion was the better part of valour?

'Oh, for God's sake,' he said roughly, 'I can see what's going through that head of yours, Isobel, and you're way off target.'

'Stop pretending that you know me!' she said, her voice high and sharp. 'Stop acting as though you can read my mind!'

'I've just told you that I had dinner with Abigail, a

fact which she omitted to mention to you, and you're putting two and two together and coming up with six.'

'You can have dinner with whomever you choose,' Isobel informed him. 'Of course I'm surprised that she never mentioned it to me, but then she probably assumed, quite rightly, that I wouldn't be particularly interested.'

'No? Because your life here was too full?'

'This is stupid.' She turned away to find that her hands were trembling and her mind was filled with unpleasant, sour images of her best friend in bed with Lorenzo Cicolla.

'Has it occurred to you that she didn't mention anything because I happened to be with a woman when I met her for dinner?'

'I see.'

'Maybe she felt a little awkward talking about me in connection with a woman. Maybe she felt that, as my ex-lover, you might be a little taken aback.'

Isobel laughed shortly. 'Why? Why would she feel that? I had my own life here.'

'If you call marriage to Jeremy a life.'

'You have no idea what sort of life we had together!'

'I can guess.'

'And of course you'd be right, wouldn't you?' she said acidly. 'After four years of absence you swan back here, make your deductions, and of course the infallible Lorenzo Cicolla would be absolutely spot-on!'

'You didn't love him. It was obvious on the day you married him. Why would that change?'

There was a tautness about his mouth when he said that.

'Answer me!' he muttered, taking a step towards her. 'You never cared for him, did you? And neither did your parents. He was a bully as a boy and the trait never deserted him. He drank, and God only knows what else he did. Run around with other women?'

'Stop it, Lorenzo!'

'Why? Why should I stop it? I want you to tell me why you married him.'

His eyes flared dangerously and she wondered, in dry-mouthed panic, how passion could turn to hatred like this.

'It's in the past,' she muttered. 'Forget it.'

'There's no getting through to you, is there, Isobel?' he asked, putting his hands on her shoulders, and she felt his fingers bite into her skin. 'You make noises about forgetting the past but, tell me, would you? If I had walked out on you then, when we were lovers, would you be prepared to smile forgivingly through it?'

'I suppose not,' Isobel said, looking down miserably.

'Then why,' he asked in a cold, brutal voice, 'do you imagine for a moment that I should?'

'Because there's no point dwelling on it, is there?'

His mouth twisted. 'And would you be mouthing all this now if I had returned empty-handed? No money in the coffers?'

'Of course.'

'Oh, I'm sure,' he sneered, and she flinched away from the look in his eyes. 'After four years I've become eligible, haven't I, Isobel? Why don't you admit it? Maybe Abigail was wrong, maybe you'd *like* me to believe that there was some dark, ulterior motive for marrying him because the truth is just too sordid. Is that it? The truth being that you married him because you wanted to make a match with someone you considered to be of the same social standing as yourself. The fact that we had been lovers was nothing more than an inconvenience.'

'Believe what you want,' she answered stubbornly.

It was like waving a red rag at a bull. His eyes glittered with savage fury and he shook her, really shook her, like a rag doll.

'You used me, Isobel,' he said through gritted teeth. 'What were you thinking when you touched me? What did you feel when we made love? That this was all something casual, a bit of a laugh? That I just wasn't rich enough for you? No more than a poor Italian boy with his poor Italian parents?'

'No!'

'Small towns breed insularity,' he muttered, ignoring her protest, his eyes burning into hers. His fingers were still biting into her flesh. In the morning there would be bruises, she thought. 'Small towns with small minds.'

'That being the case, why are you here?'

He looked at her and she felt unsteadied by his light, mesmeric eyes. 'You made a big mistake thinking that you could play with me, Isobel. No one plays with me. Do you understand? I went to America and I made my fortune, and now I have returned and here I shall stay. I will have your father's company and I will have you.'

'I won't marry you!'

He laughed coldly and his hand moved to caress the nape of her neck, his fingers soft although there was no gentleness in the gesture.

'How can you take pleasure in this?' she asked, but he didn't need to provide an answer to that one. 'You're crazy,' she muttered, wishing that he would remove himself to another part of the kitchen so that she could, at least breathe properly. The feel of his fingers on her neck was making her hair stand on end.

'Surely you have to admit that marriage would have its compensations, Isobel?' he said in a husky voice. 'You want me to make love to you as much as I want to.' He ran his fingers along her spine and her body froze as his hand found her breast. 'You see,' he whispered, rubbing her nipple with his thumb, feeling it swell to his touch, 'you can't fight me. I mean to have my way.'

'You would marry me simply for revenge? I'm not a possession, Lorenzo.' His finger continued to rub the throbbing bud of her breast and she could feel her face burning. He bent to kiss her neck, pulling her head back with his free hand.

They were both breathing heavily and when he pulled her against him, his hands moving to encircle her waist, she felt the hardness of his arousal with a shiver of longing.

'Shame,' he said coolly, smiling down at her, 'the place isn't quite right for making love, is it?'

Isobel pulled away from him and fled to the corner of the kitchen, grabbing up a tray and sticking it in front of her like a shield.

'Why don't you go into the sitting-room?' she asked on a high note.

'And let you get yourself in order?' He was still smiling. 'You do look a little ruffled.'

'I'm so glad you're enjoying yourself,' she said tightly. 'And what,' she added, on the spur of the moment, 'would your woman friend think if she could see you now? Or was the woman Abigail failed to mention no more than a passing fancy?'

He laughed. 'I thought you weren't curious about me?'

'I've always been curious about a man who is willing to sleep with two women at the same time,' she said, thinking on her feet.

The tray was beginning to feel heavy, but suddenly it didn't matter. She wanted desperately to hear about this woman. Jealousy clawed through her with sickening speed and she hated herself for it. Four years of bitter experience had not made her older and wiser, she thought, it had made her more stupid.

'Jessica,' he said, moving to relieve her of the tray, and talking in a normal voice as though, Isobel thought, discussing his damned sex-life was on a par with discussing the weather. 'She's blonde, beautiful, and she's my accountant. Satisfied?'

He walked towards the door with Isobel trailing behind him, her arms folded across her chest.

Beautiful and brainy. He had told her that he was not attracted to ornaments. Her imagination threw up at her images of a tall, leggy model who could converse about high finance with ease, and she felt slightly ill. And not in the least satisfied.

'And is she pining for you back in America?' she asked sweetly, addressing his back.

He stopped abruptly and she nearly careered into him. He was smiling with satisfied amusement.

'I knew you wouldn't let go of that topic so quickly.'

'Oh, you knew, did you?' She blushed and met his eyes with what she hoped was a steady stare.

'Of course I did. You forget—' he leaned slightly towards her, still smiling '—I know you well. You always were one to hammer away at something until you were completely satisfied. I remember a certain occasion when I arrived late to see you one evening and, despite the fact that you professed no interest whatsoever in my reasons, you gnawed away until I'd explained it all to you, right down to which side of the car the flat tyre had been on.'

That made her redden even more. It also rendered her temporarily speechless.

In one casual sentence he had sent her whirling back through time, to when life was full of heady optimism. It hurt all the more when she forced herself back to the present and back to the realisation that heady optimism was a lifetime away.

'To answer your question,' he continued in a casual voice, 'I have no idea whether Jessica is pining my absence. She has an extremely full life, an extremely demanding job and she's probably too exhausted in the evening to spend much time doing anything, including pining.'

'I'm staggered that you could tear yourself away from such an invigorating woman,' Isobel replied on a sour note. Her imagination had now elevated this other woman from merely being bright to being a positive genius, the sort who filled what little spare time she possessed pursuing some highly intellectual interest—like brain surgery.

'So am I,' he mused.

'Then why do you?' she snapped. 'Heathrow is well-stocked with planes going to America.'

'I told you,' Lorenzo said coldly, 'you won't be getting rid of me. I have business here, and I shall stay here until it is completed.'

Their eyes met in hostile understanding.

'You would give up a woman you love simply to satisfy some warped desire for revenge?' she asked on an indrawn breath.

Lorenzo didn't say anything for a while. When he finally spoke, his voice was a lazy drawl.

'Whoever mentioned giving up anyone? You'll meet Jessica yourself in due course. She's going to be coming out here to work for me.'

'You're going to bring… You intend to…'

'Stuck for words, Isobel?'

'You disgust me.' She half turned and he said viciously, under his breath,

'I didn't notice such scruples when you walked out

on me to marry Jeremy Baker. Or don't the rules of the game apply to yourself?'

'I had my reasons,' she muttered.

'What? What were they?' There was a savage urgency in his voice, and in the hard contours of his face.

'The coffee's getting cold,' she mumbled, looking away, and he turned on his heel, his mouth drawn into a tight line of anger.

Her skin felt as though it were on fire. She could see now what game he intended to play. The pieces of the jigsaw were falling into place.

He wanted her to marry him, to have her tied to his side, the possession that was once denied him; but on the sidelines he would have his mistress, this other woman.

He didn't know that she still loved him. If he knew that, then where would she be? She wouldn't let herself be hurt again. Hadn't she suffered enough? she thought with anguish. She would never marry him. Sooner or later, he would have to give up.

She followed him into the lounge where her mother, thank goodness, had not dropped off to sleep or anything inconvenient like that. She had refused to have sleeping tablets when her husband had died, was still sleeping badly most nights, and consequently had developed a habit of nodding off in the armchair in the sitting-room.

'My, you two took a long time in the kitchen,' she said mildly when they entered, and Isobel gave her a warning look which was blithely ignored.

'Did we?' Lorenzo deposited the tray on the coffee-table and shot Isobel a sideways look from under his lashes as Mrs Chandler leaned forward to pour the coffee.

'Mmm.' She handed Lorenzo his cup. 'Not that I

mind.' She handed Isobel her cup. 'I'm sure it does Isobel the world of good having an old friend to talk to.'

Isobel stifled a laugh at that one and sipped her coffee.

'Abigail,' Mrs Chandler sighed, 'is always on the road.'

'An itinerant life,' Lorenzo murmured obligingly, settling back into the chair as though in no hurry to see the front door.

'So it's refreshing for her to have you around, Lorenzo, I'm sure.' She looked at her daughter. 'Isn't it, darling?'

'Oh, extremely,' Isobel muttered. About as refreshing as bathing in a sheep-dip.

'That's nice to hear, Isobel,' Lorenzo said with a wicked grin.

'I do hope,' Mrs Chandler continued in the same pensive voice, 'that working together to sort out David's company will be possible.'

'So do I,' Lorenzo said, with rather more significance in his voice, which Isobel had no difficulty in picking up but which her mother happily missed.

'It will be so very nice to have you around, Lorenzo.' She paused and appeared to search around for the right words. 'Especially since I've decided to visit an old relative in Cornwall for a few weeks.'

'Old relative?' Isobel nearly gagged on a mouthful of coffee. 'Cornwall? What on earth are you talking about, Mother?'

'Haven't I mentioned it to you?'

'You know you haven't.'

'Oh dear, I meant to, but things have been so hectic here, what with all this business over the company.'

'What relative, Mother?' Isobel persisted. 'You can't possibly mean Aunt Dora?'

'I haven't seen her in absolutely ages, and she's always been so terribly keen to have us down.'

'She drives you crazy. She fusses.'

'She's just recovering from an operation, you know,' she said confidentially to Lorenzo. 'Her hip. Poor old thing.'

'She has a home help,' Isobel pointed out.

'But a relative would be so much nicer for her, don't you think, darling?' Mrs Chandler smiled. 'I may not be the most speedy thing in the world with my illness, but I can make a passable cup of tea and we're both so interested in the same things. Gardening, books.' She sighed. 'It will do me good, Isobel. I need to get away from here, to have a break from this house, with its memories.'

Isobel looked at her mother helplessly.

'But now?' she asked. 'Why now?'

'Why not?'

'I think it's a splendid idea,' Lorenzo said, and Isobel glowered at him.

How dared he contribute to a conversation which had nothing to do with him?

She looked at her mother, serenely sipping from her cup of coffee.

This *didn't* have anything to do with him, did it? Her mother couldn't possibly be indulging in a spot of matchmaking, could she?

She subsided into frowning, thoughtful silence, and only heard her mother's question as a vague murmur to Lorenzo in the background.

'Where are you staying?'

'In a hotel,' Lorenzo said, surprised by the question. 'The Edwardian on the outskirts of the town. Time certainly hasn't smiled kindly there.' He contemplated Mrs

Chandler over the rim of the cup while Isobel only absentmindedly tuned in to what they were saying.

She was managing quite nicely to persuade herself that there was nothing ulterior in her mother's sudden decision to go and visit Dora Gately, who was a sweet old biddy and was, in truth, recuperating from an operation on her hip. They had not seen each other for quite some time and Cornwall would be relaxing for her mother.

'Those poor people,' Mrs Chandler was saying. 'He drinks, you know, old Albert Towser. It's no great secret but he drank away a lot of the profit the place made in the boom years, and now, when belts need to be tightened, they're finding themselves terribly stretched. They're thinking of selling. The business is simply no longer there. Two factories have shut down since you were here, and there is just no call for a hotel of that size. In addition to which, the place is in a terrible state from all accounts. And, of course, no money at all to do the necessary repair work.'

Isobel had moved on from the knotty problem of wondering what her mother's motives were and was now debating whether she couldn't migrate to some other part of the world, if Lorenzo Cicolla proved to be as disastrously persistent as he intended to be. They said that the sun always shone in Australia. Wishful thinking, of course, since she would never dream of leaving her mother.

'The food's gone downhill as well,' Mrs Chandler was continuing to muse. 'Alice used to do quite a bit of the cooking, and she *always* supervised the kitchens, but she's had her hands full with Albert these past few years and she's no longer a young woman herself.'

France, Isobel thought, was closer to England, but far from Yorkshire. Maybe her mother would consider the

South of France. It was sunny there as well. No, perhaps not. What would happen to the physiotherapy course she wanted to start on later in the year? Her French left a lot to be desired.

'The food *is* pretty poor,' Lorenzo was agreeing conversationally. 'Not,' he added loyally, 'like this little establishment here—even if the apple pie's a day old.' He grinned teasingly.

Dorset. The weather would be rubbish, Isobel reflected, but there would be no Lorenzo Cicolla making her life hell and, far away from him, she could cure herself of her foolish love.

One thing was certain, she couldn't stay here and she couldn't bank on his leaving simply because she refused to marry him. He might decide to buy her father's firm, without her consent to marry him, and then while away his time dogging her every move while his leggy, blonde mistress warmed his bed on the sidelines.

'Which is why,' she heard her mother say firmly, 'and especially now that I have decided to spend some time with Dora, I think you ought to come here to stay. At least until you've found yourself a place of your own.'

At which point Isobel tuned in with horror to the gist of a conversation which had been wafting over her for the past fifteen minutes.

'You can be company,' Mrs Chandler said with a comfortable smile on her lovely face, 'for Isobel.'

CHAPTER SEVEN

ISOBEL lay on the bed and stared upwards at the ceiling. The light was switched off, so she couldn't see anything in the dark, but there was no way that she could close her eyes. She would never get to sleep anyway.

'How,' she had asked her mother an hour previously, after she had sat through arrangements between Lorenzo and her mother in a stunned silence, 'could you have invited him to stay *here*?' Lorenzo had already left, to return the following afternoon.

'It seemed logical,' Mrs Chandler had answered, standing up and heading towards her bedroom. Isobel had followed in her wake, trying to be calm. 'After all, the house is huge—much too big for just the two of us. And with me gone to stay with your aunt, you would just rattle around here. It would worry me.'

'Why? I'm fine with my own company. I don't need…'

'I would feel happier knowing that Lorenzo was here.' She had paused outside her bedroom door, and Isobel had pointedly ignored the implication that the discussion was finished, at least until the following morning.

'But this is *our* house, and Lorenzo Cicolla is—' she was close to spluttering '—a *stranger*! And to cap it all, you're going to go away and leave me…us…here!' She was spluttering and beginning to sound like a plaintive child and her mother smiled indulgently.

'He's hardly a stranger, darling. Anyone would think that you'd never laid eyes on him before,' her mother had reproved, pulling back the bedspread and then sitting

116

down at the dressing-table to remove her make-up. 'I don't know what's come over you all of a sudden, Isobel. I know you're still fraught after Jeremy's death, and your dad's. We both are. But you were very rude this evening.'

'I wasn't rude,' Isobel had said stubbornly. 'I just don't think it's a good idea to throw open the doors to any and everyone who happens to be passing by.'

'Lorenzo is an old friend!' She had faced her daughter. 'I thought it might have helped you. I thought, darling, that the company would be good for you. You're far too inclined to retreat into yourself. Besides, if you two are thrown together it might knock some sense into both of you, get you working together so that Lorenzo can go ahead and settle the deal on your father's firm. You used to be such close friends—more than that. I simply don't know what's going on here.'

And that, Isobel now thought, had been the end of that.

Lorenzo was going to be moving in. Of course she could have moved out herself, but then that would have seemed like running away, and besides, the thought of moving back into her own house, *Jeremy*'s house, as she had always considered it, wasn't appealing. She didn't know if she could face being surrounded by memories of the unhappiness that had been forced upon her, memories of the silence, the despair born out of secrets which should have remained buried in the past.

She lay in bed, seething, and when she awoke the following morning, she was heavy-eyed and bad-tempered.

It didn't help that her mother seemed thrilled at the prospect of Lorenzo coming to stay. With what seemed to Isobel indecent haste, she had packed her bags and consulted train timetables. She would leave that evening and Aunt Dora was going to have some late tea laid on, and wasn't that wonderful, my sweet, oh, it *will* be restful.

Isobel departed for the surgery on her bicycle with dark thoughts. If she happened to bump into Lorenzo Cicolla, then she would give him a piece of her mind, because she had been too taken aback the evening before to do much more than stare at them both in open-mouthed horror.

She didn't, though. She spent a tiring day at the surgery and emerged at five o'clock into a depressingly cold drizzle of rain.

Lorenzo was outside. He seemed, she thought antagonistically, to make a habit of accosting her outside her work.

She debated whether to pretend that she hadn't seen his car parked across the road, and while she was busy debating he stepped out and sprinted across the road towards her.

It was cold, and he was wearing a long black coat over his suit, which seemed to emphasise his height and muscularity.

'I hoped I might catch you before you left,' he said, not giving her time to say anything. 'I want to have a few words with you.'

'It's raining.'

'So I've noticed. Come on.'

This time she didn't try to protest. What would have been the point? He would have steamrollered her along with him like the last time anyway.

She wheeled her bicycle along the pavement, putting it between the two of them, hurrying to keep up with him.

She was soaked by the time they made it to the pub.

'You're wet,' Tom said, as if pointing out something that might have escaped them.

'Very perceptive, Tom,' Isobel muttered. 'Coffee would be nice.'

He went off to get their order and returned, saying with his usual forthrightness, 'Seems to be getting a habit, this, doesn't it? You two having a drink together.'

It was impossible to get annoyed with Tom. His bluntness was too disarming.

'We keep running into one another,' Lorenzo said, not looking at her. 'Hazards of small-town living, I guess.'

Tom nodded. 'If you could call it a hazard,' he replied, with a great deal of philosophical insight for him. 'I like it myself.' He pointed towards the table where they had last sat. 'Your table's empty. Nice and cosy too, in front of the fire. I'll bring coffee along when it's ready.'

'*Our* table?' Isobel hissed to Lorenzo once they were out of earshot. 'We've only been here twice, for heaven's sake!'

Lorenzo lowered his body into the chair and looked at her through his lashes. 'In a place this size, twice constitutes a habit.'

Tom approached them with the coffee, and they made polite noises about the weather. He himself lived above the pub with his wife and children, but his brother had a modest farm on the outskirts of the village, and consequently Tom was something of a self-proclaimed expert on the weather and its effects on various types of vegetables and livestock.

Isobel listened while he and Lorenzo conversed and, as soon as he was gone, she turned to Lorenzo and said furiously, not bothering to hide behind politeness, 'How could you?'

'How could I what?'

'You know what! How could you accept my mother's invitation to stay at the house? Especially knowing that she wasn't going to be around!'

'Nothing like coming to the point, is there?' He sipped from his glass, then carefully put it down on the table. 'But I'm glad you brought the subject up because that's precisely what I wanted to talk to you about.'

'Snap!' Isobel looked at his unsmiling face mutinously. She had had a good few hours to consider the situation, and her thoughts on the matter hadn't become any more accepting.

How was she ever going to stand having him around her, under the same roof? Without even the comforting third presence of her mother?

'You're acting like a child,' Lorenzo said coolly, and she could have hit him.

'Me? A child?' She swallowed a mouthful of coffee and then cradled the cup in her hands. 'You really want to make life as difficult as possible for me, don't you?' she asked bitterly.

'Your mother would have been hurt if I had rejected her offer. She wants this deal with your father's company to go through, which is one reason why she's throwing us together. And anyway, as far as she is concerned, why should I stay in a draughty, uncomfortable hotel room when her own house is so vast?'

It made sense, of course, but that only made Isobel angrier.

'Because you're out of my hair when you're in a draughty, uncomfortable hotel room.'

'Don't be so damned self-centred.'

'You can stay in *my* house,' she offered, clutching a sudden safety belt, and his brows met in a black frown.

'Are you quite mad?' he asked smoothly.

'It's empty!'

'Not for me, it isn't.' He swallowed a long mouthful of his drink and looked at her savagely. 'And the reason I wanted to see you before I moved in was to warn you to stop acting as though you want to kill me in front of your mother. She's going away to relax, and why don't you just allow her that sensible piece of freedom without having to worry that she'll return to find a corpse on her hands? That will achieve nothing more than unnecessarily upsetting her.'

'Don't tell me what's going to upset my mother!'

'I damn well will, because right now you're not seeing further than your own nose. I'm moving in and that's a fact, so you might as well grin and bear it.'

'I'd rather grin and bear a nuclear war,' she said through gritted teeth, and he laughed, relaxing back in the chair and giving her a long, appreciative look. Isobel reddened and said quickly, 'Why did you sell your mother's house if you had plans to return to England?'

Lorenzo looked at her thoughtfully. 'Because I had no idea when I would return, or, to be honest, where I would live.'

'Until events propelled you back to this little place.' The bitterness had crept back into her voice.

He shrugged. 'At any rate, it seemed foolish to continue maintaining an unoccupied house.'

'So I take it you're actively looking for somewhere to live?'

'Do I detect a note of optimism in your voice?' he asked lazily.

She didn't like it when he was like this, when the charm was lurking so close to the surface. He was untrustworthy, she had to remind herself, and he was hell-bent on hurting her. She glanced at him from under her lashes. Why hadn't the passing years turned him into an unappealing, overweight businessman? Maybe she wouldn't have found her senses doing somersaults if he wasn't so damned sexy.

'Curiosity,' she answered at last, and he raised his eyebrows.

'Well, to satisfy your curiosity, yes, I shall be looking for somewhere to live. Any suggestions?'

'That depends on the kind of house that you're looking for.'

'What would you recommend?'

'I don't know your tastes,' she replied succinctly.

'Don't you?'

She was beginning to feel breathless.

'I don't know what you can afford,' she said, avoiding the question and he laughed.

'I can afford anything.'

'Your best bet is to go along to John Evans on the High Street and find out what they've got.' She began making fiddly movements to indicate that she was ready to leave.

'Yes, you could do that, couldn't you?' he murmured softly, amused at her tight-lipped reaction to that.

'No.'

'Why not? You know my taste in houses, whether you want to admit it or not. Didn't we spend idle hours discussing where we'd live if we ever settled down together?'

Disastrous things were happening to her equilibrium. She didn't want to remember the past with him; she didn't want to confront the awful comparison between what they had then and what they had now.

'Right now,' he said smoothly, 'I haven't got time to visit properties.'

'Why not?'

'I have to establish a working base here so that I can

communicate with my other companies, before I get down to your father's, that is.'

'Over my dead body.'

'Jessica will be bringing over paperwork, and I shall have to install a fax machine.'

'Surely the wondrous Jessica would be able to do all that and give you ample time to find your own house? From what you say, she could run a business single-handed in between raising ten children and knocking out gourmet meals in the length of time it would take most normal people to open a can of beans.'

'Jealous?'

'Hardly.'

'You could have done something with your life, Isobel. You were destined to.' He leaned forward urgently. 'Greatness was expected from you. How could you have been satisfied with anything less?'

'Not everyone lives up to their expectations.' Her words were practically inaudible. She didn't want to talk about this and her lowered eyes and set mouth said as much.

'And there ends the subject?'

'I haven't got time to house-hunt on your behalf,' she said, ending the subject.

'On *our* behalf,' he said with smiling, steely-eyed menace. 'And I rather think you have. After all, wouldn't you like me out of here so that you can come to terms, in privacy, with the inevitable?'

He looked at her and smiled, knowing that he had trapped her.

'I'll think about it,' Isobel mumbled, standing up. She couldn't quite explain it to herself, but she felt uneasy about becoming involved in something as personal as choosing a house for Lorenzo Cicolla. It felt as though she was beginning the process of giving in to his demands, but he was right: living under the same roof as him was going to drive her insane, and she easily had more time than he had to hunt around properties.

'You'd better come back with me,' Lorenzo said as they went outside to find that the drizzle was now bordering on a downpour. He took her bike and ran towards his car, with her following him.

They were both dripping once more by the time they were inside the car. He started the engine, turned on the windscreen wipers, and it was only when they had been driving for a while that she realised that they were not headed in the right direction for her mother's house.

Her body jerked up in panic and she said, in a rushed voice, 'Where are we going?'

'The Edwardian.'

'What for?'

He looked at her sideways. 'To collect my things. Clothes, papers, my computer terminal. Any objections?'

Isobel tried to look nonchalant in the dark, but she was nervous by the time they arrived at the hotel. When he had first arrived, she had assumed, blithely, that she could more or less avoid having any contact with him, but here she was now, about to face the prospect of sharing her mother's house with him, not to mention scouring estate agents on his behalf.

The Edwardian was a large hotel on the outskirts of the town, and it was obvious that it must have been quite something in its heyday. Unfortunately, as her mother had said, its heyday had long since vanished, and as they walked into the foyer she was all too aware of those little tell-tale signs of a place that has hit on hard times. The paint needed updating, the wallpaper needed updating—even the furniture dotted about here and there looked as though it had seen much better days.

Mrs Towser was standing behind the reception desk and she looked harassed.

'So sorry to hear about your father and your husband, dear,' she said to Isobel as Lorenzo settled his bill. She looked slyly across to him. 'Your house must seem very empty without your husband around.'

'I'm staying with my mother,' Isobel answered shortly. She didn't want to encourage an interrogation from Mrs Towser, so she looked vacantly around her.

'Yes, dear. A very good idea.' She ceased looking curious, and her expression of harassment reappeared. Isobel got the feeling that she was so wrapped up in her own worries that she had little time to concern herself with other people.

Lorenzo handed her the cheque, which she perfunctorily glanced at, and it was a relief to escape the atmosphere of doom which pervaded the area around the desk.

There was no lift. They walked along a network of corridors, through archways, up some stairs, and finally arrived at the room.

'I'll wait for you outside, shall I?' Isobel suggested as he pushed open the door, and Lorenzo said with his back to her,

'Don't be ridiculous. I don't know how long I shall be. There's no point standing out there in the freezing corridor.' So she reluctantly entered and resumed her inspection of the hotel décor while he threw his things into suitcases.

Her parents had used to come here, occasionally, for Sunday lunch when she was a child. It had always been something of a treat. It seemed sad to think that the place was now a shabby building with all glamour and elegance long stripped from it.

He had finished packing. He briefly glanced around to

make sure that he was not forgetting anything, then moved to the door, where she had been standing in silence for the past fifteen minutes.

'There,' he said, leaning against the door and surveying her with a certain amount of cool amusement, 'all done, and you're unscathed by the experience.'

Isobel didn't answer. She rested her hand meaningfully on the door-knob and he covered it with his. Immediately her body froze.

'Why were you so reluctant to come here with me, Isobel?' he asked mockingly. 'Did you think that I might be overcome with lust if I found myself in a bedroom with you?'

'Perish the thought,' she said promptly.

'Of course, I'll admit that there was a time...' He coiled his fingers in her hair and she looked up at him with a small, inaudible gasp. The room seemed to be closing in and she found that she was perspiring slightly.

She had no idea how long they stayed like that, staring at each other. What was he thinking? His expression was shuttered but there was an unspoken feverish heat about him that radiated from his body.

Her eyes drifted down to his mouth, and his fingers tightened in her hair until he was hurting her.

What was needed now, she thought, was banality. She should say something, anything, to break the intense erotic atmosphere between them, but she couldn't get a word out.

She found herself straining towards him, wanting him with a depth of desire that knocked the breath out of her body.

She wanted his mouth to cover hers, she wanted his hands to explore her body, she wanted to feel the burning, sensual passion which she had known with him years before, in that age of innocence.

'Damn you, Isobel,' he said fiercely. His hand dropped and he pulled open the door.

He had wanted her, she thought numbly, following him out into the corridor. He had wanted her as badly just then as she had wanted him, but the past had come between them, that terrible secret which was like a chasm stretching into infinity.

They drove to her mother's house in a tense silence. Mrs Chandler was waiting for them. She had cooked, Isobel thought sourly, probably something special. The aroma wafted from the kitchen, and Lorenzo, she jealously noticed, switched automatically into charming mode, delighting her mother. Naturally.

'Such a wet night,' Mrs Chandler was saying. 'I thought a lovely hotpot. Though not for me. I have a taxi booked to take me to the station shortly.'

'I would have dropped you,' Lorenzo said quickly, frowning, and Mrs Chandler waved aside his protest. 'You shouldn't have gone to any trouble,' he murmured, smiling, and Isobel chipped in acidly,

'No. You shouldn't.'

Her mother pretended not to notice. She glanced down at Lorenzo's suitcases and began chatting to him about the lack of luggage.

'If you had been a woman,' she mused, walking into the hall, which was beautifully warm after the damp cold of the hotel room, 'you would have come with several trunks! Isn't that so, darling?' She looked at Isobel, who stretched her lips into a stony smile.

'I think I'll go and have a bath,' she said by way of response.

'Oh, yes. You're both rather like drowned rats!'

Isobel scowled and wished that her mother wouldn't address them both as though they were a couple of delightful children.

'Darling,' she turned to her daughter, 'do show Lorenzo up to his room. You know which one he's having.'

'Yes.' And if I forget, she told herself, I can always follow the scent of the freshly picked flowers.

She led the way, not looking back to see if he was following her, hoping that he would perhaps trip over one of his suitcases and find himself another landlady courtesy of the local hospital, but naturally he didn't. He was too strong and too graceful a mover for any such clumsy misadventure.

'Here you go.' She pushed open the bedroom door and turned to go, but his hand snapped out, curling around hers, and he said to her half-averted face,

'Watch it, Isobel. Think about your mother and not yourself.' He let her go and she fled to her own bedroom, which was just along the corridor.

Once inside the room, she leaned back against the closed door and made an effort to think calm, peaceful thoughts. If she was going to react like this, she would be a wreck inside a week. She would have to grin and bear his presence and do her damnedest to make sure that he didn't get an inkling as to what was going on inside her.

She had a quick bath, and emerged feeling not much more refreshed than before she went in.

She had wrapped her towel around her and she absent-mindedly began flicking through her wardrobe, her thoughts elsewhere.

She would have to find a house for him to live in as soon as possible. She was due some holiday and she would take it and spend the time narrowing down the possibilities. She wondered whether it could all be accomplished in the space of a day.

Nine a.m.: go to estate agents. Ten a.m.: start looking.

Five p.m.: finish looking. Six p.m.: inform him that she had found something suitable. Goodbye.

She didn't hear the door being pushed open. She was too furiously concentrating on her plan of action, so when she looked into the mirror and saw his reflection staring back at her she almost hit the ceiling.

'What are you doing here?' she asked breathlessly, clutching the towel around her.

'No towel.'

'Airing cupboard.' Her feet were glued to the ground and a feeling of panic rose into her throat as he closed the door quietly behind him and took a few steps towards her.

'Out!'

He was standing right in front of her and she wished that she had had the forethought to put on her bathrobe instead of this ineffectual little towel which barely covered her body. But then she hadn't expected him to barge into her bedroom, had she?

'I don't want you here!' she said, looking up at him.

'Do you think I want to be here?' he grated.

Her mouth parted, and he lowered his head. She knew what his intentions were even before he kissed her, but she was still shocked when she felt his lips crush hers. His tongue invaded the inside of her mouth with hunger and a little groan escaped from her throat.

His hands moved to the small of her back, pressing her against him.

She could feel the urgency of his arousal, hard against her, and her limbs began to melt.

'No!' Her voice was muffled against his mouth.

'Yes! Damn you!' He pulled her head back and kissed her throat, then lifted her and carried her across to the bed.

There was nothing gentle about him. The lines of his face were hard, aggressive, but his eyes were on fire.

She was still clutching the towel, and he pulled her hands away, pinning them above her head.

'Lorenzo!' She said his name in a shaking, husky voice, with her eyes closed. It seemed like a million years ago that she had felt this wild, reckless passion soaring through her, and as the towel fell open she arched her body up, so that her breasts could receive the moist exploration of his mouth.

She wanted him so badly that she was aching all over, so badly that she couldn't think at all, never mind think straight.

His tongue flicked over one hardened nipple and she shuddered. He took her breasts in his hands and she pressed his dark head against her, watching him as he suckled her nipples.

When he shifted to trail his tongue along her stomach she moaned, and writhed against him.

This was what she had been so afraid of. This awful, compulsive reaction, this desperate needing that had never left her. All through her long marriage to Jeremy she had kept on wanting Lorenzo. It had been a steady beat drumming at the back of her mind.

His tongue found the moist centre between her legs, and as it darted into the sweet core of her being she had to stop herself from whimpering aloud.

'Make love to me, Lorenzo,' she groaned, and he raised his head to look at her. Their eyes tangled, and with a sharp movement he stood up. It was like being cocooned under a warm blanket, only to find it snatched away from you. Isobel sat up and looked at him with bewildered eyes.

Reality hadn't quite hit her as yet. Her body was still throbbing.

'Get up,' he said shortly, and that was when reality struck her in the face. She pulled the towel around her and struggled to her feet, because lying there on the bed made her feel intensely vulnerable.

'Lorenzo...!' she began, and his voice was like a whiplash.

'When I take you, Isobel—and I will—it will be in *our* house. You will be *mine*, not on temporary loan but with a ring on your finger. You made love with me once and then married another man. Damn you, Isobel Chandler, the next time I will have you, and there will be no running away!' There was angry intent on his face and she wished that the ground would open up and swallow her whole. She couldn't find a thing to say.

He spun around on his heel and she watched in silence as he left the bedroom, quietly shutting the door behind him. Then she collapsed on to the bed, shaking.

So this was how their story ended. Anger where love should have been. She began to cry, steadily and silently, until she felt too weary to shed any more tears. Then she washed her face and applied her make-up carefully. She didn't want her mother to see that she had been crying. She didn't want Lorenzo to see that she had been crying. She would let him believe that she was fine, hunky-dory, that she too could put the whole thing down to experience, a regrettable incident.

She felt wooden as she made her way downstairs, and it was with deep relief that she was granted a temporary reprieve from him. He was still upstairs. That gave her time to get herself together.

Her mother was in the kitchen. She had made some home-made bread to take with her. Did that seem a good idea? She had also bought some smoked salmon. She was sure that Aunt Dora would love that. Was that all right? She thought it nicer than flowers.

Isobel nodded and answered and wondered miserably where all those silver linings on those clouds had gone.

She didn't look around when Lorenzo walked in, although she felt a chill run down her spine. Her mother was glancing at her watch and chatting, but with one ear open for the sound of the doorbell.

Lorenzo regarded her expressionlessly, and she looked back at him in like manner. Two ships that had once crossed in the night, but were now on impossibly parallel paths.

'I thought that I might start looking at houses for you tomorrow,' she said politely. 'Lorenzo has asked me to help him house-hunt,' she explained, turning to her mother.

'I think that's an excellent idea,' Mrs Chandler said. 'What sort of place are you looking for?'

'Old,' Lorenzo said, turning away from Isobel. If body language said something, she thought, then it was speaking volumes right now, because the twist of his body was telling her as clearly as if he had written the message in neon lettering on the table that although he might want her, beyond that there was nothing but scathing dislike. 'I rather like Tudor-style houses, and my mother absolutely insists on a garden.'

Mrs Chandler nodded approvingly. 'I see her point. There's Bearwood Cottage up for sale. I know that through Emily. Mrs Jenkins is moving down to Surrey to live with one of her daughters.'

Mrs Chandler carried on talking, discussing properties, and the words washed over her head like waves over a beach. She heard but had stopped listening. This was what it was like, she thought, when your world caved in. Even when she had married Jeremy, she had not felt quite so desolate. Perhaps at the back of her mind there had always burnt a tiny, flickering flame of hope that one day things would work out. Now the hope had been extinguished, and she felt as if she were staring into one long, dark tunnel which stretched into eternity.

She resurfaced when the doorbell went, and her mother left in a cloud of hugs and promises to call every night.

Then there were just the two of them. She couldn't begin to think how they could break the silence between them, but when Lorenzo did speak, it was in a cool, controlled voice.

He politely asked her what she intended doing about her own house, and she replied, with equal politeness, that she would be selling it.

'It's much too big for one,' she said, looking more or less through him. 'Besides, it was never much to my liking.'

The market was not good for selling houses. They discussed this for some time, and when that conversation tapered off Lorenzo told her what he thought of property in Chicago.

Was this how he imagined them together? she wondered. A life of being eaten away by love, love which she would have to keep to herself, while he treated their relationship as an ownership long awaited, a passion for revenge at last fulfilled? While his blonde amused him on the side?

They ate in silence but then, as Isobel laid down her knife and fork, she said, without looking at him, 'I just can't do it, Lorenzo. I just can't marry you, I couldn't bear it.'

He sat back and regarded her calmly, folding his arms.

'Why not, Isobel?'

'I can't marry you when there's nothing between us now but dislike. I would keep remembering the good times.'

There was a dull flush on his cheeks. 'Why would you do that? I doubt you remembered them for four years when you were with Jeremy.' His mouth twisted and she flinched.

'You'll never let me forget that, will you?' she asked, and his face hardened.

'What you did to me stayed with me for four years. Why should I let you forget anything?' He banged his fist on the table, then raked his fingers through his hair.

'It would be better if you left, if you carried on with your life in America...'

'Don't tell me what I would be better off doing!' He stood up, his eyes angry, then he stalked off and she followed towards the sitting-room, just as the telephone began to ring.

She spoke briefly, but her heart had turned to ice and she felt quite sick and disorientated. 'It's for you,' she said, her hand rigid as she held out the telephone.

'For me?'

'Yes. Jessica Tate. Apparently she phoned through to the Edwardian and was given your number here. Lucky we aren't ex-directory, wouldn't you say?'

I hate you, she thought as she handed him the telephone and heard his husky, velvety voice address the woman on the other end. I hate you for coming back into my life.

CHAPTER EIGHT

ISOBEL stood inside the beamed Tudor house and decided that, like it or not, this was going to be the house. The house which she had been looking for for the past two weeks. The house which would put an end to Lorenzo's presence under her mother's roof.

She looked around her and thought that it was in a somewhat sad state of disrepair, but there was nothing that could not be mended with enough money, and there was no shortage of that.

Mr Evans had lent her the keys so that she could look around herself, and had devoutly informed her that the only reason that it was still on the market was because most people were unwilling to move into a place which needed some work done on it.

'Some work', she quickly realised as she went from room to room, was estate agent's jargon for 'total overhaul', but it was, she had to admit, a delightful property. Large, without being sprawling, with the required picture-book garden, or at least the makings of one once the general wilderness had been cleared.

The owners, he had told her, shaking his head ruefully, had sadly been forced to sell.

'Family problems,' he had said enigmatically, and she nodded. She could sympathise with family problems. She had a very active ongoing one at the moment.

The past fortnight had been miserable. True, she had not seen a great deal of Lorenzo, but his presence had invaded every nook and cranny of the house. Every waking moment had been spent in a state of nervous tension in case he walked into the room, or worse in case she found herself alone in a room with him and had to make polite conversation.

What were his plans now? There had been no more dark threats about marriage, no more harsh demands to be told the reasons for her marriage, but the silence still unsettled her. Had the appearance of his lover made him reconsider his twisted desires for revenge? He had said nothing further after her insistence that she could never marry him, and she suspected that the quiet desperation of her words had done what no heated outburst in the past had achieved, but he didn't say and she didn't ask.

Lorenzo, when he addressed her, did so with the distance of a stranger, and that cut her to the quick. When he had returned he had made his hatred of her quite clear, but at least, in retrospect, it had indicated feeling of sorts. Now there was cool indifference in his voice when he spoke to her.

She walked up the narrow staircase into the myriad bedrooms with their curious, charming eccentricities and stood for a while at the window of the master bedroom, gazing down at the untamed garden below.

She didn't want to think about Jessica Tate but she couldn't help herself.

Two days after her telephone call, she had arrived. Lorenzo had rented a flat for her on the outskirts of the town, but that had scarcely minimised her uninvited appearances at the house.

She was keeping tabs on him. Isobel had recognised that from the moment she had first walked through the front door, full of shallow charm and even more full of significant little gestures towards Lorenzo, making it quite clear that he was *her* property.

Isobel looked around the room and thought that the house was perfect, in fact it was so perfect it was almost a shame to hand it over lock, stock and barrel to Lorenzo, but she was quietly going crazy with him living under the same roof.

She inspected the rest of the bedrooms at a leisurely pace. The windows all needed work doing on them, the walls were in dire need of repainting, and the carpets looked as though their sell-by date had been decades back.

She began drifting back downstairs and told herself sternly to concentrate on the house and not on Jessica, but she couldn't. Was that why Lorenzo had been around so little? Because all his spare time was eaten up sleeping with his mistress? She tried hard not to care but the question plagued her. She had found herself thinking about them together, making love, at the most inappropriate moments. At the frozen foods section in the supermarket, in the middle of conversations with people, and of course late at night, when everything seemed so much worse anyway.

Jessica Tate, viewed objectively, unemotionally, was the sort of woman guaranteed to put off most of her female counterparts. She exuded an aura of intelligent competence which, in combination with her impeccably groomed blonde good looks, induced an immediate reaction of wariness.

She was tall, though not as tall as Isobel, with closely cropped blonde hair and cool blue eyes which assessed everyone and everything. They had instantly assessed *her* and had seemed to decide, after some internal debate, that Isobel was not an ongoing threat.

You may have looks, those hard eyes said, but as far as intelligence goes, you're nothing compared to me.

Consequently the majority of her small talk, when it was directed towards Isobel, had been condescending and Isobel, with barely forced politeness, saw no reason to try and justify her existence in the eyes of a woman who looked as though she didn't make a habit of smiling.

'It's such a *responsibility* being promoted over and over again,' she had asserted on her first visit to the house, over a cup of tea, and scones which she had assumed were home-made, because, she had implied, what else did someone like Isobel have to do with her time when her little chores at the local surgery were finished? 'Sometimes I sit back and think how *wonderful*—' pointed cat-like look at Isobel '—it would be to throw it all in and do something completely undemanding for a few years.'

Isobel had smiled politely and murmured something innocuous, while thinking that she had never seen anyone express an observation with such insincerity in her life before.

But Lorenzo had obviously missed it because he had looked at the blonde with a veiled smile of amused indulgence.

'Although,' Jessica had resumed, crinkling her nose at Lorenzo flirtatiously, 'I would probably die of boredom after a couple of weeks.'

She was fond of making little self-disparaging comments, Isobel soon realised, which she would then quickly nullify by building herself up with a practised, bewildered shake of her head. A sort of 'I don't *want* to be terribly popular' approach. 'It's not as though I try very hard, but I just can't seem to stop everyone responding to me!'

You're just being catty, Isobel told herself now. She strolled into the kitchen and was confronted by another sad state of affairs. The dimensions were lovely, but everything had been left to rot and there were huge gaps where the paint had flaked off and something which suspiciously reminded her of mould was creeping into the edges of the walls.

Jessica was coming over to dinner later that evening. Isobel gazed at the creeping mould and thought how much she hated the prospect of having to endure at least three hours in the company of a woman who did everything possible, in the least direct way, to make her feel inadequate and unfulfilled.

'This is such a quaint little village,' she had told Isobel at a later date. 'I guess it's all gossip and wagging of tongues around here? Just like in your lovely British movies?' Her eyes, patronising, had said, What a dull life you lead, gossiping from dawn till dusk. Look at me, I'm smart and successful. Any wonder Lorenzo thinks I'm the bee's knees?

She made damn sure that finance was discussed in the most complex terms possible, and her eyes, sliding along to Isobel, would reinforce that unspoken message which she had been communicating from the very first moment she had arrived.

There was a loud bang on the front door, which knocked the thoughts out of her head, and Isobel sprinted across to open it. It could only be Mr Evans, probably here to give her a little pep talk on the charming possibilities of the cottage. He would point out the original beams, the lovely view from every window, the marvellous fireplace in the sitting-room, and he would disarmingly play down the immense amount of money needed to bring it all up to any reasonable living standard.

She opened the door with a dry smile, and was stunned to discover that the amiable Mr Evans was nowhere on the horizon.

Lorenzo looked down at her, his eyes glittering in the fast-gathering gloom of twilight.

'Oh, hello,' Isobel said, as her nervous system shifted up a couple of notches. He must have come straight from work. He was still wearing his suit, and the long, black coat which made him look like a highwayman. 'What are you doing here?' she asked automatically, and he raised his black eyebrows in a question.

'I'll give you three guesses, shall I?' he asked drily. 'Is there any chance you might stop barricading the door so that I can come in?'

Isobel stood aside and watched as he walked past her and into the centre of the hall.

It was, she thought with a little spurt of dread, the first time in two weeks that they had been alone together. Really alone. Not merely positioned in the same room, more often than not with Jessica providing a third party.

He looked around him, and she said, closing the door, 'How did you know where to find me?'

His eyes lazily made their way back to her face. 'Evans told me,' he answered, sticking his hands into the pockets of his coat. She didn't blame him either. It was freezing in the house. She herself was amply covered in jeans, vest, jumper, and her father's old Barbour which she had always loved so much. She could still feel the cold, though.

'He thought, strange though it might seem, that I would be interested in joining you here to see what I thought of the place.'

The light shone bleakly down from the naked light bulb, and it picked up all the sharp angles of his face, the intense blackness of his hair, the clever, glittering eyes. Funny how intimidating a man could be without really having to try.

'Well, I've already had a look around,' Isobel said weakly, and he moved towards her. Nothing threatening, but she still took a step backwards, and then gritted her teeth together in irritation at behaving so childishly.

'Good,' Lorenzo drawled, 'so you'll be able to give me a comprehensive guided tour.'

'Of course.' She headed off towards the staircase, very businesslike, and he followed her, his footsteps stealthy for a man of his size.

She got the vague feeling that something had changed in him, that he had reached some sort of decision, although it might well have been in her imagination.

She began pointing out the various features, which she was certain he could see for himself without having to have her play the tour guide.

'Only two bathrooms, I'm afraid,' she said, then added, because she couldn't resist, 'I don't know what your penthouse suite was like in Chicago, but houses of this age don't run to massive *en suite* dressing-rooms with separte inbuilt wardrobes for suits and shirts.'

'Don't they?' he asked softly, from nearer behind her than she had thought. 'You do surprise me with that little gem of insight.'

'Bathroom,' she said, pushing open a door. 'A bit small, I'm sure you'll find.'

'A little decrepit, at any rate,' he commented, walking in and surveying the walls and ceiling thoughtfully.

She followed the line of his gaze and murmured wryly, 'Matches the rest of the house. Apparently the owners were forced to sell. I suspect that, long before that, they'd run out of money. Or at least they'd decided to stop spending what they did have on their house.'

'Shame.'

They did the rounds of the bedrooms, which followed no formal logical pattern and required the occasional dodging under low, beamed door-frames, and after they had completed a similar circuit of downstairs, he turned to her and asked, casually, 'What do you think of it?'

They were in the sitting-room. It was the only room where any form of active residence could be glimpsed. This was in the form of yellowed net curtains precariously hanging from the windows. They were old and faded enough not to warrant their removal. Cobwebs clung to the walls and the dust which covered every square inch would have set Cinderella back by a good few weeks.

'I rather like it,' she admitted a little defiantly. 'It has atmosphere.'

'It's run down.'

'With a little restoration, it could be beautiful.'

'It would give any chartered surveyor an apoplectic fit.'

'A little painting,' she said with great understatement, glancing around her and using her imagination to restore it to its full potential. 'Some lovely old furniture, bowls of flowers.'

'Massive structural work...'

'The odd bit of structural work...'

He threw back his head and laughed at that, and she grinned at him reluctantly.

'Are you sure that you're not being persuasive because you want me out of your mother's house?' he asked.

'Of course not!'

'Or because you're secretly in Mr Evan's employ?'

'Heaven forbid! Although he *did* know my father...'

'Then why don't you sit down and tell me why you think I should invest my money in this place.'

Isobel looked around her and said matter-of-factly, 'My eyes must be failing. I can't see any chairs.'

'Who needs chairs?' He took off his coat and laid it

by the wall and pointed her towards it in a sweeping gesture, with a theatrical little bow, and she laughed, relaxing her guard. He was being friendly, she realised, and some part of her felt vaguely upset at that, though she didn't know why.

'Well,' she began, sitting down and feeling a shiver of apprehension as he lowered his lean frame next to her, 'I doubt you'll find anything as charming as this anywhere around here. It's a damned sight nicer than any of the properties I've looked around, and I've seen a lot. OK, so you'll need to have some work done on it, but what else can you expect of an old property that's had no money spent on it in years?'

'What indeed?' he murmured, and she felt that shiver of apprehension again.

'There are six bedrooms.'

'More than enough to entertain the occasional over-night guest,' he agreed, looking at her.

'And the garden would be a challenge for your mother.'

'Why didn't you and Jeremy ever have children?' he asked softly, out of the blue, and she sighed wryly, look-ing at him.

'I thought you'd given up asking those questions.'

'Because you refuse to give answers?'

'You'll have to pull out the kitchen and start from scratch. That room looks as though it might pose a se-rious health hazard.'

'You have nothing to fear from me, Isobel,' he mur-mured. 'I admit that when I first returned here I would have liked nothing better than to have made you suffer the way you once made me suffer, but you were right. All that is behind us now. I've thought about what you said, about not being able to marry me, and you're right. Revenge can be taken so far and then beyond that it becomes insanity. So what I want to say is that you're free. I'll buy your father's company, no strings attached. We can never be friends, but it's time for the past to be put to rest.'

That, she knew, should have sent her spirits soaring. Instead she felt a blinding sense of loss, the loss of the man whom she still loved to distraction, but who had now put her behind him, an unfortunate episode in his past which had once hurt but no longer did.

She knew as well, that she could tell him why she had married Jeremy, and she would have nothing to fear. He would not use the knowledge over her and, deep down, she had known that he never would.

But she would never tell him. She realised that now, with great sadness, because how could she explain her most intimate and private agony to a man who didn't love her? Her secret, like it or not, was now hers forever. There was no chance that she would ever share it with anyone because she would only share it with a man she loved, a man who returned her love, and that was the one thing Lorenzo would never do.

Sitting here, with his legs so close to hers, his body emanating warmth, reminding her of past things, she just felt ready to cry.

'In the end, he won, didn't he?' Lorenzo asked. 'He drove us apart four years ago because he hated me. The fact that you were something to pin on his jacket, something to adorn his arm, was an added bonus.'

She frowned, puzzled. 'Lorenzo, you've said that once before. That he hated you. But he had no reason to…'

'Oh, but he had.' Lorenzo took her face between his hands. 'I discovered something about him, quite by accident, you see.'

She was completely lost now. What on earth was he talking about?

'Do you remember my mother used to clean for his? A long, long time ago?'

Isobel nodded. There was a stillness in the air that made her hairs stand on end.

'One day, Emily Baker was there. She had had a little too much to drink and she was in a maudlin mood. Heaven knows, she always tended to be neurotic, from what I had seen.' He paused and looked at her, and in the half-shadows his pale eyes seemed black and bottomless. 'My mother was about to leave but she was worried about Jeremy's mother. Knowing Mama, she probably said something along the lines of, Is anything the matter? Anyway, out it all came. She began pouring her heart out. Guilt over something she had done years back.' He looked at her.

'Are you telling me that her husband was not Jeremy's father?'

'Apparently he couldn't have children.' Lorenzo sighed. 'Isn't it ironic the amount of people who seem to spawn children like rabbits, when there are others, worthwhile good men, who can't? Anyway, she had a brief affair and hence the birth nine months later of Jeremy. I suppose it was a confession that would have sunk into oblivion. Certainly Mama would never have said anything further about it, and I can't imagine that Emily would have considered it dinner-party conversation. But Jeremy walked in on the little scene. He made ugly, derogatory comments to his mother. He was shocked. She had never mentioned a word of it before.'

'But what did that have to do with you?'

'He assumed that my mother had told me, which of course she had, in the mistaken illusion that I could talk to him, lend a sympathetic ear. But Jeremy had never been one for the sympathetic ear. Months later, when it had been fermenting away inside him, he accused me of acting as though I was superior to him. He threw his parentage into my face, said that I'd probably been sniggering about it behind his back, and I did the worst possible thing. I laughed. Laughed that he could have been so off-target. But he misinterpreted my reaction, thought I was laughing at him, and he hit the roof. He said that one day he'd get even, and naturally I didn't pay a blind bit of notice to that. But he did, didn't he, Isobel?'

She nodded, digesting what he had just told her. It accounted for a lot of things, for Jeremy's sarcasm whenever Lorenzo's name was mentioned, and his recklessness, his dependence on drink. Did it all stem from that? He had never, ever discussed his parents with her and she had never had a clue about Emily Baker, but why should she? To outside eyes his parents were a happy couple, and chances were that her single sin had been a peccadillo born of depression, something that passed in time.

It had begun to rain. Autumn seemed to have been drenched with rain. She heard the steady drumming of raindrops against the window-pane.

'I suppose,' she said, 'we ought to be getting back.'

He looked at her, hesitating, then he said, standing up, 'I suppose so.'

'Isn't this awful weather?' she murmured as they walked towards the front door.

'Worse than Chicago,' he agreed, 'and that was bad enough. The winters were hard, but the summers were good. Seasons behaved themselves the way they ought to.'

She smiled and automatically raised her eyes to his, and for a split-second she thought that he was going to kiss her. But he didn't. He said slowly, 'I think I might return to Italy, make my base there.'

'Driven away by the constant rain?' she murmured

lightly, but her heart clenched tightly inside her. 'Is this your way of telling me that my efforts in finding you the perfect house have been for nothing?'

'Oh, I don't know,' he shrugged. 'I could always buy this place, and keep it for the times I return here. I shall have to oversee the company so I'll be back and forth, I should imagine. But,' he added, 'we need never cross paths again.'

Why did that hurt so much? She should be singing for joy. She opened the door, letting in a spray of rain, and ran towards her mother's car. Part of her knew that never setting eyes on him again was the best possible thing for her mental health, but there was another part, the same little desperate part that had been with her for the past four years, telling her that to glimpse him fleetingly was better than nothing.

She fumbled with the lock while he watched calmly, getting wet, and when she had settled into the driver's seat he went across to his own car, letting her leave first, then following slowly behind her.

Jessica was already there by the time they made it back to the house. There and looking none too pleased as they made their wet entry into the hall.

'Where have you been?' she asked solicitously. 'You're soaked.' She fussed around Lorenzo, who shrugged off her attentiveness with irritation.

'We were looking at a house,' he said briefly.

'Oh, yes.' She glanced at Isobel, eyes hard. 'I forgot that you were playing the estate agent. However do you find the time? I do wish I could have had someone running around to find my apartment in Chicago! It would have saved me a lot of valuable time. And was it a success?'

'We think so,' Lorenzo said, and Jessica's eyes hardened a little bit more. She didn't like the 'we' bit, it was just a mite too familiar for her, even though Isobel could have told her that she had nothing to fear on that score.

She left her in the hall, still unsuccessfully clucking around Lorenzo, and removed herself to her bedroom, where she had an overlong bath and, after eyeing her wardrobe critically, slipped on an ivory-coloured calf-length skirt and a short-sleeved, figure-hugging jumper in the same colour. The reflection staring back at her was tremendously beautiful. Isobel looked at herself without vanity and wondered why people ever imagined that looks brought happiness. In her case, it couldn't have been further from the truth.

Then she sat down on the dressing-table chair and thought about what Lorenzo had told her. Would she have reacted differently to Jeremy if she had known the true facts about him? She thought not. For the first time she contemplated her past calmly, without rancour.

She had been forced into a marriage through circumstances and, even though she had tasted the bitter fruit of unhappiness, she would have done the same thing if she had had to make the choice all over again.

In a way, it had worked to her advantage that she had not loved Jeremy. It had given her a sublime indifference to the rather unpleasant sides of his character, the tendency towards bullying, the mood swings, the bursts of unbearable arrogance. He was like a wilful child, incapable of understanding that the world did not revolve around him.

Would Lorenzo really return to Italy to live? she wondered, playing with the brush on the dressing-table. It was more than likely. Whether he ever really admitted it or not, she knew that she was the reason that he had returned to Yorkshire in the first place, back to the town that he had left behind in bitter anger. He had purged his system of her now. He was free.

Oh, God, she thought desperately, will *I* ever be free? Lorenzo was still the man who held her dreams in the palm of his hand. She could see herself in twenty years' time and she could imagine the whispers of people around her, saying to each other, She was so beautiful once. Why didn't she ever remarry? She'll never catch a man now, of course! Far too old.

There was a knock on the door and she looked up, startled. If I don't watch it, she thought grimly, I shall find myself becoming one of those awful women who live in a world of self-pity and can't see beyond their own miseries.

It was Jessica. That startled Isobel even more. Not once had the other woman ventured up to her bedroom.

'I wanted to have a word with you alone,' Jessica said, looking around her with mild curiosity. She was the sort of woman to whom even the Seven Wonders of the World would afford only mild curiosity. She stood in the centre of the room and folded her arms. 'I wanted to tell you that I've been sacked.' Her eyes narrowed to slits. 'Politely told that my accounting services are no longer required.'

'Really?'

'Please,' she drawled, 'spare me the wide-eyed innocence. We're both women of the world. When I first came here I decided that I wouldn't see you as a threat. Why should I? Sure, you have those looks, but types like you are a dime a dozen. All beauty and no brains. Look at you, stuck in this godforsaken place beyond the back of civilisation! *Not* the sort to appeal to the Lorenzo I knew.'

'Why are you telling me all this?' Isobel asked in a tight voice.

'Because I just want to warn you that you haven't won, even though you may think that you have.' Jessica was looking positively malicious. A little feline smile played on her well-painted lips.

'We really ought to be going downstairs,' Isobel decided.

'Not until I've said what I came to say. I wasted four years on that man. No one, but *no one*, takes Jessica Tate for a ride!'

The vehemence in the voice stunned Isobel back into silence. She could believe that no one had ever taken the great Jessica Tate for a ride. She looked the sort who monopolised taking other people for rides.

'It's hardly my fault that—'

'It damn well is! I don't know what happened between the two of you years ago, but whatever it was, he still wants you.' She spat that out with venom.

Wanted, Isobel thought disjointedly.

'But I haven't invested my time in that man for nothing!' She made it sound like a business venture that had gone wrong. Isobel could imagine her making up a list of the pros and cons of getting involved with him, working out whether he was worth the time and effort.

'I'm sorry,' Isobel said coldly, not feeling in the least sorry, 'if you fell in love with Lorenzo—'

'Fell in love with him?' She laughed acidly. 'I'm not some fifteen-year-old teenager, my dear! He's sexy, though, I'll admit that, but most of all he was a good catch. I suppose you thought that your ship had come in when you discovered that he was going to be in town?'

'Quite the opposite.'

'You British!' she said scathingly. 'Well, your ship may have docked but it's not going to remain too long in port. I'll make damn sure of that.' She smiled again, hugging something to herself, and Isobel looked at her uneasily.

With anyone else she would have admitted that she and Lorenzo had nothing, that any reluctant feeling he had had for her had now been extinguished, but she kept quiet.

But, throughout the evening, her eyes kept flitting back worriedly to Jessica's over-bright face, the over-wide smile.

She announced over dinner in a casual voice that she would be leaving within the week.

'No offence, but I'd be stifled here,' she said in that bursting-with-confidence tone of voice which implied that her departure would leave the community bereft, but what could she do?

Then she proceeded to launch into a monologue on what a valuable asset she was to the world of business.

Isobel remained silent, on edge, barely looking at Lorenzo, who appeared to have switched off from the conversation, wondering when she could make an exit.

She had never thought that hearing him speak to her in those neutral tones, seeing him look at her in that expressionless, courteous way, could have made her heart constrict, but it did. The past was now buried, and his manner towards her now spoke of sublime indifference.

She bleakly switched off from her surroundings too, listening to the thoughts whirling around in her head, while Jessica, who seemed to be burning with inextinguishable sparks of energy, talked about the opportunities waiting for her back in Chicago.

She *had* made a fool of herself, Isobel thought. Or at least she believed so, in rushing out here at Lorenzo's beckoning, and now she was extricating herself as efficiently as she could, so that she could think later that she had been lucky, that she had had a narrow escape.

'Of course, I shall pull strings to make sure that you get a good job,' Lorenzo said when there was a break in the conversation, and Jessica threw him a deadly smile.

'That won't be necessary. I have quite a few valuable contacts of my own.'

He shrugged, and a flash of rage crossed the hard, tight-lipped face.

This was getting distinctly uncomfortable. Isobel stood up, ready to take her leave and extricate herself from the thick, highly-charged atmosphere, but Jessica looked at her with a small smile of pleasure, and said tightly, 'Oh, before you go, Isobel.' It was the first time she had called her by her name, Isobel realised. 'There are just a few little things I feel you ought to see.' She walked across the room and picked up her briefcase which had been lying on the chair by the door.

Isobel hadn't even noticed it.

'What little things?'

'Oh, a few bits and pieces to do with your father's company. I know no deal has been formalised, but I had some spare time last week and I thought I'd mosey along and see what the company accounts looked like. I told them that the deal was more or less wrapped up and of course they believed me. Wonderful, these little hick towns.'

Lorenzo threw her a furious look but she was beyond the reach of his fury now.

'What the hell do you mean by this?' he asked, standing up so that even Jessica cringed back involuntarily. 'Does the word "unethical" mean anything to you?'

'Not always,' she said languidly, bored.

'You had no right,' Isobel said, white-faced, and Jessica laughed.

'Admittedly not,' she said unapologetically, 'but I was curious to see why Lorenzo wanted the company so badly. I wanted to see what hidden reserves there were. If it had been big enough, and if your deal had fallen through, well, let's just say I knew a certain fish that might have wanted the bait, and I knew that you would be in a desperate position with no other buyer in the field.' She was still smiling with a chilling lack of humour. 'And it was certainly an interesting forage, I can tell you!'

She clicked open the briefcase and, after a while, Isobel sat back down. She didn't like the expression of triumph on the other woman's face. It frightened her. Was it really so quiet in the room or was it her imagination? She could hear the sound of the wind outside, and inside the shuffling of the papers on Jessica's lap.

There was a tension about Lorenzo as well. She sneaked a glance at him from under her lashes and wondered what he was thinking.

'For God's sake, Jessica,' he snapped impatiently, 'is all this really necessary at—' he consulted his watch '—quarter past twelve? It's been a long day and I'm not about to stay here discussing business until all hours of the morning.'

'I won't be a minute,' Jessica said, not looking at him. After a while she glanced up with satisfaction and said, 'There. Now—' she looked at them both '—who would like to be the first to peruse these *very* interesting documents?'

She sounded like someone who was about to start an auction going, and was fairly guaranteed an enthusiastic response.

She was holding a small wad of papers in her hand,

and all of a sudden, in one sickening moment of real-isation, Isobel knew, knew with a sense of building dread what those '*very* interesting documents' were.

She had not found the incriminating evidence among Jeremy's things, had she? But that hadn't worried her. She had assumed that they would turn up sooner or later. After all, she had hardly really searched in depth for them. Too much had been going on for her to devote time to that.

How was she to have known that he hadn't concealed them in the house after all?

'Where,' she asked, white-faced, 'did you find those?'

'Oh, interested suddenly, are you?' Jessica smiled smugly. 'Accountants. You'd be surprised what we find in nooks and crannies. I was rummaging through your late husband's desk drawer, where I had been cheerfully escorted and left on my own, and imagine my amaze-ment when I discovered that it had a false bottom. I thought that sort of thing only happened in movies! Nat-urally I prised it open.' She was deriving great pleasure from telling them all this.

'What the hell is all this about, Jessica?' Lorenzo asked in a dangerously soft voice.

She didn't answer. She held out the papers and said sweetly, 'Bedtime reading for you.' She stood up and dusted herself down. 'Now, I really must be going.' She turned to Isobel. 'I won't see you again. I'm sure you'll be as sad as I am at the thought of that. Now, I'll leave you two together, shall I? There's a lot, I suspect, that you'll want to discuss.'

With that she left, closing the door behind her, and Isobel stared at Lorenzo with wide eyes. Then she did something she had never done in her life before.

She blacked out.

CHAPTER NINE

WHEN Isobel next opened her eyes, she was on the sofa, lying down. It took her a few seconds to try and work out what she was doing in this peculiar position, then she sat up suddenly, her body tense as she looked at Lorenzo's downbent head.

He was reading the papers, his long fingers flicking through them, re-reading bits, absorbing it all.

In a way it was a relief that everything would now be out in the open, at least between the two of them.

He glanced up at her with expressionless eyes and said in a hard voice, 'Why didn't you tell me?'

Isobel licked her lips. 'How could I?' she asked helplessly, and he flung the papers down on the table and began pacing the room, his movements restless, his hands shoved into his trouser pockets.

She followed him with her eyes, compulsively drinking in his movements, the angry hunch of his powerful shoulders, the tight line of his mouth.

He stopped in front of her and stared down. 'Very easily,' he said coldly, in a voice that made her flinch.

'Try and understand my position…!'

'Your "*position*" was that you allowed yourself to be blackmailed by a man intent on getting what he wanted at all costs!'

'Oh, what's the point?' she muttered, sinking down into the chair. 'What's the point in trying to explain anything to you? You don't want to understand.'

He sat down on the coffee-table in front of her and she reluctantly watched him.

'What your father did was not the end of the world,' he said in a tight voice, and her eyes flashed angrily back at him.

'Not the end of the world, no! But if it had ever become public knowledge, my parents' lives would have been destroyed. In a town of this size, where everyone knows everyone else, where my father was a big name, God help him, the publicity would have ruined him.'

'When did Jeremy find out about it?' Lorenzo asked. 'And don't,' he added icily, 'try and walk out on an explanation now. I intend to hear every word of what you've got to say, if I have to nail you to the sofa personally.'

His eyes were full of hatred. The frozen politeness which had been there before had gone.

Isobel sighed and lay back, half closing her eyes.

'He telephoned me one night at university,' she said quietly. 'He always telephoned me. I never told you because I knew you would fly into a blind rage. Jeremy—' she hesitated '—couldn't seem to let me go. He hated the fact that we were going out together. He hated your presence in my life. That night he sounded excited, on a high. He told me that he had found out something, something that could affect me personally. He said that he wanted to come up and see me to discuss it, and naturally I told him to get lost.' She laughed to herself. 'I told him that I…' She remembered what she had told him, that she was in love with Lorenzo Cicolla, but for some reason she couldn't bring herself to say that now. 'I told him that I was involved with you and that I didn't want him to contact me again.'

'You damn well should have said something to me about all that!' Lorenzo informed her, with fury in his voice, and she opened her eyes to look him fully in the face.

'It wouldn't have been worth it. Besides, I suppose I felt sorry for Jeremy. We had known each other since our childhood days, and even if he had gone a bit off the rails then there was still enough of a shared past for me to want to try and avoid hurting him. Unnecessarily.'

'So what was his next move?' He stood up and walked across to the bar in the corner of the room and poured himself a drink, offering her one, which she refused. Then he returned to where he had been sitting and swallowed the lot in one mouthful.

'He wrote to me. He told me that he had come across some papers, that he had evidence that my father had been…' Her voice faltered at this point. 'If it had been a question of another woman, I would have been concerned, but that would have been different. My mother would have been dreadfully hurt, and so would I, but people would have forgotten about it within weeks. But this was different.'

'This brought the whole question of his trustworthiness into dispute,' Lorenzo filled in for her and she nodded miserably.

'He was a pillar of the community. If it were ever known that he had been embezzling money…' There, it was out, the secret that she had clung on to for so long that it had almost become a part of her, like a dark tumour.

The silence in the room pounded in her ears and she couldn't meet Lorenzo's eyes.

'Jeremy had been going through old files. Files which should have been consigned to the incinerator, but for some reason had not been. Well, you know how Dad was a compulsive jotter. He used to say that he thought better when he could see it in front of him, so he'd jot down things. In this file were jottings. Pages of them.

Plans meticulously worked out to defraud the company. Jeremy told me that he knew how it had been done.'

'I suppose he did it between audits?'

'So I gather,' Isobel muttered, eyes still down. 'I read all the bits of paper over and over, trying to convince myself that I was mistaken, but it appeared that Dad had set up bogus companies, something like that anyway, with money being paid to non-existent suppliers.'

'You saw the accounts?'

Isobel shook her head. 'Destroyed, I suppose, but the jottings were enough. They were Dad's handwriting. On that alone... It was enough.'

'Did you confront him with it?'

'Of course not!' She looked at him, horrified at that. 'I loved my father. I loved him whatever he had done. Jeremy had the information at hand to destroy him if he wanted and I couldn't let him do that.'

'So you agreed to whatever he wanted.' It was a cold statement of fact and she winced.

'I had no choice. He was obsessed with me, and with taking me away from you, although until you told me about his background, I never fully understood the reason why.'

'So little Isobel buckled down under pressure and played the dutiful wife.' The contempt in his voice made her flush with sudden anger.

'And what,' she suggested fiercely, 'would you have suggested I did? What would you have done if I had come running to you with the story? I know what you would have done! You would have stormed up here to see Jeremy and you would have tried to thrash him into submission!'

'Are you telling me that he wouldn't have deserved it?'

'I'm telling you that it would have had as much success as plugging a dam with a toothpick! He was always prone to violent tempers, you know that! If you had confronted him, he would have done the first thing that came into his head! He would have announced his little gem of information loud and clear, to all and sundry!'

'And what else did he blackmail you into doing, Isobel?' He leaned towards her, his face dark and savage. 'Did he blackmail you into making love to him whenever he wanted you?'

She gripped the cushions on the sofa. 'Does it matter?'

'Tell me, damn you!' He dragged her head up so that she had to meet his glittering eyes.

'I...' She took a deep breath, terrified at what she saw on Lorenzo's face. 'I couldn't. He tried, but it was hopeless. I think he must have found...fulfilment with other women. He went on business trips quite a bit.' Her voice had sunk to a whisper. 'He was content to have me as a decoration, to see the envy in his friends' eyes occasionally, to know, I guess, that he had killed whatever the two of us had had.'

'Why didn't you tell me all this when I returned here?' he asked, and his voice was like a whiplash. He wasn't about to forgive her. He would never forgive her. His own impulses were not to submission. He would never really understand, she thought despairingly.

'How could I?'

'Jeremy was dead. He had no hold over you any longer.' He said that flatly, as though it made all the sense in the world, as though her continuing silence had been nothing more than stupidity on her part.

'So what...?' she asked bitterly. 'So after four years I should see you staring at me, an opponent, and confess all?' She laughed harshly, laughter on the verge of tears. 'You hate me, Lorenzo. You made that clear the minute you returned. And yet you're telling me now that I should have trusted you?'

'Did you think that I might use the information to get back at you, Isobel?' His mouth curled into a sneer. 'You insult me by implying that I would have done any such thing!'

'I...I don't suppose I thought that you would. No, deep down I knew that you wouldn't, but I wasn't about to take the chance. My mother is ill, vulnerable...' She saw another flash of immense fury in his eyes and shivered. 'Besides,' she continued defiantly, 'when you returned here, you returned a stranger. You weren't the same person I knew all those years ago! I *couldn't* confide in you. I no longer *knew* you. You talked of revenge, hatred...'

'What it boils down to, Isobel,' he grated harshly, 'is that you didn't trust me. You never trusted me.'

'That's not true!' She leaned towards him but there was no softening in his face.

'No?' he mocked. 'I could have talked to him, made him see sense.'

'He would never have seen sense. I should know, I lived with him for four years.' Her eyes clouded over with memory. 'Jeremy never really grew up. Oh, he acted the part of the adult, he could make witty conversation when it was necessary, but deep down he was like a child. If things didn't go his way, he could throw the most frightful tempers. I learned to get out of his way. I learned to keep myself apart, detached.'

'You learned to sacrifice your life. You walked out on me.'

She hung her head, not knowing what to say, tired of defending herself.

'Don't tell me that you spent all that time pining,' she muttered unsteadily. 'I should think that you quickly recovered from the body-blow to your pride. After all, you showed up here with Jessica Tate in your wake, making it obvious what your relationship with her was! Where did she fall in the queue of women, Lorenzo?'

They stared at one another, and in the semi-darkness of the room her heart skipped a beat.

She stood up. Her legs felt wobbly.

'Not so fast,' he murmured from next to her. 'When you walked out on me, you left unfinished business behind.'

'What are you talking about?'

'I'm talking about this.' He reached out and pulled her towards him, and his mouth met hers with the force of anger and desire.

Isobel groaned and struggled against him, but he wasn't letting go and, under the force of his embrace, she found her lips parting, her tongue flicking with excitement against his.

She knew what he was doing. Emotionally he had expunged her from his system, but against his will there was still desire there, and desire was what he now aimed to clear once and for all.

There was an urgency in him, emanating from his body, and with a gesture of defeat she wound her arms around his neck and surrendered to her impulses.

Why fight it? she thought to herself. If this was to be their bitter parting, then why not yield? Hadn't she fantasised about this for a long time? His image had followed her every day and every night for as long as she could remember.

He lifted her up in one swift movement and carried her across to the rug in front of the fireplace. She didn't have to see his face to know that every touch was fired by a sort of savage passion. But there was a savage passion burning inside her as well, only she knew that this would not expunge him from her system because emotionally he was still there and always would be.

He unbuttoned his shirt unsteadily, tugging it out of his trousers, then lay down next to her, holding her face between his fingers and kissing her until she gasped for breath.

'I can't stand the thought that he touched you, Isobel,' he muttered against her neck, his voice rough, and there was enough possessive passion there to send her spirits soaring, but not for long. She had hurt him, but not fatally, not as he had hurt her in the end.

His hand slipped beneath the cotton jumper and he massage her breast through the lacy bra until she writhed with pleasure.

With shaking fingers she unhooked it from the front, pulling it aside so that there was now no barrier between his fingers and the soft swell of her breasts, their nipples swollen with aching anticipation.

He groaned and pushed up the jumper, seeking her breasts like an infant searching for its source of food. She watched his dark head as his mouth fastened to her nipple and he pulled at it, drawing it into his mouth.

She knew that she would gain so much and lose so much by making love to him, but she couldn't begin to reason it out. She just knew that it was inevitable.

As he suckled on her breast, he unzipped her skirt, pulling her free of it and tossing it on one of the chairs, then her lacy underwear followed so that she was lying against him, naked.

He half raised himself to look at her, and she watched him with a mixture of sadness and pleasure. There was no concealing the primeval want in his eyes.

He stood up, still staring at her, his breath coming and going as quickly as hers was, and she looked as he undressed, taking in every smooth, hard line of his body as though she had never seen it before.

He stooped beside her, moulding her with his hands, her breasts, her stomach, her waist, then he bent and kissed her thighs, working up until his mouth had found her most private places, sending her into a vortex of raging desire. She parted her legs to accommodate the flicking of his tongue as he explored every inch of her, and when she thought that she could no longer contain the dam of excitement waiting to burst, he eased himself on her and buried his face against her neck.

She could hear him muttering her name over and over again. There was no tenderness there though.

'I don't want to feel this way about you,' he muttered unsteadily, and he looked at her with darkening eyes. 'This passion...'

And I don't want to feel this way about *you*, Lorenzo Cicolla, she told herself. I don't want to feel this overwhelming love, to know that I shall never be able to escape. If only all she felt for him was passion. Passion could be sated. It was a monster that could evaporate once it had been fed to its satisfaction, but love was something else entirely. Love ate away at you and then, when you thought that there was nothing left, it started all over again.

He cupped her neck with his hand as his mouth descended over hers. He thrust into her, his movements slow to start with, then quickening until they found a rhythm of their own and their bodies were joined in unison.

Isobel placed her hands in the small of his back and flung her head backwards as the fire that had been building in her reached its apex, filling her entire being, taking her into another orbit, at least for a while.

She was still trembling when he lay down beside her with his hand behind his head.

There had always been things to say, long ago when they were lovers. Now she listened to the silence, and knew that this would be the last time that she would ever feel that glorious body next to hers.

What was going through his head? Had he been released by their lovemaking?

He turned to her and said in a toneless voice, 'I think it's time for me to go.'

He might as well have told her that he thought it was time for him to leave planet Earth and set up camp on the moon. She could feel the tears pricking the back of her eyes and she didn't dare to look at him because that would have been courting disaster.

In all their discussions about Jeremy, he had never once mentioned feelings, he had never once hinted that he might have felt anything for her beyond all those emotions generated by lost pride. At least she had spared herself the final humiliation of having him know how much she still loved him and always had.

'I'll pack my clothes. I can be out of here within an hour.'

'Yes.' She stood up, woodenly, and began putting on her clothes. She hadn't even thought about contraception, but she knew, with a strange sense of disappointment, that she was not in a fertile period. There wasn't even a chance that this would have led to a baby.

He dressed in silence, then they faced each other across the room.

'Will you make my apologies to your mother when she returns for not staying on?' he asked.

'Yes, I will,' she said with the same feeling of unreality eating away inside her. 'Where will you go?'

'To London for a few days, then I shall fly to Italy.

You'll find another buyer for your father's company. Let Clark advise you. My days here are finished.'

Now that there was such a sense of finality between them, she had a compulsive need to keep the conversation going. Whereas before she had been too full of nervous awareness of him to be in the same room, now she would have kept him here as long as she could because she knew that this was the end of the line.

'What will you do about the cottage?' she asked, and he shrugged, moving towards the door.

'There would be no point,' he murmured. 'If and when I do come over here, I can always stay at the hotel.'

'The Edwardian?'

They smiled at each other and she felt a dart of pain.

'It is a bit grim,' he said, 'isn't it? Perhaps things there might improve.' He began walking up the stairs. It was quite black here and her eyes had to adjust to the dark shape ahead of her. At the top he turned to her and said softly, 'Goodbye, Isobel.'

She couldn't see his face. It was just too dark, and she was glad that he could not see hers.

'Goodbye, Lorenzo,' she said, hoping that her voice would see her through and not crack up in mid-sentence. 'And good luck.'

He nodded slightly and then turned away, his footsteps soft and stealthy on the carpet.

Isobel went to her room and sat on her bed with the lights switched off. She felt completely drained. After some time she heard him walk past quietly, and she had to imagine the rest. The soft click of the front door closing behind him, the throb of the engine as he started the car, the headlights beaming as he drove away. Out of this small town that had been responsible for so much, and out of her life.

*　　*　　*

The following day she felt like someone recovering from a state of shock.

'But *why* did he have to leave at such an extraordinary hour?' her mother asked when she telephoned later that day. 'Did he have a call? Is his mother ill?'

'There were a few problems that needed sorting out straight away,' Isobel replied. 'He felt that he had to go immediately.'

'Yes, I'm sure Lorenzo would have remained unless it was important,' Mrs Chandler said, ever ready to give people the benefit of the doubt. 'You'll miss him, Isobel, I know.'

She couldn't face an outright lie to counteract that one so she held her tongue and stared at the wall in front of her.

'He'll be back,' Mrs Chandler said gently.

'No. He won't.'

'My dear, if you still love him, why did you ever marry Jeremy?'

Isobel's eyes widened in surprise. 'B-Because...' she stammered, 'because it seemed like the right thing to do at the time.'

'We all make mistakes,' her mother sighed from miles away, not pressing the point. 'But Lorenzo will come back, I'm sure of it.'

When hell freezes over, Isobel thought, when the cow jumps over the moon and the dish runs away with the spoon. It was pointless dwelling on it and, when she replaced the receiver, she decided that the only thing to do would be to carry on, to smile and smile and smile for the outside world. She had had enough experience of that.

In fact, she spent the next two days smiling. It certainly convinced the patients that she was in a very good mood indeed, which was something, but the minute she

was alone the mask fell away and she found herself contemplating, without any need to disguise it, the long,
dark tunnel ahead of her. A thousand pages of a thousand calendars turning over, as the months grew into
years and the bleakness in her heart set ever harder by
the day.

What had happened to the golden girl who had it all?
she wondered. It seemed strange that everything could
slip away so completely, like sand between open fingers.
One minute the future was in front of her, promising
everything, and the next she was confined to a prison,
without hope of remission.

By the Friday she felt that she was going out of her
mind, so on the spur of the moment she decided to get
in touch with Abigail. Abigail could always be relied
upon to bring her back down to earth. For some reason,
and although she was very close to her mother, she
couldn't face talking to her about what had happened.
For a start there would be too many bits and pieces that
would have to be left out, and there wasn't much chance
that she would be able to get through an edited explanation without her mother becoming increasingly suspicious along the way.

The only problem with Abigail was, of course, her
schedule. In a fairly nomadic profession, her bases
tended to jump from one part of the country to the other,
when she *was* in the country at all.

Isobel wrinkled her brow and tried to remember what
her friend had told her about her jobs. Where was she
now? London? Manchester? Birmingham? She had been
doing something, Isobel was sure, at the Alexandra
Theatre in Birmingham, but was that now finished?

She dialled her London number. It rang three times,
and then on came the chatty, pre-recorded voice of
Abigail, informing her that she wasn't available at the

moment, but would get back to the caller 'with the speed of light'. The message breathed sincerity, and Isobel half smiled, knowing that her friend only ever got back to a few of her callers, and rarely at the speed of light.

She was mistaken, though. The telephone rang ten minutes later and Abigail said breathlessly down the line, 'I *was* in, Izzy, but I couldn't be bothered to get to the phone.' There was a massive, uninterrupted yawn down the line and Isobel said drily,

'Too much sleep is bad for you.'

'Try telling that to my nervous system,' Abigail said. 'You never phone me, Isobel, which is why—and, please, there's no need to be grateful—I'm phoning you back. What's the matter?'

Isobel sat down. In this huge, empty house, she could talk unhindered for as long as she wanted, and she really wanted to, to pour it all out, but naturally she now found that she couldn't.

'I just thought I'd find out how you were,' she said, postponing the confession.

'Thriving, now that you ask. I'm doing an absolutely marvellous play at the moment here. Not too strenuous, but with some nice, witty dialogue. It's a bit of much-needed light relief before I vanish off to distant shores. New York, to be precise.'

'Oh, what a hard life you lead,' Isobel said jokingly. 'London, New York. Next you'll be telling me that you're honing up on your Far Eastern dialects and will be flying out to Tokyo to dazzle them with your talents.' She laughed, but her fingers played compulsively with the telephone cord.

Abigail must have detected the slight nervous edge to her voice because she said seriously, 'Whatever is wrong, Izzy? I don't have to see you to know that you're not exactly on top of the world. Is it your mother? She's all right, isn't she?'

'It's me, Abby,' Isobel said flatly. 'I have no one else to turn to.' Damn, she was beginning to feel tearful. She took a deep breath and began telling her friend about Lorenzo. Really, she had meant to keep it brief. Who liked being overdosed on someone else's problems? Even a good friend's? But the more she spoke, the more she found that she had to say. It surprised her how much she had taken in of him—had she really noticed him in such agonising detail?

She never mentioned a word about Jeremy, or the reason that she had married him, but she talked and talked and talked. At the end of which, Abigail said, with her usual forthrightness, 'You're a mess.'

'Is that any way to cheer a friend up?' Isobel asked shakily. The tears which had been threatening for the past ten minutes dripped silently down her cheek and she wiped them away with the back of her hand.

'Of course, you'll have to come up here.'

'I can't.'

'Don't be ridiculous. Of course you can and of course you will. No ifs and buts. You can travel up tomorrow morning and spend the weekend with me. I'll get you a ticket to my play, you lucky, *lucky* girl.' Which had the desired effect of making Isobel smile. 'I shan't be at my flat in the morning, so you'll have to make your own way there, but you still have the spare key, don't you? Yes, I can tell you're nodding. Make your way to my flat, help yourself to my food, which won't be very appetising because I'm on a new and improved diet which, as usual, doesn't appear to be working, and then go shopping. That's an order. *Go shopping*. Buy something wonderful to wear to the theatre. It's the last night that the play's on and there will be all sorts of semi-famous faces attending. The really famous ones were there on first night, I'm afraid. We'll have a late supper when the play's finished and the applause has died down. Read my lips, Isobel: You are going to have a stupendous time!'

So at three-thirty the following afternoon, she found herself walking along Bond Street with a cold sun putting in a rare appearance to remind the country at large that it did exist, and browsing for the mandatory outfit for An Evening at the Theatre.

It was quite a few months since she had been to London. She was a country girl at heart and usually found London very claustrophobic, but right now it was wonderful. It just felt good to be somewhere different, and even if thoughts of Lorenzo continued to buzz through her head like a swarm of bees, some of her depression was lifting.

She found herself a glamorous long-sleeved dress in fine, bright green wool and was blushingly flattered when the salesperson asked her whether she was a model. Then she bought some costume jewellery, some shoes, and returned to Abigail's flat at six-thirty, far more heartened than when she had set out on the train down several hours back.

Maybe, she thought as she dressed carefully for the evening, she and her mother could spend an indefinite amount of time travelling. Maybe several years of travelling would get Lorenzo Cicolla out of her system. She flirted with the thought for a while, then ruefully decided that running away from reality never solved problems, it only generated a few more, and made it to the theatre with only minutes to spare.

Her ticket was for one of the prime seats and the place was packed. The play had received rave reviews throughout its run and there didn't appear to be a single free seat. She found herself between a refined, grey-haired woman on her left and a prosperous, overweight businessman on her right.

There was only a cast of five in the play, which relied heavily on content and not at all on stage effects, and the acting was brilliant. She found herself wishing that she had seen more of Abigail's work, but the nearest theatre to where she lived was a tiny venue, manfully upkept, but really only patronised by the town's ardent dramatic society, several school plays, and pantomimes at Christmas.

And Abigail was a star way out of that league. She had a natural way of acting that enticed you into her make-believe world and held you there for the duration.

By the time the intermission came around, everyone was on edge, wondering what would happen in the second half.

Rather than beat a path to the theatre bar to get herself an orange juice, she stayed put, reading through the programme in front of her and smiling at the lavish praise quoted about her friend by the critics. Who would have thought it? she wondered. At ten, holding hands in the playground and giggling over all the things that occupied the minds of ten-year-old girls, who would ever have imagined that their lives would have turned out this way?

She snapped shut the programme. There was no point in going over her past relentlessly. She would never be able to dodge what had happened, but it was within her hands to mould the future.

She only wished that she could make her mind listen to this piece of wisdom instead of shoving images of Lorenzo down her throat all the time.

It was a relief when the bell sounded for the end of

the interval and she could lose herself in the second half
of the play.

By the time the play had wound its way to its conclusion, the audience had worked itself up to an emotional response. There was a standing ovation as the cast
walked on to the stage and held hands, bowing to the
appreciative crowd. Bouquets of flowers were brought
on for Abigail, the only female lead in the play, and one
of the actors said, with mock dismay, 'Where's mine?'
which had everyone laughing.

She was preparing to pick her bag up when she heard
Abigail's voice, ringing out as the applause died down.

'And now, I should like to break with tradition and
do something absolutely unheard-of!'

There was a rustle of curiosity and then silence fell
over the vast, packed hall. Nothing captured an audience
more than the unexpected, and this was something totally unexpected. Isobel found that she was holding her
breath. She suspected that quite a few in the audience
were doing the same thing as well.

'I should like,' Abigail continued, 'with the kind permission of my fellow actors and yourselves, to ask my
dearest friend Isobel to step down on to the stage here
with me!'

Isobel's eyes widened in shock and she thought, Oh,
God, but she had to walk down. She felt her legs
teetering precariously as she moved past the rows of
seats, all eyes fixed on her, and as she cleared the sea
of onlookers Abigail smiled down at her and said, looking up, 'And, of course, I should also like to call Lorenzo
Cicolla on to the stage as well.'

At which point Isobel felt as though everything happening was part of some wild, improbable dream. She
didn't dare raise her eyes, but as she was ushered on to

the stage through the side and took her place next to Abigail, she saw Lorenzo making his way up.

Abigail held her hand then, when Lorenzo was on stage, she announced, with disarming charm, 'To my two good friends, who have known me since childhood and who were always destined for each other. They have been through a few setbacks but they are here now, together, and together they must stay!'

There was tumultuous cheering. It rang from every quarter of the hall, rebounding on the walls and making Isobel feel light-headed.

She hardly knew when her fingers entwined with Lorenzo's. She looked up into that beloved, handsome, dark face and someone from the crowd roared out, 'Propose to the girl!'

'Lorenzo...' Isobel said, and there was a hush.

'Isobel.' His light eyes met hers and she felt her body trembling. 'Will you marry me?'

CHAPTER TEN

'WE HAVE to get out of here,' Lorenzo said. 'We have to talk.'

They were backstage, swirled off among the cast and the various assortment of people—in this case vastly outnumbering the members of the cast—who were heartily congratulating themselves on their performances.

Abigail walked over to them, her face flushed with success, and with a small, satisfied smile on her lips.

'I hope you didn't mind my impromptu behaviour,' she said, grinning and not looking too worried.

Isobel had moved away from Lorenzo. She still felt as though she was caught up in some elaborate dream, and was therefore finding it easy to disregard what had sounded like a proposal of marriage half an hour ago.

Dream or no dream, there was no way that he had meant a word of it anyway.

Standing in front of a crowd of hundreds, what else could he do? In fact, thinking about it, she rather blamed Abigail after all.

'You're an incorrigible romantic, Abby,' she said, not looking at Lorenzo, but very much aware of him standing next to her in his dark suit, impeccably handsome and very unnerving.

'I try my best,' Abigail replied, with a modest, thoughtful nod. 'I guess you two would like to have some time together?' she asked.

'Yes,' Lorenzo murmured, at the very same time that Isobel shook her head and murmured,

'No.'

'Well, what's it to be?' She looked at both of them with what Isobel considered a rather poor show of looking innocently bemused. 'Yes? No? Maybe? We'll mull it over and get back to you?'

The director sidled up behind her, beaming with triumph, and Isobel could see that her friend was itching to get away and do a post mortem on her performance with him, so she said wearily, 'All right,' still not looking at Lorenzo.

'I know a small restaurant quite near,' he said softly, so close to her that she bristled with awareness. 'Go away, Abigail,' he said with a slow smile, 'and in case I don't get around to telling you this, you're the most conniving female I've ever met in my life.' He was smiling though. Isobel could hear it in his voice.

He pulled her towards the exit and as soon as they were outside, with the cold air stinging her face, she turned to him and said, looking down, 'I know what marriage is for you. I know you didn't mean it.' Her voice sounded stiff and nervous, which she thought was a pretty good indication of how she was feeling.

'Oh, you *know*, do you?' he mocked, with just enough of a teasing drawl for her to risk a glance at him from under her lashes.

'Well, what else could you do? With the crowd after you for a…a…' She spluttered into silence.

'Later,' he said. 'This isn't the place for any kind of conversation. Come on.' He linked her arm through his and they walked in silence until they came to a small Italian restaurant, where the manager took one look at Lorenzo, smelled the power and wealth which he radiated, and ushered them to a discreet table in the corner of the room.

There was a small vase of carnations on the table and Lorenzo moved them.

'I want to see you when I say what I have to say, Isobel,' he murmured, which instantly made the coil in her stomach harden.

'I had no idea that she would pull a stunt like that,' Isobel mumbled. 'How did she know where to find you?'

'Savoy,' he said succinctly, staring at her intently until she felt her colour begin to rise. 'When I saw her on Broadway I took her out for a meal a couple of days later and I told her that the Savoy was the only place I stayed when I was in London. I never knew that the information would rebound on me.'

There was a warmth about him that was beginning to make her head spin, and it was a relief when the waiter came to take their order.

With typical Italian exuberance, everything they wanted was 'just beautiful' or 'a wonderful choice'.

'Was your mother all right about my hasty departure?' Lorenzo asked, and Isobel twiddled with the stem of her wine-glass.

'Yes.'

'And you? Were you all right?'

'Why on earth shouldn't I have been?'

'Because, my darling, we hardly parted on amicable terms.'

My darling. Had he called her 'my darling'? Without sarcasm?

'This is hopeless,' he said abruptly, standing up. The manager, in a flurry of alarm, flew over to their table and made a great fuss over this unexpected situation.

'There is something wrong?' he asked anxiously. 'You do not find my place agreeable?'

'Perfectly agreeable,' Lorenzo assured him, delving

into his wallet and extracting a wad of notes. 'I'm sure the food would have been exquisite, but we find that we're in no mood to eat.' He looked at her through his lashes and Isobel mumbled confused agreement, getting to her feet and wondering what was going on.

They left the restaurant, took a taxi, and arrived at the Savoy in what seemed a breathlessly short space of time.

'Why are we here?' she asked in a high-pitched voice.

'To talk.' He shot her an innocent look. 'I can't talk to you in between mouthfuls of chicken cacciatore.'

He walked inside the hotel with Isobel following in his wake and, even though she knew where he was taking her, she still balked when they arrived at his bedroom and he unlocked the door and pushed it open.

'Why do we need to talk in a bedroom?' Her voice now resembled a squeak.

How could you do this to me, Abigail? she wailed to herself.

'Keep quiet,' he ordered, shutting the door behind them and tossing the keys on to the table in the middle of the room. 'Sit down. Have a drink and listen to what I've got to say.'

He poured them both a glass of whisky and soda, which was a drink she never indulged in, but which she now gratefully swallowed because her nerves were in serious danger of seizing up completely.

'Not your favourite drink, I know,' he said, sitting next to her.

'You remember,' she whispered.

'Of course I do. I remember,' he said on a sigh, 'everything about you, Isobel. How could I forget when you've been in my mind for so long?'

She didn't look at him. She hung her head and he brushed the curtain of black hair away so that he could see her profile. She felt the feathery touch of his fingers and shivered.

'Look at me,' he said, and she turned her head so that they were facing each other on the sofa. 'I spent four years with thoughts of you eating away inside me,' he continued, and there was nothing teasing in his light eyes. They were deadly serious, inward-thinking. 'I went to Chicago and every success, every pot of gold I found at the end of every rainbow, was marred by my bitter memories of you.'

'I did what I did—!' Isobel began, and he placed his finger over her lips.

'Shh.' He brushed her hair back from her face and his hand remained there, his fingers curled into her hair, as though he couldn't bring himself to take it away. 'You have no idea how much I loved you when you threw that bombshell at me,' he murmured, which pierced her heart.

All those years ago, of course she had known that he had loved her, but to hear him say it now made her want to sob.

'You were my sun, Isobel. I adored you. I always knew that you could have had anyone. The whole eligible male population of that damned town fancied themselves in love with you!' He grinned ruefully, and she could tell that he was thinking back. 'When you told me that you were going to marry Jeremy, I suspected that there was a reason, but I guess it was easy to believe when he announced that he was more suitable for you. And when you didn't deny it...'

'How could I?'

'I see that now, but I didn't then,' Lorenzo said in that deep, caressing voice that did strange things to her nervous system. 'All I saw were two people who shared

the same background, and myself, a dangerous inter-
loper, who had had the audacity to fall in love with the
wrong girl. You have never been vain, Isobel, but what
was said about you would have made your head spin.
You always had that incredible effect on the opposite
sex, without even really seeming to realise it. It was
almost as if you cast a spell wherever you walked. I
could have killed him when he took you away from
me—killed you both! Instead I went away.'

She didn't want to interrupt. Lorenzo was travelling
down his own bitter lane of memories and she knew that
he had to say it all.

She wanted to hear, too. She wanted to hear everything, with no bits missing, even though in her heart of
hearts she knew where this confession was leading.

He had once loved her, he said. She had once been
his sun, he said. But that was a long time ago. Now all
that fierce, youthful energy had died. Wasn't that why
he could speak to her so calmly? It was easy to speak
with calm to someone when indifference was all that you
felt for them.

'At that point I suppose I nurtured vague thoughts of
returning one day, returning with all the money and
power that Jeremy had said you needed.'

'So you did.'

'So I did,' he answered steadily, 'although circumstances were rather different from what I originally had
in mind. But then life's like that, isn't it? One minute
your route's stretching out in front of you, straight and
clear, and the next minute it's dissolved into a network
of paths and trails, and you haven't got a clue where the
hell you're heading.'

He was still stroking her hair, and she wished that he
wouldn't. It disorientated her. She wanted to be calm

like him, to be able to tell him about her past in the same controlled voice, as though it was something to look back on with forgiveness, as though it no longer had the power to hurt.

'I was shocked when I heard about that car accident.'

'But you saw your chance to settle debts with me.'

'I knew that I had to return. I never once stopped to question it.'

They looked at each other. The room seemed terribly silent. He had switched on one of the table-lamps and there were a lot of half-shadows, pools of darkness.

'I thought,' he continued slowly, 'that I could bury the past once and for all, but when I saw you in that office all the old anger came rushing back. I looked at that exquisite, angelic face of yours and all I could see was you on your wedding-day. I wanted you then as I've never wanted anyone or anything in my whole life. I hadn't planned to force you into marriage, but when I looked at you I knew that I *had* to have you, that you *had* to be mine.'

'Hate is a powerful emotion, Lorenzo,' she mumbled, blinking back an embarrassing attack of tears.

'Hate?' He gave her an incredulous stare and her heart skipped a beat. 'I don't hate you, Isobel. Is that what you think?'

'Not now, perhaps.' She felt utterly miserable. 'Indifference now, perhaps.'

'How could I ever be indifferent to you?' He leaned forward and cupped her face in his hands. Strong, powerful hands that evoked a million memories for her.

Her heart was definitely doing wild things now. Soaring and swooping and flying high above the clouds. She held her breath and felt as if she was walking on the edge of a precipice.

'I'm in love with you, woman,' he said in an odd voice. 'I never stopped being in love with you. I wanted to. Dammit, I wanted to more than anything else in the world. I came back to put you into perspective but the only thing I succeeded in doing was falling even deeper in love with you all over again. But I couldn't block out the past. I had to know and, in between loving you, I wanted to damn well throttle you into telling me why you had married him.'

'Lorenzo!' She looked at him with shining eyes. 'You love me.'

She reached out tentatively and stroked his face and he groaned, bending to kiss her. His lips were hungry and searching and she clung to him, kissing him back.

'When I discovered the reason for your marriage, I saw red,' he muttered against her neck and she cradled his head in her hands. 'All I could think was: she didn't trust me enough. I came up here to London, but it's been a nightmare. At first I couldn't think straight, then I began to see the position you had found yourself in. I began to understand why you had acted the way you did. Oh, my darling…!' His voice was hoarse.

'I was imprisoned for four years,' Isobel said softly. 'All that time, the only things that kept me going were thoughts of you and my parents. I accepted marriage to Jeremy because I had no choice, but I didn't like it.'

'Didn't your parents guess?'

'I think they probably guessed,' Isobel said. 'They knew that there was something not quite right, but what could they do? Whenever they mentioned it, I backed away. I couldn't afford for either of them to suspect anything. I had done it for them, because I loved them so much, and I never regretted it. But how I regretted you. I built a future in my head, the future we should have had.'

'It must have made you terribly bitter towards him,' Lorenzo said gently, and she sighed.

'To start with. No, I suppose I was very bitter for the long course of my marriage to Jeremy, but the human being isn't capable of sustained anger. After a while, you begin to adapt the only way you can and I suppose, towards the end, I felt sorry for him, even though I knew that he had used me—used us both, in a way.'

'Poor darling Isobel.' He kissed her again, slowly and tenderly, pushing her back against the sofa. Her pulses began to quicken and she moaned as he stroked her waist through the fine material of her dress.

When he lifted her off the sofa and carried her towards the bedroom it was, she knew, the moment she had been waiting all those years for. The moment when he would touch her, without anger or unwanted desire, but with love.

He rested her on the bed, and she turned to him and said softy, 'I love you, Lorenzo Cicolla. I never stopped. Even when we argued bitterly, I still loved you. Nothing could kill that. Jeremy might have thought that by marrying me he had destroyed what we had, but he was wrong. He could never touch me, not deep inside where it counts.'

'He was unstable,' Lorenzo murmured, shrugging out of his shirt to expose his bronzed torso. He lay down beside her on his side and ran his hand along her, outlining the smooth contours of her body. 'Even before all that business happened, before he found out about his mother, there was something reckless about him. He was always like a keg of gunpowder waiting to explode.'

He unzipped her dress and she wriggled out of it,

smiling slightly as he watched her, fascinated, as if he were seeing her for the first time.

When he touched her breast she lay back flat on the bed, her breathing coming and going quickly, as if she had run a marathon.

'You're so beautiful,' he murmured. 'The worst thing was that I understood why he wanted you so desperately. You provoke some dark, masculine instinct to be put under lock and key.'

'I hope not!' She laughed. Was she really *that* beautiful? She would have to look hard at herself the next time she found herself in front of a mirror.

'No, that would be a crime, wouldn't it?' He kissed her neck, then moved down her body, kissing every inch of her, exploring her with exquisite thoroughness.

She writhed as he caressed her stomach with his lips before nuzzling the soft mound of her femininity.

There was no anger, no resentment, no feeling of being in the unwilling grip of a passion too strong to control, much as you wanted to control it.

This was like the tenderness they had shared when they were younger, before life had begun to take its toll, except that this time there was a maturity about them that had been missing then.

She reached down and curled her fingers in his hair, parting her legs and opening her body to his eager exploration.

She sighed with contentment as he moved back up to lick her full breasts, taking each nipple into his mouth and teasing it until she wanted to scream.

When he finally came into her it was like being at home, where she belonged. Her body jerked against him, building to a crescendo, and her thought processes shut down as sensation took over.

'And now,' he said later, leaning on his elbow to look at her, 'that we're alone together, and there aren't hundreds of people watching, will you marry me, my darling Isobel? For all the right reasons?'

'Will I marry you?' She laughed and stroked his cheek. 'Yes. Yes, I will marry you. I've been waiting half my life for this moment, my love!'

And this time, she thought much later, as their lovemaking carried them through the night, who knew? There might even be a baby on the way.

EPILOGUE

ISOBEL looked at the suitcase in front of her. She would never have thought that she could look at Jeremy's possessions so calmly, so contentedly, without bitterness, but she could. Lorenzo had done that, she knew. Seven months ago they had married, a quiet affair involving only relatives and a few close friends. It had been the happiest day of her life and she had made sure that she had not worn white.

She smiled and began packing the last of the clothes, which she had only now got around to doing.

Where had the time gone? She knew, of course—redecorating their cottage together, making up for lost time.

She was about to close the suitcase when she felt something hard at the bottom of it, inside a zipped pocket. Curiously, she pulled out a notebook and began to read.

Her father's notebook, full of his usual jottings. It only took fifteen minutes and at the end of it she sat back on her heels and smiled. Somewhere, deep down, she had *known* that he would never have embezzled that money. Maybe it had crossed his mind, idle notes that had changed her life, but here, in this notebook, was the rest of the story. The bank loan, the figures carefully worked out, money which had never been stolen.

Jeremy had kept it all hidden. He had chosen to show her only enough to guarantee her co-operation.

Quietly she closed the suitcase, and stood it in the corner of the room. In the morning the last bits and pieces would be disposed of to a charity shop, in preparation for the young couple moving in over the weekend.

Then she went across to the window and looked out, still smiling, still holding that notebook.

Lorenzo would smile too when he read all this. He wouldn't fly off the handle. Marriage, he was fond of telling her in a semi-grumbling voice, had tamed the tiger, had domesticated him.

And, of course, something else too.

She patted her stomach contentedly and decided that *she* hadn't tamed him, not nearly as much as the tiny baby inside her.

Historical Romance™
4 brand new titles each month
...rich, vivid
and passionate
Available on subscription every month
from the Reader Service™
GEN/04/RS2

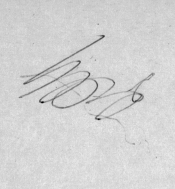